Peter Benjamin's return to the thriller with TERMS AND CONDITIONS follows a break of more than ten years. His earlier work in this genre won widespread praise. Writing as Peter Cunningham, he is the author of the acclaimed Monument novels published by Harvill. He lives in Ireland.

Terms and Conditions

Peter Benjamin

POCKET BOOKS
TOWNHOUSE

First published in Great Britain and Ireland by
Simon & Schuster/TownHouse, 2001
This edition published by Pocket/TownHouse, 2002
An imprint of Simon & Schuster UK Ltd,
and TownHouse and CountryHouse Ltd, Dublin

Simon & Schuster is a Viacom company

1 3 5 7 9 10 8 6 4 2

Simon & Schuster UK Ltd
Africa House
64–78 Kingsway
London WC2B 6AH

Simon & Schuster Australia
Sydney

TownHouse and CountryHouse Ltd
Trinity House
Charleston Road
Ranelagh
Dublin 6
Ireland

A CIP catalogue record for this book is available from the
British Library

ISBN 1-93650-18-6

Typeset by SX composing DTP, Rayleigh, Essex
Printed and bound in Great Britain by
Bookmarque Ltd, Croydon, Surrey

Jessica

PROLOGUE

New York City – Mid-1980s

I

Six months before, if she had seen the same old ache in my eyes, we would have gone back to her apartment and made love until we slept. But before Christmas I'd got married, and so the days when Minx and I had been together were now just a fond memory.

An evening in early May. The weather was still fresh enough to let you taste the salt from the sea they told us was somewhere out beyond the Verrazano Bridge, the Dow had broken new ground a week before and God was in His heaven so far as Wall Street was concerned. Her name was Carmine Dominguez, but you said Do*minx*. She was small and vivacious with a neat little body that moved with knowing understatement. I had hired her straight out of the Harvard Business School to join the team of analysts I headed up for Dolans, the business news-sheet. Dolans was fiercely independent. We reported business the way we saw it – a real hunger for the truth. And the debt-rating agencies took notice. Since the banks used the agencies' rating to fix the interest level on corporate debt, it cost someone money every time Dolans spoke.

'What's the story, Minx?'

We were sitting at a courtyard table in one of the many winebars that had opened all over downtown New York in the eighties, but were to close when junk bonds lost their shine.

'You know my comments on Trident Drug? Last month?' Minx said and fiddled with an unlit cigarette.

'What about it?'

'I got this weird call, ten days ago. Two in the morning.'

I searched Minx's face. I remembered the night I'd told

her I was getting married. I'd told her before we'd made love; our passion in the hours that followed still filled my mind, if I let it.

'Go on.'

'A man. Very strange and cold voice. Said, "Trident do a lot of good that people like you are trying to screw up, lady." Then he hung up.'

I felt a fist close around my gut.

'Then last night he called again. Same time. He said, "Before you fuck around any more with Trident Drug, think of your own health first." '

I poured us wine. I had thought our little tête-à-tête was because Minx had got a better offer somewhere else on the Street and she wanted to break the news gently to me.

'You should have told me about this before now,' I said, watching her light the cigarette.

'The first time I thought it might be some sort of weird coincidence,' she said, blowing smoke from the side of her mouth. 'Or someone playing a joke. But not after last night. Who knows I wrote these pieces? And my phone's not listed.'

There was no analyst whose insight I valued higher than Minx's. She'd written what she had about Trident because she'd found hard evidence that Trident was boosting its sales by bribing doctors at state institutions to prescribe its drugs for mentally disabled patients – for such things as high blood pressure. There was evidence that the patients had the healthiest blood pressure in North America. They lived into old age, thousands of them in twenty states, ingesting drugs they didn't need like laboratory rabbits bred for the sole purpose of enhancing the profits of Trident Drug.

I said, 'You must tell the cops.'

Minx shook her head. 'I don't want to sound crazy, but

this is a fantastic story, Joe. I mean, if Trident have hired some thug to try and spook me, and I can prove it, think of the copy that will make!'

I didn't like it, and I said so. 'Minx, do you know how much Roberto Groz stands to make next year alone on Trident share options?'

She nodded; she knew. 'At today's price, around fifteen million dollars.'

I would remember Minx from that evening for ever. The fading, New York sunlight making a band across the freckles of her nose. Her worried look. The way she thrust out her chin.

'Be careful, Minx,' I said. 'These are not people to fuck with.'

Minx shook her head, as if disappointed by my caution. 'Wall Street is dazzled by the Groz it sees on Park Avenue. The banks see an ex-NIH official on Wall Street and give him whatever he wants. The media eat out of his hand. You buy public opinion and Dr Groz is not short of cash.'

She was right. I knew. The Chairman of the Board and Chief Executive Officer of Trident Drug was becoming one of the corporate legends of the eighties. Roberto Groz's oval-shaped eyes, which told you of his East European origins, always seemed to be looking out those days from somewhere on the news-stands.

'People just see the icon,' said Minx with zeal, 'but believe me, Joe, there are even worse aspects to Dr Groz than the mental patients. He makes my flesh crawl. I mean, Trident has been indicted four times for putting unproven drugs into humans without approval. You kill people that way. And Trident has been singled out by animal rights groups as causing unnecessary pain and suffering to primates in experiments. There's more, I just know it.'

I watched the face I knew so well in love.

'You're the analyst on the stock,' I said. 'You write what you must – but I still think you should report the calls.'

'I'm setting up a tape-recorder on my phone,' Minx said. 'I want to get this guy on tape. Then I'll tell the cops. Deal?'

I never knew why, but I said, 'Deal.'

'Thanks,' Minx said and brought my hand to her cheek. 'I'll write it as I see it. People read Dolans for the truth. Happy days!' She raised her glass.

'Happy days.'

Minx was smiling because she saw the old ache in my eyes. She leant over and ran her fingers through my beard. 'Now be a good boy and run along home to your new wife, Joe Grace. And don't worry about me.'

II

'Dr Groz will go through the roof if he reads this,' said Patrick Malone. 'He'll go into fucking orbit.'

It was two weeks after Minx had told me about the calls. We were sitting in what was grandly described in Dolans as the Boardroom. Patrick Malone, the man at the other side of the chaotic desk, had been a cop in Brooklyn before he'd gone into business journalism after the war. You could still see the big, raw cop in him, even though he was now seventy.

'What's the kid got against Groz?' Malone asked. 'What's her problem?'

'She's just doing her job, Paddy,' I replied. 'She's very good at it, which is why you pay her so much.'

'Don't be saucy with me, Joe,' said Malone, showing his teeth. 'You Irish are all the same.'

He blew out his cheeks and turned in his chair to gaze out the window from which you could just see the Brooklyn Bridge, or a two-by-one slice of it. Grand sweat hoops impended from Malone's armpits.

'You hear these stories about Groz,' he said. 'He's ruthless, Joe. He's got these heavies around him, from someplace in Russia, I don't know. They say they'd walk straight through a brick wall, then come back and build it up again.'

'Chechens,' I said.

'What?' The old man frowned.

'They're from Chechnya. So is Groz. A region of Russia near the Caspian Sea, down near the Caucasus. Groz's parents came from Grozny, the capital. It's how he got his name.'

'I don't know nothing except this stuff of Minx's is dynamite,' Malone said, picking up the two-page typescript. 'Dynamite.'

'But true,' I said. 'I've been through it.'

'So Groz made big over-provisions when he took over some tinpot outfits down in South America,' Malone said, 'and now he's using those provisions to keep his last quarter's profits up – so what? Everyone does it.'

'It's part of a bigger picture on Trident, Paddy.'

'I know the pharmaceutical business, sonny. Trident Drug, Saxmann, Armentisia Laboratories, Bell Smith and Holland. It doesn't matter. They're all the same, glossy on the cover, but when you get into the small print you realize these guys don't want to cure diseases, they want to *contain* them. They don't want people to get better, they want them to tick over, using their drugs. Trident is no different. Their interest is in profits, not in cures, and certainly not in people.'

'Doesn't sound too ethical.'

'Ethical my ass! When I hear you talking ethical I know the cause is lost for sure. The pharmaceutical industry is an ethical quagmire and the most corrupt player in the whole swamp is the Food and Drug Administration of this country. More corrupt than the Mafia. Corrupt in the very way the system operates in favour of the status quo, of the big boys. Corrupt in putting internal politics and your career before the needs of millions of people. Corruption of power, that's what I'm talking about.'

A secretary came in and added another stack of paper to Malone's overflowing desk.

'So what are you going to do?' he asked, lifting up Minx's piece again. 'I've told you what I think.'

'I think we should run it,' I said.

Malone gave me a weary look; he shrugged and looked

away. 'You know I don't overrule on these things.'

I saw, for the first time ever, a furtiveness across his eyes. 'Paddy, has Groz tried to lean on you? Has he given you the heat over Minx?'

'Even if he had, do you think I'd give a shit?' asked the big ex-cop aggressively. 'Do you think I'd put the interests of some empire builder like Roberto Groz before Dolans?'

'But has he? Paddy?'

I knew it would have been easier to shift the Brooklyn Bridge than Patrick Malone.

'Yeah, there's been pressure,' said Malone quietly. 'Some big-shot lawyer got on to the Chairman. Told him Trident was being victimized.' Malone curled his lips. 'I told the Chairman to tell them go fuck themselves, all right? But that doesn't mean Minx shouldn't be careful. There's a lot of money at stake for Dr Groz. People do funny things for a lot of money, in case you hadn't noticed. Now get out of here, I got work to do.'

In the months and years that followed, I often thought back to that meeting. I should have told Malone about the calls to Minx. Because if I had, maybe then Malone would have done what he rarely did and pulled the piece on Trident. But I didn't tell Malone. I didn't because I felt that would be disloyal to Minx. Because I was too young to know better. Because I could just imagine the disappointment in Minx's face if her piece was pulled. I told no one about Minx's nocturnal caller, and then spent the next fifteen years regretting that I hadn't.

III

I had lived in New York from the age of fifteen, finished the schooling there that I'd started in Dublin, then when I was eighteen I'd gone straight into the Marines. Great years, great friends. I landed a job in Dolans when I came out in 1980 and three years later I married Lee. We lived on the Upper West Side. We were trying to make a go of it, despite the fact that gaps had opened up between us after a few months that we hadn't realized were there. I'd been looking forward to settling down when we tied the knot, getting our new apartment together, doing the kind of groundwork on the marriage that my mother would have approved of. Which to me meant kids. But Lee wasn't ready for kids. It had become an unspoken obstacle between us.

Perhaps it was because I was worrying about my marriage that I didn't think too much more about Minx. Even when she pissed on Trident again, and some of the agencies shaved Trident's ratings, I didn't worry.

'You seen *Moody's*?' Ricardo asked.

Ricardo Vegas, like me, was an assistant editor on Dolans. Women thought Ricardo looked like the young Tom Cruise and Ricardo made the most of this resemblance. We'd swapped dates, he and I – before I'd got married.

'I've seen it,' I said.

'Their downgrading will cost Trident on its long-term debt,' Ricardo said. 'Dr Groz won't be pleased.'

'Everyone worries about Dr Groz. If you ask me he runs a drugs company without very many big drugs and uses some peculiar methods to sell the ones he has.'

Ricardo fluffed out his long hair on his shoulders.

'Yet he is one hell of an impressive guy, you must admit. Son of immigrant Russians. Tough kid in Detroit, brilliant school career, first in Michigan State, then medical school. Walked straight into one of the top jobs with the National Cancer Institute at Bethesda, Maryland.'

'From where he jumped ship for an equally meteoric career in New York with Trident Drug – I know his resumé.'

'He's ex-NIH, he's got the connections,' Ricardo persisted. 'Trident gets its products approved faster by the FDA than any other pharmaceutical.'

'But what products? As Minx points out, a lot of them are running out of patent and Trident have nothing coming up to replace them.'

Ricardo winced. 'It sounds as if Dolans has a vendetta going.'

'Don't worry,' I said. 'Trident will survive Minx,' and we both laughed.

I was right. Trident lost a dollar in as many days, but then climbed back again before anyone really noticed.

IV

Then one night in mid-October when I was asleep in bed with my wife beside me, the telephone rang. Calls at three in the morning have a way of making you become instantly awake. The person on the other end told me he was a doctor on casualty duty at Lenox Hill Hospital.

'She keeps asking for you,' he said. 'I got your number out of the White Pages.'

I felt panic coming at me like a train. 'What happened?'

'I think if you can come in right now you should,' the doctor said.

'Is her life in danger?'

'Not as such.'

'Jesus! Do the police know?'

'The police brought her in here,' the doctor replied.

I pulled on jeans and a sweater and a pair of sneakers, left a note for Lee, and ran down to Broadway for a cab. I was scared. *Not as such*. I had no details of what had happened, but felt the way you do when the earth suddenly moves somewhere miles beneath you. Lenox Hill is on 77th and Park. The doctor was waiting in the lobby to Emergency when I ran in.

'We've had to sedate her,' he said, steering me down a corridor. 'She was hysterical.'

'What happened?'

The doctor took a deep breath. He was an intern, about my age. 'Seems she was at home watching TV when . . . someone she thought was a friend called downstairs. A guy. She buzzed him into the building.'

We were walking down a bright passage crowded with patients on trolleys, hooked up to drips, and doctors in green gowns and masks battling to save lives whilst New York slept.

'The guy came upstairs and still thinking he was . . . a friend, she let him into her apartment,' the doctor said and looked closely at me. 'He wasn't a friend.'

We'd come to a door. A cop in uniform sat outside, his cap in his hands. He looked tired. The doctor pushed in the door. I could see a man, another cop, I guessed, sitting beside a tiny figure in the bed. She appeared to be bandaged from the neck down.

'She's listed for surgery in the next thirty minutes,' the doctor said.

'What did he *do* to her?' I asked.

'*Joe!*'

Minx had seen me. She screamed. I went to her and she caught me and screamed. Terrified. Her grip, her eyes. She screamed into my face like something wild that's been captured for slaughter.

'*JOE!*'

'I'm here, Minx, no one's going to hurt you now,' I said.

'*JOE!* Do you know what they *DID*?'

'Who, Minx?' I shouted.

She sank back, weeping.

'It's okay now, Carmine, it's okay,' the doctor said, coming to the other side of the bed.

'Groz,' Minx whispered and looked at me from miles off. 'Groz sent him, Joe. I know it was Groz.'

The doctor sank a hypodermic needle in Minx's arm and her eyes went glassy.

'Jesus,' I gasped, standing up. 'What's *happened* to her, would someone please tell me?'

The doctor turned me away gently from the bed.

'Whatever bastard she let in,' he said quietly, 'cut off her nipples.'

I had to get out into the corridor. I lost all sense of time or place.

'Mr Grace?'

I saw this unshaven face somewhere off in the direction of Long Island.

'Yes?'

The man introduced himself as Detective something or other. He described the call from Carmine, hysterical, made from a payphone because her own had been ripped out. Where the cops had found her, in the street, in a pool of her own blood. I took in maybe one word in five.

'She was lucky she didn't bleed to death,' the detective said.

'Why did . . .' I fought for my own breath. '. . . why did she let the bastard in?'

'Because,' replied the detective, scanning me curiously, 'he said he was you.'

I took a cab back uptown. They'd used my name to get in and do it. I was sick. I didn't want to have to talk to Lee about it either – I felt too much for the woman I'd just left behind in the hospital, more than I could safely explain. I could not get the sight of Minx's face out of my sight. Nor her voice from my head. *Joe! Do you know what they DID?* The thought of what had happened to her, what it meant for her as a woman, made me bite my tongue till it bled.

I stood under the shower for ten minutes, but couldn't wash off the film of outrage. I was intact. I could run my hands down my wet body without coming to a flaw. No one had taken a knife to me because I had voiced my opinion.

I dressed quickly. The anger kept washing over me. Lee was still asleep when I left for the second time that morning and took a cab downtown. Such a man as Groz did not allow a fifteen million dollars stock bonanza to slip through his fingers. Not when all it took was some massaging of the figures to keep things humming. Or the mutilating of some perky kid.

We'd stopped at a light when I focused on where we were. In the middle of Park Avenue. Across the flowerbeds from a building I recognized.

'I'll get out here.'

Suddenly I was on a downhill without brakes, I had no say. Through the lobby, I found the name Trident on a board. Up eighty-seven floors by express elevator. I didn't care if Chechen thugs who could knock down walls were up here; I didn't care about anything. Behind a desk to one side of a walnut, panelled door, a blonde woman was arranging fresh flowers. For years afterwards I could recapture their scent. I stepped from the elevator and the woman turned to me and smiled.

'Dr Groz,' I said.

'You're expected for breakfast, sir? What name?'

The thought of Groz eating breakfast as Minx lay on the operating table of a hospital was obscene. The woman was looking at me, waiting for an answer.

'Say a friend of Carmine Dominguez,' I said and kicked in the door behind her.

No matter what your opinion of Dr Roberto Groz, the setting was spectacular. New York was everywhere below and around the vast room. Two waiters in white jackets with green epaulettes were serving bacon with scrambled eggs, and coffee to half a dozen suited men at an oval table. The men turned as one on my entrance. Groz was at the head of the table, far end. He stood up. He really did look like he'd just stepped off the cover of *Fortune*. Tall with pale but bright blue eyes and soft, curly brown hair. He was smiling as he approached me. From the breast pocket of his deep grey suit flowered a blood-red kerchief.

'Can I help you?' he enquired, but now he must have seen the look on my face for his eyes were darting from me to the waiters, telling one of them to pick up a phone, fast.

I broke his nose with the first punch. I felt it break. Groz skidded back, kicking his legs in an attempt at balance and fell heavily across his breakfast table, knocking silver dishes and coffee pots as he did so. The breakfast guests scattered like whitebait. Groz came up again, hands groping. I gave him the hardest head butt I knew how, finishing off in the nose department what I'd started. Permanently. I was shouting although I scarcely knew it. Minx's name, over and over again. So the bastard would never forget. Groz was a big man; I broke the table with him. I smashed his jaw. I caught him by the throat and slammed him back against a wall tapestry where I systematically broke his ribs down one side.

'Carmine Dominguez!' I shouted and hit him at the apex of his stomach so that his eyes popped. 'Will you remember now? Carmine Dominguez!'

It was the craziest thing I ever did. In front of eight terrified witnesses I beat one of the most powerful men in New York until no breath was left in my body. I forgot about my job and my wife and the family I had hoped to raise. I thought only about Minx. The craziest thing I ever did, but the most just.

When the guy from security stuck the gun barrel in my ear, it was the luck of God he didn't blow my head off.

PART ONE

Present Day

February–March

1

A phone rang. Miles away. On a sleety, late February Saturday morning, the type of Irish weather from which travel agents make their fortunes. Sleet whipped like flying lead over Dublin, or at least, over Temple Bar. The phone rang.

I opened one eye. Like every other part of Hanny, the nape of her neck begged to be licked. Five foot ten with blonde, short-cropped hair, her limbs were to me pure Teutonic, which is to say they had that healthy, honeyed quality I associated with larch forests and beer. She was twenty-nine, a little more than half my age, and when not in bed she wore shiny skirts that looked made of edible plastic. To complete this checklist, something I took pleasure in: a mouth like a flawless, plastic mould, perfect teeth and smiling, hazel eyes. And, oh yes, she wore a ring in the right side of her nose which she took out when we were in bed. Thirty minutes before she had reached for me, and taken me in both her hands, and we had done what both of us wanted, warm and urgent, and neither of us had really woken up.

'My phone downstairs,' I said.

Sleet hit the bedroom window in a gust that blew the curtains in. Hanny had been in the Dáil the night before, covering some political wrangle for the German media group she stringed for. She'd come home tense and we'd sat up together, and listened to Keith Jarrett on sax and Hanny had rolled herself one of her special cigarettes.

The phone. Markets didn't work Saturdays. The phone was sitting one floor below on my office desk. My schedule that Saturday was no more demanding than take out the bike – an Electra Glide Classic in vivid black; I liked that bike – and ride down into Wicklow to a little pub we had discovered, and have lunch. Get out of Dublin, sleet or not. Temple Bar was always full of tourists. They treated it like a movie set; sometimes I found them on the stairs or wandering around my office.

In the end Salman made the decision; he was a phone freak. Six months before when Hanny had moved in with me from her flat in the Financial Services Centre, the IFSC, he had come with her. Hanny still owned that flat and sometimes I wished Salman would go back and live there. Predominantly green, with black and yellow bars on his crown that widened progressively down his back and out to his wings, he had a filthy temper if ignored. Hanny called him *Wellensittich*.

I stuck my toes into slippers. The day before a broker in New York called Soby Sandbach had promised me a consultant's report he'd unearthed on a manufacturing outfit we were interested in. Soby had said he'd send it special delivery. But courier companies didn't work Saturdays. The phone rang and rang.

'I'm coming!' I said, swearing at Salman, and trundled down the first of two flights of stairs. We had stakes in a number of start-up operations, we being Grace Equity, the company I ran. We were in telecommunications, in bio-agriculture and in computers. Four individuals had put up half a million each and they made up four-fifths of the shareholders of Grace: Caulfield Cade, a Texan; Raza, an Indian, who traded only in children's toys; a London Eastender called Dave who lived in Florida and owned his own Gulfstream jet; Carson McCoy, whose twenty-five million of preference share capital had floated Grace Equity out of dry dock in the first instance. And me, of course. I owned 20 per cent because Grace Equity was my idea.

My flat was on the top floor. At ground level was a tiny Italian restaurant called Positano; in between was my office, just a room each for myself, for Tim Tully, our financial guy, and for Anne, my secretary. I picked the phone up.

'Joe. This is an unforgivable interruption.'

'Carson,' I said and checked my watch. It was still only five in the morning in New York. 'What's the weather like over Central Park?'

From his penthouse on Central Park South, McCoy owned a view of New York's square of green that was impossible to value.

'No idea,' Carson McCoy said. 'But from where I'm sitting it's a white-out over St Stephen's Green.'

I didn't get it. I had spoken to him on Thursday, the first time in two months, but he had mentioned nothing about coming to Dublin.

'I'm in the Shelbourne,' McCoy said and gave me the number of his suite. 'I know it's Saturday but I'd like to talk.'

I was irritated. I was programmed for Wicklow. 'No problem. But can we make it this morning? Like, inside an hour? I've a lunchtime meeting.'

'I'll expect you at eleven,' McCoy said.

I took the stairs back up in threes. It was a month since Hanny and I had had a whole weekend to ourselves and I was damned if anyone was going to disrupt it – Grace Equity's principal investor or not. I'd have to do something about the phone. Or about Salman. Like wring his neck. As I made my way in past the glowering budgerigar and sat on the bed, a long, honeyed arm made its way across the quilt and began, insidiously, to nibble the little hairs in the small of my back.

'Who was it?' she murmured, exploring.

'McCoy is in the Shelbourne,' I said as I pulled on my socks. 'He wants to talk.'

'On Saturday?' said Hanny and ran long fingers down into the valley below the base of my spine.

I bent and kissed her and Hanny looked up at me with a drowsy, womany, bed-captured, morning look.

'I won't be long,' I said.

I really meant it.

2

St Stephen's Green was in dress rehearsals for next year's Christmas cards. I passed a newsagent's and saw that day's local tabloid offering: a full-page photograph of a pretty woman leaving a Dublin nightclub in the company of a man with a peroxide-coloured, bullet-shaped head. 'AMAZING GRACE' the headline shrieked. She was, too, I could testify, having been married to her for five years. What I could not understand was why she still insisted on keeping my name.

I wanted to think. I did a turn of the Green, around the little lakes where ducks walked on ice, the crunching of my boots turning central Dublin into the Black Forest.

Although I had known Carson McCoy for three years, I still had no idea who he was. He was seldom photographed and apparently used aliases when he travelled. Of his domestic situation, whether or not there was a Mrs McCoy and children, or whether the fifty-five-year-old's preferences lay elsewhere, I had no idea. His background was equally vague, as occasional media profiles showed: grandparents originally from Ulster, emigrated to the States, his father had died aged twenty-six in New York. Carson McCoy had started out working on building sites on the Upper West Side. Even as a teenager he had had the physique of a man ten years older: a massive frame, great, long arms, the kind of body that makes sculptors reach for their chisels. His face was another matter. I only knew him, of course, as a man in his late middle age, but I could still imagine how angry it would have made a hulking lad of fourteen to have been born with a lip split quite as badly – and no doubt made immeasurably worse at the hands of some clumsy intern in whatever public maternity hospital McCoy had been born in. It made it difficult if you just met him, even now after many attempts by plastic surgeons in the best hospitals in the US, to look squarely in McCoy's face. No doubt this was partly where the penchant for secrecy and reclusivity had come from. The boy had seen the world stare at his face, had felt the humiliation and the sense of being outcast; the man had vowed not to be humiliated again.

At the age of twenty, he had begun buying and selling real estate in New York that no one else would touch. There were stories of the early days, mostly whispered, about how Carson McCoy had got his way. No one was around to prove this any more, but it was still said that no one had ever double-crossed him in a deal and walked away. Men disappeared. In the 1970s, McCoy had had to leave the States for eighteen months – until, that is, there were no longer certain witnesses around to testify. During that period he had gone to the Far East and consolidated his fortune. Whether or not any of this was true, most of the early New York real estate was still intact, by some accounts entire districts. Trusts owned trusts and were in turn owned by charitable foundations in Liechtenstein, Vienna and Cyprus. The *Financial Times* had dubbed him the Thomas Pynchon of international finance.

I passed the Department of Foreign Affairs, its steps blocked with snow. One day three years ago I had received a call and a week later I was sitting down in the same hotel that I was now headed for. He'd heard about me through a bank, or so he said. The terms had been tough but fair. Twenty-five-million-dollar dividend payable at one point over interbank average rates – EUROBAR – but only out of net profits. Non-cumulative, which meant: no profit, no dividend. Secured on my 20 per cent of Grace Equity;

repayable on demand. There was a lot of trust called for between two men who had never previously met. Three years later I had no regrets. Grace had never missed a payment and McCoy had never interfered. Not once.

The road outside the Shelbourne was being swept clear by a porter. I stamped snow from my boots, then made my way in by the revolving doors and to the lifts. I saw my ex-wife again, looking at me from a news-stand. My second ex-wife, to be accurate. My first, Lee, and I had split up when I left New York. Then, six months after coming home to Ireland, I had met Donna. We both had wanted the other at first sight. For ever. It lasted six years, some of them so good it hurt to remember. But then something happened, even now I'm not sure exactly what, and our marriage fell apart over one weekend. After we split up, her new companions were chosen from what could be loosely called the Celtic Pups, men under thirty-five as a rule, who had made money from computer company flotations, or had merely inherited money from people who had acquired fortunes in a similar fashion. Since then Donna – once top model Donna Rainbow, her real name – had moved on to pop stars. Today's number was called Pierce something. Pierce me, I thought and wished I hadn't left my bed and Hanny.

The heating made my nose thaw. When McCoy had first become involved with Grace Equity, I had expected him to put forward his own investment suggestions for our company. He never had. Now I expected the time had come. I wasn't apprehensive. On the contrary. With McCoy's track record, a suggestion from him promised to be as good as an insider's tip. His suite was on the top floor, at the front of the building.

'Joe, good of you to come in so quickly.'

'Welcome back to Dublin,' I said and we shook hands.

His size was again the first thing that struck me. His size and his face. Such was his destiny. I'm just over six foot one and still I was looking at his shirt collar. He walked with a slight roll, like a cowboy or a blacksmith, and led the way back through his suite. Everything was always low-key with McCoy – no big show of money, no flunkies, McCoy opened doors himself for you, and poured coffee for you, as he now did for us both. If I had his money, I'd have footmen behind every chair, I thought. I'd be with Hanny on my own island somewhere off South America.

'The waiter who brought me breakfast asked me did I gamble,' he smiled. His hands on the desk in front of him reminded me of scaled-down anvils. 'I told him I was not risk averse, so he gave me a tip for a horse. I call that style. A waiter in New York would never give you a tip for a horse.'

'You should buy some horses,' I said.

'I've thought about it,' McCoy said, sipping coffee. 'I once owned a racetrack in Florida which turned a tidy few bucks – but horses? They die.'

'You didn't tell me you were coming in,' I said. 'I could have left myself free.'

'I'm flying out in three hours,' he said, not volunteering a destination. 'That's if Dublin is open by then.'

So he was here to see me, but hadn't told me he was coming. I hate surprises.

'What can I do for you, Carson?'

'Joe, I need a favour.'

'Whatever I can do.' And I sipped the coffee.

'Perhaps the best way to explain my needs is to tell you a story.' McCoy was seated with his back to the window so that his uncomfortable face was in outline only. My attention was once again drawn to the hands, crossed on the desk, the fingers as long and thick as candles. 'Two years ago, an unusual investment opportunity came my way. Unusual on several counts: firstly the sum required was one million dollars and as you know I tend to deal in larger numbers. Second, this was an investment in a small private scientific company in the UK, in Bristol in fact, and you would also know that the trouble for me in monitoring something of that kind, a private company in Bristol in an area of business I know nothing about, would far exceed any possible dividend.'

'But you went ahead.'

'Correct. But for a completely different reason. The underlying project for which this company needed my cash was to develop a cure for AIDS.'

Snow hurried against the window of the suite.

'The inventor's name was Carlos Penn. A microbiologist. A genius by all accounts, although I never met him personally. Unconventional. Erratic and given to impulses. Bewildered by the world outside his laboratory, he found human relationships difficult. Anyway, who cares what he felt? Penn believed he had discovered how to reawaken the body's immune system. His treatment worked. In some patients, both in Bristol and in California, the virus disappeared. These patients were able to go back to a normal life, I was shown the proof. He called his drug BL-4. I gave him the money.'

McCoy put down his cup.

'Eleven months ago, Penn took his discovery to the United States. He wanted contacts with companies that would develop his discovery, that would get it licensed over there.'

I nodded that I understood. The Food and Drug Administration in the United States was the yardstick by which the rest of the world measured everything. If the FDA passed it, then it was fine everywhere else, more or less.

'But Penn did not want just any company. He wanted a scientific partner with more than money – in other words, a partner who would not keep BL-4 back for commercial convenience. I don't know if you understand the pharmaceutical industry, but they're interested not in people but in money.'

A crack opened in my memory and a bitter-sweet scent wafted out. 'So I've been told.'

'Penn was using a laboratory in the University of Southern California to analyse the blood of the patients,' said McCoy. 'One day he left USC and went back to his hotel. He has never been seen again.'

My mind was trying to get ahead of the action, to find what it was that McCoy was working towards.

'Weird story,' I said.

'Penn wasn't married. He has a sister, Constance, who lives in Bristol and who has gone through the motions. Police. Interpol. Do you know how many people go missing in the United States every year? Two thousand a week. Ninety per cent of them turn up again in a matter of days, but that leaves like ten thousand people a year who simply vanish for ever. One more is a pebble in the ocean.'

'Which is where a lot of them end up. By their own choice, too, I should think.'

'Not Penn, I'm sure of it. He lived to heal. But that's just a detail.'

'People run off the whole time with investors' money, Carson. Take it and go to faraway places. Like Venezuela.'

'This is no fraud.' McCoy took out a red file and placed it on the table between us. Slim and bound around by a rubber band, the file's centre bulged slightly. 'You see, I've got evidence in here. Somebody abducted him.'

3

I thought of Wicklow, a warm fire, a bottle of wine warming in the grate, and Hanny. I deliberately did not pick up the file.

I said, 'Okay, I may have some contacts. If you give me the full details I'll try . . .'

'Joe.' McCoy had a way of getting attention. 'I flew in last night not to ask you to ask a favour of someone else, but to ask a favour of you.'

'Me?' I asked, keeping it stupid.

'You're very modest. There are many things you never told me.'

I sat back and laughed. 'What is this?'

'You know the way I operate,' McCoy said. 'One to one. I want you to find Carlos Penn for me.'

I looked at him to make sure he was serious, but there was nothing on McCoy's shadowy face to suggest he was playing this for laughs.

'I'll help you in any way I can, of course,' I said, 'but what you need here is a professional.'

McCoy had gone over to papers on his desk and was reading: '"Joseph James Grace. Born 1955. Left Ireland in 1969 to live with relatives in New York. Reason for emigration: pending legal action in Dublin Juvenile Court. Completed schooling in New York 1973. Joined the United States Marines Corps 1974. Basic training in Camp Pendleton, then in Quantico, Virginia. Fluent in five languages, including Arabic. Moved into the Intel section 1976 under General Al Gray."'

'Carson . . .'

'"The Lebanon 1977. Force Recon. Promoted to

captain 1978. Awarded the Silver Star 1979. Left Marine Corps 1980 for position as financial analyst on Wall Street." '

'Carson, that was all years ago.'

McCoy smiled. 'Modesty, Joe. You were the best. The best don't forget.'

'I disagree, but it's irrelevant anyway, because I'm not interested.'

'Don't be impetuous. Impetuosity has cost you before, if I'm not mistaken.'

I was not going to be drawn down alleyways of this man's choosing. 'Find someone else. Period. I'm sorry.'

McCoy sighed and closed the file. 'I've been down the professional route you refer to. Look, it's eleven months now since this man disappeared. We may not have much time left.'

I tried to manage my impatience. 'I respect what you're trying to do, I admire it. I'm sorry for Mr Penn. But forget all that Marines stuff, it was a lifetime ago. I'll front the hiring of the best person there is, whoever that is. You won't have to be remotely associated with the project. No sweat. Give me the details and I'll have someone lined up to do the job within a week.'

'No deal.' He had become impatient and with it came another glimpse of the physical: his jaw grinding. He turned his face away from me; in profile its starkness reminded me of the head on a coin – one of those old coins commemorating carbuncled despots from the Middle Ages.

'Do you know what could be at stake here? There are fifty million living cases of this disease. Sixteen million deaths have already taken place – it's the worst human health disaster since the Black Death. This is not just an assignment that can be subcontracted because you are too busy with something else. I haven't talked money yet, either. But find him and you can consider that twenty-five-million-dollar seed money I gave you written off. But it must be *you*. Not some fool from a comic strip who can't tie his own laces. *You*. You go and find him. You bring him to me. Tell me we have a deal.'

I felt anger rising up in me like damp. For some reason Pierce Bullet Head or whoever he was intruded into my vision.

I said: 'Carson, I'm running a very demanding business which I think you know returns exceptionally well to its investors. I'm not some private eye. And I'm surprised, frankly, that you would try to buy me off in the way you just have. Grace Equity will repay you as it is currently doing and that won't involve me in playing Indiana Jones on the way.'

McCoy sighed. 'Have I insulted you? If I've insulted you, I apologize. I'm sorry. I really am.'

'There's no need to apologize.'

'Will you accept my apology?'

'If it makes you feel any better, yes, I accept your apology.'

'Good. Now, will you consider my request?'

I closed my eyes. 'No, Carson. Sorry. No. I'll help you hire someone, but I'm not casting for the role. Sorry.'

'Then I'm doubly sorry,' McCoy said. 'In view of your refusal, I must ask you to read this.'

I wondered for a moment if this was a set-up of some kind, some bizarre television programme where the least imaginable event was sprung on an innocent victim. I even checked around the suite, but all I saw was McCoy handing me a legal document.

'Carson . . .'

'*Read it!*'

There were two pages. The law firm was MacLattins, a big Dublin name, the same one that McCoy had used when he initially had put the money into Grace. I felt like it must feel like when you get a terminal diagnosis. Not good. 'Jesus Christ!' I threw the document back. 'Are you crazy?'

What I had just read was a legal exercise of the repayment option on the entire preference share capital of Grace Equity.

'I might ask you the same question.'

'I thought I knew you, Carson. I thought we were partners.'

'Partners do each other favours. A partner would say we have a deal.'

'Not this time.'

'Don't make me do this.'

'I'm lost for words,' I said in genuine bewilderment. 'I really am.'

'Say we have a deal. It's easy.'

'You understand what this means,' I said. 'It means refinancing the operation under pressure, which is never wise and may not in fact be possible in the time available, or alternatively, unravelling almost overnight investments that have been painstakingly assembled over three years, all because you've become fixated with some fucking scientist. We'll lose our bollox, you included.'

Carson McCoy shrugged. 'I'll ride it out.'

'You'll ride it out, but other people will be hurt, some big, me included. Does that satisfy some warped urge you have?'

'Maybe you're the one who's warped. Because Carlos Penn's no lunatic. This could be the greatest humanitarian project of the age. You choose not to become involved? I'm disappointed, Joe. You once needed me and now when things are the other way around, you turn your back.'

'You show up here on a piss-awful Saturday morning, you ask me to chase off after someone who's been missing for a year and when I decline you threaten to pull the rug from under my company. Jesus Christ!'

'As always, you sum up a situation better than almost anyone I know.' McCoy sat back. 'Look, think about it. I'm putting it all in the hands of my lawyers here. They know what to expect from you. I'm giving you a week to say we have a deal or not.'

I felt as if I'd been run over by a truck. My hands were trembling. I really did not know what to say – all I could think of was playing for time.

'I'll think about it,' I said.

'Good.' McCoy stood up. He didn't try to shake my hand. 'A few words of warning: there are some deals that no one wants but that still have to happen. This is such a deal. And as in all deals, there are terms and conditions. I expect them to be adhered to.'

I was beyond words. I too stood up, and began to walk.

'Joe!'

I turned. McCoy was holding up the red file.

'You forgot this,' he said.

I took it. I had never before felt so defeated.

4

To say that the following week was busy would be an epic understatement. Replacing twenty-five million dollars of loan capital was the only item on the agenda as far as I was concerned, by which I mean that a treatment for AIDS and an abducted scientist from Bristol did not figure high in my plans.

Late on Saturday evening I eventually caught up with Tim Tully. Tim was an unlikely-looking financial controller for an outfit like ours. Small and broad, he had a Hell's Angel look about him, complete with beard, mane and the tattoo of an eagle at the base of his throat which called for ties during formal meetings. In matters financial, however, he had the instincts of a starving Rottweiler. I'd run him down to the dog end of a poker school. Tim hadn't asked questions, had just come in straight away to Temple Bar, cracked a beer and put his feet up.

'Refinancing will hurt us,' he said. 'It will unsettle the banks. They'll want to know why McCoy is getting out. It's hardly because he needs the cash.'

We spent an hour going through the options.

'We've got three other shareholders who could easily bail out as well, if they didn't like the drift of things,' I said. 'We're in trouble.'

'Maybe, maybe not,' Tim said.

'Put yourself in Caulfield Cade's boots – what would he do? Look for a lot more information, for sure. What do we have to give him as a reason? Nothing. We can tell him the story I've just told you – but would he believe it? Would anyone?'

Tim rocked his head in partial agreement.

I said: 'There's something else driving this, something we know nothing about. Has to be. Why else would he threaten to flush away everything that has been achieved?'

'How did you leave him?'

'He gave me a week to make my mind up. Agree to find Penn or repay the loan money. The scariest thing is all the trouble he's gone to, the way he's so well prepared to pull the plug – and for what?'

I felt like getting very drunk.

'So you have to perform to his tune, or at least pretend to perform, whilst at the same time you try and find out what it is that's really going on,' Tim had said without emotion. 'What else can you do?'

'A lot,' I told him, 'starting with seeing Jenkins.'

I left him to go and update the company prospectus with a view to our meeting financial institutions as early the next week as possible.

'I'm going to kick this bastard's ass,' I said, washing Jameson over my teeth. 'I'm going to tell him where he can shove his cash.'

Hanny put down her book. 'That's the fifth time you've said that.'

'I'm very sorry, but it kind of seems worth repeating.'

'Come here.'

I turned on the sofa, put my head in her lap, closed my eyes.

'Try and relax.'

'D'you know what I saw on the way into the meeting with McCoy?'

'Hn-hn.'

'Donna's face. It's on every news-stand in Dublin.'

'I saw.'

'Who's the gobshite she's with?'

'He's the drummer with Hard Act.'

'Fuck him.'

'Are you jealous, Joe?'

'How could I be jealous of someone who costs me three and a half grand a month? I've got you.'

She bent down and kissed me.

I said, 'It just seemed to me that Donna was gloating over my misfortune. It was as if she and her stud were laughing at me. Maybe I'm going crazy.'

Hanny worked the flats of her thumbs into my temples. I began to yield.

'Joe? Can I say something?'

'Sure.'

'What if McCoy's telling the truth?'

I opened my eyes. 'I don't believe you said that.'

'What's wrong with saying that?'

'This is a stick-up, Hanny. McCoy has some other agenda. No one pisses away twenty-five million dollars on some missing nut case – that's if Carlos Penn ever existed or if he did, is really missing. I'm not getting sucked in. I'm refinancing and cutting loose. On further consideration, maybe this is the best thing that has ever happened as far as Grace Equity is concerned.'

5

Patrick Jenkins was the Senior Partner of Jenkins, Mulrooney, a medium-sized firm of Dublin solicitors, and the best corporate law firm in town. Now sixty, Jenkins was a bachelor and dressed in a way which ensured that each year he headed or came near the top of the Irish 'Best Dressed' list. He wore wide-brimmed hats with velvet bands which were made up for him in Barcelona, carried a cane and looked at the world through a Bertie Wooster-type monocle, his eye enlarged like ET's. People who were distracted by the camp diversion which Patrick's appearance guaranteed came out the other end of the case they were contesting minus everything they had gone in with. His brain was unrivalled. I had never known him to be wrong on a matter of fact. Eight out of ten of all the big American corporations made a beeline for his office as soon as they set foot in Ireland.

His office was on the top floor of a modern block near the old university. It was furnished with a Georgian sideboard and dining table and chairs, an early Victorian partner's desk and an enormous floor rug in claret and gold which I knew had been created specially for the room by V'soske-Joyce in Galway. A Jack Yeats looked down from the wall to the left of Patrick's desk, whilst the back wall was dominated by a spectacular Pauline Bewick.

We chatted about Patrick's passion, racehorses, a subject I knew something about, and the runners he hoped to have in Leopardstown at the next meeting, about the shenanigans of racehorse trainers, about the traffic, the weather and the Irish economy. Earlier, I had outlined my problem on the phone.

'The agreement with McCoy all hinged on trust,' Patrick said at last, 'and on the reasonable belief that a man reputedly worth billions would not pull the plug in this fashion.'

'If we can't refinance, do we have to unravel our portfolio in order to pay him back?' I asked. 'In other words, wind ourselves up?'

'On the face of it, that's exactly what you might have to do,' Patrick said. 'For the moment, McCoy holds the whip hand – and he knows it. Now there are considerations of natural justice to be dealt with, and he is abusing his position. However, he is the lender of the loan capital. Normally he would only demand repayment were Grace Equity insolvent or accumulating losses beyond a certain figure. No one imagined that such a lender would put a guillotine on a loan that has been performing very happily but whose repayment may now jeopardize its very security. Put simply, everyone, including McCoy, has far more to lose by his actions than he possibly stands to gain.'

I knew.

'The problem as I see it, Joe, is that if you take him on in the legal sense, your dilemma goes public. Now of course I'll get the best opinion there is from the Bar library on your chances at stopping him – and that may be our final line of defence – but in the meantime my advice to you, which I'm sure you've worked out yourself, is to find the money and take him out.'

I had to smile. No one got in and out the door here without, after some months, a discreet bill being presented, usually amounting to a sum of money that would pay for the average family's summer holiday. This morning I had coughed up in order to hear confirmed to me what I already knew.

'MacLattins will want to show zeal,' Patrick observed.

'Just direct them to us and we'll cool them off.'

He walked me out to the lift.

'Ireland is bursting with money,' he said. 'My bet is you'll be fighting off the offers.'

'I hope you're right,' I said.

'Come and have lunch in my box on Saturday,' Jenkins said. 'If the trainer is to be believed, the horse will win.'

The doors closed and I sank back down to the street.

6

Tim and I were sitting in armchairs overlooking the canal, drinking coffee from Wedgwood cups and swapping yarns about fishing marlin with the Managing Director of one of Ireland's leading investment banks. It was Tuesday morning and this was already the third such appointment. The banker joked about drinking cold beer by the neck as he chased schools of dolphin. I talked about catching salmon on the fly in the Slaney. Tim pitched in about hauling up crabs with safety pins in Ringsend. Everyone laughed. You do business like that, you pretend it's all a big game, that no one is ever desperate and that the cash is simply a detail that follows. It's called having fun. The banker was no more than thirty-five; he looked at me brightly. I'd played a lot of golf with him over the previous years when we'd done deals amounting in all to over ten million, all of them on behalf of my clients. Now I was about to ask him to refinance me.

'What can I do for you, Joe – apart from thanking you for all the fish you've brought in here?'

We all laughed again. We were all going along with the notion that it was normal that a thirty-five-year-old Dublin kid's hobby was deep-sea fishing off Haiti.

'I'm looking to replace the loan capital of Grace Equity,' I said as cheekily as I could. 'This is a preliminary meeting – there's no big rush, but it's just something we've decided to do.'

The banker's healthy young eyebrows rose.

I said, 'Here's our balance sheet. I think it speaks for itself. The loan money in question comes to twenty-five million dollars, secured on my shares in Grace. We're paying one point over EUROBAR, out of net profits.'

'And who would we be taking out . . .?'

'Carson McCoy.'

'McCoy and you are parting?'

'We're too small for him. I'd like someone on board who'll be more involved.'

'But you're parting.'

'Yes.'

'I – see.'

You can smell fear from these people, they've got glands like skunks. You can see it, too, in the way they withdraw in the eyes, and shift their bodies into defence mode and discreetly check that their wallets are still in place.

'That's – interesting, Joe. McCoy has a certain weight.'

'McCoy's played no hand, act or part in any business decision that we've made over the last three years,' I said. 'Which is one of the reasons I want him out.'

'Yet he's been a presence, albeit a sleeping presence.'

'He gave us the seed capital, he's made a good return. We now need more imaginative financing.'

The banker blinked rapidly. 'We'll look at it, certainly. I'd have to say that we're already well exposed in the venture capital area – with some of your clients, among others. But, yes, you're a friend, we'll look at it.'

'How soon?'

He gave me a wintry smile. 'You know us banks – and this is a lot of money. How soon do you need an answer?'

'I'd like an answer in principle this week.'

He nodded, but I knew whatever was now coming was bullshit and a waste of my time.

'I'll try. I have to go to the Board.'

'What'll you say?'

'I'll need a lot more information, of course . . .'

'But in principle,' I grinned. 'Come on, be straight. You won't offend me. I'd like to know.'

He sighed, the sigh of a man burdened with the custody of other people's money. 'I'll be straight with you, Joe, I'm not so sure how the bank will react to a proposal like this, no reflection on you personally, but . . .'

He tailed off.

'But what?'

The banker grimaced, as if giving hard advice hurt him. 'The fact that Carson McCoy has given you that money and left all the decisions to you has been one hell of a statement as far as your bankers are concerned. This is a man who could buy this bank out of his current account. He gives you world-class clout. I'd think very carefully about getting rid of him. Otherwise people may automatically assume the worst, they'll assume that he's getting rid of you – and that's not going to help you one little bit.'

'Thanks for the coffee,' I said.

7

I drove west out of Dublin at seven in the morning on the first Tuesday of March. The traffic was all coming the other way, gridlocked already, thousands of early commuters with their lights on. I came into open countryside around Enfield: fields that had lain under snow until a week before were now just resolutely grey and wet. The night before Hanny and I had stayed in and I had fried us up two cuts of fresh swordfish that had come in that afternoon by motorbike from Nicky's Plaice in Howth. It wasn't what you knew, it was who, my father had always said.

Six meetings, only one had shown any real interest, but they were an Irish subsidiary of a big UK bank and the local boys had no real say. The real say had come that morning: thanks for thinking of us, but at the moment this is not a proposal we can consider. Yours in mortal terror. Sometimes these people made me want to puke.

There had been moments those last ten days when I'd gone to sleep at my desk, even though I hadn't thought I was exhausted. Then I'd wake up and for the barest moment, before reality, I'd feel the old confidence that I'd always thrived on, the old surge of adrenalin and the eagerness to take on the world and everything it had to offer. Tim and I were spending eighteen hours a day trying to find a way of repaying McCoy his money and keeping us afloat. Our options were far from exhausted, but the day before there had been two calls from McCoy's Dublin lawyers, neither of which I'd returned. He was turning the screws.

I got through Enfield and thought about Hanny the night before. She'd folded her arms around me when I put the lights out.

'Joe? I've been thinking.'

'Hm?'

'I'd like to do some research on Carlos Penn – does that give you a problem?'

'No. I'd prefer if you came up with twenty-five million dollars, that's all.'

'This may help.'

'Okay.'

'I know you're angry.'

'I'm sorry, I haven't been much fun this last week.'

'Let me see what I can find out,' she had said.

Hanny – her real name was Hannelore – had been brought up in Düsseldorf by Grandfather Kleber and his wife, the parents of Hanny's journalist father. Hanny's mother had been an Olympic skier, but when Hanny was six, she and five others had been caught by melting snow on a southern slope of the Weissfluhgipfel, the peak that overlooks Davos. Hanny had no memories, only photographs of a beautiful woman with excitement in her eyes. Hanny's father had been the Moscow correspondent for *Der Spiegel*. It had broken his heart to do so, but he had sent Hanny home. She and I had known each other for three months before she told me: about the bad months in a clinic in the mountain town of Heldenbergen, north-east of Frankfurt, when she was fifteen. She'd gone to the clinic straight from hospital. She'd gone to the hospital straight from where police found her in Frankfurt, within ten minutes of death from a heroin overdose.

'Why did you do it?' I had asked.

'Because . . . I wanted to kill myself.'

'But why?'

She told me. I was the first person outside the clinic she had told. And at the moment, when Hanny told me, I had all at once seen a fragility in her that I wanted to protect with my life.

'If you ever get low like that again, promise you'll always tell me,' I said. 'Promise me.'

'I promise,' she had said.

The night before, she had tightened her arms around me and whispered in my ear: 'I have a feeling all this will work out, Joe. A good feeling.' I heard her voice and then I was asleep.

8

The flooded fields on the way west were like inland seas. I pulled into Mother Hubbard's, ordered the works and snapped open the locks on my briefcase. Grace Equity's business had to go on, Carson McCoy or not. The meeting I was on my way to had been set up for weeks.

It might seem strange to someone who didn't know Ireland that a high-tech, leading-edge company was located out here in the sticks, but there were hundreds of small success stories that the public never heard about and Interfibre was one. Leading-edge patents in mobile-communications technology. Nowadays everyone took tri-band phones and universal access for granted, but a few years ago, when such technology had been just a dream, down here in Ireland's wet Midlands the dream was becoming reality. From this small factory with less than a hundred people contracts went to five continents. A few years before when the banks didn't want to know Interfibre, I had put together an investment package of five million euros in exchange for 12½ per cent of Interfibre's equity. It only looked expensive back then if you didn't understand the way telecommunications were going. Banks were comfortable with buildings and land, but when it came to explaining that the entire planet could converse at once on a single fibre the width of a human hair, their eyes had gone as blank as a teller's window. Now a few years later the five million was worth fifteen. Interfibre was now bidding for a German software company; the meeting that morning was to discuss a rights issue for the cash needed for the job.

I finished rereading the file, drained the pot of tea, but

then, from the bottom of the briefcase, I saw McCoy's red file looking up at me. It seemed exactly as it had when I had first seen it, complete with rubber band and central bulge. The bulge now appeared sinister, like a tumor.

'Take it with you,' Tim had said.

'I don't want to have anything to do with it.'

Tim said with patience: 'There's a tape cassette in there. Maybe Interfibre can analyse it. Maybe we can learn something we don't know about McCoy.'

The cassette was the type used in Dictaphones or telephone answering machines. It sat in a little plastic box and was clipped neatly to a very short transcript of its contents. Otherwise, there were twenty typed pages and a photograph of a man whose grey hair was a mass of curls and who stared at the camera like a mad scientist from central casting. Penn had once been Penna. Argentinian. Father an inventor, of what the file was mute. Came to London after the war. Carlos born in 1957, knew what he wanted to be, even as a child. Graduate in microbiology, University of Liverpool's Medical Faculty. The file spoke of half a dozen jobs held by Carlos Penn, none exceeding six months in duration. During the 1980s, he had patented treatments for multiple sclerosis, motor neurone disease and malaria. He called them BL-1, BL-2 and BL-3. 'BL,' as the file explained, 'stands for Bristol.' For each patent a new company was formed and new investors brought in. Each company lasted only as long as the cash. It cost money to file international patents; to do tests on human beings; to use the services of reputable laboratories. Banks foreclosed. The file came across like required reading for anyone who had ever thought of investing risk capital in a patent. This was the man who was killing my business.

Then came AIDS. A special section was devoted to BL-4.

Photostat pages of dense-looking technical descriptions. There were profiles of patients – identified only by numbers – who lived in both Bristol and California.

> 'On 3rd March last year Carlos flew to Los Angeles where he met Dr Cuba Sali, a research scientist in the University of Southern California. That evening a receptionist at the Sierra Hotel, Marina Del Rey, Los Angeles, overheard part of a telephone conversation that Carlos had when he took a call at the reception desk of the hotel. Carlos was twice heard to mention the name of a Dr Gonzalez. Thirty minutes later, Carlos checked out of the Sierra. Three days later, on 6th March, Carlos telephoned his sister, Constance, in Bristol.'

All phone calls to and from the house in Bristol were automatically recorded, part of Carlos Penn's ongoing paranoia regarding the various law suits in which he was embroiled, the file explained.

'The transcript and tape of that conversation are attached. Carlos Penn has not contacted anyone since that date.'

There followed a list of the numerous attempts made by Constance to trace her brother, including the hiring of private agencies on both sides of the Atlantic.

I put the file away, paid for breakfast and went outside. It was raining. I could not tell why, but old memories were flooding back. After my first and only encounter with Dr Roberto Groz, my New York lawyer, a Bronx kid used to street fighting, had told me that either I left New York in a hurry or stayed to face a two-to-five-year sentence for aggravated assault. Groz had the best lawyers in New York on the case. Money didn't matter. Nor did winning in court, my lawyer had quietly told me. The word was, if I walked out of court a free man, I would not walk for long.

I had come home. I was still walking – or I had been up to a week before.

9

As soon as you walked in Interfibre's doors, you got the precision feel: equipment that demanded microscopic accuracy was designed and made here, and everything else took its lead from that fact. Clean, bold lines. Bright offices. I was shown straight up to the boardroom. The two founders were in their mid-fifties: Tony, the engineer, had been with Eircom before he jumped ship. Bill was the financial brain. Two Mayo men. We spent an hour reviewing the fine print of the forthcoming issue of new shares, then Tony poured coffee.

'You kept busy, Joe?' he asked.

'Busy enough,' I said.

'He has his money made, I can tell,' Bill winked at Tony. 'Tax exile written all over him. Off to Spain to work on his handicap.'

'Doubt that, somehow,' I laughed.

I saw Bill steal a look at his wristwatch. 'D'you want lunch, Joe?'

Even if I had, they weren't lunchers, I knew.

'I'll grab something on the way home,' I said. 'Thanks anyway.'

'And thank you,' Bill said, 'for your belief.'

It was still not midday.

'Do you have a moment, Tony?' I asked as we walked out along a corridor.

'Sure.'

'Do you think you could listen to a taped telephone conversation?'

Tony's office was all chrome and glass and leading-edge.

'This is the transcript,' I said as we sat down at a

conference table. The typescript was headed 'Telephone Connection 6th March'. 'It's not much, as you can see.'

Tony scanned the page. He got up and came back with a Dictaphone the size of his hand. He popped in the tape and we sat back.

There was the sound of a telephone being picked up.

'Hello, Constance? Constance?'

A man's voice.

'Carlos?'

Constance Penn.

'Constance, are you all right?'

A door opened in the background. Another man's voice could be heard.

'Carlos, what . . .'

'Constance! Listen very carefully. I . . .'

'Where are you?'

'Con . . .'

The man's voice was interrupted by three high-pitched pips.

'I'm . . .'

The call terminated in what sounded like bones being dislocated.

'That's it, I think,' I said.

'An old Europhone,' Tony said.

I looked at him.

'Payphone from a past generation.'

'What else can you tell me?'

'Give me five minutes,' Tony said, taking out the cassette and going to the door of an adjoining office.

I stood up and looked out over parkland. Although he had not spoken a dozen words, Carlos Penn had come suddenly alive for me on the tape. And then I felt fresh anger – this time with myself. People like McCoy always got what they wanted in the end.

'Sorry for all the trouble,' I said as Tony came back in.

'No problem,' said the engineer and sat down. 'Right. The call is from a Euro-Age payphone. The model T-600 to be precise.'

'I'm fascinated. How can you tell?'

'It's all in the pips. First, the pattern. Three pips close together. Then the pitch. We've measured these ones at just 600 hertz, which is how the old T-600 got its name. 600 is one of the lower frequencies used for payphone pips, when you consider that dial tone is at 450.' Tony picked up the cassette and looked at it. 'Where was the call recorded, d'you mind me asking?'

'In Bristol,' I replied.

Tony nodded. 'Makes sense. Call was made right here in Ireland, I would say.'

'In Ireland?'

'We've got a very short disconnection delay here. When you make a call, it's routed through various exchanges to your number, how many exchanges obviously depending on the distance. When you hang up, or are disconnected as happened in this case, the process of disconnection begins in the caller's local exchange and then routes all the way through to the phone at the other end. Imagine a game in which dominoes are all lined end up; you topple the first one and the whole line collapses in a wave, until the last domino falls. This is the same thing, but in this case there weren't many dominoes involved.'

'So the call couldn't have been made, for example, from the United States?'

'Not if it was recorded in Bristol. Impossible with this disconnection delay. Satellites give you a delay of a quarter of a second in each direction. Even if the call came via an ocean cable the lapse would be more than what your tape reveals, in my opinion.'

'Why Ireland?' I asked. 'Why not, I don't know, Sheffield?'

'Because Europhone didn't get to sell the old T-600 in Sheffield, or anywhere else in the UK,' Tony said with the happiness of complete certainty. 'Nor did they sell it anywhere else in Europe. Israel and the Far East, yes, but this call was made from much nearer home. You're left with Ireland.'

'With respect,' I said, 'when I've used payphones in the UK I could swear I've heard pips like those on the tape.'

Tony shook his head as if to an apprentice engineer.

'You may well have, but we've moved ahead of what they made ten or more years ago. In the modern generation of payphones the pips are only sent to the person using the phone, not the person at the other end. Older phones transmitted pips both ways. Your tape recorded pips, so they're pips from an older generation of machine, in this case from a T-600, no question. An old, forgotten museum piece in some part of Ireland.'

I said goodbye to Tony. Five minutes later I was driving east. If a microbiologist rang his sister from Ireland, even though he was meant to be in the United States, why should it be a concern of mine? Why should I bother whether or not the microbiologist had never been heard of again? Why did it matter to me whether or not Carlos Penn had discovered a successful treatment for AIDS?

Twenty-five million reasons why, I thought grimly as the rain eased and a weak sun made a much overdue appearance. Be honest, I thought. Twenty-five million and one.

10

Life is a series of people hurtling around on predetermined tracks, narrowly missing each other, time and again. Then unexpected incidents erupt like sudden gusts of wind and blow people together. Those gusts come maybe once or twice over a lifetime, and from them are forged the opportunities which determine the next ten or twenty years.

There was no precise point in my childhood that I could remember realizing that my brother John was different. He had always been like that. If I thumped John, Dad gave me six in return. Hard. John began to walk stiff-legged, without bending his knees. I was the only boy of my age I knew who understood the word haemophiliac.

We lived in Dún Laoghaire. Tom Grace, our dad, taught physical education at a school in Blackrock. His father, after whom I was named, had been a teacher who had come from the west of Ireland and had hurled for Mayo. Dad taught me to box. And to ride a horse. He'd been a boxer in his youth, a joy to watch, people used to say, with a left hook like the kick from a mule. He bought me a pony for my eighth birthday. We kept it with a farmer in Bray.

Dad met my mother in Dublin in 1946. Her father's family had been in the diplomatic business in Venice for 600 years. Mother had been sent to a convent school in Dublin to learn English and had then stayed on for twelve months. She and Dad married in 1948 and my two sisters were born over the following four years. John arrived in 1953 and I came like the last instalment in January 1955. We all took after our mother with her brown eyes and her wavy, black hair. And her unpredictable passion. She'd blow up about once every month and if you were around you soon learned how to duck. Except with John. She never threw anything at John. I could see how she felt guilty about the way he was and that that made her angry with herself.

John started to bruise as soon as he could move around. Mother learned for the first time from her father that she had had an older brother who had died as a child in Venice. Bled to death. And two uncles as well, she and Dad suddenly learned. A whole hidden pedigree of problems, a history going back on the female side. I was lucky. If they'd spotted John's haemophilia early on, no way would I have ever seen the light of day.

There was an arch pig in school called Davis. Being top of the class in the Christian Brothers, especially if you couldn't play games and walked funny, was a guarantee for disaster: by the time John was sixteen he had the undeveloped look and walk of a tailor's dummy. Davis used to stagger along behind him, mimicking John's walk, his hangers-on collapsing with laughter. One day in the playground, Davis threw a dart that he'd got in his father's pub and it stuck between my brother's shoulder blades. John couldn't reach to pull it out.

I heard his screams from the lower play-yard. I was fourteen. Every morning that we left home Mother always said the same thing to me, out of my brother's hearing: 'Keep an eye on John.' That afternoon in school I made some Dublin dentist a lot of money. But Davis's father sued the school and the school threatened to join Dad in the action.

This was the part I usually skipped. Even now it hurt me. Davis senior wanted the head of the spoiler of his son's good looks and my father was terrified of losing his job in the ensuing row. Which was why I never finished school;

which was why I was sent to the States to live with Dad's widowed sister in New York, as a temporary measure to get me away and out of sight until the trouble had blown over. But my exile had become permanent. My keenest feeling when I looked back on all that now was one of deep disappointment.

That was all in the late sixties, and John's children would not be born for another thirteen years. John came to the States in 1975 and was teaching astrophysics by the time I left the Marines and hit Wall Street. The 1980s. Era of shoulder pads and power lunches, junk bonds and cocaine. Arbitrage was in and fiscal rectitude, whatever that was, had been forgotten.

John had married Laura, a social worker, and they lived near Claremont Avenue on the Upper West Side, a ten-minute walk from Columbia. Lee and I lived within three blocks of them. John and Joe; Laura and Lee. We did things like Thanksgiving together and when Mother died and John and I came home, Lee moved in with Laura and her kids because Lee was jumpy about staying two weeks on the Upper West Side on her own.

I knew very little about the details of John's medication. I knew less about Factor VIII and nothing at all about AIDS except what I had skipped over in the *Wall Street Journal.*

'Factor VIII is a clotting agent,' Laura had told me and bit her lip. 'It's used widely by haemophiliacs.'

Midweek after Easter, an evening. From where we sat I could see the New Jersey palisades with their neon signs starting to glow and make the Hudson almost inviting. John and Laura's two small boys were watching TV. Laura was one of the most together people I had ever met. I thought she'd asked me over when John was out to help her move furniture or the like. John hated being useless like that.

Laura said, 'Factor VIII is made from blood. It's made John's life a thousand times easier in the last five years. Until now.'

'What's the problem?' I asked.

'The blood they've been using to make Factor VIII is contaminated,' Laura said grimly. 'It's got this AIDS disease in it.'

I told Laura I thought AIDS was a gay disease. Laura shook her head.

'They say it's transmitted through blood, among other things,' she said. 'It's a virus, in other words, it's a bug too small to be caught by filters. And John has it, Joe.'

It was worse than when Mother had died. John's two kids at the TV, smiling as they passed in and out to the kitchen for milk and cookies, but catching something amiss from the adults without admitting they had and with puzzled looks watching their Uncle Joe. Laura and I just sat there, trying to come to grips with something no one really yet understood or talked about. Someone we both loved had AIDS. Like cancer, when you got AIDS you died. Why? Why John? Was a point of life ever reached where you didn't have to go around, banging your head and asking . . . why?

'How come the blood companies didn't know about this?' I asked.

'That's the tragedy,' said Laura. 'They did.'

'They knew?'

She nodded.

'And the blood banks?'

'They've all known. The evidence has been there for at least three years. Haemophiliacs have been dying mysteriously. Groups at high risk from AIDS, such as gay men, have always been very good blood donors.' Laura shrugged. 'It had to have been either the blood transfusions or Factor VIII. It was obvious.'

I looked at John and Laura's two boys; I could not believe what I was hearing.

'And they did nothing? Why didn't they screen the blood coming in to them?'

'Because it would have cost too much,' said Laura with tears in her eyes. 'When John heard he was HIV, do you know what he said? He said it was the will of God. How do you tell someone like John Grace that God had nothing to do with it, and that he's going to die not because of something God did or didn't do, but because of human greed?'

John didn't die. He fought. And he was still fighting. But his two boys had grown up with the fact that their Dad was HIV positive, and they and Laura lived with this awful fact hanging over their heads like a permanent, black cloud over a mountain. I saw the strain: when John got the flu, or any infection. And I also saw the false hope when cures were talked about in the papers and when once John flew out to LA to meet some quack who reckoned he had the whole nasty thing cornered and beaten, which of course was just rubbish, as everyone knows. Fairytales, Dad would have said.

John's boys were as tall as me now, last time I saw them, which was two years before. Too long. But it was still their puzzled faces as children that day in New York that I most remembered, that and my own feeling of powerlessness. And now I had been made to remember it all again by a man whose wealth could not be measured in normal terms nor his power by the standards of normal men.

Ten years on, those memories should have withered, but driving into Dublin that afternoon I knew the reverse had happened. Ten years had simply made my memories more intense. Like a microbe burrowing up through my unconscious, they would not be denied.

And then, as Dublin's lights began to make the sky ahead pink, I suddenly realized that Carson McCoy must have known all that, otherwise he would never have picked me.

11

I was going through the motions, but inside I was dying. Bleeding cash, the lifeblood of business. I'd been so near, so very near, I thought, yet that is surely the thought of many a man in the position I now found myself in. My anger had been replaced by a dull resignation. Every path I now turned down was a predictable dead-end; and there was the added danger of the word getting out that my company was in trouble – that is, if the word was not already out and running. And as for discovering anything about McCoy's motives or why he had put me in this position, I had more information on the current whereabouts of Lord Lucan.

'I've told Jenkins to inform McCoy's lawyers that I'll do what he wants,' I said, hating myself. 'I had no choice.'

'It gives us time,' Tim said.

It was after six in the evening. We were sitting upstairs, like three people in a life-raft.

'Carlos Penn studied microbiology at the University of Liverpool in the late seventies,' Tim said. 'I asked Liverpool to e-mail me a list of all the microbiology graduates for that year, then ran the list over the databases in our computer. That made the connection to a certain Dr Alan Gold, a classmate of Carlos's. Gold is the new head of research with Trident Drug.'

Even then, after all the years that had passed, the name had an effect on me equivalent to pain.

'So Alan Gold must have known Carlos Penn,' Tim was saying. 'I wonder did Carlos go to see him first last year before he went on to Los Angeles? One current rumour is that Trident may be very close to a breakthrough on a major new drug.'

'Trident's share price in New York is on the move,' I said. 'I got a call yesterday from Soby Sandbach, who says the buying is coming from a source that is usually well informed.'

We sat around, sorting our own thoughts. Hanny curled up like a cat and put her head on my lap.

'How was Interfibre?' asked Tim. 'Predictable, I hope, if that's not too ambitious in the circumstances.'

'The rights details are on my desk,' I replied. 'I also got Tony to run the Carlos Penn tape.'

Hanny popped the cassette into the player she had been listening to. There was the sound of a telephone being picked up.

'Hello, Constance? Constance?'

'Carlos?'

'Constance, are you all right?'

The door opening and the man's voice in the background.

'Carlos, what . . .'

'Constance! Listen very carefully. I . . .'

'Where are you?'

'Con . . .'

The three, high-pitched pips.

'I'm . . .'

The crunch that resembled bones being dislocated. Maybe it had been bones, I thought.

'Tony swears the call was made from Ireland,' I said.

Hanny sat up. Tim shook his head and frowned.

'Ireland? I thought he was meant to be in the States.'

'If the call was recorded in Bristol, then Tony's sure it was made from Ireland. To do with the pips and a whole lot of other things I don't understand.'

'Tony might be mistaken,' Hanny said.

'I've already invested five million euros in Interfibre on

the basis that Tony is never mistaken,' I said. 'Not on telephones.'

Tim rummaged around in his beard for a moment.

'Do we know anything at all about HIV?' he asked at last. 'I mean, other than it's a horrible disease that kills you in the end? More to the point, who do we know who knows?'

12

Down on the quays, a church chimed eleven. I was working my way into the second half of a bottle of Jameson and browsing through *Jeffers Weekly*. Jeffers was the best business commentary there was, which didn't surprise me: Ricardo Vegas was the editor. They published each week simultaneously by satellite in New York, Tokyo and London. Old Paddy Malone of Dolans would have scratched his head in wonder. Dolans had wound up six months after Malone died. Who now remembered either, other than the handful of kids like Ricardo and myself who had been trained by Paddy Malone? The phone rang.

'Joe? It's Soby.'

'Soby, what's the story?'

There had to be a story for Soby Sandbach to call me at eleven in the evening Irish time.

'It's the Trident Drug story,' the New York broker said and for the second time that day, I felt the old twinge.

Years ago, before I'd actually met Soby but was speaking to him ten times a day on the phone, I'd tried from his deep voice that put me in mind of a barker out on Coney Island to imagine what Soby looked like. In his forties, a little chubby, of medium height, I thought. Thinning hair. Quick thinking. A dicky-bow, maybe. Quick thinking, yes, but after that and his age, the other calculations were impossibly wide of the mark, I discovered, when at last we had met. Soby Sandbach was six and a half feet tall, thin as a healthy man can afford to be, with a thick, black mop of hair. At first glance he resembled more an undertaker than an impresario. He was also that very precious thing in a broker: he was honest. He and I had done a lot of deals together. And after Black Friday in 1987 when I knew Soby had lost in three days more than he'd made in the ten years that had gone before, I'd gone out of my way to give him business.

'Go on,' I said.

'It's just broken seventeen dollars on the chart and there are buyers over,' Soby remarked with practised nonchalance.

The science of recording share movements on charts is an industry of considerable importance on Wall Street. Shares going up meet 'resistance' at certain levels, or if falling, 'support'. The fact that so many traders use charts in the first place, endow this science with all the attributes of a self-fulfilling prophecy.

'How's the rest of the market?'

'Good question. The market went sideways today, and the pharmaceutical sector actually went down. Armentisia Lab is off a full half, for example.'

I could not recall why I'd asked Soby to keep an eye on Trident for me – something instinctive, perhaps, like keeping one eye on a dog in a farmyard.

'What's the story?'

'Let's say I know someone who knows someone in the FDA. They're excited as hell in there at the moment – about what I can't find out just yet – but I will. Now you tell me, what area would cause most excitement if there was some new wonder drug coming?'

'It could be a lot of things.'

'Sure – but state the obvious.'

'Cancer,' I said.

'Yep,' Soby said, 'no doubt. And next?'

'AIDS.' Everywhere I looked. I suddenly envied Soby in New York, away from the mess I'd landed myself in.

He was saying, 'Ask yourself next, what companies are

linked most to HIV medicine? Armentisia Lab is the market leader with Viradrol. Then you have Trident. So when Armentisia moves down and Trident moves up, what do you conclude?'

'I buy your reasoning. But I don't like Trident, never have. It's run by a monster.'

'Nonetheless you are interested, otherwise you would not have asked me to watch it for you.'

'So I'm interested in monsters.'

Soby laughed. His desk had been specially crafted in Brooklyn with extra height to accommodate his knees.

'You're talking about our corporate elite here,' he said solemnly. 'Dr Groz has become an aristocrat since your day, Joe.'

'Caligula thought he was an aristocrat,' I said. 'Look, all I'm saying is I wouldn't buy Trident to save my life – but that doesn't mean I don't want to know what's happening.'

'I'm working like a hog on my contacts and they always deliver,' Soby said. 'In the meantime, I've just bought five thousand Trident at sixteen dollars ninety-five. Let me buy you some.'

'I'll have a bet with you,' I said. 'One box of Montecristo Number 1 – all right? I bet a box you'll lose money on that investment.'

'The bet's on,' Soby laughed. 'Number 1s, all right?'

'And a humidor.'

'I'm going to make enough on this to buy you and all your friends a humidor,' Soby said.

After that, I sat for five minutes, thinking about what Soby had said. Then I picked the phone up and made a call to a number in Denver, Colorado. It was time once more for some insightful analysis on Trident Drug.

13

St James's Hospital is found near the north end of Dublin's South Circular Road. Grown from the core of an old hospital into a park of numerous buildings and prefabs, its patients, should they wish to open their windows, can smell the malt from the Guinness brewery less than a mile away. From where I sat in an outer reception area, I saw my fax pinned to a file and taken into a back office. It was Harry Quinlan who had provided the introduction three days before.

'I've a pal in James's who's into all that HIV area, if you need to talk to someone,' Harry had said, drying his neck with a towel. 'He tells me that the disease is getting worse, not better as people seem to think.'

Harry worked in the Department of Foreign Affairs. His sandy hair had been cut and trimmed since the days I had first met him in Greenwich Village, an Irish kid with hair to his toes who could play a classical guitar good enough to make you weep.

'In fact, last time I met him, he told me we're as far from a cure as we are from landing on Pluto,' Harry said.

We had started to play squash when I first came back to Dublin. That day Harry was on form. He'd won three out of our four games, sprinting into every corner of the court and whacking low, mean balls that I suddenly had no energy to get to. We ordered pints and I told him my problems. Harry's eyes grew round and most undiplomatically astonished.

'What are you going to do?' he asked.

'What choice have I got? I must at least appear to do McCoy's bidding in the hope that help in the form of cash will appear from some unexpected quarter.'

We chatted some more. For Harry, a friend's problems became his own.

'You're still a mad bastard,' he said at last, 'but I hope you screw this fucker, whoever he is.'

We drank another pint, then Harry hurried back to Stephen's Green, something to do with extradition.

A notice board in the reception area spoke of the hospital's various departments and gave Dr Chris King's position as consultant in genital-urinary medicine – GUM. He had sounded most ungiving on the telephone. With a minimum of enthusiasm he had asked that I fax him the relevant parts of the Penn file so that the little time he could allocate to our meeting might be put to the maximum use. Even though he had been primed by Harry for my call, Dr King had given the impression that he thought I had more time to waste than he had.

I hated doing this. I hated doing it because I knew I was going down the road of McCoy's choosing, but as the days had gone by, the reality was that I had little option. On the one hand, three banks and two venture capital outfits – one in Dublin, one in Frankfurt – had still to come back to us, but you can't rush these things, you can't convey your own desperation. And a call the day before from MacLattins, McCoy's Dublin lawyers, had been equivalent to an ultimatum. You have agreed to act – now act. In other words, start moving or pay up. Tell us you've begun to do what you agreed you would, or join the ranks of the financial living dead. So what could I do? Apart from swear, drink whiskey, get on the bike, which I did, and drive down the M4 at 135 m.p.h.? Maybe I had hoped to be pulled in and locked up – then I couldn't oblige Mr McCoy, not from a padded cell. But it was a vain hope. No one can pull you in at 135 m.p.h. So, through Jenkins, I told McCoy's flunkies, yes, tell him I've started to make some enquiries.

I thought of Hanny, always an antidote to unpleasantness. She too had copied the Penn file, for what specifically she had not revealed. She was very professional, Hanny. Very compartmentalized. She had made a remarkable recovery from what had happened to her seven years before when she had ended up in the clean, warm clinic in Heldenbergen.

In the years afterwards, that clinic had often seemed like the only happiness Hanny had ever known. The immaculate lawns that swept down to the bubbling tributary of the River Nidder. The cheerful, bright nurses and doctors. They had been like mothers and fathers to young Hanny. With patience, over months, they had brought out all the filth in her mind, the inner poison, the dark bile that had made Hanny believe, deep down, in places she never knew existed, that she was filthy. She had wanted to be dead, she told them, choking out the words. She had wanted to be dead, but she didn't know why. The people in the clinic in Heldenbergen had, with great love and patience over many months, enabled Hanny to understand why.

It was not Hanny, it was the sickness in Grandfather Kleber's mind, they explained. His mind was warped. Perhaps the war had done it – who knew? Hanny had been given into the Klebers' care as a little girl, way before when she could remember. He had come to her at nights. She had been too frightened to cry out. He was a big, old man with whiskers and a smell from his breath of stale milk. He wore a long, white night-gown that made him look like a ghost. Hanny always went to bed bathed and fresh, but after Grandfather Kleber had been to her room she always smelt of him. Worse. He always left her filthy. She did not dare wash twice in one night, in case Grandmother asked her why. Sometimes in the same night Grandfather came twice to her. And on Sundays, after they went to the Lutheran service together, where Grandfather preached, after that when they came home and ate their *Sonntagsessen*, their Sunday lunch, Grandfather sent Hanny to her room for a rest, and then came up and lay with her on her bed in the broad daylight.

Hanny had a simple method of dealing with Grandfather Kleber. She blanked him out. Although she was there in her bedroom with him, nights and Sunday afternoons for over ten years, she was elsewhere in her mind. She skied mostly, with Mama who had died. They skied all the great *pistes* together. They sailed across the Alps where no one had skied before and came down in the evenings laughing to one another and shaking the white powder off their ski hats.

Often when Grandfather Kleber left her room, Hanny could not even remember how long it was since he had first entered it. But although Hanny thought she had blanked out Grandfather Kleber, the people in Heldenbergen had explained to her that you never really blank out something like that. You just bottle it up and lock it away. And one day it comes out when you least expect it, or don't even recognize what it is.

That happened to Hanny when she was just turned fifteen. She liked the way that heroin filled her whole mind, or emptied it, it really didn't matter which. For a few Marks all your problems were solved. Some of her friends did it, they said there was nothing wrong. Everyone had problems, after all.

Except Hanny. Although she took heroin to blot out her problems, she really didn't know what these problems were. They became an increasing part of her. Like an ache, she learned to live with them. She got used to the feeling of blackness and despair and waking up with a dread weight on her chest and the basic feeling that she was worthless.

Heroin eliminated that feeling. An overdose of heroin would eliminate the feeling permanently. There was a certain logic to what Hanny had eventually tried to do.

'Mr Grace?'

Dr King had a neat sandy beard with matching hair. He looked much too young to be in charge of a devastating disease. A little grim around the mouth, although maybe that was to be expected, Dr Christopher King – neatly printed letters inserted in a chrome-framed name-tag – ushered me into a medium-sized, carpeted office, and quietly closed the door. Serious-looking books brooded from shelves behind the desk. Dr King came softly around and seated himself. Silence seemed to be his medium, as if the ultimately impenetrable nature of the disease he dealt with was best confronted in stillness.

'How can I help you?'

'By telling me whether the stuff I faxed you makes any sense,' I replied.

Dr King allowed a shadow of irritation, or perhaps frustration, to cross his youthful face. His hair and beard were combed and trimmed neat enough to have been poured from a mould.

'There's a huge amount of bullshit around,' he said. 'Six months ago some artist in Argentina claimed he could kill the virus by heating people's blood up, then cooling it down again. There was a riot in a suburb of Buenos Aires, people with HIV trying to get him to treat them.'

Dr King pressed the middle fingers of his long, elegant hands to either side of the bridge of his nose.

'I really don't normally look at this sort of thing,' he said. 'There just isn't the time.'

That makes two of us, I thought.

'However, Harry asked me to. He said you and he were mates from way back.' Dr King smiled, a process that made him suddenly friendly. He drew the file across the desk to him. 'Do you know this man, Penn?'

'No.'

Dr King browsed over the file. 'You're not a scientist.'

'No.'

'Hmm,' frowned Dr King, like somebody trying to find the quickest route between two points on a map. 'The human immunodeficiency virus then. A nasty little beast, as we all know. It attacks cells called CD4 cells, among others. These are the cells without whose help the body's immune system becomes grossly incapacitated. HIV penetrates into the cytoplasm of the CD4 cell, and then transforms itself, if you like, into a form which enables it to penetrate into the nucleus of the cell itself. Do you smoke?'

'No thanks.'

Dr King offered over cheroots anyway. He lighted and drew on one in a way that made him somehow less pure and in the process, more accessible.

'As people's CD4 cells drop off, so does their immune system. They become vulnerable to diseases that otherwise their cellular immune system would have protected them from. A rare type of pneumonia is one example. Kaposi's sarcoma – skin cancer – is another.'

A telephone rang on Dr King's desk. He began to talk to someone, a patient, I presumed. I wondered how many times my brother had sat across the desk from a specialist like Dr King, trying to read signs of hope from his youthful face.

'You can't treat HIV by killing it, because to kill it you have also to kill the cell into which the virus has incorporated itself,' Dr King resumed, replacing the phone. 'Kill the cell and you kill the patient.' He drew the file across to him. 'What your man Penn seems to be claiming is the following. When a woman becomes pregnant, part of her immune system automatically turns down – otherwise her body would reject her child. We also know that HIV burns out the immune system.'

Dr King put on glasses, another sign of human weakness, and transferred his cheroot to the side of his mouth. The telephone on his desk rang again; he picked it up, pressed a key on the instrument, opened a drawer in his desk and dropped the receiver in.

'Penn takes these two facts,' Dr King went on. 'As far as I can make out from his theory, which is extremely technical – and remember, I'm not an immunologist – if you take the key proteins that cause this drop of the pregnant mother's immune system and make an anti-serum to it – in other words, its reverse – then the effect will also be the reverse. It will turn up the body's immune system.'

'Does that make sense?' I asked.

Dr King rocked his head doubtfully.

'Nothing in science makes sense until it's proven,' he replied. 'However, Penn clearly thought so. He extracted protein from human placenta and made from it anti-serum to itself. According to what you sent me, Penn called his anti-serum BL-4. He then made it suitable for humans and infused the result into HIV patients in trials he carried out in Bristol and California – all completely illegal, by the way. He claims that in eight out of ten cases where BL-4 was infused, the patients' CD4 cell count rose dramatically and their immune systems reawakened. He claims that subsequently HIV was absent in a majority of these patients.'

'Could this be true?'

Dr King ground out his cheroot. 'As I've said, I'm not an immunologist. However, it so happens that Penn claims he used a laboratory attached to the University of Southern California to analyse the blood samples from the patients he treated and to monitor their progress. The doctor in charge of that lab is a Dr Cuba Sali. I met her at an AIDS conference in Berlin three years ago. A very intelligent person, and very helpful. I rang her up when I read your fax.'

It occurred to me that I might have entered a parallel universe.

'Dr Sali is a scientist, she was non-committal,' Dr King was saying. 'On the one hand, yes, Penn's anti-serum did seem to work on some patients. On the other hand, there were only a total of twenty-two or twenty-three patients involved. That's a tiny number, not big enough at all from which to reach any firm, scientific conclusions. It's not statistically significant.'

'Yet, it did work,' I said.

'You have to be enormously careful in this business,' said Dr King, becoming grim again. 'When I pressed Dr Sali about the quality of the controls surrounding these trials in California, she began to wobble, quite frankly. The trials were flawed by all international standards for such things. The patients were all on other drugs as well, so that one has no absolute idea whether it was the anti-serum or a combination of the anti-serum and these other drugs that produced the results. Also the level of CD4 cells in each patient before the trials began was not precisely established. And the anti-serum did not work in all the patients. Finally, the fact that the whole thing was illegal and that the inventor is no longer around would tend to make one more than a little cautious about the entire episode.'

'But she said that the anti-serum worked in some cases?' I persisted.

'Mr Grace, I cannot tell you the number of false dawns I've personally witnessed. But yes, that's what Dr Sali said – albeit in an extremely qualified way. I got the impression she is – or was – a fan of Penn's. She mentioned his disappearance, which I presume is why you're here.'

I nodded. The woman from outside reappeared, part of a well-rehearsed intervention, I imagined, and reminded the doctor about an appointment. Dr King made an apologetic face and restored the telephone receiver to its place on his desk.

'Doctor,' I said as we stood up, 'I'm a layman, I'm trying hard to take all this in. In laymen's terms, is there any chance that Carlos Penn was on the right track?'

'Someday someone's going to succeed,' Dr King said, allowing me out before him. 'The reality is that the human immune system is like the Tower of Babel. Discussions, commands, negotiations and disputes are going on the whole time in a variety of codes and ciphers to which science has not yet found the key. Whoever succeeds will need an awful lot of luck. Frankly, your Mr Penn looks a little short in that department.'

'Assume for a wild moment that Penn's discovery worked,' I said. 'Why would someone want to remove him?'

Dr King looked at me quizzically.

'Remove him?'

'Liquidate him. Take him out of circulation. For good.'

'Are you being serious?'

'Assume I am.'

The doctor's expression suggested that it was now he who was out of his depth. 'Harry said you're a financial wizard. That's your answer, then. Money. AIDS is a huge industry, Mr Grace. It employs thousands of people, all searching for an answer, all of whose jobs will be gone the moment someone else finds what they're looking for. The biggest reputations in the business are on the line here. Drugs like Viradrol have cost hundreds of millions to develop. They sell like gold bars. If you'd spent a fortune developing and were now manufacturing the best HIV drug the market had to offer, would you be pleased if some lad turned up on your doorstep and announced that he'd found the answer in his garage?'

14

Hanny sat reading in front of the television, the sound muted. She had just taken a shower and washed her hair. Drops of water were still making bold, dark tracks down the golden slopes of her neck.

I asked, 'Where have you been?'

'Doing a little research,' she said without looking up.

I sat beside her.

'About?'

'Carlos Penn's call.'

My face must have shown my surprise.

'I told you I was going to,' Hanny said.

'Please do go on.'

Hanny put down her book. 'The date on which the call was taped was 6th March last year. Your five-million-euro telecommunications man said it was made from Ireland. So I looked up all the Irish papers for 6th March – also for the days either side, the 5th and the 7th. I didn't know what I was looking for, but I found this.'

She handed me a page with a blown-up photostat of newsprint.

GRANDSTAND FINISH. A transatlantic Gulfstream jet landed safely yesterday in an emergency landing on a racecourse outside the village of Tansey on Ireland's western seaboard. The plane, which was *en route* for Eastern Europe, was carrying only its two pilots, neither of whom was injured. – Reuter.

I looked at Hanny.

She said, 'So at least *some*thing happened on that date in Ireland – yes?'

'You mean . . . nothing *else* happened?'

'I found Tansey on a map,' Hanny said, ignoring me. 'It's within three hundred miles of Bristol so it qualifies for the telephone call. The piece says the jet had crossed the Atlantic. So did Carlos Penn in or around that date, assuming he telephoned his sister from Ireland.'

'Your cutting says there were only two pilots on board.'

'I know. So I went down to Shannon.'

'You went to Shannon?'

'I flew down there yesterday morning. I'm a reporter. This is the kind of thing we do.'

There was a quality of defiance to Hanny at certain times that precluded further questions.

'Last year on 6th March at six o'clock in the morning, the Duty Supervisor in Shannon Airport was alerted and told that a Gulfstream jet was approaching from the Atlantic, that it had reported low fuel and had requested permission to land at Shannon.'

'Okay.'

'There was thick fog at Shannon and no wind. The Duty Supervisor put the airport's emergency landing procedures into action. He spoke directly to the pilot of the plane and was informed that there were two people only on board, the pilot and a co-pilot. As is the normal procedure, Approach Control took over the last thirty miles of the jet's approach and gave the pilot his instructions. The pilot was nervous and kept referring to his low fuel position. At the last moment, because of the fog, the plane overshot the runway.'

Despite myself, I found my interest quickening.

'Shannon Control instructed the pilot to climb to four thousand feet and gave him the information he needed to fly south to Cork Airport where there was no fog. However, as the plane was turning to comply with this plan, one of its two engines cut out. The fuel supply had ceased. The pilot informed Shannon of this fact. He was scared. Without being asked, he then said that there were five people on board. Five. At that moment the pilot saw a stretch of clear ground beneath him, a racecourse. He put the Gulfstream down on it just as the fuel in his second engine ran out.'

'He said five people?'

'That's what he said. Five. The Duty Supervisor himself told me. Although, when the rescue services arrived in the village of Tansey, only the two pilots were on board. But there's something else which I think is interesting.'

'Go on.'

'The flight plan of the jet was lodged in Mexico City on 5th March last year. The operator was Aviaco, a jet charter company operating out of Monterrey.'

'But Monterey is in California.'

'With one "r" it's in California, but with two "r"s it's in Mexico,' Hanny said. She rolled out the "r"s. 'Monter-rey. An air traffic control computer system spans the whole world. Aircraft must lodge their flight plan and an alternative, safety flight plan before they take off. The origin of this plane was Monterrey, its destination was Moscow. And its alternative destination was Shannon. The name of the company in Mexico who did the hiring was Cobra Internacionale, no address given.'

'So where's the connection?'

'The Aeroflot flight from Cuba to Moscow that refuels each day at Shannon was two extra hours on the ground that morning – they could have been waiting for the people off that grounded jet.'

'Which came from Mexico.'

'I know, Joe, and I know the last alleged sighting of Carlos was in LA. But that doesn't explain the telephone call. Doesn't it at least make you sit up and wonder what's going on?'

She and I nursed our own silences for some moments.

'I've been to see the doctor,' I said eventually. 'Harry's friend who is an HIV expert.'

'And?'

'He said the chances that Carlos Penn had found the cure to AIDS is on the same scale as finding life on Mars. You can't rule it out, but it's unlikely.'

'Then why was he abducted?'

'That's an assumption.'

Hanny's face was impatient.

I said, 'Look, Carlos went to the States in the hope of signing up a company to help him develop his drug. He failed. It was the last straw. What had he left? A life insurance policy for a hundred grand. To look at an abduction scenario is to play into McCoy's hands. What we need to do is to try and figure out why McCoy is doing this in the first place.'

Hanny was shaking her head, a process which made tiny drops of golden water shimmer for an instant like a halo around her.

'Your theory is like Gruyère, Joe. All holes. You need a body and there isn't one. His call to his sister is not that of a man about to take his own life. Neither is he alone in some lonely place – we hear another man's voice in the background. Gruyère, *mein Liebling*. There is much more in this story than just sadness.'

15

I was sitting across from Tim in the lobby of the Berkeley Court. Either side of us, young men with slicked back hair chatted into mobile telephones, young women consulted Psion organizers. They were all so young, I suddenly thought. A new perspective. This was what age was really all about, it lurked in the long grass, awaiting its moment. A wave of anger surged from my viscera. What did these kids know about life? About what motivates people? What did I look like to them? A man in his mid-forties with a constantly worried look? Probably. That's the way it happened.

We had been summoned to this meeting by an Italian client, a software outfit that specialized in retail solutions. Grace Equity had already agreed in principle to take a 10 per cent stake in the company. I had spent five months on the deal.

'Maybe McCoy has AIDS,' Tim said.

I refrained from voicing an opinion. I was sick of AIDS, if such a sentiment was permitted. Two days ago, Hanny had extracted the St James's Hospital briefing from me like a wisdom tooth. She'd gone to England early that morning, leaving the flat before six to catch a Ryanair flight. I hadn't been told where she was going. This business was coming between us.

'Nothing makes sense,' I said. 'McCoy's prepared to pay twenty-five million dollars to find someone who at worst will have cost him a fraction of that. He allowed Penn to go off on his own to the US to try and set up development deals – does that make sense? McCoy himself could afford to buy a pharmaceutical company for Penn if he was that keen on Carlos's project.'

'I spoke to someone in London this morning who told me that Carson McCoy is up to his armpits in property in Seoul.'

'Korea's not where I'd be by choice, right now.'

'He has taken some major hits out there, by some accounts.'

'I don't get it,' I said.

'Joe.'

I looked around. My heart skidded, but then it always had every time I saw her – and I mean every time.

'Donna.'

'I saw you from the other side of the lobby.'

I introduced Tim. I said, 'You look well.' Much better than you do in the newspapers, I could have added, but that would have been churlish. She was a woman whose face deserved the term 'perfect'. People of both sexes just wanted to look at her all day long.

I said, 'I'd offer you a drink, but we're waiting for a client to come down.'

'I'm on my way to a reception,' she said. 'You look tired.'

'I have to work hard, I have many mouths to feed,' I said and at once regretted it.

But she said, 'Is everything all right?'

'Sure. Just overworked.'

'Good, I'm relieved,' Donna said.

'Meaning?'

'Meaning nothing.'

'Come on, Donna.'

'I'd hate to think you were in any kind of trouble, that's all.'

I knew this woman too well – now I understood why she'd taken the trouble to come over and say hello.

'What kind of trouble could I be in?' I asked, the cheeky boy, grinning. I saw Tim look away, embarrassed.

The tip of Donna's tongue emerged, just for an instant, and in that instant I felt the keen shaft of desire pierce me. She said, 'You know, gossip.'

'I don't have the time to know it.'

'Pub talk, I'm sure. It doesn't matter.'

'Go on.' She was going to tell me anyway. She was, as always, in fantastic shape, I could see. I knew how much work that took: two hours minimum every morning and a diet of rabbit food.

Donna said, 'I just heard that everything might be, shall we say, not all that well with your company, that's all. I wasn't worried.' She smiled, disarmingly, she thought. 'I know my investments are safe.'

I saw the lift doors open and a young man in a sharp double-breasted suit emerge.

'Relax, so are your excesses,' I said with all the charm I could muster. She offered her cheek. I wanted her away before my client reached us. I didn't want her attitude to contaminate him – or me – any more than it already had.

'Very pretty woman,' the Italian client said appreciatively as the woman whose bed and life I had once shared walked away across the lobby, dragging a dozen stares behind her. 'Like a model – no?'

'That's exactly what she is,' I said.

The Italian was no more than twenty-eight; he was already rich in many things.

'What it must be like to be married to such a woman, eh?' he said, shaking his head in wonder. 'Fantastic.'

'Fantastic,' I said, amazed by the huge chasm that separates the young from the old and goes by the name of experience.

16

Two hours later Tim and I sat in a pub on Haddington Road.

'You're taking it too personally,' he said.

'I'm entitled to be personal about my own business.' I twirled my finger for two more pints.

Tim's phone rang and he turned it off. 'The Italians are funny. You never know what's going on in their minds.'

'They were in, now they're out. That's not funny.'

'He used the word "postpone". It's an ill wind.'

'Tell me about it,' I said.

I liked the man opposite me. We thought the same way, most of the time. So I knew what he was now going to say.

'Look, Joe.' Tim cleared his throat. 'We're playing hardball not only with a complete bastard but with one of the wealthiest men in the world. No one wants to get on the wrong side of someone like McCoy. People are terrified of great wealth. He can fuck anyone so easily. We got into bed with him and now we must, for the moment, learn to deal with him.'

'Must we? When he decides that I must get involved in one of his crazy projects, am I meant to roll over like a fucking poodle and wag my tail?'

Tim was holding up his hand like a traffic policeman. 'Hear me out, please. None of us wants this, none of us has invited it. But if we resist, we're going to get smothered. Deals like today's Italian deal are going to start walking. Our problem is time. We have a very sexy company, but our problem is we're in too much of a hurry trying to get our divorce. We have to buy time. There is only one way to do that. You have to get out of here, you have to go and try and find this gobshite scientist, like you've agreed. Make McCoy believe you're playing ball by actually playing ball. Go wherever is necessary, to New York, to LA. Actually look for Penn. Buy us time. With time, we'll find the money to refinance Grace and tell McCoy to go fuck himself, I swear to you. But until then . . . there's no option.'

'I don't believe you're saying this.'

'Look, we've never talked a lot about your past, but I haven't been able to avoid noticing that you do have certain qualities that cut you out for this sort of thing.'

I looked at Tim. If I had been drunk I think I might have hit him. 'It's your round,' I informed him.

17

Anne, my secretary, stood up when we came into the office. It was six in the evening and she should have been on her way home. Anne was a petite, cheerful girl who was most unsuited by the worried look that now attached to her.

'Both your mobile phones have been switched off,' she said accusingly.

'Oops,' I said. Six pints does that to me. Then I saw that Anne was crying. 'Anne – what is it?'

'This came in at four o'clock.' She sniffed and picked up a letter from her desk. 'It wasn't marked private. I opened it.'

I took the letter and as fast as a coot running across water, scanned it. I sat down heavily, passed it to Tim.

'Bastards,' I said.

The letter was from the bank with whom we did our day-to-day business and with whom we had a credit facility of one million pounds. The letter used words like 'review' and 'bank policy' and 'regret'. The bottom line was that as from today, our credit facility was no longer available.

'Listen, I want to tell you both something,' I said. 'Some day this will all be five years ago. It's not worth getting upset because people behave like snakes. We'll lick this thing and we'll move on.' I knew I sounded like Davy Crockett at the Alamo. 'We're bleeding but it's something we can handle.'

I went upstairs. It was as if someone had poured cement into my trousers. But even though the ratchet had been notched up another groove and the pain was becoming worse, I could still marvel at how effective a mere cocked eyebrow was from someone like Carson McCoy. It was as if there was no integral worth or fairness to life, as if the past had never happened. I hit the door to the apartment with my fist, hard. It felt good. The door flew in. 'Bastard!'

Hanny appeared from the kitchen, eyes wide. 'Joe?'

'I'm indulging myself in an interlude of stress therapy.'

'Are you drunk?'

'No, but it's the best suggestion I've heard for three weeks.'

'I'll make you a coffee.'

She spooned a mix from a Bewley's bag into the little steel cup of the espresso machine. I sat down and switched on the television.

'Any dead bodies washed up anywhere?' I asked. 'Particularly ones with signs around their neck saying "MAD SCIENTIST"?'

The coffee machine hissed and steamed. Hanny stuck a mug under the business end, then brought it over to me.

'I don't think that's very fair, Joe,' she said quietly.

'Oh, I beg your pardon,' I said, 'I hadn't realized you'd become the referee in this thing.' Which was one of those petulant, six-pints-of-Guinness things that you say when your one million pound credit facility has been yanked without warning. And even though I knew the remark was unworthy, I kept my eyes doggedly on the small screen.

'Joe, I want to tell you where I was today.'

'Go right ahead.'

'I was in Bristol,' Hanny said, sitting down.

I didn't want to hear this, and that was the truth. Although irrationally, I felt I was being stabbed in the back.

'Nice little city, Bristol,' I said, trowelling on the sarcasm.

'I met Constance Penn, Carlos's sister,' Hanny persisted.

'She is a very sweet lady, very calm and dignified. Devastated by what has happened. Constance told me about Carlos. Everything he ever tried to do flopped. I mean, Carlos could not even tune in his own TV set. Then instead of telling me about his drug, BL-4, she took me for a drive, to a house on the outskirts of Bristol where I met a man called Gus.'

I looked at Hanny as if from another eternity.

'Gus is HIV positive. Two years ago he couldn't walk. His sister had to move into the flat with him. Gus couldn't work, he couldn't even go to the bathroom on his own. Gus's sister heard about this microbiologist, Carlos Penn, also in Bristol, who was reputed to have invented an HIV drug called BL-4. She made contact with Carlos and a course of treatment was started.'

I'd been brought to the dentist like this once, as a child, kicking and screaming.

Hanny said, 'Gus's viral load dropped. His sister moved out. He went back to work in the public library. He bought a mountain bike that he still rides at least ten miles a day. Gus is leading a normal life. He told me about the Carlos Penn he knew. Not crazy. Not deranged. A scientist of great gifts. But the scientific part of it took very much a back seat to the picture Gus painted of a man of great kindness. He told me of the trouble Carlos had gone to treat him. He had actually nursed him, Joe. He had sat at Gus's bedside whilst Gus was drowning in his own lungs and nursed him.'

My fist was beginning to throb from where I'd hit the door. The Guinness must have been wearing off.

'Constance then brought me to three other men in Bristol, all former patients of Carlos's. One of them was like Gus, leading a normal life, the other two had been midway through their treatment when Carlos disappeared, but their CD4 cells were holding up. It didn't really matter – all they wanted to do was to tell me about Carlos! Did I know where Carlos was? Was he alive? Did I *know* Carlos? No, I had to say, I don't know him, I've never met him, actually. Sorry.

'Well, that's your loss, one of these men told me, and off he went, exactly like the others, talking about Carlos the man, the healer, the man whose kindness to them could not be plumbed. A person of hypnotic simplicity. Unarguably a good man, whose only goal in life was to stop the suffering of others.'

I made the time-honoured motions of playing an invisible violin.

'One last thing that is, I think, important,' said Hanny calmly. 'When Carlos's sister drove me back to the airport, she told me that six months ago someone broke into her house and stole most of her clothes. I know it sounds crazy.'

'Sounds like it runs in the family,' I said.

Hanny, very slowly, stood up. 'Have you listened to anything I've said?'

'We're on two different tracks on this one,' I replied, trying to match her for coolness. 'I'm on this track here, running around putting out fires that are threatening to consume my business, pretending to institutions that I'm not desperate for money, watching deals I've spent months putting together disappear as if I had leprosy, coming into my office and meeting my secretary in tears because our asshole bank has just pulled the plug. That's my life at the moment and it's all being caused by an eccentric tycoon who wants me to drop everything and run off looking for his missing pet scientist.'

I went to the sideboard and returned with a bottle of Jameson.

'You, on the other hand, for reasons that I'm sure are perfectly admirable, yet elusive to me at this time, are on another track. You, as far as I can make out, have swallowed the McCoy doctrine hook, line and sinker. You've been down to Shannon, you've found a jet that came from Mexico, a delayed flight to Moscow, an air traffic controller who may have heard a panic-stricken pilot mix up his passenger inventory. You've been to Bristol and have met Carlos Penn's sister, his patients. They think he's God. And so, it seems, do you. I'm sorry if at this moment I don't share your enthusiasm, but ever since I first heard Carlos Penn's name, my life has become increasingly more difficult. Today has been no exception. I'm now going to have a drink and I would be honoured if you would join me.'

'Is that all you can say?'

'All I'm saying is that everything you just told me amounts to a whole lot of circumstantial evidence. And circumstantial evidence isn't worth a damn, my dear.'

'Is it not? Well you listen to me.' Like all women, her anger, when it appeared, was volcanic. 'Whatever I've done has been to try and help you. Do you not see that there may be a different dimension to all this than money? Circumstantial or not? Or would that be too much?'

'I want to save my business and you want me to save the fucking world,' I said and poured the Jamey.

'Fuck you!' Hanny swept the bottle from my hand. 'Of course I want you to save the world, if that's what you can do! That's what every woman wants from a man! But you're so preoccupied with money and banks and deals and, I believe, with not being seen to give in to what Carson McCoy wants, that you ignore all the other aspects of this case!'

'I don't tell you how to run your business, so I don't see

why every time we now meet you should tell me how to run mine,' I remarked and picked the whiskey bottle up from the sodden floor.

'Do you know what that's called?' Hanny cried. 'It's called living with someone. You live with someone and you get involved with their life. This is the twenty-first century. I'm not some girl who's going to say, Joe is such an amazing man that I never make any suggestions. Well, fuck you. I'm not that kind of woman. I'm an intelligent human being and if I see something I think needs saying, I say it.'

'Regardless of whether or not it may be helpful.'

'If you don't want to hear what I'm saying, you should get yourself another woman,' Hanny said.

I then said something really stupid. 'Perhaps I will.'

'Thank you, Joe.' She was breathing heavily. 'It won't be the first time, after all.'

And she went into the bedroom. Twenty minutes later, I had drunk what was left of the whiskey when I heard her behind me. I looked around. She was carrying a suitcase. I wanted to tell her to wait, for us to have one of those door threshold love scenes that no respectable movie lacks, but my blood was up and my tongue was thick with anger and whiskey. She slammed the door behind her.

'And take your fucking budgerigar!' I yelled.

It was not, all in all, the best end to a day I wished had never begun.

PART TWO

March

18

Wind from north of the Hudson whipped New York with icy venom. I sat in the back of a yellow cab, being driven into Manhattan. I felt the old rush of power as the skyline came into sight. Nothing had changed.

In the end, Tim had been right. I had no option. I didn't like it, but what I liked was no longer relevant. I'd woken up that morning, Wednesday, the morning after Hanny left, and realized that my losses were mounting – banks, business deals and now a very special woman. *Not the first time*, as her last words had reminded me. I had tried her mobile, then her flat. I left a message on both. 'It's me. Please get in touch.' I called Aer Lingus and got a seat at the front end of their flight to New York. I was going down, but I was going to go in comfort. Anyway, I needed a cure and I prefer the champagne that comes out of full-sized bottles. First, I had breakfast with Tim.

'You look gutted.'

'Fine thanks, and how are you?' I said. I told him what I was doing.

'Look, I've been thinking,' he said. 'This is blackmail. You're right to say no. I'll support you, whatever the consequences.'

'I woke up this morning and I realized what I have to do.'

'I'm serious, Joe.'

'I'm going to New York. I'm going to try and see if I can pick up the trail there. It's my territory. If Penn was there, I'll find out. Trident is the obvious place to start.'

'You sure?'

'You said it last night yourself – I have no option. We

have no cash. If McCoy keeps going the way he is, we're going to go bust.'

'I'm due some reactions this morning from sources who might come up with the funds we need,' Tim said. 'An English pension fund, a bank in Gibraltar and a venture capital outfit based in Geneva. All we need is one of them to click. Even bridging finance would do.'

'We can't wait any longer.'

'We're a top-rate outfit. Someone will see that.'

'I've got thirty minutes before I have to go and catch the plane.'

We ran over the list of outstanding business deals, the way we normally would if I was going on a normal trip, in the far-off days when normal was what happened.

'There's one other thing.'

Tim looked at me.

'Hanny and I had a row last night.'

Tim's face said he knew.

'My fault. She walked out.'

'Why don't you phone her?'

'I've tried. Got a message. Do me a favour? Find her. Tell her I'll call her from New York.'

'No problem.'

'I'll speak to you as soon as I land.' And we shook hands, because we both knew that we were going into the unknown. On the way out to Dublin Airport I had got through to Hanny's voicemail again, twice. This time I said, 'I'm sorry.'

Across the Triborough Bridge, the taxi cut down on to the East River Drive a few blocks south of Harlem. Churches. The piles of cardboard cartons. The endless traffic. People wore the ear-flaps of their caps down. I'd spoken to Tim when I landed, but he had been unable to make contact with Hanny. That bothered me. I suddenly began to think of all the other people who had let her down and hoped that now she did not see me as the latest in a series. Crossing Fifth Avenue I could look south and see the little park with its old fire watchtower. We passed the National Black Theater. Little had changed. Except me.

I had spent the three years before my first job on Wall Street working out of the compound of the American Embassy in Beirut. Developing contacts. Trying to read the minds of men whose background was the desert and goatskin tents. Trying to stay alive. One lovely evening at a busy Beirut crossroads, I bent to light my cigarette from the cupped hands of an Arab and as I did so felt the hairs of my neck fluff. Then came the thin crack of the rifle. We both tumbled. Too late. The flight path of the next bullet had already divided my Arab contact between his eyes. I often wondered after that day whether or not God intended that I should give up cigarettes.

The cab climbed an empty Claremont Avenue. John had lived near Columbia back then too; on the first trip I had booked myself in on the fold-out sofa. In warmer weather, that shop on the corner displayed its tomatoes and other greens outside, I remembered, but now your fingers would have frozen just going out to pick them. After the Marines, I thought I was qualified for nothing more than how to survive in rough terrain and storm a fortified position. Wrong – I had learned how to analyse: men, situations. My commanding officer knew someone on the board of an outfit called Dolans on Wall Street.

The granite on Grant's Tomb looked as if it could do with a good scrubbing. Nothing had changed either in John's apartment building; the appalling, speckled-egg pattern daubed on the sides of the elevator, the smell of wax on the narrow, wooden flooring lathes of the sixth-floor corridor.

'The mountain has finally come to Mohammed!'

We embraced. John was much thinner than the last time. I could feel his ribs.

'Let me have a look at you,' he said. 'God, you're so well! Laura, my little brother who beat up the world on my behalf is here!'

Laura looked as I remembered: small and neat and wearing blue jeans the way God intended for denim.

'Come on in,' she said. 'Throw your bag right there. We're watching the Buffalo Bills being massacred.'

'Jesus, what a disaster!' John wailed. 'Just before you came in they made a thirty-five-yard run into the end zone, then lost possession. Son of a bitch! Turn it off before I throw something,' he said and handed me a beer.

It was all in his face, everything you wanted to know. Beside me John had the body of a child; but then when you saw his face, you saw such kindness in there side by side with suffering that you knew John Grace was as old as mountains.

I asked, 'How're the boys?'

'Fine,' Laura said. 'Howie's in Alaska, prospecting for oil. Joseph is in Nairobi.'

'UN,' John nodded. 'World Bank. Lives in a house as big as City Hall with six people looking after him. We've been out there.'

'What did you think?'

'Fantastic,' John said. 'Joseph took us out on a game drive. The three of us and half a dozen warriors with spears. Can you imagine?'

'Long way from Blackrock.'

'That's for sure,' John said and coughed.

'And how are you?' I asked both of them.

'We're good,' John said. 'Aren't we, love?'

'We're wonderful,' Laura said.

'I'm eleven years on now,' John said. 'I didn't think I'd live eleven months when I was first told.'

'You look good.'

'Every day for eleven years I've used a mental eraser. Every day I wake up and before I sleep I sit on the side of the bed and I erase the virus.'

He coughed, trying to get up something from his lungs.

'If I can keep my chest clear, I'll probably run the marathon, damn it! You still like opera?'

'Do I look as if I've become senile?'

'Well, here's a thing. June at the Met, okay? Pavarotti's doing *Faust*. And I just happen today to have acquired four tickets. How about that?'

'You didn't tell me!' Laura cried.

'How do you know I tell you everything?' John said and winked at me. 'So, how about it? What's your girlfriend's name?'

'Hanny. And she's German, so she loves *Faust*.'

'Then she's a lucky girl that she's going out with a guy whose brother has such powerful connections,' John grinned.

I felt a wave of guilt, another one. There I was, standing on the foreshore of remorse, dripping with regret. I looked at my brother. He was so matter of fact, not bitter. I would have been bitter, I thought. I'd have been so bitter I'd have gone and knocked someone's head off.

'What's your impression of Viradrol?' I asked and cracked another beer.

John gave me an amused, sideways look. 'It's shit. But what else is there for HIV? AZT?'

'Tell me.'

'Oh, sure,' John said, 'it's probably better that it exists than not. I'm on a haemophiliacs' committee here in New York. We meet a lot of people from right across the spectrum: gays, kids, junkies. Viradrol has had some success in boosting CD4 cells in the early stages, but then they fall right back again. But why not have it, I say. It's hope.'

'At a couple of thousand dollars per course of treatment,' I remarked.

John shrugged. 'If those big companies like Armentisia were not so well in with the FDA, no way would half those drugs out there be on prescription. Why all the interest?'

'It's just for a piece of analysis,' I said lightly.

'I've never actually managed to do some insider trading, although I've always longed to,' John said. 'Is this my chance? Let's have a look.' He pointed the remote at the television and flicked up Wall Street. Trident Drug was eighteen dollars last traded. 'Hey, this is why you're in town, isn't it?'

Laura came from the kitchen with little plates of tortillas and chilli sauce, and forks and napkins.

'I think I'd rather someone else than Roberto Groz was in charge of my cash, frankly,' I said.

'That's what you guys always say,' said John, eating.

'Does the name Carlos Penn mean anything to either of you?' I asked.

'In what context?' John asked.

'Science,' I replied. 'Microbiology.'

John and Laura looked at one another, shook their heads.

'I don't think so,' John said. 'What's he got? A magic bullet?'

I had to laugh. John sounded like every other person thought they had the answer.

'We've come across so many of these so-called magic bullets,' John said, sitting forward. 'Many of them poisonous, all of them fakes. Like concentrated hydrogen peroxide. I had friends that took it until it nearly killed them, never mind AIDS. These people prey on hope. One of them in Salt Lake City boiled blood down into crystals, mixed it with herbs and lamb's piss and sold it to people who trusted him. Hundreds of people. And then there was the guy here in New York who said the answer was in shark's cartilage. Cost seven hundred bucks for a few phials. People might as well have eaten dog fish. Do you want to try the multi-vitamin approach? Or a rare plant bacteria from Iceland? No offence, but we've seen them all.'

John sat back. Suddenly he looked exhausted.

'Is he always this intense?' I asked Laura.

'Sometimes,' she smiled, but she was watching me.

'Carlos Penn was from Bristol,' I said. 'He had an HIV treatment that has been used on a few people in Bristol. Illegally.'

'Everything is illegally,' Laura said and got up to go to a bookshelf. 'The drugs underground in this business is almost as big as the legitimate industry itself.' Sitting down again, she opened a thick, green book. 'This comes out quarterly. It's a round-up of everything that's happening in the underground. Did you say Penn?'

'Carlos Penn,' I said.

Laura was scanning the index. 'Not here.'

'Look up BL-4.'

'That the drug?' Laura shook her head. 'Nope.'

'What's it all about, Joe?' asked John from the sofa.

I told them about Carlos Penn. I told them everything I knew about BL-4 and about the strange man who had invented it, and whom no one had seen for over a year. And I told them about Carson McCoy.

'What a story,' said Laura when I had finished.

John said, 'You know, even though I'm a cynic, when I

hear what you've just said, there's still a little part of me that gets excited.' He ran his hand through his thinning hair. 'But then, what you say doesn't really surprise me.'

'What doesn't?'

'That someone would take such a person out,' John replied. 'That he would disappear. A man such as you describe, if he really has a genuine contribution to make, might well be seen as an enemy by the pharmaceutical industry.'

'You're not the first person to say that.'

'I know I'd sell everything I own just to get rid of the virus,' John said. 'The pharmaceutical giants know that. So, what's the rush, then? The market is growing! When a cure does come along, it's essential the market be big enough. HIV is slowly worming its way into the previously invulnerable sectors of the population. Wait five or six more years, feeding out the same old shit you know doesn't work, and then when the infected base has become truly gigantic, launch the real cure on the biggest disease market in history.'

19

There is a little place over on Amsterdam Avenue that still serves up the best burgers in New York. Although I was on Irish time and for me it was therefore two in the morning, I wasn't tired. Neither was Ricardo Vegas by the look of him. Hair just touching his shoulders, laughing eyes. He poured beer from the cold pitcher and said:

'Run that one by me again.'

I told him what I wanted to do.

'Joe Grace and Trident?' Ricardo said. 'Wow! Is that the lamb going into the lion's den, or what?'

'You say Gold doesn't know you.'

'Right. He doesn't know me, I don't know him.'

'You sure?'

'I saw him once at some party.'

'But you didn't *meet* him.'

'Relax. No. And he's a very up sort of individual by all accounts. Smiles the whole time. Prozac, maybe. Let's face it, he could buy it trade.'

'Set up a meeting between you and him. Gold will want to be nice to *Jeffers Weekly*. If he asks why such short notice, tell him it's because Trident's suddenly hot. Gold's livelihood depends on your saying nice things about him, after all.'

'It's my ass if you screw up.'

'I won't screw up.'

'You don't have to give me the reason.'

'Just say, a question has arisen and I'm the one who has the job of answering it.'

'Well Trident is hot, now that you mention it,' said Ricardo thoughtfully. 'It's eighteen dollars bid today at the close. Is your big question, why?'

'Maybe.'

'Do I get to come in if there's a killing?'

'Would I leave you out?'

'Hey, we did dates like this once, remember?' Ricardo grinned.

'Where do you think I got the idea from?' I asked.

We talked about the old times – and the new. Ricardo was still Casanova; women still moved in and out of his Tribeca apartment like dolls on a Swiss clock, or so he said. It was after midnight when we climbed the stairs and the cold hit us as if we'd stepped into a mortuary. We said goodbye, a brief hug.

'You take care, man,' Ricardo said.

Then he got into a cab and I began the walk back to John and Laura's. I wanted another hour to go by and then I was going to try Hanny again as dawn broke over Dublin. I walked.

I had to concede that I had a knack for fucking up, where women were concerned. Here was someone I wanted for the rest of my life – so how was I now in this position, that I couldn't even get her to speak to me on the telephone? I loved her and had lost her. That bothered me far more than losing Grace Equity, I realized. Stopping on Broadway, I dialled her number as a gust of wind blew out the flaps of my coat. Why hadn't I told her that? I got her voicemail.

'Listen, I want you to know something. I love you more than anything in the world I have ever known or can imagine. Please call me, if only to say you've got this message.'

I headed west. The cold was stinging. It was making my eyes water.

20

To the left lay the Hudson, to the right, north of Yonkers, trees and fields with the sharp outline of the train hurrying across them. The thaw had begun, but the trees were still like sculpted steel and the cold spines of the fields remained in the grip of a hard frost. I looked out at the bleak river and tried to concentrate on the meeting ahead.

Deep in the Trident psyche was sure to be the equivalent of a full alert where I was concerned. It couldn't be otherwise after what had happened all those years before. I began making mental notes of the kinds of questions that Ricardo would ask.

To get to Barrymore, the station of disembarkation was Scarborough. I walked through the waiting room. The building resembled a country station somewhere in rural England on a Monday afternoon. In the Ice Age. No people, no cabs. A lot of commuters' cars waiting for their owners to flop into them after a long day in New York. I called up a cab from a phone reserved for the purpose, then when it came and we headed out on to the ice cap, I called up Soby Sandbach back in the city I had just left.

'What's it like to be sick in Ireland?' he asked.

'The same as being sick in New York,' I said. 'Why?'

'Because Trident's just traded up to eighteen dollars fifty,' the broker said. 'Even Armentisia Lab is up. Sure you don't want to change your mind about this sector? Where are you, by the way?'

'In Alaska, by the looks of things,' I said. 'What's your information?'

'Let's call it educated guesswork rather than hard

information,' Soby said. 'But I'm starting to get some information. It's slow, but it's coming.'

'Okay.'

'Here goes. When Roberto Groz became a medical doctor back in the seventies, he went straight into the NIH and was widely expected to make his career there. When he switched to Trident there was some surprise.'

'But he kept his connections with the FDA.'

'Of course. That's what makes him such an effective player. Now just say certain people in the FDA come across a drug lodged by a non-player, by someone they know is too small and has not got the resources to develop the drug. But say the drug itself is interesting. Let's face it, the FDA see hundreds of such applications every week. But this one stands out. It comes across the desk of a scientist in the FDA who rejects it on one of the countless grounds. However, this FDA scientist also knows Dr Groz.'

The hairs on the back of my neck were rising with an odd familiarity.

I said, 'The FDA reject the drug, but Groz is informed of its existence.'

'Precisely. Nothing wrong with that either, the FDA official persuades himself. The original inventor owns the patent to the drug, but lacks the contacts to develop it. Dr Groz, on the other hand, has the means but lacks the drug. It's not a big step for the FDA official to persuade himself that he's doing something right and worthwhile to put both sides together.'

'Groz is informed.'

'Groz likes the idea of this drug. He needed new drugs badly, as we both know. But when he tries to acquire this particular patent, he fails. Why? I don't know why, but that's the way the play looks to have happened. Groz failed to buy the drug.'

'Why does Groz so much want this one drug?' I asked.

'Because, my source says, it has extraordinary possibilities as a cure to HIV,' replied Soby Sandbach.

The thought of Hanny, and her trip to Bristol which I had tried to rubbish, made me feel newly ashamed.

'Who's the scientist?' I asked.

'I couldn't get the name. They'll go so far with me but no further. Question is, if Groz failed, then why is Trident stock going up? That I can't figure, but the whole thing is connected some way, that's my guess.'

I thought about the information that had come through to me the day before from Denver.

'I'm talking to an analyst who knows quite a bit about the stock in question,' I said. 'The profile of Trident is of a drugs company running out of patents. An objective valuation of Trident, taking in future loss of earnings, could be as low as ten dollars, according to my analyst. Which means, if your information is wrong, there's nothing but downside.'

Soby scoffed. 'You sometimes got to listen to your gut, I say. Tell your analyst that. Who is he, by the way?'

'Who said it was a "he"?'

We chatted for another few minutes.

Soby said, 'Anyway, looks like I can't convert you – not yet, at least. Meantime, I've bought into Trident again. Want to make that two boxes of cigars?'

'You're on,' I said. 'Keep in touch.'

I sat back and felt all the skin between my knees and my belly corrugate. I was moving beyond the circumstantial.

21

We drove twenty minutes north-east through a countryside from which people seemed to be cautiously emerging after the long winter. A man stood by a bonfire in his garden. A woman walked a dog, a red setter, which ran in demented circles, perhaps to keep warm.

'You live in New York?' the driver asked.

'Yes,' I replied, remembering I was Ricardo Vegas.

'We're country folk up here,' the driver said. 'You know what we heard was this winter's big item in New York? Paw wax for dogs. You keep a dog?'

'I keep a budgerigar,' I said.

'Budgerigars is nice,' the cabby said.

A security point, built in stone, nestled beneath rolling, man-made hills, the spoils of earth that had been gouged out when Roberto Groz built his headquarters. I said I was Ricardo Vegas, scribbled my name on a clip pad, clipped a tag-and-chain saying 'Visitor' to my lapel, and the red-and-white barrier rose. Two and a half thousand people worked in here; from here were made decisions that affected sick people right across the world.

Tim had come up with two articles on Alan Gold, one from *Fortune* in which scientists from the top drugs companies had been surveyed, and a more recent piece from *Hello*. The *Fortune* profile at best suspended judgement on Gold's achievements, whilst the social piece was mainly concerned with the British scientist's very pretty wife, his third, and their home on Long Island.

In the 1990s, when this headquarters building had been opened by the then Governor of New York, it had been much discussed in magazines concerned with avant-garde design. The cab rounded the bluff of another hill and the building came into view with the familiarity of a well-known personality now seen in the flesh. There was something of the gigantic crab in the concept: the sides soared up like so many great legs and the domed centre could easily be imagined as a beady, crustaceous head. Beneath a bridge, a river rushed in the sudden spate that had come with the first thaw. Either side of the final ascent, the lawns seemed perfect enough to play billiards on.

'Can you wait?' I asked the cabby.

'No need,' the man said. 'Ask at reception, they'll have you a cab here in two minutes. Enjoy the rest of your day.'

Wide steps led up to a vaulted, glass lobby. Looking back at the cab winding its way over the foaming river and out through Roberto Groz's hills I knew, just for a second, how it must feel to be abandoned.

'Mr Vegas has arrived,' a very pretty girl whispered to a telephone. She came out around the desk and took my coat. A tag on her shirt said 'Barbara'. Great legs, flesh-coloured tights.

'Thanks, Barbara,' I said, smiling, and she smiled back and met my eyes with what could reasonably be interpreted as interest. I was Ricardo Vegas, after all.

I sat on black leather in a pool of sunshine. That so many employees worked here was difficult to imagine. The sound of flowing water broke the air-conditioned silence. No one could be seen, apart from the pretty girl, either inside or out.

'You live around here, Barbara?'

'About thirty minutes,' she smiled.

'It's cold up here.'

'We have ways of keeping warm.'

'I bet you do.'

Perhaps the no-people effect was intended to emphasize

the company's preoccupation with the unseen, the microbes and viruses against which it did daily battle on everyone's behalf. My overriding impression was one of emptiness, in the way of an unfurnished house. There was no soul here.

'Mr Vegas?'

A white-coated woman led the way to the back of the lobby and up a set of short, wide stairs, one of a pair that swung around the source of the water sound, a stream flowing over rocks into a pond stuffed with carp. The woman set a brisk pace down a wide corridor in which the natural rock, showing the fissures and cracks of prehistory, had been incorporated.

We turned left and now the business side of the place was suddenly revealed: below us, through long, glass windows to the left, lines of trucks were backed up to the curtains of loading bays. Automatic barriers stood guard at what looked like grass mounds, but which, as cars emerged from them, were the entry and exit points for an underground car park. The other side of this corridor revealed only tinted glass and, every eight paces or so, the panelled doors of what I imagined were the offices of the top executives. It was through one such open door at the very far end of the corridor that I was shown.

'Ricardo!'

I froze. A man was standing immediately inside the door, looking out with pleasurable expectation. I cursed Ricardo.

'Alan Gold,' the man said. 'We've met before.' He was big and round. Thinning hair, grey at the temples. He too wore a white coat. 'Haven't we?' Fuck you, Ricardo, I thought.

'I don't think so,' I said as we shook hands.

'A couple of Christmases back at Salomon Brothers' Christmas bash?' said Dr Gold.

'Maybe,' I acknowledged and wondered if Dr Gold, as a top scientist, could notice my pulse rate.

'I'm sure of it,' Dr Gold said and we sat down at a cosy nest of armchairs. His accent managed to blend Hyde Park with Central.

'Let me offer you tea or a coffee, or a drink, Ricardo.'

'Tea would be just fine.'

'China, Indian or herb?'

'Herb, please.'

'Vervain, peppermint or chamomile?'

Shit! Did Ricardo drink herb tea? Did they know? I was sweating. 'Vervain,' I said.

'Didn't you once work for Dolans, the old news-sheet?' asked Gold.

'That's right,' I answered. They had done their homework. 'Seems like a long time.'

'Not for everyone,' Dr Gold smiled. 'You follow Trident, Ricardo?'

'I'd like to learn more,' I replied.

'Our stock seems to be on the move in the right direction,' said Gold. 'Do you think that move will continue?'

'Depends what's making it go up,' I replied.

Dr Gold laughed. A little more than was merited. Maybe he was on Prozac.

'We are most honoured that *Jeffers* is so interested in Trident,' he said. 'Now, how can we humble folk up here at Barrymore help you?'

'I was wondering if we could chat in a general way about the direction of Trident's growth products,' I said.

'Sure, sure,' Gold said with appropriate gravity. 'In fact you could not have come in at a better time. Trident's entry into the twenty-first century has been something of an event.'

Dr Gold began to elaborate at length. Tea arrived on a silver tray, brought by the lady in the white coat. As Dr Gold spoke of Trident's products, I made notes and realized anew that the drugs he described had been around for many years and had attracted generic imitators the moment their patents had elapsed. There was nothing new about what I was hearing; it was basically the same old Trident from my time, except bigger. Which was exactly what I'd been told. Then Dr Gold came to the future.

'Off the record?'

'Sure,' I shrugged and put down my notebook.

'One drug which Trident has currently *in utero*,' the doctor said, 'may be the drug the world has been waiting for.'

'HIV related?'

Dr Gold winced. 'I'd rather not be specific.'

'But nonetheless . . .' I said, offering him a cue.

Gold spread his hands in mock helplessness. 'We must not tempt fate.'

'What's its current status with the FDA?'

'I'm afraid I'm not allowed to discuss that either,' smiled Gold.

'Why not?'

'Dealings with the FDA are handled elsewhere in Trident.'

'You mean, by Dr Groz?'

Dr Gold just smiled.

'Is it reasonable to suppose that this is the reason Trident's stock has put on three dollars?' I asked.

'That I cannot say,' said the doctor coyly, pinching out the tip of his tongue between his teeth. 'But they say that markets are invariably wiser than men.'

We had been getting along famously, as snug as two old pals tantalizing each other with glimpses beneath the scientific skirts of the twenty-first century. It was time to kick a little ass.

'Have you ever come across a British scientist named Carlos Penn and an invention of his called BL-4?' I asked.

Dr Gold blinked.

'Penn?' he said and went ever so slightly bug-eyed.

'Carlos Penn.'

'Carlos Penn?'

It was becoming like an echo-chamber. 'Yes.'

'I don't think so . . .'

'Let me help you, Alan. Many years ago, you and he studied microbiology together in Liverpool.'

Dr Gold's mouth opened and closed. Dr Gold-fish, I thought.

'Why, yes, Carlos Penn,' Gold exclaimed. 'Liverpool. Of course.' He blinked. 'Bit of a loose cannon. Has he invented something? I'm sure I would have heard. What is your interest?'

'His name has come up in the context of possible HIV-related drugs,' I said. 'Specifically, a process using an anti-serum derived from the pregnant mother's immune system.'

'Hm-hm,' said Gold and turned his mouth down. 'Is this – generally known?'

'You might say it is, yes.'

Dr Gold suddenly looked as if he needed another dose of Prozac. 'Sorry, I can't help. But what you describe sounds a bit like something Carlos might have come up with. Now, if that's all . . .'

'When was the last time you met him?'

'Me?'

I didn't reply, just kept my eyes on his. His had closed at their centre, like those of a lizard.

'Carlos Penn?' Gold said. 'I suppose it must be nearly twenty years. A name from the past. Now . . .'

'He's disappeared, you know.'

'Oh?'

'Came here to the States last year and hasn't been seen since.'

'I'm not entirely surprised. Carlos was unpredictable. Very bright and needed a big company environment, but could never work in one. A rebel, really. An idealist.'

'Not the worst indictment of a man.'

Dr Gold looked at his watch. 'I'm very sorry, but . . .'

I asked, 'On further reflection, did you meet Carlos during his trip here last year, doctor?'

The bonhomie was truly ebbing from the doctor.

'Ricardo. I just told you, I haven't seen the guy in twenty years, remember?' He was now looking at me as if I had just come into the room. 'That time we met at Salomon's, Ricardo. Who introduced us?'

'I can't remember,' I said with a shrug which I hoped was indifferent.

'But I can,' said Dr Gold closely. 'Wasn't it Manny Obradavitch, the guy who writes the column for the *Journal*?'

'I'm sorry,' I said. 'I really can't recall. And I too am pressed for time, I have a train to catch.' I stood up. 'I mustn't hold you any longer. I really appreciate our little chat.'

The doctor bared his teeth in a smile which made him look like a salivating wolf. We shook hands. The lady in the white coat reappeared. Her smile, at least, was still standard issue. I walked with her, through the outer office. Where had Gold met Carlos last year? Because I was now sure he had. Here? In New York? Gold had been lying to me. I followed the woman out the door, into the corridor and came face to face with Dr Roberto Groz.

'I'm sorry,' I said and stepped to one side.

He was in a party of six other men, all like him in black or charcoal suits.

Groz pointed. 'I know you!'

In the good old days I had worn a beard. How could Groz know me now?

'Ricardo Vegas,' I said and we shook hands.

'Vegas,' Groz frowned, still holding my hand. 'From?'

'*Jeffers Weekly*,' I replied.

'*Jeffers?*'

He looked exactly the same Groz; the curly hair, the curving lip that gave his mouth the appearance of a perpetual smile. I wondered who had set his nose.

'Where were you before *Jeffers*?' he asked intently and let me go.

'Different places,' I said as out of the side of my eye I saw Gold come out and stand in the corridor, thirty yards away.

Gold called something out.

'Sorry, I've got a train to catch. Nice to meet you,' I said.

Son of a bitch, I thought as I regained the lobby. After more than fifteen years? Son of a *bitch*! All I wanted now was out. Barbara, the receptionist, made the call for the cab as the white-coated woman delivered me back to her. I kept one eye on the way I'd come down and the other on the man-made rural landscape outside the floor-to-ceiling windows. I was perspiring. Groz's speciality was fear. Ask Carmine Dominguez. Men with hundreds of millions of dollars at their fingertips oozed fear. Like Carson McCoy. Men who could piss away other people's dreams on a whim. I set my jaw. There was a faint whirring noise somewhere overhead. Like a bird's wing-beat. Barbara took a call, looked at me, whispered into the phone. Smiled. I walked away from her, across the empty lobby and the bird whirred again. I spun around. Maybe they had free-flying canaries in there. The kind that didn't shit. I strolled back to where I'd come from. The whirring only happened when I moved and was almost indiscernible. I looked at my watch. Four-thirty. The cabbie had said it would take two minutes and five had now passed. I moved to the window, listened for the noise and suddenly, looking up, found it. Way up, behind a bank of lights, almost invisibly, a camera was tracking me. The kind that's hooked up to a big computer. Dr Groz was watching. It wasn't going to take him very long to find out who I really was.

'Here's your cab, Mr Vegas,' Barbara said.

I stared at her as if I could not believe I was being let go.

'Your cab.'

She brought out my coat.

'Thanks,' I said.

Glossy black hair bobbed at her neck. She had a great smile, big, unblinking brown eyes that were quite far apart and one hell of a figure.

'Barbara, I have a twin brother whose name is also Ricardo,' I said. 'He's really nice. Can I tell him to call you?'

'No problem, Mr Vegas,' Barbara smiled. 'Take care.'

It was a different cab driver. He had one of those clever devices that lets the driver open the back door without getting out.

'Scarborough station,' I said, getting gratefully in.

22

The fields and woods of upstate New York seemed alien. The trees seemed to reach out at me with menace. Even the houses, instead of calm façades that had gracefully weathered the worst of winter, suddenly seemed to be staring at me with dark eyes of suspicion. Although they ought to have been the same houses that I had passed on my way from Scarborough, now both houses and countryside had acquired an indefinable air of hostility. I had not taken any particular note of the earlier route, just gained a general impression.

'How much longer to the station?' I asked the cabby.

He wore a baseball cap and checked me in his rear-view mirror. He too was perspiring.

''Bout another five minutes or so,' he replied.

'You mind turning the heat down?'

'It's five below out there,' he said.

As soon as I had walked into Trident, I had realized that old scores still lay begging to be settled, that every road eventually leads to home, and that Hanny's insistence on a higher reason behind everything was more than just feminine intuition. Had McCoy known this would happen? Because there was a connection, of that I was now sure. We swung into a long bend, came to a junction and took a left. It wasn't a busy road. I didn't remember it. Evening sun reflected redly on the windscreen of an approaching car. The cab slowed, made another left. I looked at my watch. Four-fifty and we were going back to the Hudson. West. There was a primitive compass in my head. West. In that case, the sun should have been ahead of us, not behind. We were driving east.

'Hey! This isn't the way to Scarborough!' I cried.

The cab driver had his head down, the wheel tightly gripped.

'Pull the cab in!' I ordered and looked behind.

There was a sickening inevitability about the big car on our tail. I tried to open the cab's back door. It was locked.

'*Stop!*'

We were driving straight for big steel gates with revolving spikes across the top. Beyond the gate was a building. Trident Drug. For fifteen minutes we had made a circle and were now in a dead-end at the back of Trident, whose award-winning architecture seemed less obvious from this vantage.

The cab halted in a scream of grit. The driver jumped. He passed me, running. I brought my foot up to the inside of the back door and kicked out – but the door held. Behind, the long car had pulled broadside across the road. Four men in suits emptied from it. Their appearance was that of nightclub heavies. Dark glasses and moustaches. Sallow skin and cheekbones an inch higher than you might expect in this part of upstate New York. Chechens. In a line they were advancing silently across the space between the cars. Two of them had side-arms held pointing down.

'We'd like a word with you, Mr Vegas,' one called.

I went over the seats in an awkward version of the Fosbury flop. I prayed I was right. Keys in a thick bunch hung from the steering column. Ramming the automatic shift all the way forward, I hit the ignition and stood on the pedal. Turning in the seat, steering with one hand, I saw the square face and dark glasses of a Chechen behind a gun. The man jumped. I powered up the lane. You'd like a word, my ass, I thought. The cab hit the dark car and began to swerve. My windscreen took a bullet and cracked into a massive web.

The cab's engine screamed as its revs went into red. I fought to keep her straight but I was ricocheting in reverse from one side of the road to the other. I could not chance turning forward to look, but even if I had, I knew I would see nothing since the windscreen was now white as frost. The crazy swaying had the advantage of making my cab a difficult target. I tried to correct the fatal madness that had entered the cab's backward progress. I gouged out a fencing post, then swung on in a wild criss-crossing. Several shots smacked the cab body with hammer-like impacts. Spinning out on to the quiet highway as if on glass, the cab performed two circles before coming to a rest in waste ground on the far side. The windscreen fell in.

I wrenched the ignition but nothing happened. A hundred yards away the long car was being turned. The cab steamed in the cold air like an exhausted beast. A dull, clicking sound came from the starter. I scrambled out and began to run.

Sun in my face. Road long and ominously empty. My coat made running impossible; I shed it. Looking back I saw the long car paused at the head of the spur road and the Chechens getting in. Sweat ran down my face. A lane appeared to the left, uphill. I took it. Mail boxes. A dog suddenly going crazy. Someone banged a door shut. The stark boughs of old apple trees drooped across stockade-type fencing on to the lane. The laneway made a 'V'; I went right. More mail boxes. The closing crunch behind me of limousine tyres on half-frozen grit. Gardens from these houses ran straight down now to the path I was running on, six houses in a row, cars parked in front of them, variations on a theme. The gradient levelled out, then began to fall. Another branching of the ways, left and right. Right was west. The Hudson. Funny. The Hudson was still twenty miles away. This was a quieter lane, only two houses. Nice place in summer, I thought. I passed the last house and came out on to the bank of a river.

If I listened between my own harsh breaths for half a second at a time I could hear the car's gravel-popping approach behind me like some prehistoric creature flattening the jungle in its path. I ran downstream. The river spiked and jumped with the force of the many billions of thawing gallons from upstream that had been released to swell it. I had an image of New York State in my head: the Hudson sweeping down to the greatest city in the world, being swollen on its way by streams and tributaries like the one whose bank was thudding under my feet. This was, as I had observed, a summer place. There were diving boards and wooden tables built beneath stark willows. Too narrow for a car. I looked back. The four men, Roberto Groz's hunting dogs, imported like Groz himself from the Caspian Sea, were now running too. But unlike me, they had just started.

I hit black ice and slipped. Leather shoes. The river path was as straight and unbroken as the highway I now regretted I had left. If they took me, I knew exactly what would happen – and without the remotest possibility of forgiveness. Dr Groz did not forgive. My chest burned. Gradually the Chechens' breaths were becoming more distinct.

The path had curved without the fact being noticeable. In the distance a dark shape loomed. I dug for the extra spurt, the final one, and felt an agonising weight grow in my chest. I could not see clearly either, because an apparition, or a nightmare, had reared into my path. A ten foot wall, to be exact. Some bastard's property went all the way down to the river and he'd built a wall, right across the bank.

As I looked at the wall I saw plaster on it explode. Two neat little puffs. The sound of the shots followed, loud discharges. The wall was thirty yards and nearing. Something tugged the hair above my ear. I never broke stride. I stuck my hands out in front of me and took the air in a running dive.

If I had had breath left, the water would have snatched it. The cold was immediate and painful as a vice. Yet the river served its initial purpose, because when I surfaced I could see I had been swept around the corner made by the high wall and out of sight of the Chechens. They didn't follow. Maybe they couldn't swim.

It was cold beyond experience. Breathing was not an option. I panted. Fighting to keep my head up, I could feel the blood in my body stop. I was being swept downstream past lawns and serious houses on one side, and on the other, blurred reeds and overhanging trees. It was twilight, but that alone did not account for my suddenly fuzzy vision. I'd gone weak as a glove. Although I'd come only three hundred yards at most, my hands were no use. I kicked with my remaining strength, but my feet were like two distant cement blocks. The river curved right and swept me in its course under the branches of a fallen tree. Hooking my elbows into its boughs, I hung there, partially out of the water, traumatized by cold.

It took me fifteen minutes to crawl in along the bough and to make the river bank. The effect of my water-logged clothes on my body was excruciating, as if each individual bone was being pierced by a knife, but worse – in my hands and feet there was no feeling at all. Kneeling by the trunk of the tree I began to tear at my clothes before they iced up. Numbly I dragged at buttons with my teeth. The cold was bending me double. My jacket fell off, then my shirt. I shook off my trousers and my evilly painful shoes.

I tried to rub circulation into my naked body. Trying to keep panting as if that might stimulate my blood, exhaustion began to take over. I had no idea where I was. It was dusk, about six, I vaguely guessed. A track ran beside where I stood, but there were no houses. I tried to jog on the spot, but could not tell if my legs were moving without looking down at them. They were more black than flesh. I could actually feel the bones in my arms like long pieces of steel. Suddenly I wanted to lie down. To cast around like a dumb animal looking for its final resting pace. Then I saw a blue ghost.

It shimmered towards me up the bank of the river. I crouched. The blue ghost cut through the gathering dusk like a moonbeam. I saw puffs of breath. Ghosts didn't breathe. The jogger wore a luminous blue tracksuit and had a woolly ski cap pulled down around its ears. Her ears, I could see, as she neared. Her stride was bouncy. Then I would have cried out, had I been able to. Her mouth, although set in a determined line, was nonetheless part of a pretty face I knew.

23

In my dream, I am in Lebanon. Hot, blissfully so. Sun strikes me square between my shoulder blades and bores deep goodness into my bones. Suddenly, standing in front of me – an Arab girl. I know her. She's a contact. But I can scarcely recognize her now because she has been stripped naked and beaten by Druze militia. Head shaved, eyes puffy from the beating. I gather my jacket around her and take her inside the jeep beside me. She says the same thing over and over, all the way back to the military hospital. My interpreter translates.

'She's saying, "Hold me, please. Please, just hold me."'

I came half awake. The girl's arms were around me, holding me. Transferring her life's warmth into my body. I had no doubt what would have happened had she not appeared the night before.

'Mr – Vegas?'

I had been crouching by the tree. Unable to utter. I could see my life floating away with each next breath.

'He—lp . . .'

Barbara from Trident Drug stopped in mid-stride beside the river, hand to her mouth at the sight of me. She wore mittens. Sing-Sing Prison had been built on an island not far from Barrymore. There must have been a long tradition of escapees and other such unsavoury characters in the area.

She said, 'I was about to give up looking for you!'

At that moment, about three hundred yards downstream, a powerful light came suddenly to life and began to probe. The girl and I could both hear men's voices.

'Christ!' She stripped off her pullover, beneath which

she wore the thick top of a tracksuit, and then the legs of the same tracksuit beneath which she wore the type of leggings I was used to seeing Hanny in, the type that let you see each sinew. 'Quick! But you'll have to run barefoot.'

I was, literally, frozen, I couldn't move. The light grew in size. Barbara dragged the pullover over my head, then manoeuvred my legs one at a time into the tracksuit. I was vibrating more than shaking.

'Come on!' she whispered. 'They're near!'

Picking up my clothes, she caught my wrist and pulled me after her. The voices of the searching men carried eerily over the surface of the water. With each movement, my blood began to shift again, bringing with it acute pain. I cried out. The girl put her free hand over my mouth. We rounded a corner of trees, away from the range of both the probing lights and the voices. A car was parked there. She opened it and I fell in with a sense of extravagant indifference. I nearly fainted when Barbara turned on the heater.

She lived in a condominium between Barrymore and Scarborough with another woman, a lawyer who worked in Manhattan, Barbara explained. The feeling when we got indoors was memorable. She filled me a scalding tub and brought me mugs of tea laced with whiskey. Then she helped me out of the tub and dried and then dressed me in woollen clothes and brought me to a real log fire. I was limp as a kitten. I lay down on cushions and slept for two hours. When I awoke, Barbara had made soup thick enough to trot a mouse on. Spoon by spoon, she fed me.

She said, 'I should call a doctor.'

'I don't need a doctor.'

'You sure?'

'A psychiatrist, maybe, but not a doctor.'

I sat on the sofa and watched her move about the room,

arranging the remains of my clothes in front of storage heaters.

'There was pandemonium after you left,' she said. 'Groz was screaming about a breach of security, his heavies went into overdrive. I had a bad feeling about the cab that had collected you, I hadn't seen him before.' She looked over. 'I said I wasn't feeling well and left early. That's when I found the cab and worked out what had happened.'

'How did you know where to look?'

'I jog by that river most weekends. I asked at a few houses. A woman said she had seen you run by.'

I watched the flames and felt the chill slowly ebb from me. I was scared. It had been close.

'How long have you worked for Trident?'

'About a year.'

'Nice people, I suppose.'

'Everyone's terrified of Groz. They're hypersensitive to adverse comments – or anything that might impact negatively on their share price.'

'There's been a lot of adverse comment on their HIV drug, Kontrol.'

'When it comes to Kontrol, they're paranoid,' Barbara said. 'If they ever knew I was talking to someone like you, I dread to think what would happen to me.'

'Don't worry,' I said. 'They won't.'

'I've got a friend who says she'll find me a job in Seattle. It rains there, but they're nice people. At Trident they just hired my face.'

'It's understandable,' I said, and placed a log on the fire. 'Where's the lawyer? Your friend.'

'She's in Milan,' Barbara said and smiled.

Barbara who saved my life. She cooked us omelettes and when we went to bed later on, and she held me to her, the sweetness was tinged with the sad knowledge that both of us knew we would never see the other again. Beauty lives in such isolated encounters, unfettered by what has gone before or will come after.

'Hold me,' I said. 'Just hold me.'

Memories. They slip into your consciousness when you least expect them, reminding you that you are never truly alone. I closed my eyes.

24

The American Airlines DC-10 swooped in over Santa Monica Bay and touched down in LAX as wristwatches all over California chimed noon. It was a pleasant change from New York. The palm trees cheered me up, the palm trees and the deep blue of the Pacific. Years ago, just after my first marriage, we'd come out here on vacation and I'd learned to scuba dive in Santa Barbara. And then, more recently, when I'd had to come to LA on business, I'd gone out to the racetrack in Santa Anita and imagined myself as a kid, back in Bray again, riding my pony, smelling his smells, drinking in the excitement. I sat into a cab and we went north on the 405. In Dublin it was eleven fifteen at night; Hanny would still be up – if she'd come back home. I dialled her on the new phone I'd acquired in New York, courtesy of Interfibre. It wasn't what you knew, it was who. I held for a full minute. As I disconnected, the phone began to chirp.

'Hanny?'

'It's Tim, Joe.'

'Have you found her?'

A pause. 'Yes.'

'And . . .?'

'She's staying in another flat in the IFSC with a girlfriend. She's taken a few days off work, apparently.'

'Why do you say "apparently?" '

'Well, I didn't get to speak to her directly.'

'You mean she wouldn't see you?'

'That's correct.' A pause. 'She's pretty down, Joe. Her friend told me Hanny gets like that – I didn't know.'

I did. Only too well. 'Give me her new number.'

'It's not listed. She wouldn't give it.'

' "She"?'

'The friend.'

I felt dizzy. Perhaps the ice-cold waters of upstate New York had thinned my blood. 'Tim, go back down there and get my new mobile number to her. Tell her to call me, please.'

'I'll be down there in thirty minutes,' Tim said. 'Joe, McCoy's people have been on. They want chapter and verse on what you're doing.'

'Tell them this is sensitive work, I can't talk about it.'

'I'll try. Before you go, a shaft of light, perhaps.'

'What do you mean?'

'We have some very real interest in McCoy's stake from that UK pension fund.'

I had to shake my head to focus on what Tim was saying. My business was breaking up and I didn't even recognize it when I was being hit by pieces of the flotsam.

'Call me back when you've been down to Hanny,' I said. 'I'll talk about the business then.'

We were on Wilshire, crawling. In school I'd been taught everything there is to know about St Paul and the events surrounding his conversion on the road to Damascus; and now, if I was to be honest and swallow my pride, I would have had to admit that I'd done a Pauline somersault myself. Maybe it was Dr Groz's heavies who had tipped the balance, resurrecting all the bad old memories of Wall Street. Maybe it was meeting my brother, John. Or realizing that I was in the process of losing Hanny. That, more than anything. One way or the other, I was now determined to find out what had happened to Carlos Penn, who had last been seen alive in this city by someone called Dr Cuba Sali.

I booked into the Regent in Beverly Hills, which for

fifteen years had been my LA pitstop. I then called Dr Sali to set up a meeting for that afternoon, but was diverted to her mobile. She was meant to be expecting me, thanks to Tim.

I said, 'I was wondering when I could come and speak with you about Carlos, doctor?'

'As I explained to your colleague, normally it would be no problem,' replied Dr Sali. 'But I'm on my way to Vancouver to give a paper and I'm currently dropping in to collect some slides.'

'May I ask where?'

'Rodeo Drive, Beverly Hills.'

Thirty minutes later I was sitting in the Reg Bev Wil's tearoom with a most attractive woman of about thirty-five, whose hair was very dark and short cut, whose eyes were of the Oriental variety and who was wearing a most non-medical-looking lightweight beige trouser-suit. She smelled of lavender. Two ladies in long, white aprons served us afternoon tea with a gravitas that would have suited High Mass.

'What's your interest in Carlos?' Dr Sali asked quietly, sizing me up.

My response was a general excursion around the facts, omitting the specific and including, to my own surprise, the assertion that I was doing this for 'a friend'.

'What's your impression of BL-4 as an HIV drug?' I asked.

'Carlos was always very cautious until he had much more case evidence,' replied Dr Sali. 'But, yes, there were some exciting moments, I have to say. Some patients were very weak and the treatment with BL-4 appeared to boost them at that time.'

I could not place her accent: not Oriental, not European and definitely not American.

I asked, 'Are they still alive?'

'I could have absolutely no way of knowing that. I never met them. I only processed their blood samples here in the laboratory. But from these I could see the CD4s improving and therefore what Carlos was telling me about these patients made sense.'

'Why didn't Carlos try to develop this drug himself? Why did he not apply to the FDA and try to have it tested legally?'

Dr Sali hesitated. 'But he did.'

'He did? When?'

'Early last year.'

'You mean Carlos brought this drug to the FDA?'

'Carlos had been to Bethesda and talked about BL-4,' Dr Sali said. 'The FDA gave him no encouragement to proceed with an application for their approval of BL-4 as an investigative new drug. Carlos was devastated. He could have gone to Europe and tried to develop it, but sooner or later he knew he would have to come back and try to crack the FDA nut. It's the way the industry works. Carlos decided he had to continue here with the illegal trials.'

'But the FDA knew about BL-4,' I said.

'Sure they knew,' replied Dr Sali.

I shuddered. The FDA knew about BL-4. Dr Groz knew the FDA as well as his own face in the shaving mirror.

I asked, 'Doctor, is it possible, in your opinion, that Carlos might have approached Trident Drug as possible partners for BL-4?'

'I don't think so,' Dr Sali replied. 'Carlos once told me he had had a very bad experience with Trident. About eight or nine years ago. Carlos was working on motor neurone disease. He went to someone he knew in Trident—'

'Alan Gold?'

'Maybe, I don't remember. I think Carlos already knew him. Anyway, according to Carlos, Trident tried to steal his motor neurone work. He said he would never approach Trident after that.' She made a doubtful motion with her head. 'But then, last year, I was not so sure.'

'I don't understand.'

'We had dinner. Carlos was staying in some small hotel, I can't remember the name . . .'

'Hotel Sierra? Marina Del Rey?'

'I think so. We talked about his drug. He didn't say as such that he'd been to see Trident, but I remember coming away thinking, well, maybe after all he's talking to some of those big guys.'

I was warming to Dr Sali. She had the sort of radiating intelligence that made me trust her, and in addition, taking my condition into account, she was a doctor.

She looked at her watch. 'Mr Grace, why did your friend ask you to look for Carlos?' she enquired, looking at me curiously.

'I suppose he thought I could find him,' I answered, adding, 'for my sins.'

Dr Sali's face became very soft. 'You mean, Carlos may redeem you,' she said. 'I can empathize with that.'

I stared at her. 'You're in love with him, aren't you?'

As I looked at her, her tears brimmed, then spilled.

'With every ounce of my body, with every drop of my blood,' she said simply.

We sat there, in the vaulted room surrounded by people taking afternoon tea, united in a sudden rush of understanding.

'I'm sorry if I've upset you.'

'Don't be. I miss him so much. I miss his mind, his courage. He had no fear of the unknown, you see, and that's the greatest asset that a scientist can have. Courage.

A disregard for boundaries. An interest in the human race. Carlos Penn was utterly unconventional, but he had all those qualities – and more.' She wiped her eyes, sighed. 'What happened to Carlos?'

'I'm not sure. He may have been abducted, but since it's over a year since he's been seen and there has been no word in the meantime, it's difficult to imagine that that's the case. You were the last person to see him. I'm trying to follow his last known movements. I'm on his side.'

Dr Sali leaned across and with tenderness touched my hand. 'Then I'm your friend,' she said. 'Thank you.' She joined her hands, smiled. 'I am sorry, Mr Grace, but I'm going to miss my plane.'

'It's Joe – to my friends.'

Her eyes were the lightest brown not far from green.

'Cuba.'

That lavender again. And an old, familiar feeling.

'I like "Cuba".'

'My father's idea. He thought Cuba meant freedom.'

We smiled together and I inwardly cursed whosoever arranged conferences in Vancouver.

'Cuba, one last thing. Did Carlos mention a Dr Gonzalez?'

'No, sorry. Everyone has already asked me that.'

'Do you know a Dr Gonzalez?'

'Sorry, no.'

I walked with her out through the lobby. I suddenly had an image of a ditched jet in a misty, Irish field.

'Cuba,' I said, 'can you think of any reason why Carlos might want to go to Moscow?'

'Moscow?' Dr Sali laughed. 'If he had, I'm sure he would have told me. That's my country.'

'You're from Russia?'

'Not exactly. From Azerbaijan,' she replied. 'If Carlos told me he was going to Moscow, I would have gone with him.'

There was a silence as if in this remark she had revealed too much of herself.

'I still have many contacts there,' she said as if by way of explanation. 'Now I really must go.'

'What kind of contacts?' I pressed.

'Maybe we can talk about them next time,' she said. 'Please keep me in touch with what's happening. I want to help.'

We shook hands. Then, on impulse, I kissed her cheek and to my enormous surprise, she blushed, but did not look away. I watched her drive from the covered carport that connects both sides of the Regent. Then I went up to my room to make some calls. Cuba Sali came from Azerbaijan. Groz came from Chechnya. I wondered what was going on.

25

My room overlooked the pool. I would normally have unwound down there after a flight and now the notion of allowing the California sun at my recuperating body for an hour sounded like one of the better ideas of the day; but first I wanted to call the place Carlos had spent his last night in North America.

'Hotel Sierra.'

'I want to make a room reservation,' I said.

'You want a room? For a night, or less?'

'For a night – but before I confirm, I just want to know that the hotel has a doctor on call.'

That made her think.

'You what?'

'If I'm sick, is there a doctor I can call?'

'You're sick? This is a hotel.'

'I know and I'm coming to stay with you. But if I get sick when I'm staying with you, is there a doctor?'

'How d'you mean? You think you're going to get sick?' the girl asked in a sing-song, Mexican accent.

'I'm very well,' I replied. 'I just want to know if there's a house doctor, a hotel doctor. And if so, who he is.'

'Hold on, please.'

I opened the mini-bar with my foot and took out two miniature J&Bs. Please let the doctor be called Gonzalez, I prayed.

'This is Mr Belclare,' said a man's voice. 'Can I help you?'

I tried to explain the general nature of my enquiry.

'If you want a doctor when you are here,' said Mr Belclare eventually and with a fair amount of disgust, as if someone who knew they were about to be sick was taking an unfair advantage of the hotel, 'call Dr Webster.'

'But if Dr Webster is not on duty?' I asked.

'Dr Webster is on duty,' replied Mr Belclare. 'Do you want his number?'

I wrote down the number. 'I was wondering, however, if there is a Dr Gonzalez? If there is, he's the one I'd like.'

'Why not Dr Webster?' asked Mr Belclare.

'I like Spanish doctors,' I said.

'We use only Dr Webster,' said Mr Belclare, 'and I think, sir, you should find a different hotel.' He hung up.

Gonzalez might be Webster's partner, I thought, or a year ago might have been. I called Dr Webster but he did not have and never had had either a partner or a doctor working for him by the name of Gonzalez. I felt light-headed from the Bourbon, and therefore immediately decanted a further brace of little bottles over ice. I took out the LA Yellow Pages.

26

There are a lot of doctors with the surname Gonzalez in the greater Los Angeles area.

'Could I please speak with Dr Gonzalez?'

'This is he.'

'Dr Gonzalez, my name is Grace. I'm sorry to disturb you, but I'm trying to locate a friend of mine in Los Angeles. His name is Carlos Penn and all I know is that his doctor is a Dr Gonzalez.'

'Carlos Penn?'

'Yes. Penn. Carlos Penn.'

'I don't think so. Hold on.' Dr Gonzalez then went to his filofax, or card index, or the database of his PC, or called out to someone, usually in Spanish, or as in one case just turned away from the phone and sneezed gigantically. 'Sorry, I know no one of that name.'

Those were the good calls. The ones that spoke in English. A large number of Dr Gonzalezes did not; an equally numerous group seemed to have forsaken their telephone numbers, to have left them in an inoperative condition with only the high-pitched tone of a disconnection for company. What happened to those numbers, I wondered idly, as I took a slug of Drambuie. Were they left abandoned in the middle of a vast city like puppies, whilst their owners took off without a thought? So many of them. As I doggedly dialled on, I drank three quarter-bottles of red wine and composed in my head my opening speech as founder of the Society for Abandoned Telephone Numbers. The dialling was like therapy. I would dial every mother in LA with the name Gonzalez, if needs be. It stopped me thinking about Hanny.

It was eight-thirty in the evening and I needed food. The project was going down the toilet, both in the metaphorical as well as in the physical sense. I hated drinking on my own. I needed food and a couple of hours' sleep.

'Hello.' I looked at the telephone, forgetting for a moment its purpose, or who I was calling, or why. 'Could I speak with Dr Gonzalez?'

'Yes.'

'This is you, Dr Gonzalez?'

'Yes.'

'Dr Gonzalez, my name is Grace. I'm sorry to disturb you at this hour . . .'

I gave him the usual line about Carlos and prepared to hang up.

'Okay, so what do you want me to do?' asked Dr Gonzalez in very Latino English.

I blinked. 'You know Carlos?' I asked.

'Can I call you right back?' asked the man on the other end.

'Of course,' I said and gave him the number.

I hung up and sat on the bed and nothing happened. It was maybe the way this particular Dr Gonzalez had of dealing with unwanted calls. Now, of course, I couldn't call out again because this Dr Gonzalez might be trying to reach me. My stomach was on its knees, begging for food. The phone rang.

'Mr Grace?'

'Dr Gonzalez?'

'You were about to say . . .' said Dr Gonzalez.

'You know Carlos Penn?' I asked.

'Sure.'

'Carlos? Penn?'

'*Si*, *si*, Carlos Penn, sure,' said Dr Gonzalez.

'In that case,' I said, suddenly sober, 'I wonder, doctor, if we might meet?'

'You want to meet me?'

I grabbed the pad and pencil that an hour previously I had thought I might need.

'Dr Gonzalez, yes, I do very much want to meet you,' I said. 'When would suit you?'

'This evening's okay, I guess,' said Dr Gonzalez.

'Perfect,' I said. 'I'll come over whenever you say.' I looked at the telephone book. 'Let me see, you're in Pasadena, that's—'

'No, I'll come and meet you,' said Dr Gonzalez. 'Where are you?'

'I'm in Beverly Hills,' I said.

'You know the Peninsula Hotel? You want to be standing on the kerb outside the entrance at – what? Eleven o'clock?'

'Okay. You're sure this is no problem?'

'No, it's no problem, my friend. Carry a coat or somethin' on your arm so I'll know you. You got a coat?'

'Yes, yes, I have a coat.'

'Wonderful. I'll see you then.'

'And, you know Carlos, Dr Gonzalez?' I said. 'You met him last year?'

'Sure I know Carlos,' said Dr Gonzalez, 'sure I met him,' and hung up.

I left the hotel and walked across the street to The Grill where I ate a ten-ounce fillet steak with double French fries and drank five cups of coffee. It was ten-thirty when I caught a cab over to the Peninsula. The last time I'd been in this city was four months before when I'd put together a ten million pound software deal with a bunch of clever kids out in Sun Valley. Who would have thought, I asked myself as I looked out at the city from my new perspective, who would have thought? I was convinced now that when Carlos's drug had been seen and dismissed by the FDA, someone in there had then informed Roberto Groz. But what had Groz done with Carlos? Where was the connection? Who was this Dr Gonzalez? Was Carlos still here in LA? If so, where did Dr Gonzalez fit in? We pulled up on the roadside outside the Peninsula Hotel, the deal-capital of Hollywood, and I got out. Maybe Carlos did not want to be found.

The night was balmy, just the right side of sticky. Limos came and went. I stood, trying not to appear self-conscious with my coat folded in its appointed place. The green Toyota convertible had passed me twice in five minutes. Left to right, the second time it cruised by very slowly, its soft roof in place. Without warning it appeared again, fast, and the curbside door swung open.

'Get in.'

I sat in and we pulled away with the sound of squandered rubber.

'Dr Gonzalez? I'm Joe Grace.'

'*Mucho gusto*. Just buckle your seat belt,' said Dr Gonzalez, checking his rear-view mirror. 'They see you not wearing one, the bastards pull you in.'

We were in the general direction of the 405 Freeway. Dr Gonzalez was fat and very Spanish-looking, which is to say his hair and moustache were inky black and the fleshy arms that protruded from his very colourful, short-sleeved shirt were the colour of olive oil. He wore spectacles glazed with one-way mirrors, but despite them I could see from where I sat that the doctor's eyes apportioned their field of vision between me, the road ahead and the rear-view mirror.

'Look, it's none of my business how you know Carlos, okay?' I began.

'None of anybody's business,' shrugged Dr Gonzalez and smiled toothily.

'I appreciate your coming out to meet me,' I said.

'We all got our problems, we all got to live,' said Dr Gonzalez and checked his rear-view mirror. 'Live and let live, they say. No?'

'Right,' I said. 'No problem.'

'*Muy bien*. This is going to cost you five hundred bucks,' said Dr Gonzalez without changing his tone. 'It's the purest you'll score in LA, don't let anyone tell you a lie. I just want you to put the bills up where I can see them here on the facia, then I give you the goods, no sweat and we say goodnight. Okay?'

I remembered later that we had been passing a large, illuminated sign at the moment Dr Gonzalez made that statement. The sign said, 'JESUS HEALS'.

'Look, I think there may be a mistake,' I said.

'You want to buy or no?' asked Dr Gonzalez harshly.

'I told you, I'm looking for a friend of mine.'

'Where'd you get my number?' asked Dr Gonzalez.

Despair seized my heart. 'You don't know Carlos, do you?'

'Is this some kind of set-up?'

'Just let me out of the—' I began, but then on both sides of the car, blue lights erupted like massive fireflies.

'*Hijos de putas!*' snarled the doctor and hit the floor with his foot. 'Sons of bitches!'

'Watch it!'

We'd been followed. The police car had veered to nose us into the side, but it had not nosed enough. The doctor hit it accelerating and it spun away like a piece of driftwood.

I could see from the contorted shape of Dr Gonzalez's face that he held me responsible for the outcome of the evening.

'You filthy son of a sow!' he hissed and swung the wheel. 'I kill us both now!'

'I didn't do this!' I cried as we bounced up on to a kerb with two wheels, then crashed down off it again. Straight through red lights, a truck appeared like a cliff. I stuck out my hands in front of me.

'*Bastardos!*' screamed Dr Gonzalez.

The doctor now steered with his left hand. Reaching across me he yanked open the glove compartment and began to fling its contents, books, a cap, a stethoscope, out on to the floor of the car at my feet.

'Bastards!' shouted Dr Gonzalez. 'Fucking thieves!'

He fumbled like crazy, then his hand came out holding a small box. Dragging it open with his teeth, a number of packages of clear plastic, none of them bigger than a packet of condoms, fell into his lap. We were now screaming down the centre of a two-way highway. For me to try and hi-jack the car would mean a certain crash; we were doing 70 m.p.h. The blue strobe lights were two cars behind – I could hear them wail. Dr Gonzalez opened the window. He tore each plastic package in turn with his incisors and shook the fine powder out into the hurtling night. The occasional loss of two hands on the wheel gave the already terrifying journey a flavour of apocalypse. I could see my whole life in those moments. We scraped the length of another car as we passed it – that is, a car coming against us. Red lights meant nothing to the demented Dr Gonzalez. His dedication to destroying the evidence totally absorbed him. He grunted as he chewed each packet and screamed abuse at me and at Los Angeles as he shook the damning white dust into the atmosphere.

'*Ni hablar!*' Dr Gonzalez cried. 'No fucking way!'

'Jesus . . .!'

We turned broadside of the blocking patrol cars at the

penultimate moment. We rolled. The impact when we hit the metal street light loosened each tooth in my mouth and sent pain through my head accompanied by extraordinarily vivid lights. But I was conscious a few seconds later because I could recognize the half a dozen guns that were pointing in at us.

'You guys gotta lotta explainin' to do,' panted Dr Gonzalez to the cops.

'You're both under arrest,' said a grim-faced cop whose gun was twitching at my temple.

I wondered what would have happened had I not taken Dr Gonzalez's advice to buckle up.

27

As a boy, I was drawn to wide, open spaces. The Bull Wall, the Sugarloaf, the very limit you could walk out at low tide on Sandymount Strand. My father brought me for hikes across the great Midland bogs, over tens of thousands of acres on winter days when the mist was so ambiguous that although it existed, it wouldn't wet you. We went riding together in Wicklow. We rode out in winter dawns and came back down to Bray to the smell of evening fires burning coal. I went back down there on my own as soon as I was old enough. It seemed that the sheer expanse of unpopulated space allowed my head to float free of my body. I was at peace on the bogs and mountains, alone. It was what I had most missed of Ireland when I went to live in New York. In New York you couldn't get away like that without undertaking a major trip. I longed for the space – and the mist. On hot Manhattan days, I would try to imagine the soft rain on the Bog of Allen or the feel of a horse beneath me and I would try to spirit myself back into that position.

Those were a rough approximation of my thoughts during the night I spent in the police lock-up in the centre of downtown LA. My cell was one in a long row. As the night went slowly by, the other cells filled up with the human debris of the city. I lay on a metal shelf intended as a bed.

We had been driven there in handcuffs, relieved of our personal belongings and marched in like a couple of hoodlums, which of course Dr Gonzalez was and I had come to resemble. We were charged together, then separated. I never saw him again. I never found out what happened to him, or if he was really a doctor, or if by asking about Carlos Penn I had stumbled, in one chance in a million, on some code or use of words which the doctor used to deal cocaine. Another doctor, which description gave Dr Gonzalez the benefit of the doubt, came and peered at my head and said I'd live, and told the big, black duty sergeant that I was sane enough to answer questions. I used my one call judiciously. I called the Irish Consul and asked him – no, begged him, for nothing else would have worked – to call Harry Quinlan in the Department of Foreign Affairs in Dublin and to acquaint him with my position. Poor Harry.

I tried to work out what I was going to do. My anxiety over Hanny kept intruding on my ability to think out the next move on Carlos Penn. This city was the last place he had been seen, so somewhere here lay the answer to the question of how he had disappeared, and to where. It seemed, however, that I was turning out to be the worst person in the world to find him.

Light came through high windows. I had a hangover. I knew that somewhere in this experience was a funny side – but like good wine it would take some time to appreciate. At eight that morning the Irish Consul arrived and at eight-thirty we were in a duty officer's room with forms being filled out in a civilized fashion. The Consul, whatever my connections, was stiffly polite. A career civil servant, if he was interested in how I came to be in this position, he kept such interest unvoiced. A cop came in with a brown envelope containing my belongings.

'Check them out,' he instructed.

I did so. My watch. My pen, wallet with credit cards and a thousand in cash. My new phone which looked as if a cement truck had reversed over it.

'Sign here,' said the cop, and when I had signed, said, 'Wait here.'

'Do you have a phone I could use?' I asked the diplomat. 'It's urgent.'

The Irishman sighed, took out a cellphone. 'You'll be invoiced for the call.'

'Thanks.' I pressed out Tim's number. He picked up on the first ring.

'Where have you been? I keep getting your voicemail.'

'Busy. Did you get the message to Hanny?'

'I slipped the number under her door.'

'I'll come back to you with a new number,' I said.

'Joe – the meeting went well,' Tim said.

Again I had to shake myself in order to translate. 'Good.'

'They're having a board meeting tomorrow to discuss coming in.'

'Look, Tim, I know that's great news, but I'm really worried about Hanny. I mean, you haven't actually seen her – right?'

'I have not physically seen her.'

'I want you to check out that she's okay. With your eyes. Go down to the IFSC. Break in if you have to.'

Even though his back was turned I could see the diplomat's ears twitch.

'Break in?' Tim said.

'Kick the fucking door down,' I said.

The consul turned around, his eyes enlarged.

'You're the boss,' Tim said.

I gave the diplomat back his phone and sat down on the only free chair in the room, wondering how my life could have changed so much in so few weeks. On the wall of the office were two enormous maps: one of Los Angeles and one of the United States. It was such an enormous country, the United States. It needed maps measuring yards to do it justice, which in this case it had got. I looked at the shaded conurbation of Los Angeles, in whose heart I was still, technically, incarcerated. South was San Diego. North, along the blue Pacific was Santa Barbara, and if you kept going north, Santa Cruz. Just short of Santa Cruz was Monterey.

That name rang a bell. But, of course, Hanny's jet had come from Monterrey in Mexico, not Monterey. We'd been through all that. And Monterrey, Mexico, could be found right at the other side of the map, paces away, nestling under Texas and the Rio Grande. I heard the door open and the duty officer come back in. Something caught my eye.

'You're free to go,' said the cop.

But I was staring at the map on the wall as if I had seen the face of God there.

'Mister!'

'Mr Grace,' said the Irish diplomat, clearing his throat. I'm sure he was reflecting, with regret, on certain aspects of his job.

I was staring at the big map. At Monterrey in Mexico. At a town about fifty or sixty miles to the north-east of Monterrey. All I could think of was what Hanny had found out. And of what had happened to her as a result.

'Mr Grace!' said the Consul with steel in his voice. He'd make a report on all of this. It wouldn't be auspicious.

'Jesus Christ,' I said, mainly to myself.

The little town I was looking at was called Dr Gonzalez.

28

The Delta flight had tracked south along the edge of the Gulf of California, then turned east under the Sierra Madre Occidental before landing in Mexico City. Aeromexico did the connection north. The flight was full of businessmen on their way to Monterrey, the industrial capital of the north, in the hope of prising some pesos from the tight fists of the *Regiomontanos*.

I had called Tim again, this time from a payphone in Mexico City airport, but had been diverted to his answering machine.

'It's me. I'm in Mexico, details later. This may sound a bizarre question, but did Hanny take Salman? If not, you better get in upstairs and feed him or else I'll be coming home to a corpse.'

I tried to pull down the plane's window blind, but it wouldn't come. I was flying north over the empty, northern vastness of Nuevo Leon. I was still sore from Los Angeles; my neck hurt and a six-inch sticking plaster covered a gash to my right temple. I needed twenty minutes' sleep before touchdown.

I dreamed of Harry Quinlan. The Harry of New York, one score years before. *I don't want to work on Maggie's faaaaa-m no more!* It was always Dylan then. Harry could play anything but when he heard Dylan he played nothing else. He was the kind of friend you could call at three in the morning and ask to drive across Dublin because a pretty girl needed someone to talk to. I walked along the bank of a river, searching for Harry. And for a telephone. 'You need a telephone?' asked Carlos Penn. 'Here, use mine.' I looked at Carlos. 'Where the hell have you been?' I asked with a feeling of great relief. 'Here the whole time,' Carlos replied. I asked, 'What about AIDS?' 'Give me space,' Carlos said. 'Look.' I looked to where he was pointing. To a very deep part of the river. There, in the riverbed looking up at me, was a face. Hanny's. I shouted! *Hanny!*

'*Abrochense los cinturones, por favor, señores*,' said the intercom. 'We are about to land at Monterrey.'

The man beside me ground out the cigarette he had been smoking between his thumb and forefinger and folded it into the breast pocket of his suit.

'Cerro de la Silla,' he said, leaning across to my window and pointing.

Monterrey was a bowl. The industrial might of the city belched up at the plane from its base; the rim of the bowl was made by a dramatic circle of mountains. I had got through that morning to Caulfield Cade in San Antonio, Texas, and explained the outline of my position. Caulfield, one of our investors, already knew McCoy was pulling out. Now he was driving south across the border to meet me. As the plane tilted sharply for its final descent, I saw a mountain-top formed in the distinctive shape of a saddle.

'Are you coming to Monterrey on the business?' asked the man.

'I suppose you could call it that,' I said.

'I hope you have the luck, mister,' smiled the man as the wheels of the plane touched the warm tarmac.

I had a carry-on bag only; I walked straight through and out into the arrivals hall to a bank of telephones, stuck in a credit card and punched out the number of Hanny's mobile. I imagined the pulse soaring up over the Gulf of Mexico into the stratosphere, bouncing off a satellite, then plunging downward in a great arc, seeking its chosen point within a grey, misty island in the North Atlantic.

'Yes.'

'Hanny! It's me.'

I could hear her breathing, as if she were still asleep.

'Hanny?' My throat dried out. I tried to work out what time it was in Ireland and the best I could come up with was eight in the evening. 'Hanny!'

She was there, but she wasn't speaking.

'Are you all right? Hanny? Answer me!'

Her even breaths, like kisses, from the other side of the world.

'Listen to me! I'm in Mexico. I may have found the link to Carlos we've been looking for, but it's going to take me some more time. Can you hear me?'

I strained my ear against the phone, trying to screen out the clamour of the airport, the tannoy announcements, the sudden groundswell of voices and noise that was threatening to make even her breathing inaudible.

'Hanny, it's okay if you don't want to talk, but I want to tell you something. I'm sorry. I was stupid. I didn't see anything beyond trying to refloat Grace Equity and I was very angry. Angry with McCoy, angry with myself. But a lot of things have happened since then and I want to tell you about them. I'm coming home in the next twenty-four hours, that's a promise. I'm starved for you – do you hear me? Starved. I can't live without you. There have been other women, but none of them have been like you. I swear that. I love you.'

And I listened for another thirty seconds to her breathing.

'Goodnight, Hanny.'

Then I hung up.

29

'Joe!'

The man making his way across the hall looked like a barrel with a ten-gallon stetson on the top and shitkicker boots underneath. But Caulfield Cade moved in a way that made his weight irrelevant. His strength had stood to him twenty-five years before when he had started wildcatting for oil in southern Texas. He had been an engine that never stopped, twenty hours a day, month in, month out. He still thought nothing of getting into his air-conditioned pick-up and driving three hundred miles over the border.

'Well, you haven't changed,' he said and popped his stetson back on his head the better to get a look at me, then tapped his forehead and grinned. 'How's the other guy?'

The Texan's pick-up was parked two wheels on the kerb. He threw my bag in the back.

'You sure pick out-of-the-way places,' Caulfield said. 'If this location features in any of the investment plans I'm part of, then it's gone right over my head.'

'It doesn't,' I said. 'This is personal.'

'Be my guest,' said Caulfield and we took the highway due east.

The airport squatted in tawny countryside. The highway to Monterrey cut south, but Caulfield left it at a signpost for Parque Nacional el Sabinal. We chatted about Grace Equity's investment projects. Then we discussed McCoy.

'I got your letter about McCoy,' Caulfield said.

'We think we have him taken out,' I said. 'Tim is hopeful the deal will be done in the next few days.'

'I'm backing you, not McCoy,' Caulfield said. 'You can rely on me, whatever happens.'

We were cutting through brown, barren mountain land. A group of trailers was pulled in off the road; kids with big eyes stood staring; a woman hung a line of washing out between a couple of poles.

'Did the drive down take you long?' I asked.

'It's chicken shit,' said the Texan. 'Came down Highway 35 to Laredo and crossed over. Straight run to Monterrey after that. Pity is, I can't stay over with you. Flaring off a well tomorrow morning at sunrise and I have to be there.'

'Where's this Dr Gonzalez?'

'Like a rinky-dinky little Spanish hill-town sitting on its own,' Caulfield said. 'Your Cobra Internacionale is an outfit just north of it.'

'What do they do?'

Caulfield gave me a half amused, half wary look.

'From what I can see, they do experiments on monkeys,' he replied.

'Do you mind if I use your mobile?' I asked.

'Signal's been coming and going since I crossed the border,' Caulfield said. 'But hey, this is Mexico!'

My mind was in grotesque mode and top of the billing were sudden images of Hanny: her lips like ice, her body unmoving, an old man in clerical robes standing beside her bier, his hungry eyes savouring her dead body.

'Joe?'

'Sorry.'

'I was just saying, I asked around the town, but no one seems to know much about Cobra,' Caulfield said. 'Even if they did, they're not going to tell a gringo. So we're going to have to go in cold to find out anything. Which brings me to the next question. What exactly do you want to know?'

I pressed my temples with the heels of my hands. I needed to get focused on why I was on my way through the

Mexican scrub with one of my principal investors to see a load of monkeys.

I said: 'Cobra hired a jet in Monterrey last year. On 6th March they left Monterrey with a flight plan filed for Moscow. The flight ended with an unscheduled touch-down in a field on the west coast of Ireland. I'm looking for someone I now believe was on that flight. Up to yesterday, I had no way of knowing he was on it – but Doctor Gonzalez is the connection. So I want to find out who owns Cobra. Specifically, I want to find out if they have any connection to Trident Drug.'

'The New York outfit?'

'That's them.'

'I see,' said Caulfield with a smile that said he now understood. 'Trident Drug are in demand all of a sudden. Twenty dollars a share this morning. Is this why we're down in this place?'

'I'm really not sure, Caulfield, and that's the truth,' I answered and looked at the shanty-town houses and huts we were passing either side.

'Welcome to Dr Gonzalez,' Caulfield said.

A policeman with a night-stick stood at a red light in the main square. He looked to be asleep on his feet. Two o'clock in the afternoon. The square was tree shaded and beneath the trees on iron benches sat nut-brown women and old men with silvery moustaches. The lights turned to green. After the square there was a wrought-iron, white bandstand where a young man with long, blond hair sat plucking a guitar. We left the town as abruptly as we had entered it. A group of colourful, barefoot peasants with bundles of shopping were heading north, perhaps home to the hills. I saw their high, Indian cheekbones. Two statues stood at the extremity of Dr Gonzalez, their gazes fixed on the mountains to the north.

'Here's your Cobra,' said Caulfield quietly, pulling up beside a bedraggled wire fence that marked the boundary around a low, flat building, set back in some trees about thirty-five yards from the highway.

'How do we get in?' I asked.

'We walk in,' Caulfield said. 'They're expecting us.'

There had once been asphalt on the short drive, but it had long since pitted, then covered over with the dust from the surrounding scrubland.

'Talked to a lady by telephone an hour ago,' Caulfield explained as he parked next to two other cars by glass doors. 'Dr Rosa. A veterinarian. Explained we were part of an animal rights activist group from Texas and that since we were driving through Nuevo Leon, I'd appreciate it if she could let us look around.'

'What did she say?' I asked.

'She seemed anxious to co-operate, of course,' Caulfield said.

The building was square-shaped. Cameras were wall-mounted on the front and above them spotlights; but the side windows had only wire mesh panels over them and no protective cameras or lights. Outside there had been an attempt at flowerbeds and shrubberies, but the attempt had not been sustained. The dry, caked earth and sparse grass on which Cobra Internacionale was built was reverting to its former, arid self. Caulfield pressed a button beside a metal grille; there was an exchange in Spanish and the door opened with electronic buzzing. The lobby was tiny and empty. By one window an air-conditioner rattled. An aerial photograph of the premises hung over a potted yucca tree.

'Señor Cade?'

'Dr Rosa,' Caulfield said warmly and removed his stetson with a dandified flourish. 'This is Señor Grace.'

'Señor Grace.'

Dr Rosa, a dark and small lady, held her hands clasped together before her. She was in her thirties, wore a navy skirt and a white, formal blouse. Spectacles hung by a chain around her neck. Her large eyes hovered nervously.

'How exactly can I help you?'

'Señor Grace is the better man to ask,' beamed Caulfield.

'Señor Grace?'

'Perhaps you could show us the general facilities,' I suggested.

'The animals?' asked Dr Rosa.

'Wonderful,' I said.

'Follow me, please, *señores*,' the woman said, leading the way back through doors and along a dark and musky-smelling corridor.

I could not yet identify the smell. Past a windowless office bearing Dr Rosa's name, and a canteen where several men in overalls sat around a table. Dr Rosa turned left, through a door in which an inspection window had been incorporated. The smell hit my nose like a head butt. It was that of the zoo.

A metal gate panelled in strong wire mesh barred the way to a room. Light came from a number of skylights, also meshed. Cages, three high, ran in two rows down either side. In the empty centre, which was tiled and shining, stood a number of barrels and planks and other fixtures reminiscent of a children's playground. Dr Rosa unlocked the gate and a noisy rustling and squealing erupted. Snouts pressed wire mesh and black eyes fastened on us.

'These are our children,' said Dr Rosa. 'Rhesus monkeys, *Macaca mulatta*, by their proper name. Non-human primates from the family *Cercopithecinae*. As you can see, Señor Grace, they are all clean and contented, yes?'

Caulfield and I followed the woman down the centre of

the room. The faces in the cages did look uncannily like those of children. Some monkeys were caged in pairs, others in groups of five or six, and in some cases, alone.

'Rhesus monkeys are particularly well adapted for laboratory life,' explained Dr Rosa. 'They are much easier to work with than the common marmoset, *Calithrix jacchus*, because although the marmoset is easier to breed in captivity, its lifespan is, on average, only eighteen months, whilst this bigger species can expect to live at least five years and often twice that length of time.'

Monkeys the size of large infants groomed one another, or hung from their cage perches, chewing, or played abstractedly with rubber rings and other toys; but where a cage held only a solitary occupant these monkeys appeared agitated, somersaulting endlessly, or walking in aimless circles, or, in some cases, banging their heads against the walls of their cage. In a few cages, when we paused, the monkey in solitary confinement ran at the wire mesh of its prison, its teeth bared in an expression of hate.

'I don't think they like us,' Caulfield murmured.

'Do you blame them?' I asked.

'The rhesus monkey loves herbs,' Dr Rosa was saying, taking some pellets from a bin and scattering them on the dirt floor of a cage. 'Pellets for everything nowadays, I'm afraid,' she smiled. 'These ones are flavoured with a mixture of herbs. We even have ones that taste like bananas – I know, I've tried them myself.'

The monkeys varied in appearance from very small with tender under-skin and pleading eyes to bigger and cunning. These larger specimens seemed the more aggressive.

'Where do these characters come from, Dr Rosa?' asked Caulfield pleasantly.

'All from reputable agents,' the woman affirmed.

'Mostly in India, although some of them are sourced in Malaysia and also in Peru.'

'You mean, trapped in those countries,' I remarked.

'They are a natural resource, *señor*,' replied Dr Rosa. 'They are making a great contribution to the welfare of the human race.'

'Do you ever release them from the cages?' Caulfield asked as over his shoulder a particularly aggressive monkey was baring its teeth and thrusting its face so hard against the wire mesh that it must have hurt.

'Cages are an old-fashioned concept, Señor Cade,' said Dr Rosa, in a little show of sternness. 'We refer to them as modules. Here the modules are all built to a size agreed upon by international experts. All are locked or unlocked by electronic switches activated from a control panel outside. State of the art, yes, *señor*? And better use of the walls, ceiling and floor in the modules increases the animals' psychological space. In fact, there is a good argument for believing that these monkeys are far happier here at Dr Gonzalez than they would be in the wild.'

'I've no doubt,' I said and exchanged looks with Caulfield.

'But yes, this is the monkeys' play area,' said Dr Rosa. 'Social interaction is vital. We open the modules on a rotating basis each day and the animals come and play and socialize here. These are their chairs. Their table. They even watch television.'

'I won't ask what their favourite programme is,' said Caulfield, leaning on the heavy wooden, monkey table.

'You may ask,' said Dr Rosa. 'It is hard to judge absolutely, but by and large we think the monkeys like programmes about nature and the environment best, Señor Cade.'

A door at the end of the room also incorporated a

window within it. I looked through and saw a room smaller than the one we were in. Cages ran in double rows down either wall.

'What happens in here?' I asked.

'That is our sick bay,' answered Dr Rosa.

'Seems to be busy,' I observed. 'Can we go in?'

'I am sorry. It is our policy that only Cobra personnel can enter the sick bay,' said Dr. Rosa.

'Why?' I asked.

'Because it is our policy,' said the woman firmly and led us back towards the outer gate.

'What are the monkeys mainly used for?' I asked, looking back. 'What type of experiment?'

'It varies,' replied Dr Rosa. 'It depends on what drugs the scientists are testing. For example, in the United States, before the FDA will allow humans to become involved in drugs testing, it insists on first having those drugs tested on primates.'

She opened the gate, then locked it behind us.

'So, what drugs are these monkeys we've just seen being given?' I asked.

'I don't know the names of the drugs,' replied Dr Rosa. 'But we only deal with reputable laboratories.'

'I meant, what field of medicine?' I asked and stopped so that the woman had to look at me.

'I understand,' Dr Rosa hesitated, 'as far as I know, the drugs are related to the field of immunology, *señor*.'

It was a relief to leave the monkeys' quarters and to regain the outer lobby and its rattling air-conditioning.

'Real kind of you to show us around, doctor,' Caulfield said. 'It's always our concern as animal rights activists that the animal gets a fair deal – and whilst we may not agree with what you people do, seeing that the monkeys are happy is a good second best.'

He was a class-one bullshit artist, I thought admiringly.

'Thank you,' said Dr Rosa and clasped her hands in place.

'I would like to write to whoever runs Cobra and confirm the sentiments just expressed by my colleague,' I said, taking out a pen and a notebook. 'To whom should I write?'

'You may write to me,' said Dr Rosa. 'I give you a card.'

'Pardon me, doctor, but who owns Cobra?' I asked.

'I am sorry, I cannot answer that question,' replied Dr Rosa. 'Not because I do not wish to, but because I do not know.'

'You run the company, but you don't know who you work for?' Caulfield said.

'I am a veterinarian, *señor*,' replied the woman. 'I take my instructions from an attorney who comes here once a month from Monterrey. The experiments we perform and monitor are done to the highest standard and meet the requirements of the FDA. It is none of my concern who owns Cobra. Now, if that is all . . .'

'One last question,' I said. 'We are extremely grateful for your time, doctor, but can you tell me why, on 6th March last year, Cobra chartered a jet from Aviaco in Monterrey airport with a flight plan filed to Moscow?'

'I am sorry,' replied Dr Rosa. 'I have only worked here since last September. Anything that happened before that date, I know nothing about. *Adios, señores*.'

30

'I never want to see the inside of a place like that again,' Caulfield said as the outskirts of Monterrey hoved into view.

I said, 'What comes to mind nowadays when someone talks about "the area of immunology"?'

Caulfield's wide shoulders shivered. 'AIDS, I guess,' he replied. 'AIDS knocks out your immune system.'

'So you've got a drug that helps the immune system, but the FDA say you must put it first into monkeys,' I said. 'Hardly much point in putting it into healthy monkeys, is there?'

'Christ!' Caulfield said. 'You think those poor little bastards are all HIV positive?'

'Just the ones in the sick room,' I said, thinking.

'That's obscene,' Caulfield said.

'You catch these creatures in a jungle when they're just babies with their mothers. You ship them in cages – sorry, modules – halfway across the world and put them in a shithole like we were just in, then you infect them with HIV in the name of the welfare of mankind. What a species – mankind, I mean.'

'It's not a business I want to invest in, with respect,' said Caulfield.

'I wasn't going to suggest we do,' I said.

'Good,' Caulfield exclaimed. 'There's only so many ways I want to make money and that's not one of them. Jesus! Did you see the faces of those little creatures. What about the ones that wanted to attack us? Jesus Christ.'

'I imagine if you're snatched from your mother when you're still suckling, that you turn into the monkey equivalent of a street hoodlum,' I said.

'Who'd want to be in that business?' Caulfield asked.

'A certain Dr Groz would love it,' I said.

From factories on the outskirts of Monterrey streamed *Regiomontanos* by the thousand. Cars, motor bicycles and buses fought with one another for a place on the narrow traffic arteries.

'I'll try that call,' I said, reaching for the dash-mounted telephone.

Tim was in bed, asleep, apparently. I called Harry Quinlan. Diplomats are used to working in other people's time zones, I reasoned. I could not get Hanny's face out of my mind.

'Look, this is not a reasonable request,' I began.

Harry yawned. 'This brings me back to the old days.'

I told him what I was afraid of and what I wanted him to do. Twice we were cut off – I gave him the pick-up's cellphone number and Harry called me back.

'Just make sure she's all right till I get home,' I said.

'Consider it done,' Harry said. 'And stop apologizing. You're going to be buying me pints until you die because of this.'

'Lady trouble?' Caulfield asked.

'Lady in trouble,' I answered and put the phone back.

A shanty town ran for miles along the Camino a Roma – a cardboard jungle sprawling away into the rising foothills – and then suddenly the centre of Monterrey appeared, a modern city built in pink stone and with the reassuring bell-towers of churches breaking the evening skyline. In LAX when I had bought my airline ticket, I had booked into the Hotel Monterrey on the Plaza Zaragoza. Caulfield left the pick-up and we followed the doorman's directions to a cosy restaurant on the Avenida Constitución overlooking the trickle that is the Santa Catarina River. The *cabrito al horno*, the roast kid which was the speciality of the north, was as memorable as the hotel doorman had promised.

'I'm as happy as a hog at a waterhole, Joe,' the Texan said, sitting back. 'Like your style, let me say, I like the way you can see a quality investment from ten miles on a hazy day. And I know the pressure you've come under these last weeks,' the Texan nodded. 'Oh yes, Mr McCoy has a long, long reach.'

'You were approached?'

'My bankers were. Told them where to go.' He looked at me with a lot of curiosity. 'What's going on?'

So I told him.

'Jesus,' said Caulfield when I had finished. 'I mean, the company that owns such a drug – if it works – will be the *numero uno* growth stock in the world for the next fifty years. No wonder he wants you to find Carlos.'

'Maybe. Maybe it's more convoluted than that.'

'What will you do now?'

'Sleep on it,' I said. 'I'll know what to do in the morning. Thanks again for all your help.'

'Glad to,' Caulfield said. 'If I helped in any small way, then I'm very happy.'

Evening had fallen as Caulfield drove out of Plaza Zaragoza. From the top of the Faro del Comercio, a soaring monument in concrete to Monterrey's commercial heart, vivid, green laser beams probed the city night.

I went up to my room, picked up the telephone. It was now three the next morning in Dublin. I thought of Harry Quinlan, who had played a central role in brokering the Ulster peace process and decided he could look after a lonely girl for a single night. I put the receiver back down and went out.

Music was coming from somewhere west of the Plaza Zaragoza as I left the hotel. I strolled towards the notes from a trumpet which, although it seemed just around the corner, always proved to be at least another block away. The streets narrowed. I passed the parlour of an undertaker, the little window crammed with ornamental coffins. If I looked left I could see a square where the skeleton framework of a market awaited the next day; a motor bike with two men, one with a guitar slung on his back, glided across the square parallel to the street on which I was walking. I followed the trumpet. I could not stop myself replaying my dream about Hanny. Five floors above where I walked women swapped gossip across the evening street from their wrought-iron balconies. The buildings were mellow, the stones that had been used in their construction were in pastel colours. I saw graffiti on walls, but it too was colourful. Everything seemed to smile at me and say, *Hey! It's going to be all right!* I came to the source of the music.

A church from at least the mid-eighteenth century. The crowd outside it numbered around a hundred. A procession was winding its way round and round the plaza in front of the church; it was led by the trumpeter whose tootling had drawn me from the Plaza Zaragoza; after the trumpeter came a violinist, then two guitarists. They in turn led a colourful group of men and women, the women bearing vases of flowers, the men holding great, high banners made of straw between them. I stood and watched. Something essentially wholesome and innocent about the procession and its people struck a sad chord deep within me. There was a whole section of life from whose richness I was at that moment excluded. A priest in green and white vestments emerged from the door of the church. The women began a dance as the music quickened. Then the trumpeter played a little finale, ending on a note which he held until the audience applauded, whereupon the priest led everyone back into the church. As the congregation cleared, at the other side of the plaza a youth with long, blond hair plucked the strings of his guitar.

I was left alone on the far side of the plaza. All I had to do was to cross the square and enter the church and I would be part of the congregation. Or I could stay outside and remain alone. All I needed was to connect Cobra Internacionale to Trident Drug and I would have evidence that Carlos Penn had been abducted, probably to Moscow, on the orders of Roberto Groz. Or I could remain as I was, as yet not irrevocably involved.

As the cathedral on the far side of the plaza chimed nine I reached my hotel on Plaza Zaragoza.

'A taxi,' I said.

The doorman of the Hotel Monterrey stuck his fingers into his mouth and whistled. A cab came as if drawn by magic around a far corner.

'*Gracias*,' I said to the doorman and handed him a five dollar bill. '*Por favor*, Dr Gonzalez,' I said to the driver of the cab and sat in.

31

The taxi's rear lights receded and eventually disappeared. The only sounds in the northern Mexican night were those of the cicadas and of dogs barking outside the sleeping dwellings of Dr Gonzalez. Scents of lemon thyme mingled with those of vanilla on the breeze. I inhaled deeply. I waited, listening. For a full five minutes. I'd have to figure out my way back to Monterrey later. Beirut had had dogs like these of Mexico, I remembered. Dogs followed death the world over. I slipped through the hole in the ragged, wire fence.

Stars aplenty, but no moon. I ran crouching over open ground scattered with scrub and stone. Lights shone up from the centre of the Cobra building – from the monkey room, I reckoned – but otherwise everything lay in darkness.

I gave the front of the building a wide miss; there was a fifty-fifty chance that the cameras incorporated infra-red beams which, if broken, would activate the lights. I came in to the rear, creeping along the breeze-block wall. The metal grille was bolted on over the window. I brought up my foot, aligned it with the wall and level with the lower part of the grille, and propelled my heel. The window guard spun off noisily into the darkness.

I crouched, waiting. Listening. Inside the building I could hear the occasional sound of an animal's cough, but outside, except for the cicadas and the dogs, the only noise was that of my own breath.

With a gentle crunch, the window glass gave way to my elbow. I removed the jagged remains, working them out from the window frame and placing them neatly on the ground. Then I wriggled up and in. The room I had entered was the canteen area; a couple of tables and chairs, a tall, metal cabinet with a first-aid sign. The broken window stared back at me like a gaping black eye. I let myself into the corridor.

The zoo smell was powerful. Dr Rosa's office door was locked. Unyielding. I could see the metal gate which shut off the monkey house, and beyond it, in the dim light which outside shone upwards to the sky, the shape of the rows of cages. Returning to the staff room, I opened the first-aid cabinet. The outline of shelves with boxes. My hands felt bulbs, electrical fittings, cleaning materials. On the bottom shelf, a vice-grips and a screwdriver. Back in the corridor, I forced the door to Dr Rosa's windowless office.

I did not know where to start. It was established that Cobra had hired the jet that day. Hanny had said so. Now I wanted something to make the link from Cobra to Trident. But not just a tenuous link. Ideally, I wanted the shareholders' register of Cobra which would show Trident Drug as its parent. I shook my head at my own optimism. If Cobra was so linked to Trident, Dr Groz was not going to leave a trail for someone like me to pick up. I went to work on the first of two filing cabinets.

It took longer than I would have wished to force the locks: ramming in the tip of the screwdriver, I wedged the vice-grips in behind it, then levered outward with all the strength I could summon. It took minutes of sustained effort in each case before the locking mechanisms burst. My reward was drawers of neatly filed documents. In Spanish.

I first eliminated the obvious options. The files under 'T'. Then I began the task of searching each file in turn. No doubt during the day, Dr Rosa switched on the air-conditioning, but at night her office was intensely humid.

Because it had no windows I had been able to turn on the lights without fear, but they were spotlights, shining from a central cluster, and their heat rapidly turned the office into a tropical grief-hole. I fought for my concentration as I made my way doggedly through the second drawer of the first cabinet. There was nothing to remotely make the connection I now so avidly sought. Files of reports. Of invoices. File after file of correspondence.

As a diversion, I broke into the drawers of Dr Rosa's desk. I came to a pouch holding the woman's lipstick and eye-shadow; a dousing wave of guilt suggested that dipping my hands into someone else's private life was off-limits. And anyway, the drawers yielded nothing. On the desk top was a telephone with a row of buttons down the side for the automatic dial of preselected numbers. I hit the first button and a voice in Spanish answered. I put back the phone and sat in Dr Rosa's chair, staring round the office. What if Trident had been the ones to answer the number I had just dialled? What would that prove? A firm like Cobra would obviously do work for Trident Drug. And scores of other companies like Trident. I needed more but it looked like I was not going to be able to find it.

I looked at my watch. Midnight plus thirty minutes. I did not mind methodical searching, but in different circumstances. I had been in here for five minutes over half an hour – which was half an hour longer than I had planned. I could hear absolutely nothing from the sealed office. I speeded up through the second cabinet. If I threw files on the ground as I finished them, it was more efficient. I went through and discarded 'M', 'N' and 'O'. It was a hopeless task. 'P' was a vast section and included 'Pharmacia'. I jumped straight to 'Q'; then, with a sigh, returned to 'P'. Some inbred thoroughness demanded that you finish what you begin – and properly, like a book. Like the food on your plate. Mother had always reminded us of India's starving millions, particularly on Fridays when John and I had been faced with the breaded cod that neither of us had liked. Mother and Fridays. What would she think now of what her son was doing? I shook my head. I was losing all concentration. I stared down at the file in my lap and saw that it was in English. It was headed 'Procedures'.

I flicked through the document. It laid down the rules for certain types of tests. There were fifty pages of dense headings. The document was typed on plain paper and stapled in the corner. I flicked, came to the last page, prepared to consign the document to join the impressive mound on the floor, and stared.

In a scrawling hand on the last page was the signature of Alan Gold.

I came up trembling. I could not stop it. I watched my hands shake and I laughed outright. Trident owned this place! Why else would they dictate the company's procedures?

I was jubilant. Looking around the devastation I had created, considering for a moment that I should restore order to the room, I then thought the better of it and shoved the document with Gold's signature into my jacket. Here in this building in northern Mexico, Trident were in all likelihood testing Carlos Penn's invention, BL-4, on monkeys. A second before my hand moved to the switch to kill the office lights, they died.

I was in the corridor in two strides. I listened with my entire body. Total darkness. I could see nothing, not even the monkey house twenty yards in front of me, although from the smell and the rustle of the animals, I did not need lights to know it was there. I began to make my way back in the direction of the tiny canteen. One step at a time, each step pausing before I took another, analysing each sound of the night, each time placing my foot on the ground ahead of me with infinite care. My own blood pounded noisily. Then every light in Mexico came on.

32

I knew I was being held on both sides and dragged. The blow had put me into the edge of the zone of consciousness; another millimetre and I would have gone completely. Although powerless, I was able to comprehend the sound of a metal lock being turned. The men dragging me spoke softly to one another. In English. I felt myself being let fall. I hit the floor limp because I did not want them to know I was aware. Lying face down, I fought to reassert control over my protesting body. The door lock clicked back. Then the metal gate sound echoed distantly around my head. I was alone. Or thought I was.

An intense face bared its teeth. A foot from mine. I sat up. The caged monkey's eyes shone like brown beads. I looked around me. I was in the sick bay of the monkey house. Rows of single cages. Sorry, modules. State of the art. Pulling myself to my feet, I felt my head detonate. I met the connecting door with my shoulder, but it was as solid as a wall. I looked though the observation window. Shouted. I realized with sickening certainty what was going to happen. There was a deep, metallic click.

The first monkey to emerge from its cage was small. Its body hair had come away in places leaving lurid, pink patches. I shouted to the door, to the men I could not see but knew had to be out there. My shouts made the monkey inquisitive. It hopped towards me and put its hand out.

I shouted: 'I know about Trident Drug! I know about Roberto Groz and Carlos Penn!'

I watched as one by one an assortment of monkeys shuffled or hopped from their cages to the floor.

'I'll do a deal!' I cried, knowing how stupid I must have

sounded. 'However much you're being paid, I'll pay you double!'

But there was no movement. I could well have been alone in the building – alone being a relative term, for some of my cell-mates had begun to grub in the corners for food, picking minute particles into their mouths, and some nestled into one another as if they took unkindly to being disturbed at this hour. But there was a hard core of the animals whose interest in me was unquestionable. As I shouted as loudly as I could, the monkeys began to form a closing group. Some were very thin and some had copious and ugly sores around the mouth which they picked at as they advanced. I looked up. The skylight was fifteen feet away. It had been designed so that a monkey could not get up there, leaving little chance for a man. I shouted and pounded the door. Then from the last cage in the row hopped a black monkey. Taller than the others. Like a hairy child of five or six, with a primate's head. Hissing and baring its teeth, it approached.

I could see back through the tiny window into the main monkey house which too was now swarming with the creatures. As I turned back, still shouting, the black monkey made a darting, loping run for me, scattering the others as it did so. I lashed out with my foot. The monkey swerved, squealing. It came in again, spitting and showing its sharp, white teeth. Using the claws of its hands, it raked the flesh of my leg.

'Fuck you!' I hollered and this time connected with a kick that sent the animal spinning.

The other creatures went into a frenzy. Some of them went screaming and howling into corners, some returned to their cages. But others now began to hiss and show their teeth and rake the air with their claws as, joined again by the black monkey, they closed on me.

I tried to kick the door down. Even if I got through, there was the locked metal gate. The blow to the head had taken all my strength. The black monkey, confidence regained, hissed and taunted at my left side in a move to divert my attention from the other side where two smaller primates, clearly enjoying this unscheduled diversion, began to lunge with their bared teeth. One of them bit my calf. I whirled and kicked it high into the air. From somewhere within the building came two sharp reports. I began to shout again. I chanced another look out the little window, but my momentarily turned head gave one of the smaller monkeys its opportunity: it landed on my shoulder. Screaming, I tried to rip it off, to fling it back into the sick bay, but the monkey clung ferociously to my right arm and bit at my hand as I tried to dislodge it. I yelled. With horror I felt claws on my back. Half turning my face I saw the fangs of the black monkey sink into the flesh of my shoulder. I went down. The monkeys clung with vigour. Each time I tried to dislodge a mouth, I was bitten. The black monkey, hissing lustily and dripping saliva and my blood from its bared mouth, went for the base of my throat. I caught the animal at its own throat. The monkey's teeth scored through my clenched fingers to the bone. I held on. Rolling on top of the beast, I felt it squirm and fight beneath me. My legs were being attacked. I kicked. The monkey under me spat and squealed. It caught my face. There was a massive explosion. My bloody grip knew no logic. The monkey under me suddenly went limp but I continued to wring the leathery neck with the strength of insanity.

'Joe.'

I beat the creature's head on the concrete floor.

'Joe, it's all right. It's dead,' said Caulfield Cade.

33

We sat in the pick-up. We were parked in a wooded area on the Camino a Roma, twenty miles north of Dr Gonzalez. Except for my shorts, I was naked. The multiple bite marks and scratches made my body look like I had broken out in a massive rash. Caulfield was dabbing me with diluted antiseptic. A rifle lay along the back seat. Its discharge had made a small entry wound, I had seen. The body of one man had lain sprawled across the threshold of the canteen; I had stepped over that of the second, a young man with long fair hair.

'The company is effectively run by Trident,' I said. 'I saw a procedures manual signed by Alan Gold. He's the top scientist at Trident. Those were Groz's monkeys.'

'Just try and sit still,' said Caulfield quietly.

'Some of those animals had mouth scores,' I said. 'They're HIV.'

'You need to get tests,' Caulfield nodded.

I shook. 'Another five minutes and I was dead.'

'I know,' said the Texan grimly.

'How did you find me?' I asked. 'You left me to go north to flare off an oil well.'

'I got a call,' Caulfield said. He winced.

'A call?'

'Joe, I got a call from someone called Harry Quinlan just as I was going through Laredo,' said Caulfield kindly. 'I turned around and drove straight back to Monterrey, but the doorman at the hotel told me you'd come back up north to Dr Gonzalez. I knew where you'd come.'

'Why did Harry call you?' I asked. My dream. I knew. 'What's happened?'

'It's not good, Joe,' Caulfield whispered.

'Jesus,' I said, and drowned.

'Joe,' said Caulfield as best he could. 'Your friend is dead. He was murdered two nights ago in New York. His name is Ricardo Vegas.'

PART THREE

15–30 April

34

Dublin bathed in weak April sunshine, but since the wind was from the south and the air was full of late spring scents and promise, no one was complaining. I had been in Paris overnight, meeting a manufacturer of computer software for public utilities that was engaged in a private placing. In a restaurant overlooking the Paris Bourse a most civilized Frenchman and myself discussed the merit of making governments more efficient. The Frenchman owned a highly profitable subsidiary in Stockholm, Sweden. Subject to checking Stockholm out, Grace Equity would join the placing. Now I was driving back into Dublin, savouring the air, the daffodils, the generosity of light. Around Drumcondra I got a call from Raza, my Indian investor. He was on the north-east coast of Australia and told me about a project involving a thousand square miles of real estate. He said he would e-mail the details and I promised we would speak that afternoon.

At noon Tim Tully put his Moses-like head around the door to my office.

'How was Paris?'

'We're in, subject to all their linen being clean.'

'I like it,' Tim said. He sat down and popped glasses onto his nose. 'But what I meant was, what did you eat?'

'Oysters, followed by veal done in a cream and apple sauce, followed by some sort of raspberries in pastry dish which I had to order at the start. Two bottles of very special Burgundy. I then smoked a cigar.'

'Ah,' said Tim, leaning back, eyes on the ceiling. 'I want to be there when you sign the deal, okay?'

'I had taken that for granted,' I said. 'Mid-May is pencilled. Book two seats.'

Tim wrote in his diary.

'We have been officially McCoy-less since noon yesterday, by the way,' he said.

'Excellent.'

'The Brits' money landed, we exercised our option under the original preference share agreement and paid twenty-five million dollars to McCoy's vultures. They've been over to Patrick Jenkins and executed all the documentation surrounding McCoy's stepping down from the board of Grace Equity. Jenkins made them pay his fees.'

I laughed. 'Good for Jenkins.'

Tim looked troubled. 'McCoy himself called up here yesterday, looking for you.'

'I hope you told him where to go.'

'Yes – but he asked me to give you a message: he said, tell Joe, remember we still have a deal.'

'Fuck him.'

'My sentiments entirely.'

'What else did he say?'

'Just that.' Tim picked up a newspaper, the *Wall Street Journal*. 'Not that we care any more, but there was a small piece in here yesterday about a bank in New Jersey calling in a loan on a real estate deal that was thought to involve McCoy. It was small by his standards – fifteen million dollars. Still. The loan was called in and it was noticed.'

I looked over the rooftops and saw blue sky over the Irish Sea.

Tim said, 'By the way – the Italians have been on. They want to reopen discussions.'

'How unexpected.'

'And our marlin-fishing banker has been on three times.'

'Don't tell me.'

'He's so glad McCoy is out of our picture, he was the wrong partner for Grace, the new arrangement is a master stroke. And anything we want – and I mean, anything! – we can rely on them to provide it.'

'Fuck him too.'

'God moves in mysterious ways,' Tim said, putting up files on my desk, 'but not half as mysterious as bankers.' He put his hand on the stack of files. 'Where do you want to start? We have half a dozen projects to evaluate here and all of them make my toenails curl with longing.'

I said: 'Tim, I'm taking some time off.'

Tim sat back. 'I see.'

'A month, maybe more. Starting today.'

'Okay,' said Tim, although dubiously. 'Going anywhere nice?'

'I'm not sure. But I want you to take over. I've asked Jenkins to draw up a power of attorney for you. I'll be in touch on certain matters, but as far as the day-to-day stuff is concerned, I'm out. Is that okay with you?'

'It's – fine. It's just unexpected.'

'You set up the refinancing entirely on your own. For many people you are Grace. Hire someone to help you – Dublin is full of bright kids. Have fun.'

We stood up and he gathered all the files. We shook hands.

'Joe?' Tim worried more than he let on. 'Whatever you're doing, good luck – okay?'

'I'll need every bit of it,' I said.

35

I owned an old 3-series BMW, a convertible that I'd bought in England and had had refurbished at considerable expense. I drove it when I felt too old to be riding the Harley, or sometimes I put the Harley up on a special transport trailer, hitched it to the tow-bar of the BMW, and pulled it behind me up to Donegal for a long weekend.

I put on three pullovers and took the coast road out of Dublin, enjoying the residual sense of guilt at doing this on a Wednesday morning. I was still replaying many images, none stronger than the scene on that last morning in New York when we had buried Ricardo Vegas. The cemetery had been in Queens. From where the few of us had stood among the headstones, Manhattan had lain like a brooding giant on the western horizon. Where were Ricardo's friends, I had thought? Where were the ladies of twenty years to whom Ricardo had sworn undying love? The murder had made the front page of the *New York Post*, a measure of the extent of the brutality, even in the senior city of such events. I knew without a shred of doubt that Ricardo had died because of me – Groz had wanted to send me a message. Jesus, I swore, and again my belly died. They'd skinned his face.

After Bray, the traffic thinned out. I could see fishing boats out at sea, stuck like ornaments to a still, silvery plate. I swung up into the hills and smelled a burning turf fire. The Midland bogs of my youth, with their little streams that made tunes like tiny, magic orchestras, came alive at such moments. I was at peace in a way I had forgotten, my body was in step with my mind, not even the call the night before from Soby Sandbach had managed to get my blood running any faster than its new, soft pace.

'I don't know what I have to do to get you to see the light,' Soby had said. 'Trident is twenty-three dollars traded and bid. Did you get that? Twenty-three dollars. This is becoming exciting. The rest of the sector is flat, Armentisia Lab, for example, put on ten cents and lost it just as quick. What have these guys Trident got? Something hot, that's for sure. Who cares how they got it! The market is excited because it's talking Cure – with a capital "C". I'm excited because I've been buying this stock all the way from seventeen dollars – and because I'm two boxes of Montecristo Number 1 in the bag. So if I'm excited, why am I depressed as well? I'll tell you why. Because my good pal Joe, who has done me favours in double-digit numbers down the years, is out on the touchline. What do I have to do? Do I have to get down on my knees and beg? Okay, here I am, I'm on my knees, believe me, it's a sight worth remembering, I'm on my knees and I'm begging you – buy this stock, it's going to thirty dollars, every fibre in my body says it is. Grit your teeth and get in. Don't let this come between us. There's no fun in making money on your own.'

I smiled as the sign for the pub on the road ahead came into view. Soby wanted me in to calm his nerves, not because he loved me – although I didn't doubt he did – but he was in deep now into Trident, I knew by the sound of him, and the fact that I wasn't – whatever the reason might be – was keeping him awake at night. I had not, however, been entirely idle where Trident was concerned. During my absence in the States, the analysis which I had initiated in Denver had been largely concluded. I now had a very clear financial picture of Trident in my head.

From the door of the pub you could see for fifty miles in every direction: the coast of north Wexford to the south,

Dublin Bay in the distance northwards, and to the east, the uninhabited scrubland and mountains that divides the sea from the great Midland plain.

Only one car stood in the car park. I ducked in under the wooden lintel, went down the flag-stoned corridor and into the tiny lounge. She looked up from the fire.

'Hi, Joe.'

'Hanny.'

'I've just got some real coffee.'

'For once my timing is right.'

She was wearing leggings and a sweatshirt. In the previous month she had allowed her hair to grow and now it curled over the nape of her neck. She smiled at me with a trace of sadness, then poured thick coffee into two mugs. The taint of sadness had the effect of making her beauty vulnerable, and that in turn had my heart standing on its head. We chatted for twenty minutes about all the peripheral things that had once been taken for granted: like new movies and books and the great stretch in the evenings. I saw us on a very thin ledge inching above two drops. On one side was an abyss in which we would always now be strangers to one another, on the other, a warm place of streams and heather in which we would never again be apart.

Hanny then said softly, 'How bad was it?'

'Bad.'

'I want to hear about it.'

'It was ugly, forget it. I'm trying to.'

'Don't you remember?' she asked, sudden tears in her eyes. 'I wanted to forget and look what happened. We have to remember before we can truly forget.'

I leaned back. Most of the bites were healed, although some scars were still visible on my neck.

'I was there, Hanny. Just like my brother John has been

for over a decade. I had thought I understood before how he felt – no way. Now I was there with all the other people, waiting for a laboratory report. One of *them*. I crossed the line between the great mass of untainted humanity that we all take for granted, to the group of people in the grip of an incurable disease.'

Hanny was stroking the back of my hand.

'Although it's over now, it's only over in the sense that I'm clear. But it's not – over. Let me tell you about it. I was terrified. I still am. I wake up at night and see a monkey's face two inches from mine. When I got back here I went through all the tests, got some shots of God knows what, but although the experts were non-committal, I know they thought it was probable that I was HIV positive. I'd been bitten over fifty times by diseased monkeys whose job it was to have AIDS. I'm sure they thought the outcome was somewhat inevitable.'

Hanny wiped her eyes.

'I suddenly understood a range of things that had been simply words up to then. Nothing like imminent execution to focus the mind, believe me. I thought I was going to die. I was going to begin succumbing to opportunistic infections. I was going to die from one of the most obnoxious diseases ever to ravage mankind – and basically no one out there gave a damn! I joined the condemned, Hanny. Because only the condemned really know what this whole, nightmarish business means.'

I sat forward; I looked at the scars on my wrists.

'I read for example where some idiot in the Dáil still thinks AIDS is a punishment. Sodom and Gomorrah, it was, he said. I wanted to go directly to wherever that imbecile was and choke him. Jesus! My day now started not with the financial pages but – and this is true – with a skim through the paper and the web just to check if anything new had come up overnight. Ridiculous, isn't it? Now that I was HIV positive, or thought I was, I expected something to be done!'

Hanny filled up the coffee mugs.

'You should have told me how bad it was.'

'I'd watched my brother for over ten years without really grasping what he was going through. I can grasp it now. For you're on your own in this thing in a way people don't understand. It's such a lonely place, clinics full of people I once thought of as being on the margins of society. Not any more. Now we were all in this together. We needed each other, because when you're out there on your own, it's people like yourself you want to talk to, people who understand. They're the only ones who will give you hope. They'll carry you through to wherever it is you're going, and when you shit yourself in the middle of the night as to where that place might be, you at least can say, well at least I won't be alone, at least someone else is coming with me.

'I tried to pray but I couldn't. I'd given up on God so long ago that not even a terminal disease could overcome my lack of faith. And then I suddenly thought: sweet God, what would I not give at this moment to be able to go to Bristol and to meet Carlos Penn.'

36

Hanny was standing at the window, looking in the direction of the sea.

'What can be done, Joe?'

'I'm going to look for him,' I said. 'This time I'm going to find him.'

Hanny sat down again by the fire. 'You don't need to now. Your business is safe.'

'Maybe now I need to, more than ever.'

She was looking at me from a far-off place. 'What about you and me?'

'You know how I feel.'

'This is like a process for us, isn't it? We come through, we're safe. We don't come through it . . .'

'A big prize.'

'Whatever happens, I want you to know that I'm sorry about what I said – you know, about the other women.'

'There's no need.'

'I was angry. It was – harsh.'

'I want to tell you something,' I said. 'About when I was around fourteen.'

Hanny came and sat beside me. I told her about being at school, about the first girls I met, in the usual places – the backs of cinemas, behind the public tennis courts on summer evenings – and my first kisses, how I had not even known how to do it until I'd been shown by a girl three years older. It had never been difficult for me, I had always had a girlfriend after I got started, so to speak. Girls liked me, and pretty girls liked me most. I learned a deal more than kissing even before my involuntary removal to New York, where life resumed as before. It was not, I discovered, just an Irish thing. But I always saw it on two levels: down here was me, hot-blooded and normal, who took life and what it had to offer as it came. But I was also up on another level, if you like, looking out over the heads of the girls I knew, or was with, for someone else. A psychologist would probably say I was looking for my mother.

'Please let me meet someone I like as well as love, I used to wish. Someone who respects me and whom I can respect. I tried to date girls who were interesting. Do you know what I discovered? They shied away from me. It was more difficult for me to succeed in dating an interesting girl than a pretty one. I couldn't figure it out for ages – it was like everything was upside-down. Other guys wouldn't believe me, they laughed me out of it. They spent their lives trying to persuade into bed the women I was avoiding. Crazy.

'I went into the Marines. This thing with women became something that got me down. I wanted a relationship, but all I could come with was a series of very hot affairs that burned both parties out. But, like water, desire follows the easiest course. I came to Wall Street, I met Lee, a woman whose face could have got her into movies. Even the day I married her I knew it was a mistake. We lasted fourteen months. There were four or five other Lees. I met Donna back here. I ached for someone I could come home in the evenings and just talk to. The rest is history. And then, I met you.'

Hanny smiled.

I said, 'When I woke the morning after you had gone, I knew I'd lost what I'd searched for all my life.'

Hanny thought for a long time, her eyes on the fire.

'I'm sorry for what I said,' she said at last.

'And I'm sorry about everything I said, including about Salman.'

She smiled but she was still sad. 'I thought too that we'd lost each other, Joe. I thought it was just one of those situations where the people involved find out during a crisis that they're really not meant for one another. I went right down. There were days when I didn't know what I'd do, when I wondered had I lost everything I'd gained with you. Dark days. I thought of bad solutions – yes, it's true. For a few nights I wanted to die. The old answer. I wanted to wipe it all out.'

I closed my eyes as I relived my fear, understanding anew that I had been right.

'Then, later, even when I heard about everything you went through, even though I cried when I heard, I realized that if ever we were to get back together, we would have to start all over again. It's like building something that's meant to last. We're the materials and we were up so high, then we all fell down. Now we're both still here and we're hoping to start again.'

'We can do it – if we want to do it, we can do it.'

'I know,' Hanny said, 'but do you know what I'm afraid of now? I'm afraid that just as we're about to begin again, you're going away and this time you won't come back.'

'That's not part of my plan.'

'I'm selfish now, Joe, but when I lost you, I realized I'd lost part of myself. Now that you're within reach again, I don't want to let you go.'

'I have to do this. For Carlos, for my brother, John. For someone called Minx whom you've never met. But most of all, I have to do this for myself.'

'I understand.'

'And believe me, I'll be back.'

Hanny nodded and wisps of her hair fell across her nose. 'I know you have to do it. That's what makes me so frightened.'

'We wouldn't be happy, you and me, knowing what we know, if I stayed at home,' I said.

'I know,' she said, 'I know.'

'It will be all right,' I said. 'Not many people get the opportunity that you and I have, to do something that is an absolute right. A good beyond question.'

'I'm afraid,' Hanny said. 'Do you want to know the truth? I'm afraid for you, but even more, I'm afraid for me and what it will be like for me if you don't come back, Joe. Can a human being be more selfish than that?'

'I'm selfish too,' I said. 'I'm coming back with Carlos Penn, if he still exists. I'm coming back to you. You and me, we need time together.'

She put her arms around my neck and rested her cheek beside mine. 'I dream of when we're old,' she whispered. 'You and me. I'll see you down the garden in your vegetable plot and I'll be in the house watching you and I'll feel so proud that we made it through together. Promise we'll make it through.'

'I promise,' I told her. 'I promise with all my heart.'

37

Harry Quinlan puffed air from one cheek to the other.

'Why isn't Carlos Penn all over the papers?' he asked eventually. 'Why hasn't the world outside Bristol heard about him and what he has achieved?'

The pub was one we'd discovered west of Dublin twenty years ago and had sworn not to tell anyone else about. It was built on the edge of a bog into which it was, with supreme grace, gently slipping. On a scale of one to ten, the pints were around fifteen and rising.

'Why? Because there's no real scientific data,' I said. 'Because what Carlos has is an unproven idea. Because his concept may be just a brilliant, scientific whimsy, but nothing more. Because, like cures at Lourdes, it's easy to say that cases like the ones Hanny saw in Bristol are the exception to prove the rule. Because Carlos Penn is, or was, a maverick. And because he's disappeared. But he's a good man, of that I'm sure. That's why I'm going to find him – because however off the wall he may be, he has at least given people hope.'

Harry looked out the window. He had one of those faces which was exactly the same as it had been thirty years before, and probably then it had been the same as when he had been a schoolboy: slightly upward-curving eyes giving him a playfully demonic look and a curving nose. He munched peanuts.

'Naturally it should be the concern of any government if one of its citizens has been abducted to another country. Unfortunately in a place like Russia there's a limit to the amount one can find out and, as far as I can make out, the Brits have run into a stone wall. And they obviously can't go in demanding things and banging the table, so to speak, without the most compelling evidence to support their case.'

'But the evidence, although circumstantial, is most compelling. My bet is that Groz could not get his hands on Carlos's treatment because Carlos refused to sell it to him. Groz couldn't steal the patent and then develop it in the United States, because the patent laws would prevent him. So what was left to Groz to do? Where might he develop such a stolen drug without having the inconvenient problems that are associated with international law?'

'This is the part I don't like,' Harry said.

'Russia,' I said. 'Has to be. It's where Groz is most at home. It's where the jet was headed. Groz can do what he likes in Russia. It's a crazy place, money is the only law. The Russians have got all the scientific apparatus of a superstate, but they have no hard cash. Along comes Groz with a stolen patent. Perfect.'

'Do the Russians have the know-how to develop it?' Harry asked.

'They have Carlos,' I replied. 'Groz sets up a deal whereby Trident licences back the discovery from the Russians. Everyone is happy. Groz gets the drug, the Russians get the hard currency from the licence deal, and the prestige. The only loser is Carlos, the owner of the patent.'

Harry shook out the last of the nuts.

'It's messy,' he said. 'Could the Russians somehow lodge their own patent from what they manage to steal?'

'The whole area of patents is a minefield,' I said. 'Inventors find their discoveries being challenged the whole time by imitators and if your patent is not watertight you lose it. My bet is the Russians will lodge new patents for the developed drug which will be close to the original discovery but will conveniently vary in some details. Because Carlos is in captivity, or worse, there will be no one to challenge these Russians patents. How could you challenge someone in Russia anyway? It's still like a fourteenth-century kingdom run by despots. And Carlos Penn? Who's he? He gets taken out one morning when he's no longer needed and gets a bullet in the back of the head. But my belief is that we'd have heard something by now about a Russian invention in the HIV field if Carlos was dead and no longer needed. He's still alive is my bet.'

Harry looked at me with something approaching tender regret.

'Although the circumstantial evidence is appealing,' he said, 'it remains circumstantial. Foreign Affairs can't get involved.'

'You have contacts, Harry. All those dinners. Come on!'

'You are right about Russia. It's still the great unknown. The police are either incompetent or utterly corrupt. Almost invariably our requests to Moscow go unanswered.' Harry's countenance suggested he deplored such behaviour. 'The country is at best mercurial, at worst volcanic. Putin is no different at this stage to most of the Soviet leaders he has replaced: an effigy maintained by scheming courtiers at the head of a crumbling power base. The country is, in effect, a multiplicity of fiefdoms. We hear about men like Vladimir Zhiranovsky, tsars of the far right, but we rarely hear, for example, about Anatole Petrowski, a political boss from Kiev whose influence over the secret police is absolute. Think of J. Edgar Hoover without the dresses and twice as mean, and you have Petrowski. Sources in the IMF estimate that he has a personal stash in Switzerland of five hundred million dollars – and they should know since it's their money he's stealing in the first place. What I'm trying to say here is that there are no rules in Russia. It's not like any place else. But it is the place you propose to go to find Carlos Penn.' Harry must have seen the expression on my face. He sighed. 'So I have acquired a telephone number for you.'

'That's more like it.'

'Its owner lives in a Moscow suburb. Don't ask me which. He is a retired KGB colonel and he will be expecting you to call.'

'Name?'

'Just Aleksandr, which I'm sure is not his name at all. You are to say you are Uncle Vanya. It all sounds very Chekovian.'

'What does Aleksandr do?'

'What does any retired KGB colonel living on a rouble pension in Moscow do?' Harry asked. 'He becomes an entrepreneur. Aleksandr is a member of the curious Association of Veterans of Foreign Intelligence. Essentially, they'll sell anything, including once-classified information.'

'Has a price been mentioned?' I asked.

'No. But I understand that a thousand dollars would buy an evening with Lenin himself.' Harry shook his head. 'You're going to the Wild East, you know. The commerce of the country is completely ruled by organized crime. Whereas communism at least ruled by the pretence of ideology, these new Russians don't even bother to pretend they have a political philosophy – unless racism comes under that heading.'

Harry's eyes were very blue; he fixed them on me. 'You really are going to go through with this, aren't you?'

'Yes,' I said. 'Yes, I am. If he's there, I'm going to find him.'

'You're completely fucking mad,' Harry said. 'But if you had said anything else I would have been disappointed.'

We walked out into the Midlands night. Long, dramatic

washes of purple sky marked the end of the Irish day.

'One thing worries me,' Harry said. 'Not about Penn, but about you. They know about you, Joe. If your suspicions are correct, all it takes from your Dr Groz is one telephone call to his minister friend, Petrowski, and every border guard in Russia will be primed for your arrival.'

'Primed for the arrival of Joe Grace, maybe,' I said. 'That won't be a problem.'

Harry winced. 'You've been dealing on the illegal passport market, you bastard.'

'Of course I haven't.'

'I wish I believed you,' Harry sighed. 'We're all big boys now. I wouldn't have made that connection in Moscow for anyone else, you know that. You also know it's non-attributable. I've used up quite a few shots from my locker in getting a line to Mr Aleksandr.'

'A rare example of Foreign Affairs being useful,' I said.

'Just don't expect miracles,' Harry said. 'And remember, it's one thing getting you out of the slammer in LA. But you go into Moscow and you're on your own.'

We reached the cars. Wind rustled through an invisible field of snipe grass.

'Do you know something?' Harry asked. 'In a funny old way, I really envy you this. Makes me mad too, I suppose.'

'The world is the strangest place,' I said. 'It stands you on your head and suddenly you see what you've always been looking for.'

'Good luck,' Harry said.

I watched as he climbed into his car. Then I walked to mine, wondering if I really should have my head examined.

38

Just the tiniest beat of a wire brush on a cymbal and the key of a piano crept from the speakers of the sound system. I could see my own reflection in the otherwise blank screen of the television at the foot of the bed. The phone rang.

'It's me.'

'Hi.'

'I just wanted to say goodbye again.'

'It's not goodbye, it's, see you in a week or so.'

'Joe?'

'Hm?'

'You love me, don't you?'

'I love you very much.'

'Not as much as I love you. Joe?'

'Hm?'

'Can I go to sleep with the phone just like this on the pillow beside me? – that way, I'll hear your breath and you'll hear mine.'

'Good idea.'

'Goodnight, Joe.'

'Sweet dreams, Hanny.'

'See you in a week or so.'

'See you really soon.'

I kissed her to sleep. Her breath and the sound of the wire brush. Like footsteps. Into the deep night. I did not dare move the phone in case I awoke her. I dozed sitting upright. Men all over Dublin. With the ones they loved. Holding tight to their happiness. Until the first sounds of the delivery trucks that marked the new day.

39

One moment I was looking down at the colourful checkerboard of agricultural Europe; the next the terrain had become a great, dark plain, broken only by occasional knots of cities and the glint of rivers reflecting the late April sun.

The Ilyushin 86 had been conceived by men who had served their apprenticeship designing ships. Wide companionways swept down from the cabin to the luggage holds; the crew commuted down to the kitchen in lifts. At Shannon I had been one of only two passengers boarding the flight as it refuelled between Havana and Moscow. If Hanny was right, this was the way they had taken Carlos Penn to the east.

The hostesses came down the plane, checking visas and currency declarations. My declaration spoke of five hundred dollars; it did not mention the five hundred thousand dollars stitched into the leather belt of my trousers. My old Marines issue belt. It still fitted, just. And yes, my visa was in order. Grandfather Grace would have been amused. Born in Achill in 1870, he was christened Seosamh Macgreana. I was called after him – in English. But my smart new passport, issued against the Irish version of my birth certificate, spoke of Seosamh Macgreana, of Temple Bar, Dublin 2. A call to Bombay had looked after the invitation I needed to acquire a visa. Raza's brother owned a jeans manufacturing factory in Moscow. The letter cordially inviting Mr Macgreana to visit the plant in Nizhny Novgorod had been faxed to Dublin. Two days later the Russian Embassy's consular section in Dublin had issued Seosamh Macgreana's visa application to the same address.

We were skimming over waste ground, buildings with rusty roofs, a river. The wheels touched concrete with sharp squeals.

'Welcome to Moscow,' said the girl in Russian, in Spanish and in English.

As we disembarked I thought about John. The night before Laura had called to say he had been taken into hospital.

'But he's in good spirits,' Laura said. 'He says to remind you about Pavarotti in June.'

'Tell him I'll be there,' I had replied. 'I promise.'

It was a way of life for Laura, I thought. A way of death. As for me, my promises were mounting.

In the Golden Circle lounge at Shannon before the flight, I had spent an hour on the telephone to Denver, Colorado. In the previous dozen years, I'm sure no week had gone by when we had not spoken. But we'd never met in that time. Minx lived in Denver's western suburbs, just where the foothills of the Rockies begin. She often described the setting: from her house she could see no other building or sign of human existence. The way she wanted it. The solitude enabled her to concentrate without interruption on the work at which she excelled. That was her story. In all the years, she had never suggested once that I might drop by on one of my trips, take in Denver on my way west. Catch up. Sometimes that made me sad. And sometimes it made me mad all over again with Dr Roberto Groz.

'It's a high-risk strategy if they have a drug that works,' I had said to Minx from Shannon. 'And it's hard to think they would go out on such a limb if the drug doesn't work.'

'Groz is a gambler,' Minx said. 'He may be making a big play because he likes the idea.'

'Still.'

'You're the only one who can call it,' Minx had said. 'But otherwise, I'd bet everything that my analysis is right.'

Peering out from under what looked like the rim of a frying pan, the immigration official in Sheremetyevo Airport examined my passport, yawned, applied his stamp. Customs officials and men lurked around the edges of the baggage hall, scanning arrivals. Thirty minutes passed. Outside the area you could hear the awaiting crowd. On-duty soldiers with guns and in long coats took furtive drags from cigarettes. Cubans and Russians sat side by side on the edge of the baggage carousel, inured to such delays. There were no trolleys. I carried my case through.

'Metropole Hotel,' I told the taxi.

It was more like a leftover colonial landscape than anything I had imagined. Old buildings with wrought-iron porches that might have been in French Indo-China. Clapboard houses that resembled the outskirts of Bombay. The grey reinforced concrete edifices to progress, towering blocks that increased in density as they met the start of Leningradskoe Shosse. The taxi, a Volga, stank of petrol. Traffic increased as we crossed a busy interchange. Water below and to the right. Teams in fours and eights, rowing.

'Cigarette?'

The driver offered back the pack from which he was chain smoking, cigarettes with a heavy, Turkish aroma.

'They'd kill me,' I said in the pidgin Russian I still remembered.

The driver grinned into his mirror from dirty front teeth. Dark glasses. A friendly weasel.

'*Umri s ulybkoi na ustakh!*' he grinned. 'Die happy.' He pointed. 'Kremlin,' he said.

It was familiar yet still wondrous, a lustrous cluster, the gold from its domes drawing everything to it. The taxi swept down into the heart of the city. Like Paris – without the cafés and the crowds, I thought. Vast thoroughfares. Cobblestones. Nineteenth-century imperial architecture. In a courtyard, a great, imperial lion in bronze reared from its plinth, indomitable, although the base of the plinth had begun to crumble and soon the magnificent creature would be lying in the refuse that was already blown around its feet. Traffic slowed to walking pace, then to a crawl. Trolley-buses overflowed with passengers either side of the belching Volga. I had opened both rear windows; everything smelled of the fuel, now mixed with exhaust fumes. Prospekt Marksa widened into Maneznaja Place. We stopped opposite a statue of Marx who looked like everyone's idea of a grandfather. The kerbside door was opened.

'Welcome to the Metropole, sir,' smiled a young doorman.

'Will you be staying with us long, Mr Macgreana?' asked the receptionist.

'A few days.'

A porter brought me up to the fourth floor and presented a reception chit to a woman in her fifties with suspicious eyes whose position was at a desk outside the lifts. She handed the porter a key.

'*Zhelayu vam priyatnovo vremya pripavozhdenya v Moskve!*' she said. 'Enjoy your stay in Moscow!'

There were two wide beds. An enormous bathroom in green marble and gold taps. This in a country where some people still had to queue to eat. Maybe the shortages were all western propaganda, I thought. I stood ten minutes under the shower trying to de-gasoline myself. Dripping, I sat on a bed and dialled a number.

'*Da?*'

'I would like to speak to Aleksandr, please.'

'*Da.*'

'Aleksandr, this is Uncle Vanya,' I said.

'Ah, Uncle Vanya, I was expecting you,' said a man's voice.

'Wonderful,' I said and shook my head in wonder.

40

The lobby of the Metropole was a wide 'L', the long part a series of tall plants dividing armchairs and sofas, the nib a bar serving cocktails. Every few yards beneath the palms sat very expensive-looking young women. Photographic models awaiting their cameras, perhaps. Perhaps not. A little apart, lingering behind the palms, were their pimps in baggy trousers, loose jackets and tieless shirts. They all wore stubble and looked like Italian footballers on a day off.

'It's the house of whores,' said a man, pulling out a chair beside me, sitting down and helping himself to the contents of the bowl of chips. 'But so is Moscow nowadays, all of it.'

Small, about mid-sixties, his face was sallow-smooth and slightly chubby. He had a line of white-grey hair connecting either ear and running down over his collar, but otherwise was shiningly bald. He clicked his fingers at the waiter.

'A Jack Daniels, double, rocks,' he said in English.

He looked all around the lobby carefully, before returning the attention of his clear, blue eyes to me.

'Are you alone, Uncle Vanya?'

'Yes,' I said, 'and my name is Joe.'

'For me you are Uncle Vanya. But pleased to meet you,' the man said and shook hands 'Call me Aleksandr.' He gestured around him. 'When perestroika came the first thing happened was everyone became a hard-currency prostitute. At the beginning they wanted the money but they didn't really accept the fact that they were whores. Piano teachers, was the standard line. "This is just something I am doing on the side to keep my old grandfather in food and fuel for the winter." Now they don't even bother with that line, they're just whores, period. Personally, I think that's a mistake. I would much prefer to be fucking a piano teacher. Cheers!'

Aleksandr took a mighty swallow from his drink and clicked his fingers at the young waiter again.

'Where did you learn your English?' I asked.

Aleksandr smiled. 'You don't want to know anything about me, Uncle Vanya. I know Tower Bridge and Brooklyn Bridge the same. I could take you on a guided tour of the Cotswolds or the hills of Virginia. But I'm probably too old now to think of anything else than the essentials in life.' Aleksandr counted off his fingers. 'Money, food, somewhere to sleep, decent vodka and a woman to keep you warm, in that order.'

'How are you making out?' I asked as further drinks arrived and I signed the chit.

'Life is a journey, Uncle Vanya. When you are my age, you just want to get there, you understand? You see this place? These people? Every person you see here, other than you and me and those few businessmen, the others are all Mafia. Every one. This is the best hotel in Moscow and the only people who can afford to come into it are criminals. How do you think I feel about that? Lenin addressed the crowd from the balcony of the breakfast room in this hotel, now the scum of the earth flash their dollar bills and work their whores in these historic surroundings. But where are the people Lenin fought for? They are outside shuffling the streets, clutching their shopping bags, trying to trade perhaps a silver spoon or a picture frame for a loaf of bread. It's worse than the worst excesses of Stalin. It's worse than it was under the Tsars. Russia now is like a gigantic sewer. Only the bacteria survive.'

The waiter had brought more drinks in response to some signal from Aleksandr. I signed the chit. A red-haired man in a dark suit entered the bar from the lobby and sat on his own in the far corner, behind Aleksandr.

'I spent my life in the service of my country and what do I get? A pension that's not enough, literally, to buy food for my cat. My wife is dead. I live alone. I'm old, our kids are all gone. I rent my *dacha* to make the only money that keeps me from starving, but that means I have to spend all my time in this filthy, fucking city. My friends, those that are still alive, are all in the same position. We share our vodka, our bread. We even share our whores. We have to. We just want to get there, to the end of the journey, you understand?'

Aleksandr had acquired a comfortable glow. He crossed his legs, showing correctly pressed trousers, smart, plaid-design socks and Church leather shoes, highly polished.

'You find yourself in a bad position, what do you do? You trade what you have. What do guys like me have? Forty years in the Lubyanka, you learn something, yes? Sure you do. You make connections. They changed the name of this system, but that's all. How does it still work? Of course it works because the same hundreds of thousands of people are still in the same jobs making it work, that's how. Nothing has changed except the names and the reward for loyalty. Before, you could expect to be looked after, now – nothing!'

Aleksandr shrugged and watched the waiter replace the bowl of chips.

'So you sell that most precious of all commodities, Uncle Vanya. You sell your loyalty. Now, what is it you want to buy?'

'I am looking for this man.' I put a small envelope on the table.

Aleksandr put on spectacles and took out the photograph.

'Who is he?'

I told him the outline I had prepared: Carlos's name, his profession, the fact that he might currently be a guest of one of the many arms of Russian science, in the same way that an inmate of Mountjoy is a guest of the Irish nation.

'Why do you want to find him?' asked Aleksandr.

'Because I believe he's a good man,' I replied.

Aleksandr put his head back and roared with laughter.

'Okay, okay,' he said, wiping the tears from his face. 'One of the marvellous things about my new position is that I need not ask why any more. Before, everything was the why. Now, I don't give a fuck for the why. Has this guy got a nuclear secret? Does he know the inner secrets of the Pentagon? Was he seen taking photographs of Russian submarines in some Baltic port? Who cares? He's a good man! Beautiful. You just want information and you are prepared to pay for it, I take it? Yes?'

'Of course.'

'What could be simpler? One important question. Is this individual's whereabouts the subject of an official enquiry from your government? A protest of any kind?'

'No,' I replied.

'No questions about him from Washington to Moscow?'

'He's a missing person, so the police in the UK and Interpol have all been informed of his disappearance. Maybe they've been on to the police here, I can't say.'

'How important is he?'

'Important to me.'

'But not to your government?'

'Not that I am aware of.'

'Good,' Aleksandr said. 'It's crucial, you know. When

something becomes official, between governments, it often becomes harder to find out all you might want. Not impossible, of course, just harder. Now we go to the gents' room and you pay me two thousand dollars in cash. If you don't trust me, then no hard feelings, I've enjoyed the drinks, thanks and goodbye.'

'I trust you,' I said.

'A good decision,' Aleksandr said. 'One thing I never do is cheat in this business. It's not worth it. I will immediately start to make enquiries and I will call you here with a preliminary report within forty-eight hours, latest. We assume your friend is actually in Russia and that he is alive. Money is like a fountain. It trickles down from the top. My estimate is that to find him, on top of what I take to feed myself and my cat, will cost you another grand.'

'That's no problem.'

'Plus a bonus to myself of a grand for taking such risks on your friend's behalf.'

'What's the extra grand for?' I asked.

'To keep my old grandfather in food and fuel for the winter,' Aleksandr replied. He turned, clicking his fingers for the waiter. When he turned back to me he was halfway to his feet. Through clenched teeth he said, 'Just get up. Now. And walk with me out to the men's room as if we were friends from the old days.'

I got up. The red-haired man on his own in the corner scrutinized his newspaper. In the empty toilet, Aleksandr went down the row of cubicles, pushing in each door.

'Bastards!' he said tightly. 'If it's not the scum from the Mafia, it's the Interior Ministry. I recognize the one in the bar. A pig. A major in the Interior Ministry named Marat.' Aleksandr looked curiously at me. 'You sure your enquiry about your friend has not gone through official channels, Uncle Vanya?'

'As sure as I can be,' I replied.

I gave him the cash. Aleksandr separated it into different pockets and shoved a fold of bills into each sock. He washed his hands. As we left the men's room, I glanced back into the bar, but Aleksandr's red-haired acquaintance had vanished.

'This used to be a great country,' said Aleksandr as we walked by marble pillars and palm trees bedded in great brass urns. 'We are masters of technology. Our scientists can split the atom, orbit the earth. We have a love of literature that can only be compared to the Frenchman's love of wine. What other nation so reveres its writers? None. We have the greatest army in the world. The most magnificent cities. Art of which everyone is envious. Our country is fertile and occupies one-sixth of the earth's surface. You would think, therefore, would you not, Uncle Vanya, that a country so abundant in all the riches the world has to offer could at least feed its own people?'

A blue-liveried doorman sprang into action.

'A taxi,' Aleksandr said to the man on the kerb. 'You see, the money is not three minutes in my pocket and I have to spend it,' he laughed. 'That is also a Russian trait. Live for today.'

A black Volvo cut away from a nearby taxi rank.

'Two days, Uncle Vanya, don't worry. I will ring you in two days,' Aleksandr said. '*Poka!* We'll meet again!'

I watched the taxi until it became lost in the traffic on Prospekt Marksa. Then I went back into the hotel.

41

On Novy Arbat, it had just stopped raining. The hawkers selling watches and rings and priceless icons for a dollar, and glass jars of caviar, flicked back the plastic covers of their stalls and resumed business.

I went down into the Metro. It was lunchtime, Wednesday. Commerce below ground in Moscow was at least as vigorous as that above. Every space was crammed with people dealing. Cigarettes. CDs. Cosmetics and tights. Caviar. Hash smoke sat sick-sweet on the air. The occupants of cardboard shelters stared out, traumatized. I passed a plastic bucket-full of disposable syringes and took the first train north-east to Lubyanka.

Aleksandr had said forty-eight hours. Today I had got to grips with the Metro. The purple line went to Proletarskaya. I found a fifteenth-century monastery complete with monks in the middle of grim, high-rise apartment blocks. The gardens were overgrown, the way in littered with years of rubbish. But the church's tiled façade was still intact and they were saying mass in the Eastern rite as I arrived. I had kneeled at the back of the church and prayed in the way I had once been taught. In simple words, the way Mother would have. For John. Dear God, please help John Grace. And if You must take him to You, then please save him from suffering. Amen.

Business in the Metropole was in full swing. I got into my room and called Tim.

'How's business?'

He gave me a run-down on what was happening. I could hear a new confidence in Tim's voice as he told me about two deals he had passed on and one he had decided to go with.

'By the way, that Dr Sali called here this morning from LA looking for you. I told her I didn't know where you were, but I'd try and find out. What do you want me to do if she calls again?'

I thought of the intelligent face and for a moment recalled the scent of lavender.

'Just say I've come to her home town to find a friend of hers,' I said.

Tim said: 'I'm also hearing the weirdest story about Carson McCoy. I know it's only of academic interest now, but it runs like this: McCoy owns a real estate company in New York that is central to his whole empire. About five years ago this company issued a huge amount of junk bonds, like a billion dollars' worth, to finance some mega real estate deals in the Far East. At the same time, through a sister company based in Bermuda, McCoy masterminded a dawn raid on none other than Armentisia Lab. He figured they had an AIDS drug and he spent – or this Bermuda trust spent – more than five billion dollars on their stock at twenty dollars a share. If it is him, he's their biggest single shareholder. And biggest loser.'

'Their AIDS drug is called Viradrol,' I said.

'Which has been overshadowed by Trident's Kontrol. The market says it all. Trident is bid at twenty-five dollars today and Armentisia is still at ten dollars, half what McCoy paid for it,' Tim said. 'But it's not only Armentisia that's gone wrong – his Far East property portfolio is sick as a parrot. By my informant's estimate, it could take his New York operation down with it. So he's hurting big all over.'

'I'm heartbroken,' I said.

'Makes it all the stranger why he'd want to piss away his investment in Grace,' said Tim.

I didn't say so, but the way I was beginning to see it, it wasn't really that strange at all.

'Anyway – just thought you'd want to know,' Tim said. 'How are you getting on?'

'I'm waiting,' I said.

Next day was showery too. I spoke at length with Hanny, as if she were upstairs in Temple Bar and I was at my desk on the floor below. It was beautiful in Dublin, she told me. I could imagine.

'I'll be home in a few days,' was the last thing I said.

Rain washed the face of the White House. I took a cab up to the Lenin Hills and stood looking down on the great city as showers and sunshine chased each other across it. Lenin's wedding-cake-like buildings speared the skyline and the Moskva River slunk like a shining serpent around the Olympic Stadium. Was Carlos somewhere in this panorama? In fear of his life? I wondered if Aleksandr's enquiries were bearing fruit. Another cab took me from the Lenin Hills to the Kremlin. I stood looking at the huddle of magnificent churches to God's glory. At the Tsar Cannon, so huge it never worked. Like Russia itself. At the gold and silver and icons of the Kremlin's Armoury. At Fabergé's triumphs of miniaturization. As I returned to the Metropole, the Kremlin's clock struck the hour and crowds hurried down to Lenin's Tomb.

I fully expected the message light on the telephone to be flashing when I got in. It wasn't. I poured myself a drink and checked the switchboard anyway. No calls. I kicked my shoes off and lay on the bed. Surfed the movie channels. It was eleven at night and still bright daylight outside. I watched the window grow gradually dark.

Midnight chimed in Red Square.

Aleksandr did not call.

42

The black Volvo passed the Yuri Gagarin statue on Prospekt Mira. From the back of a truck pulled into the hard shoulder of an interchange, two men were selling oranges to a crowd.

Friday. Noon. Aleksandr had not called. Neither did he pick up his telephone. I had called him at four o'clock the morning before, when most people are at home, if that's where they're going to be. The number had rung out.

I had had enough of Russian architecture. Of trudging people who never smiled. Of shamefully crumbling eighteenth-century façades. Of art galleries run by pretty sharks. Of meals alone which always began with the same tables laden with hors d'oeuvres. Of sweet *pirozhkis*. Of the Metropole pimps and whores who now smiled at me familiarly every time I appeared. Trying to wear me down, perhaps. Trying to discover what exactly it was that turned on the lonely man from the fourth floor.

I had called Soby the night before when it had still been mid-afternoon on Wall Street.

'So, the mountain is finally moving! Where are you now? – Don't tell me. Siberia.'

'Closer than you might think,' I said.

Soby clicked his monitor and groaned. 'Please. Come in with your father, my son, and let me introduce you to the stock that will make your fortune, currently trading at twenty-five dollars and looking as rosy as Jerusalem in the evening light.'

I had to laugh. 'I'm an Irish Roman Catholic,' I said, 'or I was.'

'So I understand the error of your ways, which is why I

look after you so good,' Soby said. 'Look, I'll tell you what I'm going to do, I'm going to buy you ten thousand Trident and if you don't want to pay me, I don't care. It's a present from me to you. That way you can't say no. Have you ever had a better offer?'

I had been nursing a hungry impulse for forty-eight hours and now I decided it was time to let it nibble.

'Don't do that,' I said, 'because I have a market order for you.'

'Aaaah.' Soby's sigh of relief. 'The things that make an old man happy. Speak.'

'Sell ten thousand Trident at twenty-five dollars.'

The intake of breath must have been audible in New Jersey. I had just told Soby to go short ten thousand Trident, to sell shares I didn't have. The theory was that when the market fell I would buy the shares back in at a lower figure – which was just like buying first and then selling, except in reverse.

'Stop fuckin' with me, Joe.'

'I'm not fuckin' with you, I've given you an order.'

It's not easy to hear someone go white on the phone, but I was right, I had no doubt.

'Joe,' Soby's voice had dropped into the whisper zone. 'What do you know?'

'Nothing concrete, I'd tell you if I did, but my gut says this is all a bubble.' I thought of Minx's profile on the company. 'Trident is a dead cat, Soby.'

'Is your gut connected to your head? Because everywhere I turn people are talking this stock up. I've got a big position.'

'If I were you I'd take my profits.'

'It's one thing to take profits, it's another to go short,' Soby said. 'If this market is what I think it is, you're going to lose your ass.'

'Do it, Soby.'

He let out a monumental grunt, then I heard him put the order into the market.

'You've done me more favours than anyone I can think of,' Soby said. 'D'you know what this does to me? It hurts me. I'm not joking. It's like my own son came home and told me, I was past it – can you understand that? Is that what you want to do – humiliate me in front of myself?'

I imagined the mournful face on another continent, and the restless night he now knew he faced, whether he sold his own stock or not.

'I hate this business. You sold ten thousand Trident at twenty-five dollars, five cents. May God have mercy on your soul,' Soby had said.

An hour earlier, five dollars had electrified the doorman at the Metropole. As I had stood waiting, the man had run down the line of waiting taxis, questioning.

'It was a black Volvo,' I told him. 'Monday, about five o'clock.'

I described Aleksandr. There weren't all that many black Volvo taxis in Moscow.

The car was not on the line, but one of the waiting taxis nodded to the doorman and called his depot on the radiophone. Seven minutes later Aleksandr's cab had pulled up outside the door.

I had believed Aleksandr when the Russian said he was no cheat; I knew cheats.

Block after block of apartments went by. At gas stations, cars waiting in lines, some a hundred yards long. The Volvo swung off Prospekt Mira and into a dense development, a whole city with playgrounds and shops and apartment blocks that shut out the horizon. The driver came to a crossing, paused in thought, drumming his fingers on the wheel, then made a left and then another left, down an alley between two twenty-floor buildings where washing hung from balconies and cars were parked along the kerb with signs saying '*Prodayotsya*'. For Sale.

Right at the end of the alley, then left. We pulled up at the wide forecourt to a building.

'*Tuda*,' the driver pointed. '*On poshol tuda*.'

'He went into this building?' I said.

'*Da, da. Tuda poshol*,' the man replied.

'Wait here,' I said getting out and giving the driver the palms down. 'You wait here.'

'*Da*. No-problem,' the man said.

Women with children in strollers sat outside on seats in the concrete wilderness. They might have been in any inner city. Anywhere.

The building was eighteen floors high. I counted them. And a block deep. Broken windows on the first few floors. Aleksandr was all I knew. And his phone number. The chances of his real name being Aleksandr nudged zero. I went to mail boxes in the lobby and tried to discern the names in the six high, twenty-foot long row. At least the 'A' in Cyrillic and in Roman were the same.

'Can you help me?' I asked in Russian.

A woman had emerged from a closet-type room, an archetypal matriarch in Paisley apron, grey hair in a scarf. She was four foot nothing in both directions. She carried a broom like a prop in a movie about Russian peasant women. She did not respond to my question and said something in a dialect I did not recognize.

'I'm looking for a friend,' I explained. 'Aleksandr. Aleksandr?'

The woman looked at me suspiciously.

'A small man, no hair,' I said. I thought about mentioning KGB, then thought again. 'Bald. Bald,' I said and patted my head.

The woman muttered something darkly and disappeared back through the door. I went out across the forecourt to the running Volvo.

'You come in with me,' I said to the driver. 'You ask where he lives.'

'*Ni v koyem sluchaye!*' the driver replied emphatically. 'No way!' He tapped the steering wheel of the Volvo. '*Stay here.*'

'Ten dollars,' I said and flashed the bill.

'No ten dollars,' the man replied. 'No dollars. You look.'

He was pointing at a wall to one side. I looked. Three adolescent heads disappeared below the parapet.

'They wait,' the driver said and pointed at himself, then made elaborate finger movements to show himself walking into the apartment block. 'They take.' He gestured to his car. 'I wait,' he grinned and picked up the army revolver he had been concealing beneath the fold of his jacket on his lap.

I walked back across the forecourt. Kids were thumping a football against a wall where a chalk goal was drawn. Where would an ex-KGB colonel live in such a building, I wondered. High or low? Where would I live in here, I thought, if given the choice? High, it had to be. As high as possible. Above the noise and the dust and the petty crime. Up where there was a view and you could drink your Jack Daniels and dream of the old days in the Cotswolds or the hills of Virginia.

The elevator was in the middle of the building, down past the door occupied by the woman with the broom. It smelt of piss. I hit the top button and the car scraped itself up eighteen agonizing floors.

The top floor had corridors stretching in three directions and was lit intermittently by light bulbs that flickered like dying candles. I picked the corridor that seemed to point south. None of the doors had names. Passing, I heard televisions or radios on. The voices of women reprimanding children. A telephone ringing. I stopped. A telephone. From along the corridor I could hear a telephone ringing in a flat.

I took out my new cellphone and rang Aleksandr's number. It had yet again been acquired for me by Interfibre who by now must have thought that my wear and tear in this department was excessive. With this new little number I could talk to people on bicycles in Beijing, provided they had telephones. Then I began to jog down the first corridor, listening. I had no way of knowing where Aleksandr kept his phone, or how big the apartments were. They could not be that big. Maybe Aleksandr kept his telephone buried under a cushion. I reached the end of the corridor. A telephone somewhere was ringing. A door. I cut my own machine but the telephone inside the door rang on.

Second corridor. I pressed redial and ran on the balls of my feel, listening. The phone in my hand rang and rang, but none of the flats had a ringing phone. Suddenly there was a voice I recognized. I stopped. 'It's no sacrifice,' the voice sang. Elton John, eighteen floors up in the suburbs of Moscow. The global village. The phone in my hand was still ringing. I ran back to the lift and started down the third corridor.

On the seventeenth floor, third corridor, a telephone inside a door rang.

'*Da?*' answered a man two feet away from me.

The telephone in my hand continued to ring. I ran back to the elevator. Sixteenth floor. A man was screaming at his wife; she was giving back as good as she got. Next corridor. A drunk lay stretched, snoring, in the doorway of a flat. No ringing telephones.

I took the stairs down as it was quicker than the

unlubricated elevator car. The taxi driver must have got the address wrong. Floor fifteen. Three corridors, one in complete darkness. Blank. I wondered would the batteries run out, yet the phone in my hand rang crisply. Fourteen. Two men emerged from a door and walked forward threateningly. I beat it down the stairs. This would not work. One more floor. Lucky thirteen. At the very end of the first corridor a telephone was ringing. And ringing. I pressed the 'end' button on the mobile and cut the connection. Feet away from me the ringing stopped. I pressed redial. The ringing inside the door started up again. My mouth dried out. Aleksandr.

I put the phone away. So Aleksandr wasn't at home. Had he taken my money and gone for the last binge of a lifetime to someone's country *dacha*? Maybe taken his remaining friends? Treated them all to some girls on his unexpected windfall? It seemed unlikely that any contact of Harry's would be so unreliable. And yet.

I redialled the number. The phone inside the door rang. The door must have been wafer thin. It was a flush door with a handle and three locks. I pressed down the handle. The door opened into complete darkness.

'Aleksandr?' I called and cut the phone off.

A sudden clatter came from my right. My hand found the light switch on the wall and I dropped, rolling. It took me seconds to get my bearings. A bad smell. General dishevelment. I had come to a halt at a sofa. My head was level with something cold. My eyes began to see in the gloom. Another head. Familiar. Bald.

'Aleksandr?' I asked.

The once stocky throat had been cut in a new moon. It leered. Where the knife had been first punched up in under the ear, the wound had been enlarged by something tearing at it. Small bite marks of something working in under the jaw and feeding on the soft top of the windpipe. And the eyes were gone.

I got up, gasping. At the other side of the room, licking its whiskers and eyeing me speculatively, sat a large, tabby cat.

43

The Volvo pulled up outside the Lubyanka.

'I'll walk from here,' I told the driver and paid him in dollars.

'You are good man,' the driver said happily.

'Don't count on it,' I said and tried to get the fresh air to sort out my head.

As soon as life gave a little, I thought, as soon as the obstacles began to fall and the path appeared clear, some higher authority rubbed his or her hands and pressed the destruct button. It was hubris to a Greek, Murphy's law to an Irishman. What was it to a Russian? It hardly mattered to Aleksandr, KGB entrepreneur, I thought bitterly.

The old KGB headquarters in Lubyanka looked out balefully on the square where once the statue of Dzerzhinsky, the father of secret terror, had stood. Now his plinth was empty and topped with a cross. Do we all come back to a God in the end I wondered, as I walked past a store selling toys and down Prospekt Marksa to the Metropole? Was the revival of religion in Russia a grand metaphor for us all?

I saw the pink-and-white outline of the Bolshoi on Sverdlov Square with the Metropole opposite. The ferocity of all the attacks was consistent. On Ricardo. On me in Mexico. Now on Aleksandr.

I paused for traffic at the Maly Theatre and looked across at my hotel. The elegant, neo-classical buildings, the somehow vibrant smell of gasoline. The cobblestones. Add some tables and chairs, a few waiters rushing around serving Muscovites watching the world go by and you could have the Paris of the East. As run by Don Corleone.

Something caught my eye. A flash of colour. Instead of crossing when the traffic stopped, I walked on, past the Maly until I was standing outside the porticos of the Bolshoi. Across busy Prospekt Marksa, looking at his watch, a red-haired man in a dark suit stood outside the Metropole. Waiting. As I watched, the man took out a cellphone and spoke into it. I focused on the other end of the block; at the side of the Metropole facing Sverdlov Square, stood two men in long coats. One of them was speaking into a telephone. They too were waiting.

In some things you can only do your best, I thought, as I entered the hotel, looking neither left nor right. The woman on my floor gave me an odd look as she handed me the room key.

I paused a moment before entering the bedroom. All my old antennae were back as if after a long hibernation. Carefully I put the key in the door, then kicked it open and leaped into the room.

A startled face looked up at me.

'Are you trying to scare me to death?' asked Dr Cuba Sali.

44

She asked, 'Are you alone?'

She was dressed all in black, and the effect was to make her face seem almost luminous.

I said, 'I was.'

I remembered my first impression of her in LA had been a physical one, the way she moved, like an athlete; and now this was the quality I saw again.

I said, 'Moscow is full of surprises.'

'When I heard where you were, I had to come here,' Cuba said. 'I owe it to Carlos. If he really is in Moscow, it's the one place on earth I can probably find him. I took the first plane.'

I looked enquiringly at her. 'I don't get it.'

'You will – soon,' she said, but now she was worried. 'Joe, I've got contacts here and since I've arrived, they've told me that the person whose life is in most immediate danger is yours.'

I thought of the men in the street outside. I thought of Aleksandr.

'I was beginning to work that out myself,' I said.

'You have two options,' Cuba said. 'The first is, go home now. I mean, in the next hour. My friends here can guarantee a safe car to the airport and they'll get you through immigration – but you must leave now.'

'No way. I haven't come this far to run when it starts getting rough,' I said. 'And the second option?'

She sighed. Then she checked around the room. Her eyes, brown going on green, were even more oval-shaped than I had remembered from Los Angeles. 'Leave this hotel now. Don't check out or take luggage, just leave. The cocktail bar in the lobby has an exit directly to the street.

I'll meet you outside it in exactly five minutes.' She paused at the door of my room. 'By the way, where have you been all afternoon?'

'Feeding the cat,' I said.

Nine minutes later we were walking together along the Arbat.

'What makes you think he's in Russia?' Cuba asked, scanning the street ahead the whole time as we walked.

I told her about all that had happened since we had last met.

'Hi-yi!' she said when I came to the part about the laboratory in Dr Gonzalez. She looked at my wrists. 'You okay?'

'I'm clear, thank God,' I said.

'Thank God,' she repeated and blessed herself the Eastern way.

Then I told her about Aleksandr, late colonel of the KGB and entrepreneur.

'I'm not surprised,' Cuba said, putting on a pair of RayBans. 'From what I hear already, we're going to need more than a few old military jocks to sort this thing out.' She looked at her watch. 'We have to meet someone. By the way, I hope you like Haydn.'

The Arbat was going full throttle. Stall-holders, prostitutes, cafés full of men with dark glasses sitting over thimble-sized cups of Turkish coffee. A yellow-and-blue police car went screaming through an intersection, its strobes and sirens at full throttle.

'Your turn to tell me what's going on,' I said, checking over my right shoulder, as we turned into a side street.

'I've got family here, a brother,' Cuba said. 'If Carlos is alive and in Russia, then Volodya will find him.'

'What does your brother do?'

'He's a businessman.'

Outside the Tchaikovsky Conservatoire on Ulitsa Gercena, under the statue of the master, the hawkers were selling CDs and albums and tapes of classical music. We walked through the gates and into the foyer. A handsome man in his early forties with fair, tousled hair turned as we came in.

'Try not to speak English that can be heard,' Cuba said quietly. 'This is my brother, Mikhail Vladimir. He is called Volodya. Volodya, Mr Grace.'

Volodya was well built and compact. Fit. He wore an open-necked, blue silk shirt beneath an Armani silk suit that had cost someone three grand, minimum.

'My name is Joe,' I said. 'As in Uncle Joe Stalin.'

Volodya was not a smiler. His alert grey eyes flitted from me to the room behind us. He acknowledged someone with a nod. Then he spoke rapidly to his sister in a language that wasn't Russian.

'We're being followed.' Cuba kept her face relaxed. 'Don't turn around, please.'

I said, 'Who?'

Volodya spoke to her again, at the same time analysing me carefully.

Cuba explained, 'He says Petrowski's men soaked your friend out in Babushkin.'

I looked at her. 'How does he know?'

'It is Volodya's business to know what happens in Moscow.'

Daylight filtered in through high windows as we entered the main chamber, diamond-shaped and crammed full of people. The quartet was already on stage. We took our places on upright, cane-bottomed chairs, two rows from the front: first Cuba, then me, then Volodya. As Volodya sat down the silk jacket above his hip rippled and I briefly saw the outline of a gun.

Hearing the soul-deep chords of the cellos, letting myself flow with the slow passion of the music, I tried but failed to get the image of Aleksandr out of my mind. I was exhausted as well as confused. Applause. Cuba smiled at me. There was a glowing quality to her skin that had me wondering what it tasted like.

'Wasn't that good?' she smiled, leaning across.

'It made me forget for a moment where I am,' I said. 'Or why.'

'Music does that,' she replied. She composed her face attentively for the musicians. 'Watch where Volodya goes, please.'

I turned to the chair next to me. It was empty. Although the audience were clearing their throats and the quartet was about to begin its next piece, Volodya was thirty yards away, leaving the auditorium through a side door.

'We wait two minutes,' Cuba said. 'Then we follow him.'

'Where?' I asked.

'Where you will be safe,' Cuba replied.

Deep, urgent strings erupted, energy unleashed. I edged my way out across the other concert-goers. Trying to scan the back of the hall from the corners of my eyes and without turning my head, but failing to see anyone back there, I reached the exit door. As I stepped through, a hand grabbed my elbow.

'Come on!' Cuba cried.

A dim corridor, full of stacked chairs. I was propelled forward, past an open door where I glimpsed the backs of the string quartet, bent in concentration over Haydn.

'*Toropis!* Hurry!' hissed a voice.

One door led backstage, another to steps and an outside yard. An old man with white handlebar moustaches, kitted out in the dress uniform of an army officer, stood to attention for us; a long sabre, its hilt gleaming, hung at his side. Volodya pressed some money into his hand.

'*Da zdraistvuet Azerbaidzhan!*' cried the old man in a ringing voice.

At the base of the steps a black 7-series BMW was revving.

'What did he say?' I asked Cuba as she scrambled in.

'He said, long live the Republic of Azerbaijan,' Cuba answered as gates opened and we screamed up an alley and out on to Prospekt Kalinina.

45

We never dropped below 60 m.p.h. Once, at a roundabout, we were flagged down by an aggressive traffic cop with a striped traffic baton, then quickly and respectfully waved on. In a long loop underneath the Kremlin, we went south, crossing the Moskva River twice before heading west on Entuziastov Shosse. Volodya, now smoking a cigar, took and made telephone calls, all of them, as far as I could make out, in Azeri. Our driver kept switching his eyes between the road ahead and the rear-view mirror.

'All right?' Cuba enquired.

'I'm sorry I didn't have time to buy a CD,' I said.

The driver rapped out something. Volodya paused in his telephone conversation and spoke. Without breaking speed the driver hit the central grass reservation of the highway, turned 180 degrees and, to the blares of Zhigulis and Ladas, hit the concrete inch-perfect and barrelled back in the direction we had just come. We left the highway and fifteen minutes later were driving unhurriedly through leafy suburbs. There was a comfortable, if threadbare, feeling to the district. Most of the gates were locked. Weeds grew from footpaths and from cracks in the road asphalt. It was like Foxrock when the money ran out.

It was nine-thirty in the evening and still bright daylight. Electronic gates eased open and we drove up an avenue with grass gone to seed on both sides. A three-tier, drab, modern office building with a concrete canopy over its entrance came into view. It was built in what I was beginning to recognize as Mature Socialist style: glass and prefabricated concrete sections that looked as if they'd all been used somewhere before. Opposite the door stood two parked Mercedes, a Volga and a Zil limousine. Half a dozen men in suits and dark glasses who had been lounging by the cars straightened up. Getting out of the car, walking into the building, I looked back and realized that none of the cars, including the BMW I had just arrived in, had licence plates.

The ground floor was a raw shell, a building either just constructed, which seemed unlikely, or in the process of evacuation. Everything had been stripped. Barrels lay around. Planks. Wires hung nakedly from walls and ceilings. There was a smell of chemicals.

'Please.' Volodya ushered me ahead of him up a wide flight of stairs. The floor above ground level was a wide corridor, one side decked out completely with modern art, the other a row of glass-fronted, empty offices stretching the length of the building. Three men stood guard at a door. Mohair suits. Moustaches. Shades and guns. One of them pointed at me.

'*Ruki-k-stenke!*' he said and indicated that I should lean, arms out, against the wall.

Hard fingers probed the entire surface of my body, including my crotch, backside and the inside of my shirt collar. Volodya preceded Cuba and myself through another doorway and into a room where on TV a soccer match was in progress. Closed-circuit TV screens showed black and white scenes of the entrance, the gates and the outer office. Four men got to their feet. One of them, his moustache making him look like a mournful sea-lion, had a submachine-gun strapped to his hip. Volodya embraced him, then each of the other men in turn. Then he beckoned us to follow him into a smaller office from where you could see back through one-way glass into the room we had just left. There were a few armchairs and a sofa, all finished in violet velour. In central place on the back wall was a gold-framed, colour photograph of a heavy-set woman with greying hair and wearing spectacles.

'Our mother,' Cuba said.

Removing his jacket and gun belt like someone after a hard day at the office, Volodya went to the drinks cabinet and took out a bottle of vodka, shot glasses and cans of ice-cold Miller. I saw dark blue tattoos, like rings, circling the middle fingers of the Azeri's right hand.

'*Da zdraistvuet Azerbaidzhan!*' Volodya said and tossed back a shot of vodka.

'*Da zdraistvuet Azerbaidzhan!*' I said and drank.

Volodya kicked off his shoes and flopped down on the sofa with a can of the beer. He looked up at me with unconcealed suspicion. 'You police, mister?' he asked in English as he flamed alight a Marlboro.

'I'm a businessman.' I said.

'Businessman.' Volodya nodded and tapped a finger to his chest. 'I businessman.'

In the outer office, Volodya's guards were watching the soccer, drinking tea and sucking cubes of sugar. Volodya sat back, belched, then began to speak very rapidly to Cuba as if I was not in the room. I could see her breath shorten. Then she spoke, at first in reasoned tones, then heated. Volodya shook his head. Cuba shouted at him, gesticulating in my direction. She was crying. Just the kind of family scene you hate to be in on. Volodya got up abruptly and went to the adjoining room where he sat, his arm around the shoulders of the big man with the moustaches.

'This is my fault, I know,' I said.

Cuba sighed and dried her eyes. 'What Volodya did earlier he would do for very few people. It was because I asked him to. His position is very difficult, you must understand. He wants to help me, but he has a business to run.'

I felt the sinking feeling to which I was becoming accustomed. I didn't think I needed to ask the type of business Volodya was in.

'And . . .'

'He says you'll be safe here,' Cuba said. 'There's a bedroom next door, it's yours until you have to go. He will have your luggage collected from the Metropole and will pay your bill there.'

'But . . .'

'But he says we don't know for sure if Carlos is in Russia or even alive. He says he is too busy to get involved in something like this, that it puts his business in danger. He says he thinks you should go home to Ireland. But I've asked him to at least make enquiries about Carlos and to allow you to stay here until those enquiries are complete.'

I watched the Azeri in the other room. He had taken a machine-gun from the big man and was examining it. I recognized the weapon from Beirut: a Soviet PK, based on the Kalashnikov rifle, the standard such weapon employed by what used to be called the Warsaw Pact armies and which had occasionally found its way into Syria and further south. Volodya handed the heavy gun back. Then he took from the other Azeri, a blond man, a gun I knew quite well. It was a Heckler & Koch MP5K, a nasty little weapon that could fit in a car's glove compartment and discharge 650 rounds a minute. I'd used that little number several times in training, but never on active service.

'Doesn't what happened to Aleksandr out in Babushkin suggest that Carlos is alive?' I said.

'Volodya says his name was Dimitri Shishkin. He was a retired KGB colonel. Volodya says he deserves what he got.'

The image of the dead Aleksandr, now Dimitri, made me wince anew.

'They gouged the poor bastard's eyes out,' I said. 'Does Volodya think he deserved that too?'

'Some killers do that,' said Cuba without emotion. 'They think their image will be recorded in their victim's eyes if they don't. It's an old belief.'

I was suddenly exhausted. Volodya was standing by the door, his men behind him.

'*Spokoynoy nochi!*' he said with a thin smile.

'What does *spokoynoy nochi* mean?' I asked when they were gone.

'It means sweet dreams,' Cuba said.

'Do you think he really will make enquiries?' I asked.

'Hope rises with the sun,' Cuba said.

46

Soby told me afterwards about those trading days, days he would never forget. I won't forget them either. I feel I was right there with him on Wall Street as the drama unfolded.

I was correct about the fact that he couldn't sleep – and my initial sale of ten thousand Trident two days before, whilst not a big one, had nonetheless contributed to Soby's lying in bed at two in the morning, trying to quiet the fireworks in his head.

He had spent all his life battling against the urge that dogs the lives of short-term stock traders everywhere: Soby always tried to force himself to cut his losses and run his profits. Mostly, he succeeded. It sounded easy in theory, but in practice, 95 per cent of people who bought and sold stocks did exactly the opposite. They saw a profit and grabbed it, then watched their stock soar beyond reach. Or they bought a stock and when it fell, instead of admitting they were wrong, they held on. The world is full of amateurs with more money than sense, Soby knew. He was a pro. He'd operated with success for forty years in one of the world's most dense jungles. He'd been in with the rest of the pack on some of the great killings; and equally, when computers had taken over in 1987 and it had been only the Chairman of the Federal Reserve himself between the markets and Armageddon, Soby had lost his shirt. But this was different. This was like the real, good old days, Soby sensed. This could be the big one.

Yet he was unhappy. After I'd gone short the night before, he'd taken his wife out to Maxwell's Plum, a ritual they'd observed for three decades. They'd come here to 64th and 1st the night he proposed to her, when even the suit he wore was borrowed – but she'd taken his hand and said: 'Any man who takes me to Maxwell's Plum is good enough for me.' And they always ate the same thing – Soby called a month in advance and made sure it was on the menu: hot asparagus, sole on the bone, salad with a roquefort dressing, ice cream. Coffee. Some things in life were invariable – if you were lucky. Love and marriage. A good restaurant. A bull market on Wall Street.

'Soby, you haven't spoken all evening,' she said.

And he apologized, said he'd had a rough day, warmed up the remnants of an earlier conversation about their only son, a doctor in Chicago, and then drifted off again as his wife described a letter from her grandchild, each word recounted in precious detail.

'Are you losing money?' she asked him.

'What?'

'Are you losing money? You're always like this when you're losing money.'

'On the contrary,' Soby said and called for the check.

Next morning, he came in and saw Trident trade in a range between twenty-five and twenty-six dollars. He had opened his position eight weeks before at sixteen dollars fifty and subsequently had bought the stock each time it had broken new ground on the chart, trading on margin, which is to say, he only needed to put down and maintain 10 per cent of the market value of his position, never a problem if you're a bull in a rising market. Soby now held a position of five hundred thousand Trident shares at an average price of twenty-two dollars fifty, an investment that had required him to pay in a little over one million dollars in cash to the market. His exposure, however, was to the whole 100 per cent of the position and for Soby that meant every time the market moved ten cents up or down he made or lost fifty thousand dollars.

He watched Trident blip on the screen from twenty-five dollars ninety to twenty-five dollars eighty and felt his stomach do a cartwheel. He should take his profit – at this stage more than one and a half million dollars – and bring his wife to Grand Cayman for a week. He had often thought, on bad days, of giving it all up, of walking away with whatever he had on a particular day. Of moving west. His wife had gone to college in San Diego and liked the climate there. Their grandchild – and maybe grandchildren – could not all fit in the Central Park South apartment when they would come to stay; there came a time in life when it was time to change. He made a call. And as he did so, he told me later, he said between clenched teeth, 'Fuck you, Joe! Fuck you for ever.'

47

I could not sleep. It was warm and humid in the little bedroom suite that adjoined Volodya's office. I took a shower and lay on the bed covered by a single sheet. After two fitful hours I made my way out into the office. Two Azeris sat in the next room which served as the guardroom. Six feet from me, I could see the closed-circuit screens switching between the guard on the ground floor, another man with a gun patrolling the trading area and the locked gates of the property. On my cellphone, I pressed out the number in New York.

'Hello?'

'It's me,' I said softly.

'Joe.'

The tone of Laura's voice, the shorthand that said it all.

'How is he?'

'Not good,' Laura said factually. 'They can't keep the fluid off his lungs.'

'I'm thinking of you both the whole time,' I said. 'Of the old days.'

'The terrible Grace brothers,' Laura said and her voice broke.

The line hung empty in our silence.

'Do the boys know?' I asked.

'Howie's home,' Laura said. 'Joseph's on his way.'

'Jesus,' I said.

'It's worse for you,' Laura said. 'It's always worse when you're not beside a situation. In a way we've been preparing ourselves for this all these years. So we're thinking of you too, okay?'

'Okay.'

'Where are you?' Laura asked.

'A long way from home, wherever that is.'

'You sound tired. You should get some sleep.'

'Tell that guy of yours we have an appointment in June with Pavarotti. Okay? Tell him I hate people who don't keep appointments.'

'I'll tell him, Joe. I'll tell him.'

I pressed the 'end' button. I lay down on the bed.

First I cried.

Then at last I slept.

48

Work in Volodya's office began early. It seemed as if I had barely closed my eyes when I was awoken by the sound of voices out in the guardroom.

I showered and dressed. Cuba was sitting at the table in Volodya's office. Three men were on duty in the guardroom next door. The big man with the moustache waved a greeting to me. I had been watching them the night before and was getting to know their names. This one was Pasha. The younger man with blond hair was Yury, and the smaller, quieter of the trio had been called Vassya by Volodya.

'In Baku, breakfast is the most important meal of the day,' Cuba said.

A coffee pot stood beside a samovar alongside plates of pale yellow cheese, of sliced, cold meats, of tomatoes and of oily calamari and a basket crammed with crisp, brown loaves that had been baked somewhere in Moscow whilst I had slept. I watched as Cuba, using chopsticks, ate translucent rounds of calamari.

I asked, 'Do you use those at home?'

She smiled. 'Only when I eat Chinese, but there was once a time I used nothing else.'

She saw my quizzical look.

'Papa was a merchant in Baku.'

I wondered what 'merchant' meant in the context.

'He was a good man,' Cuba said, as if by way of reprimand. 'He did his best for his family.'

Cuba held her coffee cup between both hands and leaned back.

She had been their first child, born at the height of the Cold War. Papa was a good man, got involved with a feud over trade between Azeris and Armenians. Armenians are dirt, Cuba said. One of them, Nobu, a killer, demanded protection for the goods Papa was shipping. Papa refused. Nobu tried to kill him. Papa had to flee for his life with his wife and little daughter Cuba across the Caspian Sea to Krasnovodsk in Turkmenistan. It was 1967.

She was called Cuba because Papa revered Fidel and Che, champions of the people. Che's dashing portrait in his black beret had always hung in the pride of place at home. Cuba meant freedom to the old man. Papa wanted Cuba to be free.

He had been a dreamer. In his youth, the long-jump champion of his entire district, so good they wanted him to go and be trained in Moscow; but he didn't want to, so he pretended he had pulled a tendon, even developed a limp.

Mother's father was in the flower and fruit trade in Moscow and he suggested they all move there. In Moscow, Cuba became an athlete like Papa, won everything she entered in. First in her class, too, excelled at science subjects and when she was fifteen decided she wanted to be a doctor. But Papa did not want her to be confined within the structures of Soviet medicine, he wanted her to go to the United States. At the time, Cuba agreed. When she was sixteen, Papa got her out through Turkey. Cost all the money he had. There were friends in Brooklyn, in Brighton Beach. Everyone in Russia knew of Brighton Beach. A bit like certain suburbs of Moscow to them, a place you got to go and lie low. Cuba lay low for two years, got a visa, went to medical school and graduated top of her year.

Meanwhile, Volodya had been born. A year after Cuba left, on Mother's birthday, Papa brought her and Volodya out to a local restaurant. A man walked up behind Papa halfway through the meal and cut his throat. In front of his wife and child. Nobu had also come to Moscow.

'Volodya pretends he doesn't remember,' Cuba said, 'but I know – I know. He cannot ever forget.'

Papa died without ever seeing Cuba since the day he sent her to the States.

'That still makes me sad,' she told me. 'If only I could have met him again, for an hour, for a minute.'

I could feel the grief at her core, still beating there.

Volodya was only a child then. Helped in the business as children do, but they had nothing, he and his mother. They had to find a place to live. The authorities took away their residence permit and tried to split them up, to send Volodya to a school and to send Mother back to Azerbaijan. Papa had been *mafiosi*, they said. A mobster. The family of *mafiosi* were criminals and had no rights, they said. Volodya and his mother became like mice. They learned how to hide. Volodya never went to school. The authorities forgot about them, Cuba said.

I watched men come and go in the outer office, thought of Dublin and Tim. Hanny.

Volodya grew into his teens on the streets. Mother taught him the lessons he would have learned in school. Then he was caught stealing a car and was sent to prison in Kristi. They put him in a gang that were forced to lay railroad ties in –26° centigrade. It killed a lot of men. It almost killed him.

When they let him out, they thought they had broken him. They were nearly right. Mother nursed him for six months. Your spirit is strong, she told him. When the spirit is strong, the body rallies to it. Somehow he survived.

Then one day Volodya thought of Cuba. Mother always spoke of her daughter in the States, so much so it had become something of a dream. Cuba did not seem a real person to Volodya, but he decided to find out if she was. He wrote to her in Brighton Beach, New York.

Cuba was by then a doctor, was working in the University of Southern California and training to become an immunologist. She did not know Papa was dead and had for years been trying to make contact with her family in Baku. Those were the Brezhnev years. Russia was like a sealed tomb. Some people with relatives abroad had contact with them only once or twice every ten years.

Three months after the letter was posted in Moscow, it found its way to Cuba in California. She replied by return and two weeks after that, when Volodya opened the exotic letter with the US postmark, two fifty dollar bills fell out. It was a miracle – two miracles, in fact: one, that the letter had not been intercepted by the authorities, and two, that it contained so much money.

Cuba changed Volodya's life. She made everything possible. With the money she began to channel to them, Volodya got into business. He wanted to be a businessman like Papa, but soon he came up against Armenians in the lower echelons of Nobu's empire. One summer's day at a trotting race in the Moscow hippodrome, Nobu left the stands and went into the men's room. Volodya was waiting there. He killed him. Shot the old Armenian six times in the chest and head. And the next generation – because Nobu's son, also Nobu, now took over – carried on in Moscow what had been started in Baku twenty years before.

Because Volodya had money he also now had *blat*, influence with the right people in the Moscow Communist Party. Suddenly, from being a nobody on the outside, Volodya was an inside player. He had never been to school, but that did not stop him being a quick learner. He learned that money can buy anything. *Anything*. Money and power. An old mobster from Baku had once said that money and power were like the breasts on a beautiful woman. Take one away and you were left with something incomplete, but with both you could conquer the world.

Volodya never forgot those lessons. And he never forgot that without Cuba none of it would have been possible. She had been like a second mother, he told her.

'Volodya makes a lot of money now because he works with the authorities. All the business you read about government cracking down on crime, it's just propaganda. The government *is* crime in Russia; crime *is* the government. But Nobu too is out there, trying to do deals with people like Marat. Always waiting for the moment to settle the old business. Volodya knows Marat well, but he doesn't want to do anything that might jeopardize that position and let Nobu in.'

'How much will Volodya do to find Carlos?' I asked, feeling as if I was suddenly getting involved in much more than I had bargained for.

'If Carlos is in Russia, Volodya will find out where. Because I asked him to. Because he knows I love Carlos. That much Volodya has agreed to but no more. Until then, we must wait.'

49

Another day had gone by during which I had strolled down the wide corridor with the modern art on one side and the glass-fronted offices on the other, looking in at young men and women, smartly dressed, often two to a desk, working at computers. Over thirty people. Printers chattering out green print-outs. At desks in a larger room, working in front of monitors and key-and-lamp systems, were the traders. White shirts, red braces. Cigarettes. The howls and the cries. The scene could have been Wall Street rather than the Moscow headquarters of Azeri organized crime.

The men in the car pool looked up as I came out. A chopper clattered over the building but no one bothered with it.

Who owned this building in a country where the laws of ownership did not exist, I wondered. Who allowed Volodya to come in here and make this place his own? Some obscure branch of a sprawling ministry or another department in the endless departments of the Communist Party, I imagined. You could not operate in this fledgling environment unless you had grown up barefoot on its streets.

I walked out into the high grass and heard crickets. I sat down. There were wild daisies in the grass. And birds. The air smelled of pure, early summer – pollen, a mixture of herbs, the warmth that the raw earth gives off to celebrate the end of winter.

Now it was after three in the morning, midnight in Dublin. I couldn't sleep. Volodya spent each night in a different place, a security measure he had practised for twenty years, Cuba told me. Tonight, wherever he was, she had gone with him – to meet other members of their extended family. I went into Volodya's office and switched on the desk light. Through the one-way mirror I could see Yury, the young, blond-haired Azeri, feet up on a table, dozing in front of the three closed-circuit screens that flicked between dead images of the building and the grounds. I pressed out Tim's number.

'No names. It's me.'

'You okay?'

'I'm not sure. I can't explain. Anything I should know?'

'Hanny called me three times today to know how you are. She said to tell you she's booked Mrs Duff's – whatever that means.'

'I know what it means.'

'I thought you might.' Tim's voice was echoey. 'Listen, this is probably the last thing you want to hear – but McCoy was on again and he left you a message.'

I felt something akin to a stone drop through my digestive system. I had forgotten about McCoy. 'What do you mean, a message?'

'He said, he knew you weren't here, but he asked me to turn on the tape and record a message for you. It's heavy stuff, Joe. Don't bother with it, but I had to tell you.'

'Let me hear it.'

'Seriously, it's bullshit.'

'Run it, Tim.'

I could hear Tim sighing as he regretted having told me in the first place. 'Here goes.'

'Joe, you know who this is. I understand what you have done, money-wise, but please don't think that changes our agreement. We had a deal. I could have pulled the plug on Grace Equity two months ago. If I had, now there would be nothing. But we did a deal, we agreed terms and conditions and I stood back because you had agreed to fulfil your part of our bargain. Now I have learned that you are still engaged in searching for Carlos Penn. I have no doubt you will find him. You must still bring him to me, Joe. That is our arrangement. If you do not, if you find this man and fail to honour your side of our bargain, no place on earth will be safe for you or yours, believe me, so help you God.'

I listened to the stillness of the Russian night. I had, I realized, known in some deep part of me, that this would happen.

'Joe . . . ?'

'It's okay, Tim. I've dealt with worse.'

We chatted for another minute.

I asked, 'How much cash can we lay our hands on at the moment?'

'Using all our facilities? Couple of million.'

'Draw down as much as you can, get the cash in one place,' I said. 'Call the board – Caulfield, Raza and Dave. Tell them I have an idea. Then call Minx in Denver, tell her what I'm proposing to do. I want her to chart Trident, hour by hour – okay?'

I spoke and Tim made notes for ten minutes.

'It's a big bet,' he said at one point.

'I agree. But it's the only bet in town.'

'We're going to need a lot of cash,' Tim said.

'That's where the three boys come in. Explain everything. Ask them to chip in a float of five million dollars between them.'

'Got it,' Tim said.

It took another five minutes to sort a few more details, but then, essentially, the strategy was complete. We said goodnight and I sat there at the desk of probably the only person now in the world who could save Carlos Penn, realizing that if I was wrong, I had just pissed away my livelihood. The closed-circuit screens drew my eyes. There was a time when I might have wondered whether or not I had been brought this far by an obsession with old scores, whether I was being carried along by the vein of uncontrollable emotion which had come down to me from my mother. Not any more. There was a time when I used to genuinely wonder at people who averred that there was more to life than making money. Only losers thought like that, was my view, and I hated fucking losers. Now I knew more, or at least, enough to know that I had known very little back then.

I needed sleep. As much as I might try to pretend, McCoy's threat had taken my wind away. *No place on earth will be safe for you or yours, believe me, so help you God*. Tomorrow would take every trick I knew – performed now in a culture of which I knew nothing – to persuade Volodya that his best interests lay with me.

I had taken the first steps in the instructions I had given Tim. All I needed now was a little luck. I leaned forward to switch off the desk light and I stared. On the middle of the three closed-circuit screens in the adjoining room, two figures in balaclavas were scaling the outer gates.

50

I looked to the next room. Yury was still inert. I looked again at the screen, but on automatic mode it had now switched to another part of the compound. Yet, I had been sure.

'Hey! Yury! Wake up!'

I came into his room and shook him. Yury jumped to his feet, gun in his hands, looking at me warily. He had very clear, green eyes.

'I've just seen someone climbing the gates,' I said and pointed at his closed-circuit screens. I made the motion of someone covering their head with a mask. I pointed urgently outside. '*Terrorista!*'

Yury turned slowly to the still screens. He turned back to me, his expression hung between scepticism and derision.

'At least two men—' I held up two fingers, struggling with my Russian '—came in over the gates.' At that moment the screen flicked to the intact gates. 'Here! Here!' I pointed. 'Go and tell your comrades! Now!'

Yury sighed patiently, beckoned me to follow him and shuffled ahead down the corridor, speaking into a hand-held radio transmitter. Another voice spoke to him in a crackle of static.

'*Da, da.*'

The big general office was silent. At the door where I'd been frisked the day before, Yury switched on the lights. I didn't think that was a good idea, because it meant we were suddenly targets if I was right – but Yury was in charge and he had a gun. He walked slowly down by the rows of empty desks and silent computer screens. At the end of the office, at the top of the stairs, a big window allowed sight of the illuminated forecourt of the building. A couple of cars stood there, that was all. Perhaps what I had seen was just Volodya's men sneaking in after being on the town without leave. But if so, where had they been? At a fancy-dress?

Yury turned and shrugged as if my nerves had got the better of me. He turned to walk down the stairs and as he did so his hand-held transmitter came alive.

'*YURY!*'

The burst of semi-automatic fire was deafening. We both hit the stairs, rolling. One glass door burst inwards, carrying with it the body of an Azeri guard. Yury lay flat by the far wall and began firing out into the night, his barrel end spitting yellow and red.

He screamed into the radio: '*Vassya! Pasha!*'

To the accompaniment of rolling thunder, lead funnelled through the air a foot above my head. The barrage was coming from about forty metres out. I thought about what Cuba had told me and knew that it had to be Nobu's men. A burst from Yury's Heckler & Koch struck one of the parked cars and it went up in flames, briefly illuminating at least four figures. The dead guard was lying across his gun, a Uzi. I belly crawled into him, dragged the weapon snout first to me, propped the stock on the dead man's chest and loosed off most of a clip in the general direction of the attacking fire. I heard shouts behind and above me and saw big Pasha, naked but for blue jeans, and barefoot, fling himself down at the top of the stairs and begin firing long bursts from the PK.

'*Yury!*'

Pasha was shouting at Yury and urging him to get me to higher ground. Machine-gun fire strafed the entire front of the building in a prolonged, six- or seven-second frenzy. I saw a pair of eyes glide from left to right outside, dark eyes under darker ringlets. The Armenian was trying to manoeuvre across the front of the building to get a better angle on me and Yury. Behind me Pasha let off three short stabs from the PK and the figure outside coughed and folded.

'*Hiya!*'

Emboldened, the bare-chested Pasha was springing down the stairs to us, leaping from one side to the other, the machine-gun in the air, eyes enlivened. He was magnificent, like a sculpture of a man in action – magnificent but mad, I thought. The volley caught him square and seemed for a moment to hang him there, as if lead could defy gravity. Pasha seemed to go in two directions, his upper half back and upwards, from the waist down, to the left.

'*Pasha!*'

Yury was scrambling to his feet. I rolled and took him by the knees as a fresh fusillade crackled through the space which his body had intended to occupy. On the stairs, still inexplicably suspended, I could see Pasha look up, as if trying to follow his soul. Yury was swearing and crying. His gun had jammed and he screamed out.

'*Vassya!*'

At the top of the stairs, Vassya, smaller and more cautious, crept forward and arched his arm. An AK-74 rifle landed on top of us. Yury snatched it, rammed up the magazine and fired a long discharge into the night. I could see outside, at a distance, men assembling what looked like a grenade launcher beside one of the cars.

'Jesus,' I said.

Lying flat at the top of the stairs, Vassya was shouting into a mobile telephone. Below him, Pasha's blood was finding its way down to the hall, one step at a time. Then I heard engines. Headlights split the foreground and shadows broke up, running. I let out a few bursts from the Uzi and a grey figure pitched headlong. A pair of top-of-the-range jeeps had pinned down the remainder of the attacking force. I heard a shout. The jeeps revved wildly in reverse.

'Get down!'

In the beat of silence that followed, I knew exactly what was coming. The centre of the forecourt erupted in a mesmerizing ball of orange flame as the grenade detonated. All the upper windows of the building fragmented. When I sat up I couldn't hear. Even had I been able to, I could not have understood what Volodya was saying. He was standing outside over the Armenian whom Pasha had shot but who was still alive. Volodya shot him at close range in the back of the head. Twice. Then he looked up and saw me watching. He walked over.

'I have found your friend,' he said.

I had never seen a face so drained of mercy.

Volodya said, 'He is being held in the Urals.'

PART FOUR

51

We crossed Moscow southwards in the mist of early morning. The city still slept. In some cases the upper storeys of apartment blocks were lost in the low cloud, their dim, high lights like circling aircraft. Emptiness made the wide outlying highways of Moscow seem even wider. The black pumps of a deserted petrol station appeared. We pulled up beside a Mercedes sedan, its engine running and Cuba, her head covered in a scarf, got out. Vassya opened the door and she got in beside me, then we drove out of the empty forecourt.

'Volodya?' I asked.

'He's travelling separately,' she said. 'The situation is too dangerous.' She looked at me. 'That was Nobu's younger brother who was killed last night.'

I thought about the dark eyes gliding across my field of fire. The younger brother, full of bravado, trying to make a name for himself. Ensuring only that the blood feud would haemorrhage on for another generation. And I thought about my discussion the night before with Volodya.

He had been sitting in his office on his own, staring into space, drinking vodka. Outside men were quietly going about the tasks of caring for the dead.

'Volodya? Can I speak to you about something important?'

The Azeri looked at me, or to be more exact, through me.

I said, 'We're both businessmen, so we both know some things are beyond value, you cannot buy them – like health, do you understand what I'm saying?'

He shrugged.

'Carlos Penn is like that. He may have the answers to the sufferings of millions of people, but even if he doesn't he's a good man. He's beyond value, or at least his freedom is. There's good and bad in the world. You know that, I know that. We make choices. What has happened to Carlos is bad – much worse than bad, in fact. This is a good thing we're doing. You can help us.'

Volodya stood up. 'You see tonight? Tonight bad. You see all this? You think this all come from stupid? No way! You think this all come from make enemies in Moscow? Forget, mister. No way, Volodya. Forget.'

He drank three mouthfuls of vodka straight from the neck of the bottle.

'I thought you said you were a businessman,' I said quietly.

The Azeri looked at me balefully.

'Volodya businessman, *da*,' he said.

'You couldn't trade turkeys at Christmas in my country,' I said. 'Where I come from you need it up here to make the real money.' I tapped my head. 'Not knives or guns. I'm talking serious money, Volodya.'

Volodya looked to see if it was a joke.

'What you say?' he asked, his face tight.

'How much do you think a successful HIV drug is worth?' I asked. 'I'll tell you. Hundreds of millions of dollars.'

'How you do?' Volodya asked narrowly. 'How you get this drug?'

'You think you've got to own the drug? You think you've got to own something before you can make money on it? You know nothing. You think you're a big businessman?' I stood up. 'I'll tell you something – by not helping us to free Carlos, you're pissing away the only chance you'll ever have of getting into the really big time.'

Volodya looked at me narrowly. 'You want me to kill you?' he asked slowly. 'No prob-lem.'

'Forget it,' I said. 'I'm in the wrong place.'

His fist came down hard on the table. 'You tell!' he yelled.

I sat down slowly. I reached across and took a piece of paper. 'There are two ways of making money on the stock market,' I began. 'One: you buy and when the market goes up, then you sell. The people who do that are called bulls. Or you can do the opposite – first you sell and when the market falls, then you buy. The people who do this are called bears.'

'Bears,' he said.

'Like Russian bears,' I said. 'And here's my plan.'

It took him all of two minutes to grasp it. And during that time the questions he asked were all highly relevant – like how fluid the market was, how much stock could be shifted and how we would be guaranteed to get paid. And he asked me who would put up the risk capital. I told him I would. And that his job was to get Carlos out.

'What part of all do I get?' Volodya asked.

'If we go into this as partners, we split my profits fifty-fifty,' I replied.

Volodya had nodded. 'Fifty-fifty.'

Every time the car hit a pothole, the vibration went up my spinal column to the roots of my scalp. At crossroads, armed men were supervising the transfer of the contents of one articulated truck to another. I had spoken briefly to Hanny on my cellphone, and had told her that I was going to be on the move for a few days. The sound of her voice had made me ache with longing. We went straight through the intersection's red light at 70 m.p.h. As sunrise came, Yury switched on the radio and listened to the news.

Different parts of my life were playing though my head, like a newsreel, but all interconnected, all relaying on the one channel at the same time. The faces of my parents, scenes from my Marine training days, the face of Donna, my second wife, the comforting sound of my brother's laughter, and the door to a cage, swinging slowly open. I jerked awake.

'Try to sleep.'

'Sure.'

We drove between low buildings and straight out on to the tarmac of Domodedovo Airfield. The plane was an Aeroflot hopper, four turbo-prop engines already turning. My right shoulder, bandaged where flying glass had lacerated it, stung. I was also beginning to swell up nicely in my left wrist, on whose surface the path of a stray bullet had left its wandering path, something I hadn't noticed during the attack. Cuba and I climbed the steps, Vassya came up last and pulled the door in. There was just the three of us plus two pilots in the plane. I saw Yury as he drove out of the airfield. We took off and climbed above the mist. The early light was exquisite.

Volodya had taken the decision. Not that he had discussed it with me, but I could sense the change in him, the look on his face as they had carried his two men upstairs and laid them out. The machine-gun fire had as good as sliced Pasha in two. We had all stood in a circle as an older man, one of the guards from the compound, recited prayers over the dead men.

As we vibrated eastward, I marvelled, not for the first time in my life, at the ability of the living to shrug off the near presence of death and to carry on. It had something to do with survival, a jungle thing, but I had seen it in the Middle East and I had seen it again the night before – the way men can operate in circumstances which no textbook would admit. In the end, I thought, it allowed man to do what he must, regardless of death: walk on the moon, drive Formula-1 cars, push the very limits of existence to a point where life and death are so close as to be indistinguishable. But it was in the aftermath that the devil lay. In the long nights when you thought you were safe, when you woke up with no one but yourself for company. Then, without warning, the faces of the Pashas took shape, as if their right to recognition was long overdue, as if they were saying, 'You tried to forget us, but we won't allow you to.' That was the worst. And I'd been there often enough to know that sooner or later the faces always returned.

I awoke to cloud beneath us. I must have slept for nearly two hours. Vassya handed me coffee. I peered out and in a brief clearance saw the rolling outline of the European/ Asian divide, to one side, west, green foothills and rivers; to the other the mountains, and then an abrupt black wall in the atmosphere, like an encroaching storm cloud.

'Smoke,' Cuba said and wrinkled her nose. 'If you don't smoke already, you will by the time you leave the Urals.'

I asked her about the set-up and what we could expect – that is, other than the Mafia, the people from the Interior Ministry and the Red Army.

'Volodya does a lot of business over here,' Cuba explained. 'He is one of the biggest buyers of copper in the Urals, there are factories producing the product he wants. He needs men to keep in touch with the managers, with the directors of the factories. A Chechen gang based in St Petersburg have recently tried to muscle in on Volodya's copper trade. It is a very dangerous time.'

Outside the day had been lost to tar-like cloud.

'Volodya has been told that a western scientist, a man, has been working in the old Soviet Academy of Science in Yekaterinburg for nearly a year. He is a prisoner. He is kept by men assigned directly from Petrowski. He is brought every day to the laboratory. No one thinks it strange over here. This sort of thing has been happening for years. Under Brezhnev, they killed tens of thousands of people in the name of science. No one bothered to notice this case until Volodya asked.'

I sipped the bitter-sweet coffee.

Cuba then said: 'People the world over have been conditioned by governments, by culture, to expect success only from the expenditure of billions of dollars. It makes people feel good to think that way – they think they're getting something for their taxes. But the drug for AIDS is not going to come from billions of dollars, or from men who are now more concerned with politics than with a cure to the virus. Like HIV itself, the drug is going to come from the least obvious place, and at a time when no one expects it. It's going to come from a man like Carlos Penn.'

'Does Volodya believe that?' I asked.

'Volodya told me to tell you: this is a business deal. He expects you to honour your side of the bargain,' Cuba said. 'Fifty-fifty.'

The wheels skidded along the apron of a small airfield. When we stepped out, the smog made it look like five on a December evening rather than a late April dawn. Headlights made their way to the plane. They belonged to a Mitsubishi jeep. Two men of the type I was becoming used to got out and stood either end of the big vehicle. A third man, whose dense, black moustache looked as if it had been stuck on that morning for the part, greeted Cuba with a kiss to her cheeks. He was going a little thin on top. His eyes looked black in this light, his jacket was open and his big belly thrust out. He embraced Vassya, turned to me.

'Joe, this is Vovo,' Cuba said. 'Since my childhood, one of our greatest friends.'

Vovo looked at me circumspectly. Then we all got into the jeep and drove out.

The landscape was grim: tall chimneys belching smoke, dozens of ferro-concrete apartment blocks, workers on foot, men and women, with grimed faces. There were a lot of buses. Men in cloth caps were hitch-hiking lifts. Vovo gestured like an Arab while speaking. He produced photographs and handed them to Cuba. As she took them I watched his eyes go to her breasts.

'Look,' Cuba said and handed me the pics.

They were amateur efforts, slightly blurred and askew. They showed a man getting into a car. Getting out. Always at least three other men around him. But despite the distance at which the photographer had stood, the subject of the shots was the same as had looked out at me from the red file McCoy had given me two and a half months before, the scientist from central casting.

Vovo elaborated.

'Carlos is guarded day and night,' Cuba said. 'Vovo says it's going to be impossible to get to him.'

The extent of Yekaterinburg's industrial might was beginning to seem limitless when suddenly there was bright sunshine and we stopped at traffic lights on a tree-lined avenue opposite a magnificent rococo building with delicate pediments and intricate arches. The jeep made a succession of sharp left and right turns, down streets becoming progressively more narrow. Old women sat begging at corners. The houses were often wooden constructions; big, solid pine buildings, their window frames and portals carved in great detail. Abruptly we turned into an open gateway. We went through, into a concreted yard, and two men rushed to the ten-foot steel gates and dragged them shut behind us.

'Welcome to Yekaterinburg,' Cuba said.

52

When Soby spoke to me about 'usually well-informed sources' or 'someone who knows someone', it was usually a specific mole within an institution who was feeding him and whom the broker wanted to protect. In this case, she was the daughter of his wife's sister and worked as a secretary in the sprawling Washington institution known as the Food and Drug Administration. Quite by chance, fifteen years ago she and Soby had met at a family reunion to which Soby had been dragged along. She was then in her thirties, unmarried, with a laugh like a neighing horse. Her name was Florence.

'As in Renaissance,' she had said and laughed.

Apart from the laugh, Soby had liked her. They had chatted with increased interest for much of a long, balmy September afternoon. Afterwards, they kept in touch. Soby helped Florence invest her modest funds. He told his wife about her, not that he divulged client business on a regular basis to his wife, but the client in this case had insisted.

'I don't want her to think that I'm your mistress,' as Florence had put it, neighing in a high octave.

Over the years, without any specific intention, just in the way of a general relationship, Soby and Florence had chatted like business people, maybe once a month. Soby had discussed Coke, IBM, WalMart and Microsoft; Florence, for her part, had shared gossip that affected the FDA. She worked as an internal auditor in CDER, the FDA's Center for Drug Evaluation and Research. It wouldn't be fair to Soby to say that there was an ulterior motive. Information was his business and, if the truth be known, their tête-à-têtes made Florence feel a little less lonely.

Three months before, she had relayed the first instalment of gossip she'd picked up regarding Trident. Florence's source was a secretary in the Pharmacology/Toxicology Section of CDER which dealt with the application process for investigational new drugs (IND). The name Trident had been mentioned to Florence.

'D'you know them?' she had asked Soby.

'Sure.' Soby clicked his screen. Trident was last traded fourteen dollars. 'Sure I do.'

'Seems there's a lot of stuff coming in from them over at IND right now,' Florence said.

'You don't say,' said Soby.

'Maybe something to do with AIDS,' Florence said.

That's how it started. Soby never let on he was excited, just told Florence what an interesting job she had, how he admired all the good they were doing down there, how Wall Street could do with a bit of the FDA's compassion.

I said later, 'You told her that?'

Soby made a face. 'The day I bought at sixteen dollars,' he said. 'Okay, okay. Look, she was coming at me – right?'

And as the weeks went by, Florence kept coming. The story began filling out. She told of an HIV drug brought to the FDA by a small-time scientist, of how, although the application never made it up the line, certain people with CDER – 'No friends of mine,' Florence said – were paid by different drugs companies, bribed was the better word, to sift through all the rejected applications and to send on anything worthwhile. In that business no one paid more than Trident. Its CEO was Dr Roberto Groz. The word was that thanks to the FDA, Trident was sitting on something real hot.

But now Soby, who should have been celebrating thirty years in a happy marriage, had spent the night before sleepless in Manhattan. He made the call.

'I got some friends to whom an AIDS drug would be of major personal importance,' he said, unhappy that he was, even if only by implication, lying to Florence. Still. What was the point in everyone being unhappy? 'It would be most useful to know anything you hear on this matter, as soon as you hear it.'

'I heard nothing, otherwise I'd have called you,' Florence said.

'Could you, you know – ask, d'you think?' Soby said, wincing, knowing he was pushing it.

But Florence said, 'No problem, I'll talk t'ya, Soby.'

Soby blew out his cheeks in miniature balloons. When in the trading room he might as well have been on a desert island, nothing intruded. The other traders' voices now surged back for a moment. It was time to get out, he decided. He was getting too old. Then he felt a spike as the screen changed before his eyes.

'Hey, Soby!' a man thirty years his junior called from across the room. 'D'you see Trident? It's just broken twenty-six on the upside!'

When Tim came on from Dublin to tell Soby that he'd wired two million dollars into Soby's client account for the credit of Grace Equity, Soby's first reaction was to gloat.

'So he's seen the light!' Soby said, referring to the order I'd already given him days before and assuming I was now reversing it.

And then Tim told him to sell two hundred and fifty thousand Trident short at twenty-five dollars or better.

'Aw, shit,' was all Soby could say as he worked the order. 'Aw, shit.'

53

Eight hours had passed. Nothing had happened. Vovo had disappeared almost as soon as he had installed us in the ramshackle, fortified building in central Yekaterinburg. In a room with low beams and a large, empty fireplace, his men served up pilaf. The stew came in a massive, earthenware cauldron and smelled like formaldehyde. Using their hands, the men ate hungrily. White and purple onions; garlic; mutton; yellow carrots; round, pink rice and everything swimming in the thick fat boiled from sheeps' tails, Cuba explained. They were men of a different order to Volodya's guards in Moscow, to Vassya who sat a little apart, watching everything. These locals had the shifty looks of touts at a greyhound track. They ate furtively, stealing quick looks at Cuba and myself. My spirits, momentarily raised during the flight east, now fell even further. I could tell when men's hearts were fully invested in a project; or like now, when they were not.

I had been given a room at the back to sleep in with Vassya. Cuba's was along the corridor. I put aside my unfinished plate as the door opened and Vovo came in. He was drunk, I saw straight off.

'*Za uspehk vashevo vizita!*' Vovo toasted, pouring from a bottle into shot glasses. He looked fondly at Cuba. 'To the success of your visit!'

'*Za nash uspehk!*' Cuba said. 'To our success!'

'*Da zdraistvuet Azerbaidzhan!*' Vovo said and tossed back another vodka.

'*Da zdraistvuet Azerbaidzhan!*' I said and drank.

'God to bless Ireland, mister,' Vovo said, glasses again brimming.

'A Nation Once Again!' I said.

Vovo upturned the glass on his mouth, then he sat beside Cuba and began to speak to her in the insistent way of the very drunk, catching her hands in his and attempting to kiss them. At first Cuba laughed it off, pretending what he was saying was all a joke, but then, as Vovo became more earnest, Cuba too became firmer. I could see the other men suppressing laughs. At last Cuba got up from the table, came over, sat beside me and put her arm around my shoulder.

'I'm sorry about this,' she said quietly, 'but I've told him you're my boyfriend.'

'My pleasure.'

'Otherwise he'll persecute me. It's been the same for years with me and Vovo. He thinks I should have stayed in Russia and married him.'

Vovo was looking murderously in my direction; I grinned back. Vovo then asked something and made a gesture towards me.

'What's he saying?'

'Take no notice.'

'Please.'

'He's asking how much you're paying him for this service,' Cuba said.

'Tell him, my deal is with Volodya.'

Vovo turned away from the table and spat, then drank.

'What's he saying now?'

'He wants to know, if some of his soldiers get killed will you pay for their widows to be looked after?'

Vovo said something and Cuba looked away. I saw Vassya go on alert.

'What was that about?'

'Nothing.'

'Come on, I need to know, Cuba.'

Cuba winced. 'Vovo says it's not worth all the trouble. He doesn't care who gets AIDS or who doesn't. He thinks it's a disease of scum and Carlos is no better if he's involved in trying to cure it.'

Vovo looked at me darkly. I met his eye.

'Tell him,' I said, 'that his job is to follow Volodya's orders.'

Cuba spoke. Vovo dropped his gaze, turned away, then he suddenly caught up the vodka bottle by the neck and smashed it into the empty fire grate.

'I'm going to bed,' Cuba said.

54

It was midnight. I had stayed up, chatting with Vassya. I liked him. He told me about growing up in Moscow, about his family, his girlfriend, his hopes for the future. I told him about Ireland, about Hanny. My life. We talked for over an hour. Nothing would happen, I knew, until Volodya arrived. Most of Vovo's men were asleep in chairs around the room. Vovo too was asleep, drilling out machine-like snores through the brush of his moustache. I knew men like Vovo from the Marines. The trick was to find the good in them – and it was always there, however small the quantity. All at once he sat up, wiped his face on his hand and squinted around him. Then he left the room.

I tried to wonder what the chances were of getting Carlos out in one piece. At best, one in three, I concluded. And that was only the start of it: he then had to be smuggled to the West, an issue I assumed Volodya had addressed. Carlos plus Cuba plus myself. Everything hinged on Volodya's ability to come up with a plan.

I heard some shouts, then the door burst open and Cuba walked in, followed by a scowling Vovo. She said something sharp to him, then turned to me.

'He doesn't get the message,' she sighed. 'He came into my room and said if I was your boyfriend, why then was I sleeping alone.'

'Sleep in my room,' I said. 'Vassya will change.'

'Sorry about this.' She turned to Vovo, spoke to him shortly, then left.

Some of the men had come awake and were looking at Vovo with amusement. He paced the room for all of a minute, like a caged bear. Then he came over and not so much spoke to me as jammed his face into the space two inches from mine and exhaled a mixture of vodka and vituperation. I had no idea what he was saying, but Vassya's eyes had gone wary.

'Cuba,' Vovo said and tapped my chest with a meaty finger. 'Cuba.' He tapped his own chest. He made a see-saw motion with his hands whilst at the same time hitching up his shoulders. Then he pulled up a chair to the corner of the table and sat down heavily.

'Cuba,' he said, rolling up the right sleeve of his shirt, revealing an arm the size of a heavyweight thigh and covered in mats of black, curly hair. He looked darkly at me. Vassya said something, but Vovo cut him short. He barked something and pointed for me to sit down. He wanted to arm-wrestle me for Cuba's affections.

'I don't want to fight you, Vovo,' I said helplessly. 'I want to fight *with* you. Against the people who are holding Carlos.'

But Vovo was waiting.

'I don't want to fight you,' I said again. 'You are a very strong man, okay? You win.'

However, Vovo was programmed in one direction only now. His eyes rolled when he looked at me. I thought of Cuba, now asleep, and what awaited her if I flunked this test in Vovo's eyes.

'Jesus Christ,' I sighed. It hurt even to roll my sleeve up. I sat across the corner of the table.

Vovo poured two glasses of vodka, then grunted something.

'May the best man win, I suppose,' I sighed.

We drank.

I drew in my chair, brought in my forearm so that the hairs on it touched Vovo's, then went into the grip.

The Azeri's arm was like a wall. He smiled at me,

watching my eyes. I feinted forward, exploring the parameters of Vovo's strength, but there wasn't a centimetre of movement from the twelve o'clock position of both our arms. Although my shoulder ached, its strength was still intact, mostly. I deliberately relaxed to draw Vovo forward, catching the huge man a little by surprise at such an early opening. Vovo blinked, lunged down to five minutes after the hour. I stopped him and brought both our fists back to the vertical.

'Call it quits?' I asked.

'*Poshol na khui!*' said Vovo and calmly brought up his glass to his lips with his free hand. I was sure it meant, 'Go fuck yourself!'

I knew I couldn't win, no matter what the outcome; but neither could I lose. Vovo's strength was immense but it was disorganized, I thought. A bit like Russia. And the man was drunk.

There came a time in arm-wrestling when, unless you lifted weights for a living, you had to go for the kill, or else the power in your arm would be squandered simply from holding the position. I struck. Vovo smiled. He let me force him down to the ten minutes before the hour position on his side of the clock, then he calmly levered my arm back up to where it had been.

He smiled. 'No prob-lem.' But he was sweating.

Now Vovo struck. I gave him nothing and counter-attacked. My elbow on the table was hurting like hell – worse than my shoulder. Vovo was grimacing now. He began to curse. I struck harder, like pulling down a very heavy weight, and then what I had feared would happen, did. Vovo's arm began to give, slowly, half a centimetre at a time. The Azeri stopped me at the point where if he conceded any more it would be over.

'Call it quits?' I panted.

'*Blyad!*' Vovo said from gritted teeth.

Vovo began an agonizing last attack, putting all his strength into the effort, bringing me up half the distance he had lost. But his timing was wrong. I thrust down and Vovo's arm went back to its point of last resistance.

Vovo was fumbling about on the table. Incredulously I thought he was going to have a drink. He twisted a fraction, then I felt red hot pain in my ribs. My left hand went across and grabbed Vovo's hand that was stabbing me in the chest with the handle end of a knife.

'Fuck you!' I cried out in pain.

'*Fuck you!*' Vovo cried wildly.

With the body attack the Azeri had managed to get my playing arm back up to where we had started. He was still trying to stab, but I kept his knife hand pinned to the table, wondering if my ribs were broken.

I was dimly aware of the other people in the room, all now awake. I burst down powerfully. Vovo's arm began to quiver.

'Vovo . . .' I said, fighting for the words.

The Azeri's brown eyes were small and pained. He must have been as aware as me of the audience.

'*Quits?*' he gasped.

'Quits,' I said.

He collapsed back, grabbed the bottle of vodka and gulped from it. From the corner of my eye, I saw Vassya quietly return the pistol inside his jacket.

55

There were two hard, narrow beds. A wooden chair. Bare floorboards with gaps between them into which cock-roaches scuttled. Thin curtains that did not cover the whole window. A toilet, with its seat broken, a basin. Cuba was lying in the semi darkness, hands behind her head. I told her what had happened.

'Vovo is an oaf,' she said quietly. 'Volodya sent him out here from Moscow because in Moscow he was a joke. You sent Vovo down the Arbat for a pack of cigarettes and two days later he called you from St Petersburg.'

'He's just jealous,' I said.

Cuba gave a derisory snort. 'Vovo once worked for Papa in the Moscow flower market. You have to keep a man like that who has worked for you all his life. The job here in the Urals was the one where nothing could go wrong. All he has ever had to do is to make sure that the money gets to the right people in the steel and copper works. He has never had to fight.'

All noise in the outer room had ceased. When I had left him, Vovo was slumped across the table, snoring loudly. Somewhere far off was the regular sound of machinery, as in a steel mill.

'You never know with men,' I said. 'You get the most insignificant little guy who's been the butt of everyone's jokes in training, then you put him into a combat-type situation and he's suddenly everyone's inspiration.'

She asked me about the Marines and I told her.

'I was once in love with a soldier,' Cuba said, a faraway look on her face.

Cuba Sali was nearly sixteen, dark in the Azeri way,

most attractive. Vovo wasn't the only local trying to turn her head, there were many others like Vovo for whom Cuba had no time. One day she was helping her father load flowers into his truck at the Moscow market when a young man from another stall came up to lend a hand. Papa knew him. He was Dimitri, his father – another stall-holder – was from Minsk. Dimitri was a corporal in the Red Army, on leave from Afghanistan. Cuba saw a tenderness in his eyes, something beyond mere desire. She went home that night and slept so deeply that when she awoke, she said, she was not even sure who she was.

That was the beginning of it. Soon, they could not see enough of one another. Dimitri was fair haired and blue eyed. After the first week, he told Cuba he loved her, and three days later she told him she felt the same way. At the end of that week, faced with imminent trans-shipment back to Afghanistan, Dimitri proposed. Cuba said she would think about it. She went home and told her parents.

He was her first boyfriend, she was floating on air. Although she had not responded there and then to Dimitri, she knew her answer in her heart. And there was a precedent: her mother had married three weeks short of her sixteenth birthday – Cuba was now older than her mother had then been. She waited until Papa came home and finished his evening meal, until his slippers were on and he was sitting with her mother on the sofa by the electric fire. She told them of her decision.

Her father's reaction was one of disbelief.

'You cannot do this!'

'Papa, I am nearly sixteen!' Cuba cried.

That wasn't the point. What about her career in medicine? He had made arrangements for her to be received in New York, it was all highly fraught, money had been paid. But she could become a doctor in Russia just as easily, Cuba said. Papa blew up. His ideal was under threat. All his life he had slaved, but not for this. Cuba told him she would be happy to be Dimitri's wife, that her life was her own. Papa became furious, accused her of squandering the chances he had worked for. Throughout the discussion, even when Cuba pleaded with her to do so, her mother never said a word. Cuba walked out.

Next day she told Dimitri that she loved him dearly and would marry him – but not yet. Her parents were against it and she wanted time to persuade them. Dimitri was crestfallen. Faced with shipping out the following week, he begged her to marry him there and then. Over the next two days tearful scenes took place – between Cuba and Dimitri, between Cuba and her father. Papa would have none of it. He at last came to a compromise of sorts with Cuba: they would wait. Cuba then convinced Dimitri that it was the same whether they got married now or later, either way they would always be together; and in the end, he accepted what she said.

'The night before he shipped out, we slept together,' said Cuba, matter of factly. 'I was never more in love. He left our house at five the next morning to get into barracks on time. I never saw him again.'

They didn't hear about his death for six months, the way of these things in Russia. Even then, the official explanation was hazy, although everyone assumed Dimitri had been killed in an incident involving local freedom fighters. Some time after that, by appointment Cuba met a soldier in a café near the Kremlin and heard that Dimitri had been killed when a tank that was being loaded on a transporter slipped off and fell on him, killing him instantly. That saddened Cuba most: if he had been killed in action, by the people he had been shipped out to oppose and contain, there might have been some reason to it. But to have been killed by carelessness, which was what had happened, seemed to her inexcusably crass.

'A few months later, I went to the States.' Cuba's eyes narrowed. 'For years – until I met Carlos, in fact – I thought of Dimitri most days and blamed myself for not having married him. It sounds illogical, but I was convinced that if we had got married, he would not have been killed. He might have been allowed to ship back to Moscow early in order to see his new bride, or the fact that he was now a married man would have somehow meant that he was not in that place at that time. It's crazy, but I believed that if I'd married him, I could have somehow protected him, my energy could have flowed thousands of miles and kept him safe.

'And I was so angry. Not with my father, because at least he'd come out and stated his opinion, however selfish I thought it was at the time. No, I was angry with my mother. She must have known I was so much in love, yet she said nothing. She'd married Papa at fifteen, she knew what infatuation was. Hers was a betrayal. When I left Russia and knew that I would in all likelihood never see my parents again, although my sorrow was genuine where Papa was concerned, with my mother it was not. She let me down. It took me a long time to forgive her for that.' Cuba smiled sadly. 'What are mothers for if not to stand up for love? But then I met Carlos.'

I lay on the other bed. What she told me brought me back to another life, and had stirred feelings within me which I thought I had forgotten.

As if reading my mind, Cuba said, 'I imagine men talk like this the night before a battle, in the trenches or in the jungle. It's easy when you're bound by a common purpose, isn't it? Look at us, we don't know each other and I've just dumped my most inner secrets on you.'

I reached for her hand. 'I wanted to hear.'

'How about you?' Cuba asked. 'Did your mother stand up for you?'

'She stood up for me,' I said. 'She screamed so loud I thought the whole neighbourhood would hear.'

I described the incident in school when the dart had been thrown at John, and what I'd done. It wasn't, of course, the first time that my brother had been bullied, nor that I had responded. I had been taught to box by my father, I knew from the age of ten how to hit and how to hurt. Even when I hadn't yet started to grow, I could whip out a left jab and make a boy two years older howl. It was a wonder. The realm of fear did not exist – I was feared. And of course, I used this ability, this fear, to trade my way through primary school, then secondary.

Problems. Complaints arose, I was hauled in before the dean when I was in my first year of secondary school.

'This is not the first time, is it?' he said, meaning that in my old school there had been the odd fracas as well for which I'd been roasted. 'I take a very hard line,' said the dean, a priest with a milky complexion and red hair. 'Keep your fists in your pockets. I don't want to see you in here again.'

I idolized my dad, I told Cuba. Such a great man to have as a father. He was my hero, it was that simple. When we went off on our treks down into the Midlands, across the heather bogs, or climbed the hills in Wicklow, I wanted the days to be unending, I wanted to be like his shadow. My worship for him was so intense that some nights I could not sleep.

And then, the incident in school. I knew I was wrong, of course, that I should have gone the official complaint route – but somehow I felt that justice was on my side. I reasoned that Dad would see it that way too and support me.

What happened subsequently turned my world upside down. Any money Dad had was put aside for John. He was terrified he'd lose his job. There wasn't a moment to address the fact that I might have been morally justified, however misled. It was my mother who stood up for me. I'll never forget her. She was possessed of this magnificent sense of outrage which now surged up like a tempest and engulfed us all. There was mayhem. She confronted my father, but he just blubbered and stammered and wrung his hands. This was the man whose shadow I had wanted to be. He sat in the kitchen, his head in his hands and he wept.

'I was sent to New York. It was so needless. But I was sent. Like you, I went over it in my mind for years, and each time I thought of what happened, my mind would skip the details. The truth was, it was too painful for me, even for a moment, to dwell on the fact that my father had not been my hero.'

Cuba brought my hand to her lips. 'My turn to say thank you.'

'I've never told anyone that before,' I said. 'No one.'

She kept my hand by her face. 'D'you know the truth? Me neither.'

It had taken us both long years and many miles to find this moment in this unlikely place, and although we both understood it was ephemeral, that we were both here for just one purpose and that when that purpose was fulfilled – or not – we would, in all probability, never see one another again; although we knew this, nevertheless we also grasped the relevance of the instant.

I went to sleep, my hand to her face. At some time during the night I came awake and was aware of the cicadas outside and then of the fact, which seemed so natural, that she was beside me, her body in sleep fitted to mine. The night beyond the thin curtains had begun to change at the edges as darkness began its first steps towards dilution. I kissed Cuba's cheek. Dawn was creeping into the Urals.

56

In my sleep, I heard an overhead clatter of what I thought were helicopters. I was awake at once. Light, four-thirty. I decided I must have been wrong about the choppers, for the only sound now was that of the ever-present mill, somewhere miles away. My ribs hurt. As I watched Cuba, she came half awake, and smiled with her eyes still closed, the fact of where she was not yet a reality. Suddenly the sound of men hurrying down the hall outside and a familiar voice broke the silence.

'Cuba!'

Volodya Sali came into the little bedroom.

'Cuba! *Nam vsem nado pogovorit!*' he cried. 'We need to discuss what's happening!'

He took in the two of us at a glance. He had not shaved for days and his blond hair was tousled. '*Bystro!*'

Now that the moment had come, I felt intensely alive, the way I always had before action. I swung out of bed and pulling on a shirt, ran along the corridor with Volodya, into the big room where the men were already standing at the central table. A pot of coffee was going around followed by a bottle of vodka. Vovo looked grim, with red eyes and a general air of dishevelment. Volodya, mug in hand, Vassya one side of him and Yury the other, was leaning over a map of Yekaterinburg. He'd found the heat in Moscow worse than he ever remembered, I heard him say to Cuba. By looking for Carlos, we had opened an anthill of activity and now the Interior Police, led by Marat, had been joined by Nobu's people in an attempt to find me.

'They think you're still in Moscow,' Cuba explained.

Volodya looked up from the map. 'Big-problem,' he said. 'Big-problem.'

Vovo had spread out photographs on the table. We gathered round. The shots were of buildings. Volodya began to speak in Russian, using his hands, whirling them around his head, using a marker to circle points on the map, relating the photographs to the places circled.

'Carlos is held at this building here,' Cuba explained, pointing to what looked like a shot of an apartment building. 'It is in the outskirts of Yekaterinburg, an old hotel that was once used by the Academy of Soviet Engineers.'

Vassya asked a question and Volodya answered, referring to the photographs.

'This photo shows the Academy of Sciences where Carlos is brought every day,' Cuba explained, pointing to a photograph of a nondescript building with a statue in front of it. 'It is a twenty-minute drive to the Academy from the old hotel. At least ten militiamen are in both locations at all times.'

Volodya continued his briefing and the room tingled under the impact of his authority. That morning Petrowski himself was due to arrive from Moscow, Cuba translated. He would be travelling with an American businessman. They were due at nine at the Academy.

Groz, I thought. Home at last.

Petrowski would, as always, be accompanied by troops from the special Omon guards. In Afghanistan, they had been the elite. So, everything had changed, Volodya said. With the heat so intense, and with Nobu also involved, waiting was out of the question. We either struck now or forgot it. In addition, Volodya speculated, the arrival of Petrowski and Groz – if indeed it were he – meant a new development so far as Carlos was concerned. They could be about to move him out, or worse.

A low murmur rippled through the assembled men.

Volodya reviewed the plans. Cuba explained that Volodya's original scheme had been to attack the convoy carrying Carlos as it arrived at the Academy. Although in principle the idea was sound, it was now no longer workable since by then Petrowski's men would have arrived and the numbers against us would be simply too great. Volodya spoke rapidly. Carlos would have to be snatched before he ever left the hotel, from within the hotel compound itself. This presented its own problems, since there was one entrance only, which meant that the escape route could be blocked. Vovo was unhappy. He explained that he had sounded out trying to buy off the militiamen guarding the hotel, but that they were all terrified of Petrowski.

'We're going to do it now – or not at all,' Volodya stated.

'If we do free him, what then?' I asked.

Volodya spoke rapidly.

'He wanted to fly all of us out by air to Poland in a private plane,' Cuba said. 'That's impossible now. Petrowski could have the plane shot down in five minutes.'

'Not air,' Volodya said. '*Gruzovik*. Truck. You understand?'

'I understand.'

Volodya went around each man in turn as their leader. A fellow Azeri. Each man when asked, nodded his assent. Then his eyes fell on me.

'Fifty-fifty?'

I nodded. 'We have a deal.'

The Azeri extended his hand. I saw again the tattoos.

'Businessman,' he said.

We shook.

57

Four vehicles stood in the walled-off yard – a Mercedes and an old Volga, and two wide-wheeled Mitsubishi jeeps, gleaming, aggressive-looking twins with the drivers already in place. At a command from Volodya, Cuba and I peeled off into one jeep, Vovo and two guards into another. Volodya stood with three men by the Mercedes. The remaining four Azeris crammed into the fuming Volga.

'Joe.' Volodya came over, a cigarette in his lips. '*Na vsyakiy sluchai*,' he said and handed me a pistol and a brick of magazines.

I thanked him.

He looked at me for a moment. Then he turned to his driver.

'*Poekhali!*' he cried and we began to move out.

'What does *na vsyakiy sluchai* mean?' I asked Cuba as we pulled out of the yard.

'It means, "Just in case",' she said.

We drove in fast convoy through the sleeping streets of Yekaterinburg. Although light, the sun was still low and night accumulations of smog still clung to the wooden houses. They seemed defiant, these structures, as if in proud memory of the pioneers who had been sent out to this barren place a century ago and carved their homes from the forest.

I examined the gun I had been given. A Beretta machine pistol which discharged its fire in three-round bursts. Hinged to the front of the frame was a folding front grip for the left hand. This was a weapon. I rammed up one magazine into the bottom of the butt, pocketed the rest, checked the safety and sat back, the feel of the gun's steel snout reassuring.

Suddenly we were turning off the deserted highway, the jeeps and the Mercedes in front, the Volga last. Abruptly the under-wheel concrete became uneven as if the ground were subsiding. Grass grew in spikes from cracks. Even the sudden trees, only recently in bloom, looked neglected. Through the narrow neck of an entrance, the convoy made its way on a winding, broken road with sharp islands of concrete standing like inverted stalactites in the centre of yawning potholes. I looked back and saw that the Volga had stayed out on the road, the men from it already deployed.

'This hotel was built for the use of Soviet engineers visiting industrial plants in Sverdlovsk, as Yekaterinburg used to be called,' Cuba whispered. 'Like everything else, it has been allowed to fall apart.'

Where shrubberies and lawns had once been, now everything grew wild and weedy. For four hundred metres the avenue wound bumpily through sprawling vegetation. I could see why Volodya would not come in here by choice – the escape was too easy to block. Suddenly we swung around trees to the front door of an ugly concrete building, some of its windows broken, the paint peeling off in crusts.

Volodya, Vovo and six men were already out and the vehicles had reversed to the door in an arc. Some of Vovo's men took up defensive positions with rifles and sub-machine guns behind their vehicles. I saw Vovo pull the ring from a grenade, lob it at the front doors of the building, then duck.

The blast violated the morning. Glass, metal and dust rolled out and made everything vibrate. I hinged out the front grip on the Beretta. As I looked up, Vovo and

Volodya were rushing the building. Less than thirty seconds had elapsed.

Guns immediately began to chatter. The men behind the cars opened up, firing at the overhead windows, shooting at nothing, so far as I could see, until from one window on the first floor the head and shoulders of a man fell out through the window and lay there, slumped in the jagged frame.

From where the entrance doors had stood, a woman appeared. She looked crazed, black, bushy hair everyway, blood in streaks down her face. She screamed.

'*Otodvintes!*' cried one of Vovo's men to her. 'Move away!'

But she stood there, screaming, fingering the blood. From somewhere inside a gun spoke and she crumpled. Vovo's men kept up their assault on the windows in prolonged bursts. Then, just as I discerned movement inside the doors, there came from the entrance avenue the sound of further gunfire.

Vovo emerged first from the house, a Uzi looking like a toy in his hands. I shouted. Vovo and I saw the first incoming jeep at the same time. Its driver wore a black military beret. Behind Vovo, Volodya had emerged, then Vassya, pushing a white-haired man along in front of him. A second jeep was arriving behind the first. From the door of the jeep, I began firing clips.

Vovo's men who had provided cover moved around to the back of their revving cars. Vovo moved fast. He had the back door of the Mercedes ajar and was dragging a missile launcher from it. The doors of the two incoming jeeps were opening. Flame roared from the barrel of Vovo's telescope-like weapon and the first jeep jumped three feet in the air, aflame.

'*Poekhali!*' Volodya was screaming. 'Let's go!'

The half-dressed, white-haired man was cowering in the shelter of the doorway. I saw another jeep career into view and hurtle straight across the front of the building through the field of fire. Three men had already disembarked from it and were wriggling across the cement, combat-style. Volodya was crouched on one knee, holding a pistol two-handed and emptying successive magazines at the soldiers' positions. Bullets whined by.

'Joe!'

Volodya was beckoning frantically for the jeep. At that moment the windscreen ahead of me popped and the driver fell silently across the passenger seat.

'Joe!'

'Open the rear doors!' I shouted as I saw two black berets come in wide to my right. Cuba scrambled back.

I crouched between the front seats, firing directly out where the windscreen should be. Kicking open the driver's door, I used my leg to heave the dead man out. Then I dropped into his seat. I kept firing. Wrenching the gears into reverse, I lurched back for the doors, bumping over the driver's body in the process.

'Joe!'

I whirled around at Cuba's cry. A soldier had materialized from nowhere at the rear. He was aiming. I knew I could not get the Beretta around in time. I swore. Then the soldier seemed to cough. He crumpled. I looked the other way. Vovo was lowering his gun hand.

'Thanks, Vovo,' I said, ramming the jeep backwards for the building, ejecting the spent magazine from the pistol and slamming in another.

'We're going to be killed,' I heard an unfamiliar voice cry.

'Carlos! Climb in!' Cuba was yelling.

As I watched, Vovo stepped out one pace from the Merc to get a better line-up on his target. To Vovo's left, hidden from the big Azeri, jumped a man with bright red hair. Marat.

'Vovo!' I cried.

Vovo looked at me. It was the wrong decision. Vovo's head was snapped back as if by garotte. He began to stagger. A red patch appeared high in his face. I saw Marat retreat around the corner of the building as my bullets tore the plaster work from the gable where he had stood.

Volodya had one arm of Carlos, Vassya the other. They ran with him the ten yards and threw him up into the jeep. Cuba began hauling Carlos further in. In one wing mirror, I saw Volodya dart out and snatch the missile launcher from Vovo's dead hands; in the other I saw Marat appear at the opposite end of the building to the one I had last seen him at. I loosed off a long burst and the red head once more ducked out of sight.

'*Drive*' Volodya cried and I felt the jeep rock as he leapt on board.

I floored the pedal, screamed for the bend, firing out in both directions at black berets until the Beretta clicked. Vassya sprinted after us, caught the swinging door and clutched his way on board the jeep.

'Lie flat on the floor!' Cuba was yelling to Carlos.

Coming straight at us up the avenue was a further military jeep.

'Watch out,' Volodya said.

Mounting the missile launcher on the back of the front seat, he discharged it. I felt heat singe the side of my face. Ahead of us on the avenue there was a sunburst and the jeep disintegrated.

'Shit!' I swore, wrenching the wheel to avoid airborne, flaming debris.

'Cuba, what is happening? Why are you here?' asked the voice from the floor.

'Relax,' she told him as we bumped out along the avenue. The entrance gate loomed ahead. 'You're bleeding,' she said to Volodya.

'*Nichevo!*' Volodya said. 'It's nothing.'

Bullets thumped our bodywork, but now they were coming from behind. I was coaxing all the power I could from the screaming Mitsubishi. I looked back. A jeep-load of pursuing soldiers had rounded the bend of the avenue. Ahead I could see the remains of the Volga with one man lying dead across its open door. A jeep lay on its back, wheels spinning. It looked like a dead dog. Without warning, Vassya cried out behind me, caught at his shoulder, spun around and fell out the back on to the roadway. I halted. The space to the oncoming jeep was shrinking. Volodya and I locked eyes. It was strange, I thought later, that two men who had known each other for such a relatively short time, could know each other so well.

'*Drive.*' Volodya spoke.

I put my foot down. Cuba dragged the doors over, but as she did so both back windows shattered, scattering glass shards viciously inside the jeep. We crashed out on to the highway. It was busier now with the first buses taking workers to the factories.

'Which way?' I asked grimly, trying not to think of the price we had paid to get thus far.

Volodya indicated left, away from Yekaterinburg. His face had gone strange. In my wing mirror I saw that from the opposite direction, two black limousines had turned off the highway and into the devastated entrance I had just left.

I drove west. Then, as if Volodya's wounds had lain low until escape from the hotel was certain, one moment he was giving me directions, the next he was lying in Cuba's arms, ashen. She turned him over and tore off his shirt.

'He's got a serious back wound,' she said calmly. 'A bullet or perhaps glass. Perhaps a pneumothorax – a collapsed lung.'

'We need a hospital,' I said, wrenching the wheel of the jeep and passing three crawling trucks.

'Out of the question. Either Marat or Nobu's men would find us in five minutes,' Cuba said. 'We've got to stay with the plan.'

'Then try to ask him where I'm meant to be going,' I said as we reached an intersection where long lines of cars and buses rolled in both directions. Dust and fumes blew in through the absent windscreen.

'Trucks, Volodya says,' Cuba said. 'Look for a yard with trucks.'

'But which way?'

She asked the question in Azeri and I could hear Volodya gasp the words.

'He says straight on,' Cuba said and I shot across through a gap in traffic, checking my wing mirrors for the tell-tale jeeps I knew must soon follow.

'Carlos?' I called, searching left and right as the blunt prows of Ladas went by. 'We need to find a truck yard.'

Carlos scrambled over the seat. His face was speckled red where it had stopped arrows of window glass. He was a slight if plump man, with the round, science-like spectacles and mat of head curls of his photographs. The road was crammed either side with factories, warehouses. Women stood at bus stops, shapeless men's jackets over their drab frocks, heavy work boots, kerchiefs over their heads.

'What about my sister?' Carlos blurted.

'What are you talking about?' I asked.

'My sister is being held somewhere nearby,' Carlos said. 'They promised me I would be brought to her today.'

'Carlos,' I said, 'your sister is in Bristol. Where she's been for the past year, waiting for you to come home.'

Carlos looked at me in disbelief. Then he covered his face with his hands and began to weep.

I nearly missed the wire fence with the line of trucks parked at its other side. I swung straight in through open gates. A man appeared, running, beckoning me to follow. I saw a wide ramp. The man ran straight up it, beckoning all the time. An open container was backed up to the other end. The signalling man ran into it and I followed into the darkness, hearing the hum of my tyres on the metal floor. I turned in my seat. Immediately, a forklift with high packages on pallets appeared and raced at us, dropped its pallets and screeched out again.

'Get some water,' Cuba cried. 'Someone get some water!'

A relay of forklifts was rapidly filling the rest of the metal box. I edged to the back.

'Water!' I cried to the man who had led us in. 'Medicine!'

A siren erupted. I was grabbed and pushed back down between pallets. The siren noise grew deafening. A vehicle had drawn up outside. From the jeep, only one or two shafts of light could now be seen as the forklifts completed the loading. I felt sweat cascading down my face. The container doors were slammed and bolted home. I fumbled another clip into the Beretta.

'*Ei, ti!*' said a voice outside. 'Hey you! Have you seen a jeep?'

'A jeep?' asked the man who had just pushed me back in. 'What kind of a jeep?'

'Does it matter what kind of a fucking jeep?' asked the questioner.

'I've seen no jeep.'

'What are these tyre marks, then?'

'They're the marks of the fucking forklift, what do you think they are?' answered the man indignantly.

The sudden roar of an engine seemed to come from within the container. I realized we had been hitched all the time to a truck cab.

'What's in the container?' I heard the questioner ask.

'Copper rods,' the man replied. 'Here, why don't you come into the office and talk to my boss.'

The jeep lurched as the container jerked away from the ramp, horn blaring. At any moment I expected the sound of gunfire, the impact of lead. I kept the Beretta cocked on my wrist, determined to make it very expensive for them.

But there was no gunfire, no lead. We drove.

58

Soby was in at six-thirty. Two other traders were already in place, checking out Tokyo and Sydney, their mugs of Starbucks steaming beside their screens.

'You'll love this, Soby,' one of them laughed.

Soby clicked on his screen. Trident leapt out at him, traded overnight in Tokyo at thirty dollars. New York would open with every short position running for cover as virgin chart ground was broken in the path of this rampaging bull. Soby's phone was ticking its red message eye. Soby frowned. He hadn't left the desk until ten-thirty the night before – who could have been ringing him in the meantime?

'Soby, it's me,' said Florence's voice, recorded at one o'clock the previous morning. 'No matter what time you get this message, call me at home,' and she left a 202 area code number. Washington DC. Soby obeyed.

'Soby,' she said.

He at once caught the uneasiness in her voice.

'Are you at your desk?'

Soby confirmed his position.

'I'll call ya there in five minutes,' Florence said.

Soby's digestive system felt as if he'd swallowed a cue ball. He checked his screen again. Some early trading was taking place and Trident was steady at thirty dollars – but Soby as usual took little comfort from the overnight surge for several reasons: the first was that the day before, Tim Tully, acting on behalf of Grace Equity in Dublin, had sold Trident short on three different occasions and in considerable volume. Our short position in Trident, executed at twenty-six, twenty-six fifty and twenty-seven dollars fifty now amounted to nearly a million units of Trident stock. The overnight movement meant that Grace was losing nearly three million dollars on the position, the effect of which would be an immediate margin call that morning, probably for five million dollars, the way the market was moving. But there was another reason, apart from the fact that his friend was losing money, to make Soby unhappy. Despite Tim's vigorous selling of shares Grace did not own, Soby himself had been unable to resist going in again the night before on the long side for his own account. The price he'd bought at was twenty-seven dollars, increasing his average price to over twenty-four dollars. Now his dilemma was whether the inevitable market correction would bring in nervous sellers and stop the bull run dead in its tracks, or worse, reverse it. There was still no hard news about a drug, the rising Trident price was fuelled purely by rumour and chart-driven speculation. Soby was what the market liked to term, if not a stale bull, then suddenly a very nervous one. He actually jumped as the phone flashed.

'I'm calling from a payphone,' Florence said.

Her anxiety was contagious; Soby suddenly wanted to sell everything and go home. But he managed to say, 'I'm listening.'

Florence was doing well under the circumstances, Soby later admitted. Although afraid, she was calm. A good lady, Soby would observe with some pride. Now she told him she feared her phone might be tapped, that there was general consternation in the FDA since midday the day before. It was as if all hell had broken loose as soon as he'd asked her to find out things about Trident. Not that the two things were connected, Florence assured him – it just felt like that.

'What did you hear?' Soby asked, keeping it casual.

Soby couldn't ever say she'd told him this, Florence whispered, but the info she'd been getting had come through a colleague in IND who worked in Pharmacology/Toxicology with a certain Dr Clarence Moss. Florence spoke as if just to voice the name might bring FBI agents from the walls of the phone booth. Dr Clarence Moss, a divorcé, had enjoyed several liaisons with female secretaries in his department, but in the case of Florence's contact, he had left her high and dry six months ago for a fresh inductee. Never so much as said thank you and goodbye, just dropped her. And so this one-time friend of the IND executive, a woman with a lot of self-respect who had enjoyed, among other trips, two weekends off Grand Cayman in Dr Clarence Moss's fifty-foot sloop, had turned to Florence a few months ago and talked. About Dr Moss's contacts within the pharmacological industry, about the doctor's not easily explained wealth which, this lady implied, might be of interest to the IRS, and about Trident.

Soby went cold. He had always known what he had been hearing was a tad irregular, but this had Grand Jury written all over it.

Then yesterday, Florence went on, a touch breathless, Dr Clarence Moss had disappeared. His desk at the FDA had been emptied, his files were gone. The phone in his DC apartment didn't answer, there was no explanation. And so, when the head of Pharmacology/Toxicology had called in Florence's contact and she had revealed what she knew of Dr Clarence Moss's work habits and lifestyle, a major internal investigation had been launched. The performance of Trident on Wall Street was being closely linked to Moss's disappearance. Everyone was being tight-lipped, Florence said, but this spelt Trouble with a capital 'T' for anyone associated with Moss. It was only a matter of time before the media found out. She thought Soby would like to know first.

'I appreciate it,' Soby said, 'I really do.'

'I'm not goin' to be able to call ya again, Soby,' Florence said, 'not until all this has died down.'

'I understand,' Soby told her.

When they had said goodbye, he sat in front of his screen, wondering how fast he could realize his entire long position – that is, sell it all and take his profit. He tried to stop his hands trembling as he reached for the phone. And even as he did, Trident traded at thirty-one dollars per share.

59

Half of one day had gone by. An hour into our journey, when the truck had cleared the suburbs of Yekaterinburg, the vehicle had halted, a panel the size of a family Bible had slid open and a bag had been hurriedly handed up to us. It had contained a first-aid kit, a flask of water and a bottle of vodka. On the back seat of the jeep, the only place in the moving container there was light, Volodya had lain, fighting for each breath like a man with a weight on his chest. On the shelf of the jeep sat his guns, a Smith & Wesson revolver and a Korth .357 Magnum, together with a clip of hundred dollar bills and his mobile telephone.

'He's got a condition known as tension pneumothorax,' Cuba said. 'He was hit in his mid-back and his lung was punctured and has collapsed. Air has been trapped between his chest wall and the damaged lung and this is now displacing into the good lung on the other side. If I don't perform a surgical procedure to release the trapped air, he's going to die.'

She spoke calmly and without emotion.

'I need a flexible tube of some kind, about the diameter of my little finger and six inches long. I need it fast.'

Carlos and I hunted around the jeep, but found nothing. Nothing either, to meet Cuba's specification, on the floor of the container. We turned out our pockets. Carlos shook his head.

'Open the bonnet of the jeep,' I said.

Carlos sprung the lid and I felt around in the gloom through coils of oily rubber and plastic. I clasped one end of a slender hose and yanked it free, then its other end until I was holding a semi-transparent length of plastic piping, dripping petrol. Carlos took it and wiped it as clean as he could on his shirt. I swigged a mouthful of vodka, then blew the alcohol through the pipe into my cupped hand. I used what I caught on the outside of the hose, then repeated the procedure three times.

Cuba said, 'I need the water.'

She held out her hands and I poured a half-cupful of vodka into them for her to disinfect.

'Let's do it,' she said as Carlos stood there with the water jerrycan.

Carlos helped me carry Volodya out of the jeep and turn him face down on the bonnet. Using the scalpel from the first-aid kit, Cuba sliced off the bandages she had already bound him in to staunch the blood, doused Volodya's back with vodka and with great care, began to cut away layers of flesh around the narrow entry wound.

He gasped each time she cut, then he passed out. Despite my attempts to swab it, blood flowed everywhere. The cavity Cuba had now opened was, at surface level, the diameter of an Irish pound coin. She sank in her thumb and forefinger, grimacing with concentration. I watched her try to get purchase as I swabbed the welling blood. It was no good, she couldn't grip whatever it was that was in there.

'Glass, I think,' she said. 'Still, maybe better than a bullet.'

Again using the scalpel, Cuba cut finely and more deeply. Blood leapt from a new vein.

'Come on, Volodya,' she cried. 'Leave it go!'

This time she drove in so far I thought she was going to go through him. Then ever so gingerly, centimetres at a time, she withdrew a sparkling and jagged glass shard, four inches in length. As I mopped frantically at the increased blood flow, Cuba immediately fed the tube into the wound. The blood seemed to check. Cuba positioned the end of the tube into the neck of the water jerrycan that Carlos was holding. Small bubbles appeared.

'How about that?' she said with a big smile. 'Not bad for a girl who hasn't done a surgical procedure in six years.'

Volodya was breathing with noticeable relief, even as Cuba packed the wound with antibiotic powder and gauze.

'What are his chances?' I asked when she sat back at last, exhausted.

'Like your deal,' she said. 'Fifty-fifty.'

60

We were heading west, for the Baltic. Volodya did not even breathe now, he gasped. He lay on the back seat, propped up on bundled clothes. The trauma of the impromptu operation had now replaced the wound as the cause for concern. The air stank, but we could not risk leaving on the jeep's fan for fear of running down the battery; and to start the vehicle's engine in the confines of the container would have been to suffocate us all.

Suddenly we stopped. Cuba bathed the sweat from Volodya's face. I tightened my grip on the Beretta. Again the floor panel opened. Sweet air swam in. A plastic water bottle was thrust through, then a paper bag, full of bread.

'*Akei?*' asked a voice quietly. 'Okay?'

The panel closed and the truck restarted.

We drank thirstily and tore the bread into hunks. The closeness was smothering. An alarming quantity of blood lay stickily all over the back seat and floor. We took turns in fanning Volodya's face.

Carlos and I sat on the bonnet. The jarring undulations of the road that pierced into every square inch of the container were somewhat reduced by the suspension of the jeep.

'I would never have worked for them had I not thought that Constance had been captured too,' Carlos said. 'But they knew so much I assumed she was being held. They brought me her clothes.'

'You did the right thing,' I told him.

'I had resigned myself to the fact that I would never come home,' Carlos said. 'That they would kill me, eventually. What else could they do, having stolen from me everything I knew?'

I nodded in the darkness that I understood, and Carlos spoke. We lumbered west.

He told me about his life and his background, fleshing out the substance of what I already knew. A childhood in Buenos Aires, then the family had moved to England. Carlos had won a scholarship to medical school in Liverpool and had led his class in each year on his way through. What McCoy's file had not conveyed was the man's sincerity. When Carlos spoke about his embryonic discovery, BL-4, it was with passion. He had a vision of what the drug might one day do, but he had spent his whole life in pharmacology and his most ardent desire was that BL-4 would not be taken over by one of the big companies. He wanted to take it as far as he could on his own – the whole way, if necessary. When early on he got bogged down in the FDA, he didn't despair. He would conduct his own trials and go back to the FDA when the drug was more advanced. That's when the approaches came: from Trident and Armentisia Lab.

'Armentisia too?' I asked.

Armentisia had, in fact, been there before Trident, but Carlos had told both companies he was not interested. Then out of the blue he got this approach from a private American investor named Carson McCoy.

I couldn't believe what I was hearing. 'You mean – McCoy came to you?'

'I can't remember what his story was, but it appeared to me he was one of these philanthropic Americans to whom a million dollars is not really all that much cash.'

I almost smiled, but I think I was too surprised by what I was hearing. The thought of McCoy and philanthropy being spoken in the same sentence verged on the amusing – but I had to hand it to the American, you had to move very fast to keep up with him.

Carlos described how McCoy offered to fund the development of BL-4 on a private basis. Then, twelve months before, in the course of a trip to California to evaluate results on bloods which Cuba was doing, Carlos was contacted out of the blue by Carson McCoy.

'He was so plausible, so kind, I liked the man. He contacted me in Los Angeles and told me he had decided to set up a laboratory in Mexico, that he had unlimited funds to develop viral drugs.'

I gasped as it hit me. McCoy and Groz had conspired together to abduct Carlos. And of course they had taken him to Mexico – far better to do the dirty work in the lonely foothills of the Sierra Madres than in the United States.

'I was taken to this place called Cobra where I was overpowered, then pumped full of sedatives,' Carlos said. 'When I came to I was being driven in a very old car in countryside I could not recognize.'

'Ireland,' I said.

'I needed a toilet, so we stopped at an old bar somewhere. I found a phone in the hall to the toilet and managed to speak briefly to Constance,' Carlos said. 'Then we were on an Aeroflot flight and I knew I was going to Russia.'

The truck hit a rough patch of road and the jeep bounced.

They brought him to Yekaterinburg and put him to work. The conditions were appalling. Carlos needed to make the anti-serum, so he asked for human placenta. But they knew that certain proteins were found in aborted foetuses, so they brought him those. He refused to use them. He said go ahead, shoot me. They almost did. It was the little victories that kept him going, he said. They accepted he would not use foetuses.

'*Vsyo budet khorosho, Volodenka*,' Cuba soothed inside the jeep. 'Volodya, it's going to be all right.'

Alan Gold came to the Urals twice to evaluate progress. Carlos pleaded with Gold to help him escape, but Gold was in so deep with Trident he was beyond reason. Carlos found him not very knowledgeable about HIV either. Gold could not seem to understand that you could not rush, that rushing always led to mistakes and problems. The problems were numerous. For patients, they brought Carlos drug addicts from Moscow and St Petersburg, but they were so debilitated in other ways that the experiments were a waste of time. They came with male prostitutes, Romanians and Czechs, mostly. Kids who did not know where they were in most cases. They just knew they were going to die. They were all housed in the hotel with Carlos. It was completely unsuitable. These boys had pneumocystis, some of them had appalling sarcomas. The kitchen people would not feed them, the guards wanted nothing to do with them. Their food was being thrown to them as if they were dangerous animals in a zoo. They were cooped up in this place, about thirty kids. One day they broke out. The guards refused to recapture them because that would mean coming into physical contact. They shot the whole lot of them before they could reach the road.

Once they brought in a truckload of North Koreans who had been deliberately infected. These men had been loggers, working as slaves in Siberian lumber camps. The Russians rounded up fifty of them, transfused HIV-infected blood into them and then brought them west to the Urals. Ten of them died on the journey. The others were too ill from other things for Carlos to experiment on them, but he knew what would happen to the patients if he said that. So he pretended to do trials on them. It was hopeless. Those that didn't die were shot like dogs.

'Did the anti-serum never work?' I asked.

Carlos explained that in a few cases, yes, it had. But that was when everything went as it should, even in the midst of such chaos. There were continual problems. But the trials were crazy. No one had bothered to find out what medication these patients were already on. So some of them just died. Some of them were drug- and alcohol-dependent, presenting its own problems. There was no heroin, just some mescaline in the lab, which Carlos gave to a couple of the worst cases, but that was soon gone.

Gold began to accuse Carlos of delaying progress. There were threats to both Carlos, and to Constance whom Carlos believed was being held in Moscow. Carlos did his best to work under the conditions, despite the fact that in the lab the ability of the technicians to analyse the patients' blood samples was very basic. Carlos had to train them from the start in the need to document everything. They would do infusions with BL-4 and then take a batch of blood and the samples would get lost or broken, or the results would be mysteriously out of synch. The Russian lab people continually took short-cuts because they had been told to save time.

'A month ago they brought in boys from Romania. Most of them should still have been in school. It was heartbreaking.' Carlos shuddered. 'Then yesterday, for no reason, a man appeared and ordered them out in front of the hotel.'

'Red hair?'

'How did you know?'

'I'm learning.'

'He shot them as we looked out the windows.' Carlos shook his head as if still dazed by the experience. 'Boys. He shot them because I assume the programme had been terminated for some reason and he had no further use for them.'

Carlos put his face in his hands.

'Why do we try to save human life if this is what we human beings do to each other?' he asked. 'Why go to the trouble of prolonging something that has become so debased? We are not worth saving, is the answer. The virus will conquer, because as a species, we deserve to become extinct.'

'What have the Russians got after a year?' I asked quietly, trying not to let it show that my livelihood depended on the answer to the question.

'Probably at this stage enough to claim they have a process that boosts CD4s. Probably enough to license something to Trident and allow Trident to develop the drug.'

I felt light-headed. We'd lost.

'But it's not a drug yet, not by a long shot,' Carlos said. 'It's going to take much more time. I explained that fact to Gold again and again. And each time he kept telling me, time was the one thing they did not have.'

'Oh boy,' I said and grinned. 'If only Soby could be here.'

61

The noise had become part of our heads. After ten hours we could ride the bumps reflexively. Volodya's shallow breath was still there as the engine of the big truck paused between its gears. Conditions were deteriorating. Flies had discovered Volodya's stale blood; I had used some of our precious water to sluice down the seats and floor of the jeep. We had stopped twice in the past hour: once for a police highway patrol and once for the driver to smuggle in more water and food to the container. We had all three stooped over the tiny trapdoor and sucked in blessed night air.

'*Isho dolgo?*' Cuba whispered to the driver. 'How much longer?'

'Twelve hours,' came the man's reply.

He seemed frightened, as if the Russian night, no matter how vast and empty, had ears. Cuba asked him if we would be passing near a hospital, but the man told her it was too risky. Petrowski's bulls were searching everywhere. And Nobu's local affiliates. Cars. Helicopters. Volodya would have to wait until we reached Estonia.

Some time in the following three hours, the truck stopped yet again. Voices. My hand tightened on the Beretta. The sound of diesel flowing into the tank. Men laughed. The engine restarted and we lurched forward.

I fought to keep track of time as we bumped and droned across the endless steppe. I dozed and snapped awake, hot steel shooting up my neck. Volodya did not appear to change. We took turns to keep the flies off the Azeri's pallid face. Each breath Volodya took made his chest leap a little and seemed to be his last until the next, desperate gulp came.

I slept at the wheel of the jeep, fitfully, the sides of the container rushing in and out at me, my head begging to fly. I was not in transit from the Urals to the Baltic, but in a room of blinding white. A strong smell of antiseptic, curtains round a bed. I was in a group of five. The face in the bed I knew like my own. We sat around him, waiting for the next breath. It did not come. We watched his chest, at the same time both fearful and glad. It was over. No more pain. Then we held each other tightly as the woman put her hand around the thin wrist, warm for the last time to her touch. We were all connected, all five. One circuit. That could not be broken by anything, least of all death. Who would have thought that something so feared and ugly could be attended by such sweetness? Birds sang outside the evening window.

62

I jumped awake and my head hit the roof of the jeep. The images from my dream had entombed my heart in despair, for the significance of what I had dreamed was clear. Cuba and Carlos were both asleep, Cuba on the back seat beside Volodya, Carlos outside, tucked into the front wheel of the jeep. I took out my cellphone and switched it on. There was a strong signal. I pressed out the number.

'Hello?'

'Laura, it's me.' I had to shout to make myself heard above the truck. 'How is John?'

I couldn't make out the substance of her reply, but thought I heard a catch in her voice. My knees gave out.

'Laura? What's happened?' I asked, seeing again the whiteness from my dream, believing now that I had, over a distance of continents, been somehow with him as he set out on his last journey.

But then the line opened up, clear as a church bell and I just sat there dumbly, uncomprehending. Laura was laughing.

'. . . I said, he's pulled through. His temperature is back to normal, he's sitting up and he's eating.'

Funny things, tears. They seemed determined to come out, whether for grief or joy.

'Thank God,' I said, wondering at myself, even as I said it. Old habits die hard. 'Thank God.'

'Joe? Where are you?'

'The truth is, I don't know.'

'Well, Tim Tully has been on three times in the last few hours from Dublin, wondering if you'd been in touch.'

Tim's name sounded like a tone from a different galaxy,

one of these sonar impulses snatched back from the far reaches of the heavens.

'What did he want?'

'He said it's critical you call him without delay,' Laura said.

'He said "critical"?'

'That's what he said.'

I told Laura I loved them all and hung up. I knew I shouldn't have been using a cellphone since both Nobu's and Petrowski's scanners must have been working overtime. Nevertheless, Tim had said critical. I called Dublin and prayed he'd be there and would pick up. The power of prayer.

'It's me.'

'Holy Christ!' Tim said.

I said, 'Is Hanny okay?'

'Hanny's fine,' Tim said. 'I'm the one to worry about. I've aged ten years today. Where are you?'

'Long story. What's yours?'

'Joe, we're losing our shirt on these fucking Trident shorts,' Tim said. 'It's just broken through thirty-five dollars a share.'

63

That day Soby committed the stock trader's equivalent of mortal sin. Having sold out half his position in Trident at thirty-one dollars and 50 per cent of what was left at thirty-one dollars sixty, he then watched as Trident rose like the rocket carrying the Space Shuttle, first to thirty-four, then thirty-five dollars a share. The only news on the Reuters screen was that Trident would make a statement that evening on a new drug which was still in evaluation. During the morning Soby bought back nearly four hundred thousand Trident at an average price of thirty-two dollars fifty, using his new purchases to cancel out his sales of earlier and taking a hefty loss, half a million bucks, on the transaction. Everything was relative, however. Apart from that hiccup, Soby was now back in the situation he had started the day, the owner of five hundred thousand Trident at an average price of twenty-four dollars – except that Trident was now last traded at thirty-five dollars. Soby was making overall the bones of five and a half million dollars – and most of it since last night.

'It's goin' to forty dollars!' said a trader across the desk.

'Fifty dollars if their statement says they've cured AIDS,' said another.

Soby personally authorized a ten million dollar margin call on Grace Equity in Dublin; Tim Tully, utilizing an account in Citibank, paid the money within fifteen minutes of the demand.

'Jesus wept,' Soby said as Trident traded at thirty-five dollars fifty twice, then twice again. 'This is too bad to be true.'

What he meant was that he had never before seen

anyone lose money quite so spectacularly as we were then losing ours, but that at the same time, he could not believe that I had been so wrong or had let a personal vendetta get in the way of my trading decisions. And so, even before the phone rang, Soby had made a decision which, had he taken it an hour beforehand, would have gone down as one of the great moves of timing ever seen on Wall Street, but even so, as it was, ensured that he would live to tell the tale. He decided, whether or not Trident was going to one hundred dollars a share, that he did not want to be in any longer. He had, of course, made the same decision that morning, but had been weak enough to reverse it. Now he actually got up from his desk and went to the men's room. There, he rinsed his hands and face, dried himself with a paper towel, looked at his reflection in the mirror – gaunt, mournful, unhappy – and said, 'Do it, you stupid sonofabitch! *Do it!*'

In Dublin at almost that precise moment, Tim Tully made a telephone call to Denver, Colorado.

'We're losing our ass,' he spoke. 'Joe said to call you.'

The voice on the other end was rock steady. 'Sell the bastard,' Minx said. 'Sell it to hell.'

When Soby re-emerged to the clamour of the trading room, someone was calling, 'Soby! On six!'

He hit the key.

'Have you seen the news?'

He had to funnel in on the voice before he recognized it; Florence had said she would not be calling again.

'News?' Soby said, his eyes eating the screen two feet away.

'Oh, Soby, it's not good,' Florence said, 'I just hope there was nothing I said, or that you picked up on, that caused this to happen, because . . .'

Soby didn't hear the end of what she was saying. His eyes had hit the screen.

Washington DC. High-ranking FDA employee found dead near Potomac. More.

Now here was the thing, as Soby often said afterwards. Had he not known the background, the announcement would have meant nothing. There was no name. No one at that point could have said that a dead body near the Potomac River could have had any bearing on the announcement about a new drug due that evening from a company in upstate New York called Trident. As it was, Soby reckoned he had all of a two-minute start. He nearly made it. Selling in lots of ten thousand shares, he got fifty thousand away at thirty-five dollars and the same number at thirty-four dollars eighty. Nice and quiet. There was other news around. The dollar was trading at new heights on foreign exchanges. Madonna had a new boyfriend.

And then Soby's floor trader said the words that instilled fear into a thousand hearts.

'There's somethin' goin' on here, Soby, maybe it's a technical hitch, but the bid's showin' thirty-two dollars.'

'Take it,' Soby ordered.

'You're crazy,' the man said, 'like I said, it's gotta be technical, we're goin' to forty dollars tonight with this one.'

'Take it!' Soby rasped. 'Hit the fuckin' bid!'

But even as he spoke, he heard someone across the room crying, 'Soby! They're saying there's some FDA guy put a shooter in his mouth down in DC and it's connected someway to Trident!'

Soby, although breathless all of a sudden, was calm. He smiled, he said later, broadly. And he kept smiling as he fed his sell orders in.

'I knew it,' he said, 'I fuckin' knew it.'

The colleague at the next desk, so unused to merriment from his esteemed associate, leaned over at one stage and asked, what was it that Soby knew.

'I knew that sonofabitch in Ireland had somethin' up his sleeve,' Soby said. He looked at the man. 'D'you know what this is costin' me?'

The trader nodded sympathetically. He was a decent man and went by the dictum, 'There but for the grace of God go I.'

'How much?' he asked.

'Two boxes of Montecristo and a humidor,' Soby said and began to laugh.

64

Twice in the course of the morning we stopped, once to take on more fuel, and once for the trapdoor to be opened and for food to be given in. The air was like champagne. We drank it in and felt the badness flow from the cramped space.

And Volodya had made it. His fever had passed and he was breathing easily. Conscious now, he was half-sitting up, able to take in what was going on – which wasn't a lot. The flies, the murky, ever-trundling mausoleum that had become our new home, the smell of the blood which we had not been able to remove. On the second stop, the driver came and crouched beneath us, talking to Cuba, using place names that I recognized.

'It seems we have by-passed Moscow to the north and are now near Kalinin,' Cuba explained. 'We will cross the Volga and travel north for a hundred miles, and turn east for Pskov. We will then be in sight of Estonia.'

'How long more will it take?' asked Carlos.

'He says another six or seven hours,' Cuba said. 'He has a short-wave radio and has heard other drivers further east talking about troop movements and every vehicle being stopped. He hopes to enter Estonia this evening by a little-used route.'

As she spoke, there was the sound of a helicopter somewhere in the vicinity. The driver whispered urgently and dropped down further. He was a dark-skinned man with blue eyes and a drooping, sorrowful moustache that seemed to anticipate the worst. The trapdoor clicked to. We could hear him climb up into the cab. We restarted.

There had been no signal on my cellphone for three

hours – not that I had kept it switched on all the time, but on the few occasions I had checked it, it had been unable to find a network. I wondered how that world was getting on. I thought of Hanny mostly and all the things I wanted to tell her – things about myself that I had discovered. And I wanted some day soon to introduce her to Carlos and Cuba and to Volodya. Something important had happened since I had left Ireland for Moscow, something had changed. I wanted Hanny to be part of that change.

Another stop, and by the sounds and the light outside it was mid-afternoon. The driver brought a flask of hot water, gave Cuba his update in his usual, lighthearted way, restarted the truck. Cuba poured the water into the lid of the flask, stirred sugar into it and blew it cooler before bringing the cup to Volodya's lips. Carlos sat in the front seat, gazing at Cuba. His look had the radiance I remembered as a child, of people sitting in church, staring at a statue of the Virgin or at the exposed Host: a look of awe and adoration. She, in turn, smiled at Carlos with unlimited benevolence. Sometimes they chatted quietly, laughing. No barriers. Her intelligence was like a strong undercurrent to her beauty. She had come all this way for him. He was a lucky man, I thought.

And what about me and Hanny? She too had been guided as if by an unwavering light to the true good at the core of the muddle I'd been dropped into. You could travel all your life and not find women like these, I realized. They changed everything, day and night, life and death, they made stubborn men pray for another chance and they held the gift of great love for those strong enough to find it.

Carlos got out of the jeep, stretched and came to sit beside me.

'What will you do when you get home to Bristol?' I asked.

'Try to develop the anti-serum,' he said. 'Obviously I believe in it, but it still needs to be proved conclusively that it works. That means going back to where I was a year ago. Finding a company with the money needed to develop BL-4 who will use it the way I want – which means retail it to people who need it, at a price they can afford and without any delay.'

'How long will that take?' I asked.

'Three years at least,' Carlos said. 'Perhaps more. We havc to start from scratch again with the FDA. There must be proper facilities, trained scientists, trials done to international specifications. It will cost millions. I believe it will work. But there is always the possibility with this virus that it will produce a defence you least expect and that you thought impossible.'

After some time, Cuba came to join us.

'You know something strange?' she said. 'I love this big, crazy country. I loved it as a child and I love it now, no matter what has happened. One day it will get better. A country is its people and people want order, in the end. They want justice. They want a safe place to live and bring up their kids. Food to eat. Warmth. Safety. All the usual things. Sometimes that takes a country a hundred years to achieve. But in the end, the goodness is what counts.'

65

We had pulled up. I strained to sift through the sounds outside. No traffic of a busy city. Or sound of fuel pumps. No talk between the driver and the people of the place in which he had come to a halt. Nothing. The floor panel dropped open.

'Psst!'

Cuba went to the square of light and kneeled. There was the sound of rain.

'*Da?*'

The driver spoke urgently.

'He says we are almost on the border with Estonia,' Cuba whispered. 'But there are vehicles on the road half a mile ahead. He is not sure whose. He has pulled in here to see if they will go away.'

The man left the panel open. I heard his footsteps outside on the hard surface of the road. Then there was a single shot, like a powerful whip-crack. I heard a shout. All at once, the sound of many vehicles was deafening.

'*Shto zdes proiskhodit?*' cried Cuba out the hole in the floor. 'What is happening?'

I seized the Beretta. Motioning Cuba and Carlos to get down under the jeep, I stepped into it, caught up Volodya as gently as I could and manoeuvred him out, then laid him on the floor next to the trapdoor. But the metal holding bar on the back of the container was being levered down. I heard both doors thrown back as tiny shafts of daylight found their way into the long, metal box. There were gruff commands. One by one the pallets were dragged out and pitched on to the road. I steadied my firing hand on the front wing of the jeep. With the removal of each pallet, the sound of rain, and of the vehicles, became clearer. After nearly forty hours, to see the sky again and to hear rain should have been a joy. I tried to adjust my eyes to the light. I could see hooks pull the last pallet slowly out and pitch it down with a crash.

'Grace?'

I knew the voice.

'You can either all come out now, on the count of five, or else I get these men to demonstrate their grenades,' said Dr Roberto Groz.

66

Cuba went first. I threw the Beretta on to the road. Then Carlos and I lifted Volodya down. It was a pine forest. The rain was bringing out the scent from the trees, delicious if the circumstances were somewhat different. Rain bathed the roadside. You looked left and right and saw just the reddish outline of the bark soon lost in the darkness of woods.

Groz was totally out of place. He wore a long, dark woollen coat. A white collar, a tie. His black shoes gleamed, his trousers were creased. A Chechen held an umbrella over Groz's brown, curly head. He should have been going to a board meeting on Wall Street, not standing in a Baltic forest, surrounded by a phalanx of Chechens. They all, except Groz, carried guns. Outside the ring of Chechens a further circle of black-bereted soldiers with rifles had formed. Their jeeps and cars blocked the road either side of the container. Sprawled to one side, his mouth gaping and pink under his sorrowful moustache, lay the dead body of our driver. Standing over him, red hair bared to the rain, dressed in a black leather coat, was Marat. I instinctively did a head count: four Chechens plus Groz, six militia, Marat. Ten to one. Unattractive odds.

The militia body-searched each of us thoroughly, and when they came to Cuba, there was much laughter. A soldier found my cellphone in my breast pocket. He held it aloft.

'Such things don't work here, Grace,' said Groz with a tired smile, 'just in case you were thinking of using it to get help. I've tried mine. Perhaps another small miscalculation?'

He hitched a shoulder and the soldier dropped the

phone back in my coat. Marat snapped out an order and two of the militia came over and grabbed Volodya. They threw him down on the grass by the roadside. One took out and levelled a pistol. Cuba screamed.

'*Stop!*'

She rushed across and threw herself on Volodya.

'You will not shoot him like a dog!'

Marat laughed and the two men dragged her off.

'For Nobu,' I heard Marat say as the man brought his pistol to Volodya's pale, defiant face.

A sudden crackle of radio static filled the beat of time in which the pistol shot had been expected. Marat held up his hand for quiet. I saw the Armenian's trigger finger relax. Marat was listening intently to a short-wave hand-held. He spoke to Groz. The chairman and the chief executive officer of Trident Drug frowned, then nodded. Marat spoke urgently to the men and three of them peeled off to the jeeps and started them.

'Load him in,' whispered Groz from gritted teeth, motioning Carlos and myself to Volodya. 'Hurry!'

Then, in the haste to get out of there, to avoid who- or whatever it was that Marat had heard on his radio, there was a golden moment. Marat was still digesting what he had heard, Marat's men and the Chechens were reacting to the order to get loaded up, Groz's attention was on Carlos and myself, and on Volodya. No one, for several seconds, bothered with Cuba. Several seconds was all she needed. One moment she was beside me, the next she was twenty yards away. Marat whirled. He fired two shots from reflex, but I could see the bullets kick up ground well behind and to the left of Cuba's shrinking heels.

'Stop her,' Groz spoke.

Rifles clattered, but Cuba's athleticism, something I had accepted as inherent to her but had had no occasion to see proven, was now ratified in spectacular fashion. Like a character in a cartoon she was literally disappearing from our vision. One of the militia readied and sought the shot, but Marat knew he was too late.

'Leave her,' Groz was saying. 'Come on.'

Cuba had now rounded the bend of the road west.

'That's the girl,' I said and turned with what I knew was a big grin.

Then I saw Groz's cold face multiply into frames beyond number and night fell.

67

It was the air on my face that brought me round. I was kneeling on stony ground. I dry retched.

'Stand him up.'

Uncompromising hands hauled me to my feet. I steadied myself on the wing of a jeep. Despite the fact that I could guess what was coming, and that my head throbbed, and that my legs were refusing to co-operate with my brain, I was able, albeit briefly, to marvel at the view. The convoy had come to a halt at a pass between mountains. For hundreds of miles the vista was of trees and lakes and rolling hills.

'So the chickens do really come home to roost.' Groz was standing in front of me, smiling quietly and rubbing his jaw. 'I should have pursued you all the way before. That was my mistake. But I evidently learn better from my mistakes than you do.'

Carlos was standing to one side, Volodya was lying on the ground. I wondered if the Azeri was dead and then reckoned I would have heard the gunshot. Only Marat and three Chechens had disembarked, the others were still in the jeeps whose engines were running. They had not planned to waste time on this stop.

'What are you going to do with Carlos?' I asked.

Groz looked at me, then shrugged as if to say it no longer mattered whether I knew or not.

'He's going back to the Urals to finish what you interrupted. It's primitive, but I shall oversee certain upgrading of his facilities. What a pity you won't be around to see the outcome.'

'You're crazy, Groz,' I said.

'Words, Grace, words. History will be the judge of

which of us is the crazy one.' Groz turned to the Chechen nearest him and snapped his fingers. The Chechen placed a heavy revolver into Groz's hand.

'Now I'm going to indulge myself,' Groz said quietly.

The other two Chechens grabbed me on each side and hauled me over to stand on the rough ground away from the jeeps. All the saliva drained from my mouth.

'Groz!'

Carlos had taken two steps over the road. Marat clicked off the safety on his Heckler & Koch.

Carlos said: 'You don't have a drug yet! I'll do whatever you want, but only if you let these people go.'

Groz turned his eyes.

'I don't need to do deals with you, you idiot.'

The gun was two feet from my temple and level.

'Goodbye, Grace.'

I saw Groz's finger squeeze and I thought of Hanny. And then, like a trapped bird, the telephone in my pocket sang. Its tone rang out over the pine-clad Estonian border mountains like a miniature, electronic symphony. Groz's two eyebrows met. No more than me had he anticipated a signal up here above the hills and forests. I saw his trigger finger ease a millimetre. The bird in my pocket sang. And sang. For some reason, I thought of Salman.

'Your phone's ringing,' Groz said, puzzled. 'How is that possible?'

'You obviously need to upgrade your own equipment,' I said.

'Answer it!' he snapped.

I looked to either side, to the two big Chechens each with one of my arms held by the wrist. Groz nodded.

'Hello?' I said, shaking myself free, the phone to my ear.

'Joe, it's Tim.'

'Hello, Tim.'

'Are you all right?'

'Well, let's say, I'm glad you called.'

'Look,' Tim said, 'I know you may be otherwise tied up, but I just had to call you with this news. You won't believe what's happening in New York. Are you listening?'

'Shoot.'

'You're not going to believe this, but Trident Drug has just fallen out of fucking bed!'

I felt my chest fill in a way it had not since January.

'Go on.'

'The selling began in Tokyo last night,' Tim said. 'It went down like a knife to thirty dollars before the New York market even opened. We're making a fortune. Last night in Washington, a top virologist in the FDA committed suicide, apparently because he was selling information to Dr Groz and then trading in Trident stock himself. Politicians are calling for a special enquiry. But the big story is Dr Alan Gold. He's currently out on half a million dollars bail having confessed this morning to his part in kidnapping Carlos Penn.'

I willed myself to keep my eyes on Groz; his blue eyes behind his gun hand still unwavering.

Tim was saying: 'It's the only item on all the news bulletins. It's crazy!'

'That's the best news I've heard today,' I said.

'Hold on,' Tim said. 'I've got Soby on the other line.'

I could hear Tim speaking into the other phone. I could not keep the wide grin off my face, despite the gun muzzle three inches from it.

'What are you calling it now, Soby?' Tim cried. 'Joe? Did you catch that? Trident is trading at twenty-one dollars! It's a rout!'

'What's happening?' asked Groz.

'I'm just listening to music,' I said.

'*Please repeat!*' Tim cried to his other phone. 'Christ Almighty! Joe? Trident's just traded at eighteen dollars with sellers over!'

'Carlos.'

I could see Carlos from the corner of my eye.

'Tell Volodya he's now a legitimate millionaire,' I said.

'Joe? What do you want to do, Soby is asking?' Tim was bawling. 'He thinks this could be just a market correction. He says you should grab your profits.'

'Tell him to call you back when the stock is ten dollars traded,' I said.

'*What?*'

'You heard.'

I heard Tim shout to Soby.

'Soby says you're crazy,' Tim said.

'Tell him I already know that,' I said, 'and ask him where he'd like to send my new humidor.'

'So, we don't buy in,' Tim said with more than a hint of exasperation.

'We don't buy in,' I said.

Groz was transfixed.

'What is it?' he rasped and his finger tightened.

I held the telephone out to him. 'It's for you,' I said.

Groz looked at the telephone as if it might be trained to bite. He put his hand out for the phone. I handed it over. There was but a fraction of a second needed for him to focus on the instrument. His eyes twitched. I hit him with the top of my head and heard the revolver discharge like thunder beside my eardrum. Even as Groz was falling, I was back on the first Chechen, taking him stiff-armed across the throat. Pivoting, I kicked the other full in his stomach making his dark glasses pop off.

The men with Marat were searching for a target with their guns. As I dived I saw Carlos dragging Volodya in beneath the jeep. But now the other jeeps were emptying. Bullets began gouging up jagged lines across the mountain. Marat's troops were weaving towards us. I scrambled wildly back for Groz's inert body. Abruptly, one of the men with Marat fell backwards, hands on his throat. As I grabbed the pistol from Groz's unconscious hand, I could hear Tim's indignant voice coming from the abandoned phone.

'Joe? Joe? What's going on there, Joe?'

I rolled for the jeep and loosed off one shot as I did so. It caught Marat and he arched. One for Aleksandr, you bastard, I swore. I rolled twice more. And one for Vovo, I said as I squeezed off the second shot, just before I made the big wheel. Marat threw both hands to his head, spun and pitched forward. I was aware of gunfire coming from outside our circle. The Chechens and the militia were diving for cover, too, from fire that was pinning them down by their vehicles. A Chechen in dark glasses holding a sub-machine gun, stood up and unclipped the ring from a grenade. Before he could hurl it, he doubled over and fell. I pressed my face to the ground. The man exploded.

I could see blue berets weaving from rock to rock fifty yards out. Two of Marat's men tried to make a break for it, back along the road to the leading jeeps. They fell to a barrage of shots.

Suddenly one of the soldiers on the road jumped to his feet, threw down his rifle and stuck his hands in the air. The others did the same, one by one. Then the Chechens.

From over the skyline a helicopter erupted. It swooped down and settled on the road surface, twenty yards away.

All at once there were soldiers either side, shouting commands, picking up weapons, checking bodies. Carlos and I helped Volodya out and to his feet. Cuba was running over from the helicopter beside a young officer in combat gear.

'We're okay, Cuba,' I called. 'We made it.'

I could see she was weeping.

The officer, his khaki tunic set off by a blue silk kerchief around his neck, strode over to us.

'You are in the Republic of Estonia,' he said in an American accent. 'You are all under arrest.'

68

From the top floor of the village town hall you could see a mile away to a south-facing slope where a man with a horse was cutting hay in the sunlight. It was such a gradual thing. Inch by inch the swathe fell behind the horse-drawn blade. The sun flitted in and out of clouds, bringing great bands of colour to the hills and making the wings of seagulls luminous.

Too many people were crowded into the upstairs room. Apart from Cuba, Volodya, Carlos and myself, there was Groz, and two Chechens, and four young, alert Estonian soldiers with rifles, guarding the door. Four more soldiers stood outside, I could see, every time the door opened. The floor was bare boards. An old roll-top desk and ancient leather chair stood in one corner. Volodya was in the only other chair with Cuba beside him. Carlos stood in a corner. Groz paced the floor impatiently. As the door opened again and the young officer who had taken us in entered, Groz stepped up to him.

'Captain, we need to have a business conversation,' he said.

The officer stopped and slowly turned to look at Groz.

'What did you say?'

Groz said, 'I'm sure Estonia levies fines and so forth on people who stray without permission into its territory, and so I wish to make it clear that the means to pay such fines exist.'

'Are you trying to bribe me, you shithole?' the officer asked.

'Quite the opposite, sir,' Groz smiled, undeterred. 'I'm simply trying to put the situation in a business context.

Why? Because I am a businessman and so, no offence intended.'

'Jesus Christ,' the officer said in disgust. 'I left the States and came here to get away from sleaze-bags like you.' He turned to Volodya in the chair. 'I'm arranging for this man to be transferred immediately to a military hospital. We're waiting for an ambulance to arrive from Voru.'

'I'll go with him,' Cuba said.

'Captain!'

The officer turned to Groz.

'I need to use your telephone,' Groz said.

'The telephones are out,' the officer said. 'But even if they were working, who were you going to call? Your lawyer?'

'Grace, what about your phone?' Groz asked.

'I gave it to you,' I said.

'Jesus Christ!' Groz swore.

The soldiers at the door laughed. Whether or not they understood, they were enjoying the show at Groz's expense.

An official came to the door and announced that the ambulance had arrived. Four soldiers carried in a litter and lifted Volodya on to it. He was one shade of pale away from death, but still he managed a smile as he was carried out past me.

'Tell him, we'll have a business meeting soon,' I said to Cuba. 'In Ireland. I have a few projects he might like to look at to invest his profits in.'

She kissed me lightly on the cheek, then put her arms around Carlos and held him tightly before she left the room.

'These people are in the dark ages,' Groz said. 'It's a tinpot country. I could buy it, the whole thing. I could write a cheque now and buy Estonia.' He jumped to his feet. 'I got to use a telephone,' he said, not addressing anyone, and walked to the door.

Two soldiers put up their rifles, blocking the way.

'I got to use a telephone, you dumb bastards!' Groz yelled.

The soldiers shoved Groz back.

'This is ridiculous,' Groz said to himself. He walked over to the street window and stood with his head down, breathing hard. 'I probably employ more people than live within fifty miles of this place. I need to use a phone.'

The four soldiers were getting real value from the situation. They spoke to each other from the sides of their mouths and laughed.

Groz walked back to them. 'I need to use a telephone! You understand? Tell your superior officer I want to talk to the army commander in Estonia. The head man. Tell him to get the Commander in Chief on the telephone and that Dr Roberto Groz wants to talk to him.'

The troops grinned.

'*Pozovite polkovnika!*' Groz yelled in Russian. 'Get your superior officer in here! Fast!'

'Fast!' one of the soldiers said and the others laughed outright.

Groz sat on an upright chair. At last his eyes found me. 'Just wait until word gets up the line that I'm here and watch what happens. I guarantee you, I'll be in New York this evening and you and your *mafiosi* will be on your way to a jail in Siberia.'

I said, 'You spent a year trying to squeeze a drug out of Carlos but you failed.'

Groz laughed, genuinely amused.

'Do you think it matters now whether Trident has a drug or not? The important thing is that the public believes we have. Which in fact we may well have if we can perfect the little we've learned from this emotional cripple.' He looked at Carlos. 'But as long as the public believes it, the stock will continue to rise. That's all I care about. If you're really a businessman, you'll understand.'

'I understand perfectly,' I said. 'You're the one who doesn't understand.'

Groz shook his head. 'Have you any idea how much I'm worth?'

'Net, probably in the region of six hundred million dollars,' I said. 'But only if Trident holds up over forty dollars a share.'

'You're smart, but how smart?' Groz smiled. 'The average price at which I hold Trident is twenty bucks. Do you know how many Trident I own? Between trusts and different family accounts? Two hundred and fifty million. I'm sure you can work it out.'

'But you borrowed cash to buy those shares, Groz,' I said. 'You pledged all your other assets too. You owe at least three hundred million dollars to the banks, is my bet.'

Groz shrugged. 'Big numbers scare you, I think, Grace,' he said.

'The charts would scare me if I held Trident and it broke thirty dollars on the downside,' I said. 'The charts look as if it will then fall all the way to twenty dollars very fast. Every computer-enhanced trading operation in New York will sell the shit out of it through twenty dollars. Then fifteen. Without a drug, it's doubtful if Trident is even worth fifteen dollars.'

Groz smiled in exasperation and shook his head.

'You're full of shit, Grace,' he said. 'Who told you that?'

'Someone you probably don't even remember,' I said. 'She was once a perky kid but you took away her zest for life because even back then she had you spotted for the scumbag you really are. But now it's her turn and I imagine she's really enjoying it.'

He looked at me with genuine bewilderment. 'Who are you talking about?'

'Do you not remember? Carmine Dominguez.'

A shadow of fear crept into Groz's face before he caught hold of it and shook himself free.

'I live in the present,' he said. 'You live in the past.'

'On the contrary. I live very much in the present. Which is why at under fifteen dollars a share, I'm a buyer of Trident.'

Groz looked at me sharply.

'What do you mean?'

'I'm a buyer of Trident under fifteen dollars,' I said. 'Under fifteen dollars I start to buy in the shares I sold at thirty dollars. Everyone's doing it. Grace Equity, Minx, half of Wall Street by the sound of things. Even Volodya, ask him next time you see him. Nothing like the quantities that you wallow in, of course. Just a million shares here and there. We're grateful to you for the opportunity, by the way.'

'You're a pygmy,' Groz said despairingly, shaking his head and looking at his watch like a man outside the office whose wife is late again with the car.

All at once the door opened and the officer walked back in.

'Captain, you're doing a good job,' said Groz calmly, 'but if I were to tell you that sums of money at least as large as the gross national product of this country could depend on my making a phone call, then I'm sure you could find a way of helping me out.'

Ignoring him, the officer turned to me. 'Is this yours?' he asked, holding up my cellphone.

'Thank you.'

The Estonian handed me my telephone, shrugged and left the room.

'Okay, Grace,' Groz sighed. 'How much? I'll call my bank first and have them transfer whatever you want. It's a business transaction, I understand. I don't hold it against you, I'd probably do the same. It's a market, everything is a market. You own something, you sell it to the highest bidder. We both understand.' Groz snapped his fingers impatiently. 'Come on, Grace! How much? Just say it. I need that phone.'

I handed Groz the telephone. 'Be my guest.'

Groz looked at me with grave suspicion. Then he took the telephone. The room fell quiet. The Chechens and the soldiers stared. We all looked as Groz pressed out the numbers.

'It's Dr Groz!' he said in a ringing, confident voice. He smiled disdainfully at me. 'How is the market this morning?'

Groz's eyebrows twitched once.

'I'm in . . . Eastern Europe,' he replied to the question. He laughed. 'Best not to say where exactly, you know these people. What? You have? I'm sorry I've been out of contact, but there have been a few . . . technical problems over here that I've had to sort out. So, how are we looking this afternoon – or morning as it is with you?'

The smile never quite left Groz's face. It seemed pinned there by something less reliable than muscle. He blinked once or twice.

'I see,' he said quietly. 'No. I'll call you.'

Groz stood, his weird half-smile under a perplexed frown.

'It traded down to twelve dollars,' he said to me as if we both might be interested in a curious phenomenon. 'It's been suspended. The whole market's down. If Trident opens again it's expected to be less than ten dollars.'

Groz handed me back the telephone. He walked back to

the window. You might almost feel sorry for him, I thought.

One moment he was standing there. The next there was a terrific explosion of glass.

I rushed to the window. So did the soldiers, dragging me back.

Before they did so, I had time to see the inert, black-suited figure twisted uncomfortably on the road below.

PART FIVE

69

The profits to Grace Equity for the short positions established in Trident Drug amounted to just over fourteen million dollars – enough, I decided, to justify ringing Tim and instructing him to charter a jet out of Dublin and to come to Narva in Estonia and bring me home. At noon the Citation-2 touched down in Narva. An official of the Estonian Immigration Service walked me to the steps of the plane. There had been minimal complications in allowing me to leave – thanks in no small measure to Harry Quinlan's representations from Dublin. Estonia hopes one day soon to become a member of the European Union and so the Estonian government is keen, all things being equal, to build up its stock of favours and credits with existing EU members such as Ireland.

When I got on board, Tim was sitting in a leather swivel chair with two glasses and a bottle of Jameson on the teak-finished table in front of him. At twelve-twenty we took off and clinked our glasses.

'The phone has been going non-stop,' Tim said. 'All the board have been on, Caulfield three times. They're over the moon.'

'You told them the plans?' I said as outside the window the coastline of the Baltic became lost in cloud.

'Whatever you want to do, that's for them.' Tim consulted a notebook. 'So: ten million dollars goes in as seed capital to the John Grace Foundation, a charitable research organization whose object is to fund and develop a cure to HIV. Chairman of the Board of Directors: John Grace. Chief Executive Officer: Dr Cuba Sali. Head of Research: Dr Carlos Penn. Board members: the existing board of Grace Equity including myself and a Mr Volodya Sali.' Tim looked up. 'Have I got all that right?'

'Spot on,' I said and treated my gums and vocal cords to a long overdue reunion with Jameson.

The night before, I had sat with Cuba and Volodya in the hospital in Narva and suggested my plan. Volodya, still pale, but getting stronger with each hour, had smiled from ear to ear.

'I like it,' he had said. 'I like this new way of getting rich.'

Just over two million dollars had been transferred to an account in his name in New York, c/o Soby Sandbach, Wall Street.

'What will you do now?' I asked the Azeri. I saw Cuba's look of concern. 'You don't have to go back to Moscow. You've enough cash in New York to start a new life there.'

Volodya's eyes became fixed on the distance.

'Moscow is home,' he said at last. 'Maybe I'll go to New York one day, but in the meantime I go home.'

That had saddened me, I must admit – why, I find it hard to explain, because I should not have been naïve enough to believe that someone like Volodya could ever operate out of his own environment. What made me sad was the thought of the inevitable: a fine young man with a brain like quicksilver and courage beyond dispute would end up some day in the next ten years, lying in a pool of blood on a Moscow pavement as the next round in the generational vendetta was played out. The night before, I had left him and his sister in the hospital in Estonia, a sense of despair creeping in to replace the euphoria on which I had been riding up to then.

I had also called Minx in Denver. I had just got her voicemail.

'Hi, I'm going into the mountains for a couple of weeks.

Leave a message and I'll probably call you when I get back.'

That had stopped me in my tracks too: the fact that she had not even stayed to go over the details of what we had achieved together, or to hear that Groz was dead. My image was still of the sunny kid with freckles on her nose. Nothing could bring her back.

Tim had put away his notes and was glowing fetchingly from the Jameson.

'The pieces have been falling into place as far as Carson McCoy is concerned,' he told me, stretching out his legs and going into recall mode.

Two years ago, Tim informed me, Carson McCoy had bought in massively to Armentisia Pharmaceutical on the back of their new anti-AIDS drug, Viradrol. The tycoon, using the collateral of his real estate, had levered a five billion dollar stake in Armentisia through a Bahamas-based trust. But almost as soon as Viradrol had been launched, its efficacy began to be questioned by the medical profession, the AIDS population and anyone else with an interest in healthcare. Armentisia sank from twenty dollars, the price at which McCoy had invested, to ten dollars. Simultaneously, a slump in Far East property values, notably in Seoul, Korea, meant that McCoy's real estate – the backbone of his collateral for his Armentisia investment – began to look sick. McCoy needed a solution. He looked around ever more desperately and suddenly found someone in a not too dissimilar position to himself. That someone was Dr Roberto Groz.

'So they were in this together from as far back as that,' I said.

Groz was heavily exposed to Trident stock, just as McCoy was to Armentisia. They met. McCoy proposed a mega-merger. The result – call it Armentisia–Trident –

would have been one of the biggest players in the pharmaceutical world. Thousands of jobs could have been shed, earnings would have soared, the stock market would have loved them. But Groz was playing a different game. Although he told McCoy the deal was on, he said it was only so on one condition: Trident was convinced that an unknown British scientist based in Bristol held the answer to the HIV virus. He was a maverick, his name, Dr Carlos Penn. Groz was intrigued by Carlos's ideas, for although Penn had been shunned by most of the scientific community as being impossible to work with, the head of Trident drug had studied some of Carlos's more revolutionary ideas and concluded that with the right management structure behind him, Carlos was a gold mine waiting to be cashed in. However, all efforts to entice Carlos to work for Trident failed. Groz confided in McCoy: if McCoy could succeed where Groz had failed and bring Carlos Penn on side, Groz would agree to the merger.

But when McCoy arranged an approach to Carlos through Armentisia, he discovered that the reaction was exactly the same. The scientist wanted nothing to do with big business. McCoy therefore had to find another strategy. Posing as a philanthropist, he made a one million dollar investment in Carlos's company. The strategy worked. McCoy won Carlos's confidence. McCoy was poised to scoop the results of Carlos's discovery – whenever that came about.

Whenever, however, was the problem. Both McCoy and Groz needed results fast – for different reasons: the banks were pressing McCoy heavily to realize some collateral in order to reduce their exposure to his Armentisia investment; Groz was losing millions on his Trident stock and he too was being pressed by his bankers.

Groz came up with the solution. They would abduct

Carlos and literally squeeze the drug out of him. McCoy agreed. Groz provided the location: the Trident subsidiary, Cobra Internacionale in Dr Gonzalez, Mexico. McCoy contacted Carlos and asked him to come to Dr Gonzalez in conditions of utmost secrecy, saying that he had set up a special laboratory there. Carlos went to Mexico.

But here the plans of these two high-class con-artists parted ways, Tim said. Groz realized that when he had Carlos in his safekeeping, he had no need of McCoy. With Carlos's discovery, Trident would have the world at its feet and Groz would be a billionaire. So instead of incarcerating Carlos in Mexico, which had been the original plan agreed between the two men, Groz lifted him to Russia, to the Urals, where McCoy would never find him.

I understood it now. All McCoy had to go on was the tape-recorded conversation made by Carlos's sister. McCoy had the resources to find out exactly where the call was made from. He knew it was made from Ireland. But, of course, he couldn't go through official channels without risking exposing his part in the conspiracy. So he turned to the one person in Ireland he thought he could rely on to get to the bottom of something like this. He enlisted me.

'I think he genuinely believed you would deliver Carlos into his hands,' Tim said. 'He didn't think you would be able to refinance Grace Equity in such a short time-frame.'

'He also promised me that if I found Carlos and failed to deliver him, then he would find me and kill me,' I observed.

'I shouldn't worry too much about that happening,' Tim replied. 'Last week McCoy's main New York property company defaulted on a debt repayment. This morning all McCoy's property companies filed for bankruptcy protection in New York. He was last seen boarding a private jet in Newark with a flight plan filed to São Paulo, Brazil.'

We had burst through cloud and now, for the first time in hours, had a view of land. It was worth waiting for. The green of Ireland, the vastness of County Mayo.

'Sligo Airport in three minutes, folks. Buckle up, please,' said the pilot.

There had been times when I had almost believed this moment would never happen. Almost, but never fully. Deep down I had always known I would be coming home.

70

I sometimes complained about the Irish weather, but I had to concede that on a good day in early May Ireland wins the race for the world's most beautiful country – by a distance. Hanny was waiting on the tarmac in Sligo. The top was down on the BMW and the seats were warm from the sun. I said goodbye to Tim and he climbed the steps of the Citation jet. As we drove slowly out of the airport, the little plane took off and then, no doubt instructed by Tim, did a fly-past over us, waggling its wings.

Queen Medb's tomb brooded in the late afternoon sunlight. I was drawn to it each time I came west, my feet found their way up the stony sides of Medb's mountain, as often as not; but today, not. Hanny drove. Her hair was gathered in a short scarf, knotted at her bare throat. We cleared Sligo. We drove north.

We had so much to share in the days ahead. Only three months had gone by since this thing had first started, but within that twelve-week period, light years had been travelled by both of us. I had so much to tell her, about the people I had met, the insights I had gained – into myself, above all. I was surer than I had ever been that Hanny and I were the genuine article – but it would take time for both of us to want the same thing. This week was just a start. I'd lay plans this week. Nowhere better in the world existed to lay such plans than Mrs Duff's on McSwyne's Bay in Donegal.

We passed through Bundoran and Ballyshannon – where only a slender neck of land separates the Republic from the North – and Donegal Town. It was just after seven o'clock, but the sun was still high when we spiralled down the little headland, the lane ever winding, and then turned in the direction of the ocean on a long boreen, between hedges of fuchsia and montbretia, red and gold, and crunched in at last over the gravelled drive of McSwyne's Bay Cottage.

It was a place we had discovered a couple of years before, during one of those weekends when you just take off without any fixed plan, no reservations or commitments, just a vague idea of the region into which you are headed. That weekend we had ended up in the tourist office in Donegal Town, looking without enthusiasm through brochures of B&Bs, wondering if we might not be better off cutting our losses and heading back south to the more proven spots of Connemara. The woman in the tourist office had been in her sixties, she wore tortoise-shell spectacles and an aura of unlimited, motherly competence.

'There is a wee place,' she said, looking around the empty office conspiratorially, 'but it's not, you know, registered.'

Oh, we said.

'The owner doesn't advertise. Her only guests are those who have heard of her by word of mouth,' said the woman. 'And there are only three rooms.'

But – what's it like? we asked.

'It's like heaven on earth,' the woman smiled. 'Would you like me to give her a ring?'

And so we had first come to McSwyne's Bay Cottage. It had been a summer cottage for its owners, the Duffs, and they had come up from Dublin during summer weekends for a score of years. Mrs Duff had been forty-five when her husband, a wealthy lawyer, had died. Mrs Duff had sold the house in Dublin, moved to the cottage and created paradise on her own terms.

Hanny parked to the left of the low front door and I got out and gorged on the view. It was anticipating moments like this that had kept me going those last weeks. The prospect I now beheld had flashed through the smog of the Urals and the grey grimness of suburban Moscow: a narrow estuary, bathed in golden, evening light, tiny coves in which I knew the heads of seals would soon appear, a sense of utter peace and settlement that I craved more than anything.

Mrs Duff showed us to our room – *our* room, as in 'Your room is still down here'. Inside the rose-strewn cottage lay a modern, comfortable house built in traditional style. There was a wide kitchen with an Aga, which led on to a big conservatory in which meals were served. Mrs Duff, when pressed, admitted to being a master chef, but during the summer months she took in culinary helpers as trainees. Our bedroom was on the ocean side and had double doors opening on to a private patio paved in Liscannor.

'We have three other guests,' our hostess told us, 'a couple from Belfast in one room and an American gentleman who is on his own. They're all out tonight, gone to Killybegs and Donegal Town, so you have the place to yourselves.'

Hanny said she wanted to nap and I opened the french windows and walked over the garden and down to the stony shore. There had been times when I had come here but had been unable to switch off completely; I hoped this time would be different. I felt the warm breeze on my face and thanked God that I had been spared for this. I bent and cupped the North Atlantic to my face and tasted salt. I realized how much John and Laura would love this place. I made a note, as I walked back up through the knee-high meadow, to arrange that before the first meeting of the

John Grace Foundation, he and I would spend a long weekend here in McSwyne's Bay Cottage, doing nothing more than hanging out – celebrating being alive, in other words.

The meal was served by a New Zealander named Becky. The menu offered no choice – little point when the starter was a mousse of salmon and prawns, the main course sea-bass, caught that morning in the sea beneath the cottage, and new potatoes and a salad from Mrs Duff's garden. The wine was a Meursault. For dessert, Carrigeen Moss. These are easy details to remember. Every moment of that first evening was etched as if by chisel into my hungry memory. We went to bed at midnight.

My dream was a stream of interactive, buzzing faces, with a background of gunfire and engine sounds. The noise at first seemed like the breach of a gun being drawn back. I was awake, sitting up, searching for my coordinates, feet on the floor, before I realized I had heard a footfall on gravel. Stepping into shorts, I pushed the unclosed french windows six inches and slid out to the patio. The gravel noise was repeated. I had no time now to regret that something precious was about to be shattered; all I wanted to do was to protect the woman in the bed I had left and myself, in that order. Dropping down, part of the shadows, I moved around the gable of the house. There was a half moon, high in the heavens, some cloud. The moon's reflection on the bay added to the luminosity of the night. A man, I saw, was on his knees at the back of my BMW, engaged in doing something beneath the chassis.

I checked the night shades all around for movement, then I covered the short distance to the car in three strides. Reaching down for his neck, I dragged him out and at the same time wrenched his right arm up at an acute angle into his back between his shoulder blades as I slammed him face down across the boot.

'Hey! Hey! Hey! Hey!' he cried out.

I let go his arm and turned him over. He was small-set and in his late thirties. His face was transfixed by fear.

'Hey, I was only lookin'!' he shouted in an American accent.

I felt my stomach do an unplanned workout. Nevertheless, with one hand on his throat, I went over him quickly for a weapon. He was clean.

'What do you mean, "lookin'"?'

'I'm – I'm staying here,' he stammered. 'I've – I've got a BMW myself back home and I was just lookin' underneath at the twin exhaust to see if yours and mine checked out.'

I stood up and let him go. I apologized. He must have been an easy-going guy, for he insisted the fault had been his, that he had had no business going near other people's cars. We shook hands and he went inside. But I went back in by the french doors and got in beside Hanny realizing that I had a long way still to come down from the unforgiving heights I had recently visited. It would take more than a few hours in McSwyne's Bay Cottage to chill me out. Sure, one day there would be a funny side to what had just happened out at my car, but for the moment I went to sleep feeling slightly ashamed.

71

Our days, blessed with good weather, became seamless. We walked all the way out to St John's Point with the picnic made up by Mrs Duff – tiny squares of homemade brown bread, with leaves of Donegal smoked salmon, come immediately to mind – or sat on the tiny beach that lay on the lee side of the point, or wandered in Killybegs among the trawlers from whose rear decks white nets by the mile spewed onto waiting trucks. I made a fire on the beach at Fintragh and spit-roasted a lobster. One day we rode a couple of horses along the shore, another we walked on tiny Teelin Pier. From a narrow cliff track on the great, sheer heights of Bunglass beneath Slieve League, we leaned into the wind and picked out below and in the distance the island of Rathlin O'Birne. It seems now, looking back, as if it was all one long, joyous day, not almost ten. Each evening, except for two on which we went into Killybegs, we ate the mainly fish dishes prepared by Mrs Duff and Becky. Each morning we awoke around nine and out on the little patio ate royal breakfasts, watching little skiffs buff their way out among the warm seacaps, or followed the daily arrival on the near shore of an artist complete with his easel and canvas, his chair, his wide-brimmed straw hat. Each morning he worked his subject with complete absorption, then around noon packed everything back into his car and left. It made one think about life's priorities.

The couple from Belfast were invisible. Sometimes we heard them leaving in the early morning and once we heard their distinctive voices not far from our bedroom window, discussing with Mrs Duff nothing more demanding than the weather. I began to relax. I even played golf one day, nine holes with Hanny as my caddy. 'You're the best-looking caddy in the world,' I told her. During the first few days, I kept in touch with Tim, slipping out of the room before Hanny came to and phoning him from the garden; and again around five, just to get my daily adrenalin fix of money and markets, the ongoing servicing of my umbilical cord to the great institution known as capitalism. Not that much was going on to demand my close and continuous attention: it would have been hard to find someone as good as Tim to run the nuts and bolts of an outfit like Grace Equity. He reported all the calls that had come in for me, none of which seemed out of the ordinary. On the fourth day I skipped the evening conference with Tim. Two days later, I didn't call him again. I didn't even bother to charge my mobile.

We took it very gently with each other, Hanny and me. In one way, it was startling to us that we had lived together for three years and had known so little about one another. At the time, of course, before any of this had happened, we had thought that we knew one another intimately, but nothing had come to test that knowledge. Carlos Penn had been the test. Now we knew a lot more than we had ever guessed – and some of that was scary; not the stuff each had learned about the other, but about ourselves.

In Hanny's case, her dejection after she walked out on me had taken a couple of days to hit home. First, there had been the sustaining euphoria of anger. She had gone to her flat, confident of her own righteousness, as she put it. But then the practicalities of what she had wanted me to do had overtaken her position of principle and all she had been left with was unsustainable pride.

'I felt I was alone on an island that I had made out of sorrow, just for myself,' she said.

Her gloom had thickened, wrapping her in it like fog. She went down. And yes, she told me, there was a point she recognized from her adolescent years, which she thought she had left behind for ever – a bad, dark, lonely place with no windows or doors.

'Was it ever – you know, close?' I asked her.

'I knew you would come back,' she told me. 'I knew we would get together again, perhaps in a different, stronger way, but I knew it would happen.'

I had no way of knowing now whether that fairly reflected what had really happened – but in a way it didn't matter. What mattered was the reality, and that was what we were taking each day in Donegal and building into something for the future.

I told Hanny about Cuba, about how in the midst of the great mass of Russia I had come to terms with the fact that the great hero in my life had let me down. In that accommodation, I had lost a little of myself.

'What part?' Hanny asked.

'A good question. A little pride, I think. A little of my own self-worth, something I have to make up on my own. But I saw, too, that for years I was this man going around with a lump of unexplained anger in my heart. I thought it was my resentment against the people who had pressed for my removal from school, the parents of the boy I beat up and the authorities – all those had stood against me and meant that I had had to go away. Now I understand that my anger was against my father. He should have taken a stand for justice and fairness on my behalf, not put me on a plane and changed my entire life just because he was afraid of losing his job.'

'But did he really have an option?' Hanny asked.

'Heroes always have an option,' I told her, and kissed her on the nose.

'Cuba is such a beautiful name,' Hanny said.

I agreed.

'Is she beautiful too?' Hanny asked me.

Women are extraordinary creatures. From the myriad atmosphere, they can pick up the tiniest scintilla of wandering emotion and nail it with unnerving accuracy to the notice board of the heart.

'Not as beautiful as you,' I replied, which was almost the absolute truth.

72

I began to run every day, a sign, if I admitted it, that I was becoming restless. Soon we would have to think about when we were going back to Dublin – although the long, warm days of May were holding us in Donegal beyond my expectations. In Mrs Duff's, you stayed or left when you wanted, there were no rules, often the other two rooms were empty, she had few advance bookings and wasn't worried by the fact.

I ran every morning, for about ninety minutes. Some days my route took me along by the foreshore, easier when the tide was out; or I struck north, crossing the Killybegs Road and up quiet tracks, past forestry plantations and fields with ruined castles and megalithic tombs. On Sunday morning I left Hanny showering and set out. Tim had called the evening before, casual on the face of it, just to see how we were getting on, and to say that everything was fine in Dublin, Salman was still warbling, the vessel of commerce over which Tim presided was still on its charted course, give or take. More or less. Yet, when I probed a little, yes, there were a few matters he wouldn't mind discussing, face to face, he said, some opportunities he was considering. Attractive on the face of it. One in software, one in real estate. I'd told Tim I'd be in touch – but the time was coming to return to Dublin. I didn't want to leave Mrs Duff's over-full with her hospitality. I would talk this morning to Hanny. She had her job too, to go back to, they must have been wondering where she was. We would, I reckoned, go south on Tuesday morning.

That morning I'd gone all the way to St John's Point, taking a path I'd discovered through fields on the way down to the extremity of the peninsula, then back by the road, where I now was, sun in my face, the sweat from back and chest in two large spreading patches on my shirt. I'd met no one. The artist to whom we'd grown accustomed this last week was absent – perhaps because it was Sunday, or more likely, he was a tourist whose seven days were up and at this moment he was waking up in Manchester or Manhattan with his quiet, liberating mornings by the water now a precious memory.

McSwyne's Bay Cottage came into view. I loved it then, the sense of anticipation, the feeling of real excitement that a place I treasured and a person I loved were coming once again into my reach. Some mornings, at this distance, which was a shrinking five hundred yards, I could get the smell of baking bread, or the newly lit turf fire – for even in midsummer Mrs Duff kept a fire on the go in the central sitting room, more for the burning turf's aroma than for the heat. This morning there were no smells. Sunday again. Mrs Duff went to pray in Donegal on Sundays, a round trip of two hours plus. She arrived back around twelve-thirty to preside over lunch, if it was needed. Today, it was not. Hanny and I were going to drive over to Fintragh with a picnic and spend the day lying in the sand dunes, watching the gulls and breathing in the scent of wildflowers.

'I'm back.'

I came in through the french windows. She wasn't in the room, or the bathroom. I could smell her, though. And the bed on her side was still warm to my hand.

'Hanny?'

I walked back out to the patio and looked towards the water; sometimes she walked down there with a book. Not this morning, that I could see. I went back in and showered, expecting her to come in at any moment.

Dressing in shorts and sandals, I went into the house, walking from room to room. The conservatory was a blazing suntrap on a morning like this. She was sure to be curled up kitten-like in a corner.

'D'you see Hanny?' I asked Becky, the New Zealander, who was putting on an apron. A bag with milk and the Sunday papers which she'd just brought with her from Dukineely lay on the kitchen table.

'I just passed her,' Becky said.

'Where?'

'She was in a car about a mile from here. I was cycling from Killybegs. They passed me.'

'*They?*'

73

Fear rushed up out of the ground and wrapped me in its net. The girl was staring at me.

'Who – for Christ's sake?'

'Hanny and a man.' The girl was alarmed. 'Is there something . . .'

I couldn't hear and my eyesight had become momentarily unreliable. Simultaneously, I had a primal urge to throw up. Making a fist, I brought it down hard on the table. Becky jumped.

'I'm sorry, Becky. Take this very slowly. Describe what you saw and try not to leave anything out.'

Thirty minutes before, just when I must have been jogging back to the cottage, Becky had reached the top of the lane, that is, where the turn-off from the Killybegs Road down to Mrs Duff's occurs. As she did so, a car drove up from the cottage and emerged onto the main road. It had to pause before proceeding. Becky thought the car was red, but hadn't noted the number. She was on the other side of the main road, turning off it on her bicycle. As the car paused, she saw Hanny in the passenger seat, looking at her. Becky saw a man at the wheel. The car turned for Killybegs.

'Were there any guests other than ourselves here last night?' I asked, already knowing the answer.

'Just you,' Becky replied.

'When you saw Henny in the car, did she say anything – or try to say anything?'

Becky thought. 'She looked at me and her mouth was open, now that I think of it, but I assumed she was talking to the driver.'

'Describe the driver.'

'I couldn't see, he was in shadow.'

'He? How do you know it was a man?'

'That was my impression. I think it was his size.'

'His – size?'

'Well, I got the impression he was a big man, because the upper half of him was well up in the car, like I said, in shadow.' The girl nodded. 'Yes, he was a big man.'

A big man. One half of me hunted like a demented gnat for rational explanations, as the other stood there, shaking and knowing with complete accuracy what had taken place. The innocent, gnat-like half refused to believe the absurd, the other had already passed the point of disbelief and was howling with rage that the inevitable had come to pass.

I thumbed the telephone directory, hands trembling. The two nearest Garda stations were Dunkineely and Killybegs. I wondered as I rang them how I was going to explain what I knew had happened. I was already imagining their sceptical faces as they pondered the word 'abduction' on a perfectly calm, sunny and peaceful May morning. I needn't have worried: neither station replied. And then my cellphone rang.

'*Hanny?*'

I knew it had to be.

'Joe?'

I prayed for the rational, that she had decided to go into Killybegs, that a local farmer had given her a lift. I prayed, but I knew that she would never have gone without leaving a note to say she had done so.

'Where are you?'

'At the little harbour.'

'Teelin?'

'Yes.'

'With who?'

There was a muffled noise.

'Hanny? Are you all right?'

'Quickly, Joe.'

The call was disconnected.

I stood there, trying to make the right call. Becky's hand was on my arm.

'Why don't you try and tell me what's happened?'

'My wife's been abducted,' I said slowly. 'She's in Teelin harbour. I want you to get on to the Gardai in Donegal Town and tell them to come out here as quickly as possible. Tell them a very dangerous criminal has kidnapped her.' I saw the girl's face, knotted in concern. 'I'll explain later.'

I scribbled down my cellphone number for Becky. Thirty seconds later I was gunning up the lane, trying to recoup the focus I'd spent the last ten days trying to lose. I was one mile on the main road to Killybegs when I realized something: I had never before referred to Hanny as my wife.

74

I hurled the BMW through the narrow streets of Killybegs and out the cliff road of the peninsula. Mountains towered ahead and to my right. I thumbed out Tim's mobile number as I drove, but got his answering machine. I should never have dropped my guard to the extent I had. Once a man like McCoy became fixated on something – whether success or revenge – he would kill in order to achieve it. I left the coast and veered right at the turn for Kilcar. Over the barren foothills, suddenly Carrick village came into sight in the valley, a bright clutch of houses gleaming out of the velvet green like a brooch in a jeweller's window. Carrick was deserted, the community were at prayer. In desperation I scanned the street for a Garda car or the comfort of a blue uniform; except for a dog, there was no one. Swinging left in the middle of the village, I took the road out to Teelin Pier.

It had, in another century, been an important coast-guard station and a centre for cod fishing. Today it was a deserted arm of grey, nineteenth-century mass concrete jutting out into the water. On the land end were some modern sheds, local industry attracted by heavy financial incentives into this Irish-speaking pocket of Donegal. I saw the red Escort first and my heart sank: the car had been parked every morning for the past week opposite Mrs Duff's. The artist's car. Then I saw the boat. It was a long, sleek ocean-going power craft, over forty feet in length, and was standing by in shadow under the pier's steps, white foam bubbling at its stern.

I pulled up fifty feet from the Escort and as I got out, the doors of the other car opened and Hanny emerged, slowly.

Then, from the same door, came Carson McCoy. He was wearing the same wide-brimmed straw hat that he had for the last week of mornings. In other circumstances, I might have laughed – at my own gullibility. Then I saw that he had Hanny tethered by a leash, both her hands tied in front of her.

'We had a deal, Joe,' he called. 'You broke your end. Sorry, but there's a price.'

'Leave her go, Carson,' I said, walking towards them. 'What you do to me is between us – but she's not harmed you.'

'She's just bait, Joe,' he said, and I saw the glint of a gun coming up behind Hanny's neck, 'and I'll blow her away like bait if you don't stand exactly where you are.'

I stopped and strained to hear any sound of help from the land behind me, the wail of sirens or the engines of cars, but all I could hear was gulls and the soft lapping of seawater. I could see that the leash which tied Hanny's wrists was looped around McCoy's left wrist.

'Why didn't you bring him to me, Joe?' McCoy asked, his face pained. 'It would have meant so much. I heard what you're planning for him – but surely we both wanted the same thing? A drug that works? I'll find him anyway, now, with or without you. But you've cost me so much, Joe, and it's all been so *fucking* unnecessary.'

'Why do this?' I asked. 'What's the point?'

'I have a simple philosophy,' McCoy said. 'I always keep my side of a deal, regardless of what it costs me. I told you that. Many years ago I learned that it pays in the long run to have this attitude. You knew what the terms of our deal were, you knew the conditions. Now, down the steps!' he called. I could see him scanning the road behind me for activity. He rammed the gun severely into Hanny's neck. 'Do it!'

I made my way to the top of the steps and as I did so, the boat churned up white water and began to glide in to receive me. It was much bigger than I had thought initially and the whole open section of the stern was taken up by something that was covered in a large, green tarpaulin.

'Where are we going?'

'To feed mackerel,' McCoy said. 'Walk.'

The steps numbered twelve or fourteen to the waterline. Where the water lapped the bottom steps, I could see green slime. I went down slowly, aware of McCoy bringing Hanny after me, maybe two steps behind. Sunlight glinted on the deck and superstructure of the yacht. I could see a man bringing her stern in to us: his dark glasses, an Oriental head. I made to slip, too realistically, for my head struck the sharp edge of the step behind me.

'Fuck you! Get up!'

Hanny's feet were at my eye level. I knew what I had to do and inwardly apologized to her for it. Scooping her by the ankles, I rolled. I could feel the rushing air on my face. I kept her held. There was a moment of resistance, then McCoy toppled too. I hit the water, felt something dense strike my shoulder. Sank. I came up first, choking. On the rear deck of the boat, the man now held a rifle. But he was looking at the pier, not at us. Faces came into view above, two Gardai. McCoy broke water, the gun in his left hand. He aimed it at me and I dived. The shot was like thunder. I came up again, beside him, and could see that the leather strap was no longer on his wrist. The Gardai were shouting and coming down the steps. McCoy was too close to me to fire, so he drove down with the gun and caught me on the side of the head.

'Go!' he shouted to the boat. 'Go!'

I heard the engines roar. I was finding it difficult to tread water, and all of a sudden felt my shoulder in agony.

McCoy made to lash out again. I heard him shout. Then with dread I grasped the fact that Hanny had not surfaced. I dived. I found I could use only my left arm to swim. Bubbles were streaming up beneath me. I surfaced again, unmindful of McCoy, sucked in a chestful of air, dived. This time my chest could burst before I'd come up without her. I met her hair first. Her eyes were staring. I saw the leash where it had wrapped itself around an old anchor chain. With her hands bound she had been unable to free it. Pulling it with all my strength, I fell back as it came free. We both shot up, level with the bottom steps of the pier.

I hauled her in and we sat, heaving for breath. I untied her wrists. Then, trying to figure out what had happened, I slowly climbed the steps. I stared. Beside the open doors of the patrol car lay two bodies in blue uniform, their caps on the ground beside them. I turned. The yacht had disappeared. But my BMW was gone.

I heard the chatter of a short-wave radio from the Garda patrol car.

'Hanny?'

Hanny was peeling off her wet jumper. She was exhausted. Staggering over to the seawall, she sat down.

But I was in attack mode. It was as if the theft of my car, a minor misdemeanour in the canon of McCoy's epic crimes, was the point beyond which I was not prepared to let him go. Perhaps it was that. Or else, perhaps like McCoy, I was now set to go the full distance in this thing. Whatever it took.

'Are you all right?' I asked.

Hanny was shivering. She nodded. 'I'm okay.'

'Can you drive?' I asked, going to her. 'I've hurt my shoulder.'

She looked up at me. 'Are you sure you want to, Joe?'

'I'm sure.'

'Then I can drive,' she said, getting up.

In the Escort, we left the harbour by the only road. Every move pained me, yet I could look around and see the boat on which we were meant to be aboard, a mile out already from the harbour and shrinking by the moment. Hanny's hair was slicked back like someone who has just taken an invigorating dip. The road was narrow and deserted. I wondered what his back-up plan was – someone like McCoy always had a back-up plan. The road levelled out and as I saw the white and blue of a Garda patrol car coming towards us, I simultaneously saw my own car climbing high up the mountain to my left.

'Don't say anything,' I said.

'But the Guards . . .' Hanny began.

'Say nothing!'

I could imagine the length of time it would take to explain the circumstances – two dead Guards on the pier, the fact that Hanny, the person reported as abducted, was now driving someone else's car – time during which the man I now had to stop would be away for ever. Or until he came back again to settle his side of the deal.

The patrol car came level with us. Hanny smiled. The driver rolled down his window.

'What's the water like?' he grinned.

'It's nice, Guard,' she said and we drove on.

McCoy too must have seen the patrol car, one reason why he may have taken the mountain road.

'Left,' I said to Hanny and she turned uphill.

The first mile was almost straight and steep enough in places to make the nose of the car seem to rear up. Then we came to a bend with houses and swung around them, a corkscrew. We gunned on, ever steeper, and sometimes my knees were level with my chin. As we breasted the next rise, I saw the tail-lights of the BMW, now barely fifty yards ahead of us – and then I saw the reason. An aluminium gate swung open across the road, a blue rope hanging from it. He had had to get out and untie the rope to open the gate. It had cost him a full minute. But why was he coming up here in the first place? This road led up across the cliffs, but nowhere else.

'We have him,' I said to Hanny.

We climbed again, this time more on track than road, and when our nose came down again it was to reveal an undulating black ribbon of tarmac that clung to the unprotected side of a sheer drop and wound on along the cliff out of sight. The gap to my car was less than thirty yards now. The BMW rounded a bend and disappeared. We came up to the bend, which at its apex rose sharply, denying onward vision for the length of time it took to negotiate it. I had a glimpse to my left of spray rising from the sea, somewhere vertical miles below. Hanny screamed. The BMW was coming for us hard, in reverse.

'Jesus!'

He hit us with the tow-bar on the left wing and skittled us backwards towards the edge.

'Joe!'

I felt us go over. He came up again and struck us with another splintering blow that jarred my head, first back, then forward into the windscreen. I felt the car slide. The BMW was lost from sight. I kicked out the door and looked directly down into the distant North Atlantic. Hanny's door was jammed. She looked at me.

'Lean back!'

For the moment, my pain was sublimated to my desire for life. I came to Hanny's window with the heel of my boot. On the second kick it went out in noiseless slow motion. The car shuddered as it pitched seawards another foot. Hanny scrambled out. I came after her, unmindful of shards of window glass in my face and hands. The car was impaled like a toy on the sharp end of a boulder, swaying to and fro above the abyss. As we clawed back for the road it slipped a metre and then dangled, as if held by invisible threads, over the sheer drop.

I began to run – not back downhill, as anyone sane might have, to where the proper authorities might at last deal with what had taken place, but in the direction McCoy had taken. I knew he had to stop the car a hundred yards ahead. I ran and Hanny ran beside me. I was wondering afresh what McCoy was going to do, when I heard the sound. The blades chopping the air somewhere out to sea on my left made a unique vibration and pitch, one that I had lived with for years. The road dipped and rose. My breath was coming in strangled gasps and the pain down my right side had now returned with a vengeance. I climbed the final rise and saw what I had moments before known I would see: McCoy standing on the cliff side, his arms in the air, and the small, black shape of a helicopter circling in from the sky to meet him. I saw too the boat out at sea from which the chopper had come, and my car, parked to the right, pulled up on a steep bank of earth to give the chopper room to land.

I ran for him and even a hundred yards out could feel the air whooshing across the clifftop from the chopper as it came in. His size, his face. Both these aspects of the man which had impressed themselves anew at each meeting, now, bizarrely in the circumstances, registered again, as if appearances were important up here, as if even when life and death were involved, as they were now for sure, certain procedures of recognition had to be gone through first. I was fifty yards out. The chopper was hovering and sinking. McCoy turned. He was such a big-framed, physically impressive man. Majestic would have been a good word in other circumstances. Broad in the shoulders, wide in the chest. Nearly fifteen years older than me, yet, I knew with dismay, even as he stood his ground awaiting me, that in the shape I was now, I was no match for him. Not that logic was playing a part in my actions, any more than it was in his. The chopper stayed three feet off the ground and the door swung open. I could hear nothing. Yet McCoy stood his ground for me. I dived at his ankles, but he saw me coming, stepped to one side almost daintily and kicked me full in the chest.

'*Get in!*'

I heard the pilot scream at him. But McCoy, given the proximity of the six hundred-foot drop, could not resist one more effort, and so he stepped and kicked again. But this time I rolled. I felt the gravity take over my momentum. A jarring pain in the small of my back, as if one of a long series, punched my breath out and made my eyes stare. If he came at me again, I was helpless. But then I saw two spectacles I am unlikely ever to forget: McCoy was clambering into the helicopter at the same time as a blur of red flashed from right to left. The freewheeling BMW took the chopper's landing rails beneath the tow-bar and without pause hurtled both of them over the edge. I heard nothing. The noise of the explosion was muted at first, then a roaring fireball rocketed all the way up to my eye level, like a beautiful balloon, before dissolving into the atmosphere. I turned right. Hanny was standing, staring at what she had done.

'My car,' I said.

From the road to my right grew the sound of engines. A Garda patrol vehicle was coming into view. I was going to have to do a lot of explaining.

POSTSCRIPT

I am still the Chairman of Grace Equity, although we no longer operate from Temple Bar – last year we moved our offices into the Irish Financial Services Centre. It was a decision that in the end made itself: having taken on three bright kids to look over the volume of deals coming into us, we decided to become respectable. I now work from a large office overlooking the River Liffey. I spend on average two days a week in the office, the rest of the time I work from home.

Home, by the way, is Howth. Yes, I moved too. I sit in a big front room that overlooks Dublin Bay, listening to jazz, working at my laptop and rerunning all the events that I was a part of. I like being this near the sea. I'm thinking of joining a scuba-diving club and bringing my certificate up to date.

Trident Drug was very lucky not to go bust. But the banks stepped in and sacked the Board, then hired a professional fixer to sort the mess out. They changed their name too: to Scarborough Laboratories. Last I noticed, they were traded at around thirty dollars.

Soby retired, moved with his wife to San Diego and bought a small ocean-front property. The grandchildren come out to stay. Soby learned how to play golf and bridge. He began to take an interest in the West Coast stock-market. Last I heard, he was planning to rent a small office suite in downtown San Diego – nothing too large, just a little diversion from golf and bridge and home life, a couple of days a week. I received the cigars but not the humidor, by the way. If ever I'm in San Diego, I intend to look Soby up and slag him about that.

I haven't spoken to Minx for about six months, but through the grapevine I have learned that one of the major killings in the Trident crash was made out of Denver. I'm both glad and sad: glad that she made a worthwhile pile out of the stock she knew so well; sad that it looks like we'll never meet now. Some things are not meant to be.

A lot of media attention followed the deaths of Groz and McCoy and the subsequent break-up of the McCoy property empire. He had a wife all the time, an attractive lady in her early thirties who never had any idea of what had been going on. She mustn't have lamented her husband's passing too much. She inherited about twenty million dollars under a trust settlement and remarried within six months.

The media, however, went into frenzy mode for three or four weeks, both sides of the Atlantic. The FDA launched its own enquiry and for a time Congress held the whip hand. But like everything else, the moment passed. I had a bad few weeks from the media, but in deciding not to speak to them, in deciding that if anyone was going to tell the true story, it was going to be me, I think I did what was absolutely right. Of course, stories were published that were so wide of the mark they were laughable. I ignored them. Eventually the attention waned. And eventually, I've got around to doing what I said I would.

Writing this has kept me busy this last year or so. Writing, and keeping up to date with the activities of the John Grace Foundation. It's most encouraging. We've attracted a lot more funding since the initial whip-around. Carlos Penn works mostly out of a laboratory in LA, right beside Cuba's office. He tells me official trials will start next year. He promises nothing, just follows what he believes in, and that's good enough for me.

These last two Christmases by special delivery from

Moscow, I've received a present of five kilos of Beluga caviar. You've got to eat the stuff or it goes off, so the first Christmas I asked Harry Quinlan and Tim and Anne, my secretary, to come out and help me. We drank chilled vodka with twists of lime. Hanny sang a Russian song. It was a good night. And the Christmas just gone by, when the package arrived again I decided to keep the tradition up, although this time Hanny wasn't here. I sent word through Cuba to ask Volodya to come over to Ireland, even just for a long weekend; but she came back to say he couldn't.

'Pressure of business,' she told me.

I might have guessed.

The guests of honour, however, were John and Laura Grace from New York. I'd never seen John looking better, never. It was the best Christmas present I could possibly have had.

Hanny's got some good assignments in Germany over the last six months – she enjoys being back there. Doing what she's so good at. Months go by without us seeing each other, then she flies in and it's as if she's never been away. Harry gives me sidelong glances and I tell him to stop mothering the be-Jesus out of me. When the time comes for Hanny and me to do the big thing, then we'll know that time, I tell him. Meanwhile, it's something to do with freedom. A concept we've both invested a lot in.

Light is going down behind Dublin, as I type these words. It's early February, almost exactly two years since I got that telephone call. I often think about what might have happened if I hadn't answered the phone that morning, if I'd stayed in bed. And then I look over at Salman in his new position overlooking the Irish Sea and I realize that life is something you catch only once as it goes by. And that despite everything that happened, I'm one of the very lucky ones.